MAJOR ARCANA

MAJOR ARCANA

— a novel —

John Pistelli

Belt Publishing

This is a work of fiction. Unless otherwise indicated, all the names, characters, places, events, and incidents in this book are either the product of the author's imagination or used in a fictional manner. Any resemblance to actual persons, living or dead, or actual events is purely coincidental.

Printed in the United States of America
First edition 2025

ISBN: 9781953368928

Belt Publishing
6101 Penn Avenue, Suite 201
Pittsburgh, PA 15206
www.beltpublishing.com

This book is dedicated with thanks to those who supported it during its writing and serialization.

Seldom   Trying for Love
Fantasy dealt them out as gods
Two or three men   looked only human

But you alone
Superhuman   apparently
I had to be caught in the weak eddy
Of your drivelling humanity
To love you most

—Mina Loy, *Songs to Joannes*

PROLOGUE

CHAPTER Ø

Q. E. D.

He pulled the revolver from his army jacket. That was the first strange thing bystanders reported witnessing before they saw the gun: the olive drab World War II "Ike" jacket with its large front pockets and gold insignia on the lapel. Oversized, it hung oddly, unbuttoned, over his T-shirt and jeans.

They'd bought it together in his mother's vintage store. He couldn't bring himself to go when his mother would be there—he hadn't told his mother about her yet, still less introduced them—so he took her after hours, around 10 at night, and entered with the spare shop key his mother had given him in case of emergencies.

She said he should get "something good for you to wear when you do it," and, as soon as she saw the army jacket, she insisted he had to have it, even though it cost $150. He looked skeptically into the shop mirror at how it draped over him. A man now dead, with planks for shoulders, a man of the type they used to call barrel-chested, a man from what they hailed as the Greatest Generation, had once worn this coat back in what they called the American century. She circled his own thin chest with her arms and whispered warmly in his ear that she would buy it for him. (It was only the second time she'd ever touched him.) Her breath smelled spicy, like the crystallized ginger she chewed to settle her perpetually upset stomach. She met his eyes in the mirror and spread the fingers of one hand over one of the coat's front pockets. The remnants of her chipped nail polish, pale green, didn't match but off-rhymed with the army olive. He brought his own hand up and laced his fingers with hers. He carefully recorded the sale in the ledger next to the register—his mother didn't trust machines to be the sole custodians of her data—and she left the cash on the counter. She only explained her choice later that night, not to his face. For strategic reasons, they rarely texted, but at three in the morning, she sent him a passage from Yeats:

Why should we honour those that die upon the field of battle? A man may show as reckless a courage in entering into the abyss of himself.

He threw the jacket on over his blank white T-shirt—it was the first of November anyway, a wintry barb riding the air—and dropped the small revolver into the left front pocket. The gun came from her too, but she didn't tell him where she'd found it. He walked from his dorm, one of the latest constructed and furthest from everything, up at the top of what everyone jokingly called Cardiac Hill, down to the center of campus.

At the change of classes, around 3:00 p.m., he stood with his back to the door of the little Chapel in the center of the green. He faced front and stared up all 42 stories of the main campus building, what they called the Cathedral, and into the cloudy gray sky beyond. Wind blew down the expanse between the two Gothic façades, the towering Cathedral and the tiny Chapel. Bright leaves skittered at his sneakers, stained green from cutting the grass at his mother's house just that weekend, probably for the last time before winter. No, I won't *ever* do it again, he caught himself thinking. I won't do it again.

He pushed his hand into his pocket and cocked the revolver, just as she'd shown him. Though the jacket's thick material muffled the click, it sounded to him like a crack of thunder from the clouds. A droplet of sweat trickled coldly over his ribs. He worried he might faint—he hadn't eaten in two days; he wanted to avoid, if he could, the rumored voiding of the bowels—so he did it right away.

In one motion, as he'd practiced in the dorm-room mirror, he slipped the gun with his right hand from his left front pocket and lifted it upside down, with his finger inside the trigger guard, straining his wrist, to his right eye. The metal burned with cold against his tightly shut eyelid. With one eye, he saw the milling crowds of his fellow students lift their heads from their phones and turn in his direction, alerted in waves that rippled out from the susurrus of those nearest him.

He pulled the trigger. He collapsed into the musty heap of the army jacket. Blood sprayed the limestone wall of the Chapel in a slashing arc like the sigil of an order or a party pledged to death.

The second strange thing bystanders reported witnessing—beyond the enormous, unspeakable fact of the act itself—was how calmly *she* stood, her spiral-scarred face concealed in its black medical mask, 10 feet in front of him, her phone held in both hands at arm's length, a fresh coat of black on her fingernails. She was recording the whole thing. She didn't flinch at the shot or at the cries and shrieks of the bystanders.

She was rumored to have whispered something in the tinnitus haze hanging in the air just after the shot, but given the way the mask muffled her speech, no one could agree on what she'd said, except that it was in a foreign language. Later, social media commenters, consulting various of the phone videos that later went viral, offered "*Ave atque vale*," "*Morituri te salutant*," and "*Eli, Eli, lama sabachthani*" as candidates for her mysterious statement. What she'd actually said, as her own video, when everyone saw it, would eventually prove, was, "*Quod erat demonstrandum*."

PART ONE

CHAPTER 1
The Logic of My Face

Simon Magnus felt two ways about teaching in what they called the Cathedral. As an aesthete since childhood, Simon Magnus would never deny the enlivening, elevating effect—the effervescence in the pit of the stomach—Simon Magnus experienced almost every time Simon Magnus looked up at the Cathedral posted against the sky, almost every time Simon Magnus passed through the revolving door into the vast common room, where students studied at wooden tables or on stone ledges amid marble pillars supporting a 50-foot vault. Simon Magnus could not fail, however, to contemplate the contrast between the Cathedral's imposing greatness and what Simon Magnus was tasked with doing inside its limestone grandeur.

Simon Magnus's adolescent ambitions toward high culture had been shared by the men of the city themselves early in the 20th century, when they'd raised this Gothic Revival monument to the best that had been thought and said, even though the city's wealth was based not on humanistic knowledge but on the soot-skied production of steel. (In homage to comic-book conurbations, which rarely shared a name with their mundane models, Simon Magnus in fact privately thought of it as Steel City.) Simon Magnus and the Cathedral *qua* institution had, however, each together, betrayed this ambition.

Who was Simon Magnus? A writer famed for a few hideous comic books written before the age of 30, now, in middle age, not having written a creative word since then, a permanent adjunct professor teaching classes on the exact same type of material, and to students too uneducated to read books without pictures in them.

(Simon Magnus had not gone to college SimonMagnusself.)

In a tiny, cell-like classroom cradled in the Cathedral's vastness, Simon Magnus taught in the dark. Simon Magnus kept the blinds lowered and the lights off. The only illumination in the room came from the projection onto the whiteboard of Simon Magnus's laptop screen. Simon Magnus showed Simon Magnus's class pages from the graphic novels Simon Magnus had assigned—the course was named Studies in the Graphic Novel—to incite discussion, to invite close scrutiny of the words and pictures. Sometimes, though, the students had plainly failed to read the books at all before the day appointed to discuss them; Simon Magnus would then pull up illicit electronic versions from pirate sites hosted in countries with lax or indifferently enforced copyright laws. Simon Magnus remained unruffled as ads for pornography and mail-order brides flashed on the screen, as women with spread legs and parted lips flickered across the students' jaded faces. Simon Magnus would spend the hour reading the comic books to them, interpolating the occasional question at intervals between the panels to try, however vainly, to keep them awake. A class joker once shouted, "Wait! Scroll back up! It says Nadia is waiting for you." Uneasy laughter deep in the Cathedral.

Given their fates, anyone who followed the news would have imagined that Jacob Morrow and Ash del Greco had sat in the back of that classroom, slumped and sullen, darkly whispering to each other as they planned their fatal *geste*. Instead, they'd sat in the middle of the front row. They spoke often and intelligently—more often and more intelligently than anyone else in the room, in fact—both of them witty, provoking Simon Magnus's wit in turn. They were quick to laugh, making references and jokes no one understood but themselves and, occasionally, their professor. The girl seemed morose only in her style of dress, the boy not at all, if "girl" and "boy" quite captured the distinction between them. "Boy" seeming especially questionable given the typical composition of Simon Magnus's classes, or all humanities classes nowadays really. Simon Magnus typically addressed the sudents as a collective, to appreciative, if slightly wary, chuckles, as "girls, gays, and theys."

Jacob Morrow and Ash del Greco made, Simon Magnus thought, an odd pair. Simon Magnus supposed they were dating, though Simon Magnus had never seen them touch one another.

The boy was lanky, otherwise nondescript, with long brown hair, streaked naturally with light threads of blond; it hung down around his narrow shoulders. He always wore a blank white T-shirt. In late August and September, he'd worn cutoff jean shorts and sport sandals on bare feet; then, as the weather cooled, he changed over to full-length jeans and sneakers. He looked every inch an American boy, of the athletic variety, even, straight out of the suburbs, no trace of bohemia in him, which made his references to philosophy and literature incongruous, unexpected.

The girl, on the other hand, looked as if she'd spoken of Nietzsche immediately upon exiting the birth canal. She was short, meager, not thin exactly but somehow stunted, persistently fetal; her stark uniform, black from the thick frames of the huge glasses that covered half her face to the knee-high boots on her tiny feet, gave her an air of command. She wore baggy black cargo pants tucked into the tops of her boots in a martial style. Pandemic protocols had waned—they were still somewhere on the books, no longer entirely enforced—but, almost alone, she wore a medical mask to every meeting, always black. Her mask invariably also carried some handmade symbol or rune: an arabesque, a question mark, an injunction, or a challenge. These messages were always painted in white onto the black masks. Then there was the delicate matter of her face itself, squarish and jowly and outsized atop a slender and fragile-looking neck. The right side of her face was burned and furrowed in a spiral scar at the cheek, the earlobe gone, as if melted into the jawbone. She had drawn in red a continuation of the scar's spiral lines on the side of the mask that partially concealed it. On the first day of class, her mask had read, *I'M STILL WORKING OUT THE LOGIC OF MY FACE.*

Simon Magnus hadn't looked at the roster before the first meeting; protocol now dictated that students, whom some were now calling "learners" instead, introduce themselves, name and pronoun, often in defiance of what the roster recorded, so what was the point of looking at it before hearing from the incarnations of the data it so imperfectly recorded? When she introduced herself on that first day, therefore, Simon Magnus narrowed Simon Magnus's eyes at her so violently that the whole room became perceptibly unnerved.

"I knew a 'del Greco' once," Simon Magnus finally said, faltering, nervous—the worst tone for the first day of class. It would be her father's name, Simon Magnus reflected, not her mother's; Simon Magnus may have borne a maternal surname, a matronymic, but few others did. Where had Diane del Greco said she was from? Simon Magnus asked SimonMagnusself. She had never named the place.

"It's a common Italian surname," Ash del Greco replied. "It means 'from Greece.'"

Simon Magnus recovered enough to banter gently: "Are you from Greece?"

"I'm from the suburbs. That's a country of its own."

The mystery of this girl—Simon Magnus had clocked her as a they/them when she'd entered the room, but she'd introduced herself as, "She, or whatever"—provoked Simon Magnus enough to google her that night. Online, he found, she was some kind of what they called an influencer; she made videos on literature and cultural theory and the occult. Sometimes she essayed, but at other times, she seemed to be chanting, almost attempting hypnosis on her audience, which, according to her videos' public view counters, numbered in the hundreds of thousands. Like her Studies in the Graphic Novel professor, she taught in the dark, recording her exhortations and explications only by the glow her phone cast back on her, its lighted square doubled in her massive glasses, its eerie blue light rippling over her spiral-scarred cheek. She said in every video—it appeared even to be her clumsy catchphrase—"The human mind is superior to the totality of the real." This is what Valerie Karns would be doing if Valerie Karns were a teenager now, if Valerie Karns had not jumped off a bridge three decades ago, Simon Magnus thought—Valerie Karns, Simon Magnus's first love, who had taught Simon Magnus Tarot on a dirty carpet when they were teenagers in a dark forest.

Simon Magnus found something inexorably fascinating about Ash del Greco. She reminded Simon Magnus of someone, but of whom? Not Valerie Karns, her precocious occultism notwithstanding. The face nagged, even showed up in Simon Magnus's dreams over the first few weeks of the semester, but never conveyed the right name from the past to Simon Magnus. It wasn't the del Greco he had once known. It wasn't Diane del Greco's face. That face had been immortalized as Mina Mars, the hero's beloved consort, in what they called Simon Magnus's masterpiece, *Overman 3000.* Simon Magnus had last seen that face twisted by an unsurvivable grief and rage, accusing Simon Magnus of what amounted to murder, screaming to Simon Magnus, "You killed my precious baby!" This could not be Diane del Greco's living child. Diane del Greco had had a glossy cascade of dark hair and a body all curve and no plane.

Simon Magnus's fascination with Ash del Greco certainly wasn't sexual. Even if she hadn't been barely out of her teens, there would have been the matter of how thoroughly she de-eroticized her already meager body with her baggy black clothes, not to mention the severe and vaguely hostile messages she bore on her face. *YOU CAUSED THIS*, her mask said one day. On another, it read, *DEATH IS ONLY A RUMOR*. A third commanded its reader: *YOU ARE THE AUTHOR OF YOUR LIFE*. Simon Magnus began writing them down on the third day of class. After Jacob Morrow's death, Simon Magnus committed them to memory and burned the paper. When investigators contacted Simon Magnus to inquire about her messages later, Simon Magnus said, "I never noticed them."

The other students stared at the back of her head—at her spiky, close-cropped hair, dyed an unnaturally deep black—with angry puzzlement as she told Simon Magnus how the angelic souls of the gay boys in the shōjo manga on the syllabus echoed Plato and Wilde or how the hermetic worldview of certain occult comic-book writers (to whom Simon Magnus had SimonMagnusself once upon a time been compared) accorded or failed to accord with Hegel's philosophy of history. Simon Magnus could detect that she knew Simon Magnus's work—she seemed to allude to it constantly by asking questions that could have no other relevance—though she allowed this to remain unspoken.

The classroom had been difficult in the years just before the pandemic; some students came ready to interrogate the writer about the work. What about the homophobia of *Marsh Man* (had Simon Magnus meant to analogize same-gender desire to cross-species sex in the classic issue, "The Love That Dare Not Speak Its Name"?) and the transphobia of *Ratman: Fools' Errand* (did Simon Magnus understand the enormity of the harm caused by the image of The Fool in a pink tutu anally violating Sparrow?) and the misogyny of *Overman 3000* (whatever Simon Magnus intended or realized, Mina Mars's climactically exploding womb reduced womanhood to birth and motherhood to sacrifice). In the pandemic's aftermath, however, the ideological ardor had dimmed along with everything else.

Other than her general strangeness and brilliance, Simon Magnus couldn't say what fascination Ash del Greco held for Simon Magnus. It was like when you dream of someone distinct but can't remember whom, as if you dreamed of someone you knew very well but knew only in the dream. Ash del Greco was like that: a shadowy figure, known but elusive, somehow in the corner of Simon Magnus's eye even when Simon Magnus stared straight at her, which Simon Magnus often couldn't help but do.

Simon Magnus had taken less notice of the vaguer and perhaps even somewhat etherial Jacob Morrow, though the boy too could raise those humble picture-books on the syllabus to the level of Plato and Hegel, Wilde and Nietzsche. Whenever he spoke, he raised his head and brushed his hair out of his eyes with his long tapered fingers. Simon Magnus remembered this gesture the instant Simon Magnus saw the video, because Jacob Morrow had used the barrel of the revolver to nudge the fringe of brown, blond-streaked hair away before he'd pressed the metal to the flesh of his right eyelid.

Jacob Morrow killed himself in the middle of the fall semester on the Wednesday between Simon Magnus's twice-a-week Tuesday/Thursday graphic novel class. The Tuesday before Jacob Morrow's public suicide, he wore the army jacket to class over his white T-shirt, a strange detail the adjunct professor noted at the time. The same day, Ash del Greco's mask read, *THE TRUE WAR IS A SPIRITUAL WAR.*

CHAPTER 2
Parts of Speech

Partly Simon Magnus did it out of contempt.

These spoiled children—rewarded for their supposed transgression of no-longer-enforced gender and sexual norms by mawkish school administrators, celebrated by an ever-more-illiterate popular culture that transformed even Simon Magnus's own comic-book innovations into pap for the masses, hailed as courageous by a corporate news and political media otherwise pledged to the lies of commerce and empire—what had these spoiled children ever suffered? Simon Magnus had been kicked half to death in the street for wearing a long lacy dress once.

They should, Simon Magnus thought, be *made* to suffer. Suffering must be the passkey to any and every more unusual style of individuation, not to mention any serious achievement in the arts. Most people ought not even attempt to transgress, first, because the world requires its preponderance of normal natures to replicate the species and sustain civilization, and, second, because most will botch it with their incorrigible bad taste. These brevetted brats with their pronoun stickers, they—they/them!—were not the losers but the winners of the social game, the game of power, a game for which Simon Magnus always at least tried to have, yes, contempt. Art—including the art of life—was a different game altogether, one where, as the man said, you had to lose your life to save it.

They had intruded, these spoiled children, on Simon Magnus's academic idyll. Simon Magnus, who had run away from the provinces to the great world, to what they called Cosmopolis in the comic books, hadn't wanted to come to live in this small world, proud and post-industrial—what the comic books wouldn't even have deigned to call Steel City.

Simon Magnus regretted the work Simon Magnus had written when Simon Magnus was barely older than these children: *Marsh Man*, *Ratman: Fools' Errand*, *Overman 3000*. Simon Magnus did not regret these works' putative homophobia or transphobia or misogyny; these were, Simon Magnus believed, authentic feelings and therefore authentically available for artistic expression, damn the moralists and the censors. Once translated for popular consumption, however, their visionary air of fantasy, even amid proceedings as grotesque as The Fool's rape of Sparrow, or Overman and Mina Mars's child exploding from her womb, seems to have addicted two whole generations to a belief that they could alter and order reality by fiat. In deference to public sensitivities, the company had affixed a warning label to Simon Magnus's books: *Suggested for Mature Readers*. Mature readers, however, never arrived.

Perhaps—it ought to be admitted—this was what Simon Magnus had meant when Simon Magnus promised Marco Cohen they would change the world with *Overman 3000*, that they would introduce to everybody the secrets of occult perception previously hoarded by elites and outcasts. Unlike elites and outcasts, however, "everybody" seemed to want a world without agony and so without interest.

Simon Magnus would never write a comic book again after *Overman 3000*. Simon Magnus would never write any stories again, since the stories Simon Magnus had written, and the visions Simon Magnus had seen as Simon Magnus wrote, had come true, true in every hideous possible way, not only the obvious—the dead child, the ruined marriage—but also a decade's worth of comic books and then movies framed in imitation of Simon Magnus's own foul moods and heinous anxieties and sweaty aspiration to have comic books taken seriously as "art." Simon Magnus, who had run away to Cosmopolis to become a poet!

After *Overman 3000* and the private disaster it occasioned, Simon Magnus had drowned Simon Magnus's book and would never write again. (Simon Magnus, never anything less than pretentious, who in fact often offered classroom defenses of the "pretentious" as a category to skeptical students, would actually reply by email to requests for interviews in the comics press with the line, "This rough magic I here abjure.") How, then, could Simon Magnus refuse the offer of a teaching position extended by academics impressed by the symbolic richness and formal intricacy of Simon Magnus's work rather than by the supposed "maturity" of its vaunted anal rape and exploding womb, which had once so impressed superhero comics' incorrigibly jejune fan club?

(It had been Ellen Chandler who'd gotten Simon Magnus the teaching position in Steel City two decades before, just after *Overman 3000* and the catastrophe by the ocean and just before she decided never to speak to Simon Magnus again.)

Simon Magnus found the impulse once satisfied by granting interviews in the fan press or speaking at comic-book conventions to be more than appeased by heading a classroom, however, especially in the early days, when the students came to class with opinions more lightly held, a cynicism easy enough to convert into some measure of awe by displays of wit and knowledge.

Not having gone to college SimonMagnusself—having run away to Cosmopolis to become a poet, having had a 40-issue run on *Marsh Man* and a savage beating in the street for imperfectly concealed transvestitism as Simon Magnus's Yale College and Simon Magnus's Harvard—Simon Magnus knew Simon Magnus had, upon arrival in Steel City, to add to Simon Magnus's stock of knowledge.

The university library, a concrete Brutalist bunker fluorescent white on the interior, looked like a hospital inside a prison in a garrison state, or so Simon Magnus judged; Simon Magnus entered once and then never again. Luckily, this modest city offered a vast public library just across the street from the university library, a library gifted to the city in its soot-skied days by one of the steel magnates, whose well-stocked stacks were dim and whose front was

Beaux-Arts—kitsch, perhaps, but hadn't Simon Magnus learned the hard way that avant-garde brutality could never sustain a life?

Simon Magnus grew to love Steel City and the university, to love the sheer drama of the Gothic Cathedral and its junior partner, the Gothic Chapel—the Chapel before which Jacob Morrow had done it—the two structures twinned at the center of campus, the former one of the tallest university buildings in the world, a Cathedral large enough to contain the expansion of mind beckoned by the education delivered within its walls, the latter in all its limestone quaintness another magnate's gift, a Chapel on the lawn of a secular college, its windows decorated in universalist splendor with stained-glass portraits of Abraham Lincoln, Florence Nightingale, and Emily Dickinson.

Simon Magnus resented Simon Magnus's permanent relegation to classes on comics, but Simon Magnus still fed on the intelligence, or at least the energy of the students. Living alone in a modest studio apartment near the campus, determined never again to love as never again to write, since both love and writing had ended for Simon Magnus in the same conflagration by the ocean, Simon Magnus gave SimonMagnusself a PhD-level education several times over. Simon Magnus even came to appreciate, as Simon Magnus never thought Simon Magnus would—Simon Magnus, who had never been to college—the long patience and stately rhythm of accurate and imaginative scholarship.

All possibilities for major pleasure had vanished from Simon Magnus's life after *Overman 3000*, after that hell on earth that its composition caused to erupt by the ocean at the turn of the millennium, but Simon Magnus derived the height of minor pleasures in that first decade teaching. Simon Magnus would wander around the campus in fall or spring, beneath the colonnade of trees in front of the Beaux-Arts facade of the public library as the branches burst into autumnal flame or wetly budded pale green in the spring thaw. Simon Magnus would sit on benches at intervals to appreciate books as magisterially learned as Auerbach's *Mimesis* or Frye's *Anatomy of Criticism*, Bakhtin's *Dialogic Imagination*, or Lukács's *Theory of the Novel*. Simon Magnus, who had never gone to college SimonMagnusself, was seduced by scholarship.

(To encourage the director of undergraduate studies to keep renewing Simon Magnus's contract—little difficulty here, since Simon Magnus's students generally appreciated Simon Magnus, not least because Simon Magnus had no interest in grades, because Simon Magnus tended to give the girls, gays, and theys nothing but As—Simon Magnus even presented a paper at a conference hosted by the department once, the first and last thing Simon Magnus had written since *Overman 3000*. The paper was titled "Pamela Colman Smith: First and Best Comic-Book Artist?" How could anyone deny that the artist who'd transformed the Tarot with her fantastical *ligne claire* had illustrated anything other than a portable graphic novel, with narrative constituents the user could rearrange at will for purposes of illumination and divination, just as God, if there was a God, could look up and down and back and forth through the rotating crystal of eternity? Wasn't this fifth-dimensional perception of fourth-dimensional realities the philosophical secret of comics as a form? The audience of professors and graduate students clapped quietly, politely, and asked in the Q&A if Smith was a lesbian, if Smith was a woman of color, if Smith had resented Yeats.)

About a decade ago came the students seduced by politics, seduced, as far as Simon Magnus could see, through a screen. Simon Magnus was not one for the internet. Simon Magnus's first forays into the digital wilderness brought Simon Magnus into contact with too many commentaries on Simon Magnus: not only absurd fan theories on message boards taking Simon Magnus's books as literal cryptograms rather than open-ended symbols ("Was The Fool really Ratman in disguise when he sodomized Sparrow?") but also ideological critique across the social and even video platforms. Simon Magnus watched a girl who couldn't have been older than 15, with hair the color of toilet cleanser, sitting in front of a bookshelf filled with toys as she assembled textual evidence from every part of *Marsh Man*, *Ratman: Fools' Errand*, and *Overman 3000* to establish what she called Simon Magnus's "terror of the feminine."

Was she, however, a "she," despite very nearly resembling a "she," notwithstanding her hair color, which resembled nothing human? Did she harbor some terror of the feminine herself? Simon Magnus, after encountering those whom he privately called the pronoun people for the first time, suspected she might. Confronted with these students' injunction to twist the language in Simon Magnus's own mouth, as if they had insinuated their fingers onto Simon Magnus's own tongue, not to mention Simon Magnus's eyes, which surely retained rights of private observation and judgment, Simon Magnus was reminded less of the youthful Simon Magnus, alone and bleeding in a lacy dress on the concrete, but of the exercise in dominance that had brought the long-vanished "boy" in the dress down to "his" knees.

(Simon Magnus, who had not gone to college, had been very nearly college-aged when writing those first *Marsh Man* scripts, hammering on the old typewriter at the end of Ellen Chandler's bed, wearing Ellen Chandler's peignoir, laughing to SimonMagnusself as Simon Magnus robed the boggy behemoth, the anti-hero from the fens, in his murdered mother's wedding dress. Simon Magnus had been these kids' ages when Simon Magnus had set out to change the world.)

Simon Magnus had not worn a dress (publicly) since moving to Steel City. Simon Magnus looked as Simon Magnus thought the college classroom required

Simon Magnus to look: blazers and button-down shirts and corduroy pants, a small, neatly trimmed beard and thinning, graying hair swept back from the forehead. Stared down by students who came to class bristling with neologistic pronouns and armed with the internet's bill of indictment against Simon Magnus's corpus—and not even the *right* bill of indictment, for Simon Magnus had literally murdered a baby, while these children were bitching and moaning about merely textual transgressions—students convinced that Simon Magnus was no more than the almost-dead white male whose condemnatory obituary they had already written, Simon Magnus thought to SimonMagnusself, Oh no, *élèves*: two can play at this game.

Despite having kept for over 10 years to SimonMagnusself, despite having avoided any attention-grabbing interventions in the life of the university community, despite having only quietly hoped for three to four classes a semester, enough to keep busy, to keep remorse and regret at bay—there was no need for money; the royalties on the comics and Mother Magnus's inheritance more than paid for the small book-crammed studio apartment near campus—Simon Magnus suddenly, toward the middle of the 21st century's second decade, announced SimonMagnusself.

Simon Magnus, adjunct professor though Simon Magnus was, became the first member of the English faculty to declare publicly, in a mass email and then in one of the open-to-all department meetings Simon Magnus had never before attended, that Simon Magnus was party to no gender and would henceforward use "they/them" pronouns. Simon Magnus also moved to make compulsory for faculty, students, and even staff in the department to declare their own pronouns on all official department communication.

Two Shakespeare scholars who had been mortal enemies for 40 years and who both refused to retire—a withered octogenarian New Critic in a rumpled brown suit (author of *The Art Itself Is Nature: Tension and Reconciliation in Shakespeare's Late Romances*) and a sexagenarian second-wave lesbian separatist feminist with the tips of her chopped hair dyed purple (who had written *My Foot My Tutor: Shakespearean Images of Sex-Class Subordination*)—vehemently protested. In a shaky voice, the old man grumbled about clarity in communication; a colleague who had apprenticed in deconstructionism in the 1980s, and who'd authored *(De)Facing It: Conrad's Allegories of Inscription*, reminded him that ambiguity and aporia were the essence of the literary. The feminist more forcefully, albeit in a longtime smoker's rasp, expressed her resentment at receiving this high-handed lecture on gender from a man, but, after all, Simon Magnus was *not* a man, which was the whole point of this conversation, as the younger faculty protested. Their informal ringleader, a 40-year-old silver-haired queer theorist turned digital humanist in silver-framed glasses, author of *Feeling Superficial: Posthuman Data Affects*, asked the two elderly and near-elderly holdouts, the New Critic and the second-wave feminist, what it would cost them to be kind. In the end, only the two Shakespeare scholars voted no; Simon Magnus's motion was adopted. The second-wave feminist was put on administrative leave pending a review of her case; the New Critic was enjoined, at long last, to retire.

A month later, Simon Magnus advanced the cause, inspired by that apocryphal student of Heraclitus's who'd surpassed the master by arguing that you couldn't even step into the same river *once*, so protean were both yourself and the river. Simon Magnus next called for the total elimination of binary gender pronouns—the old "he" and "she"—in official communication (and not "preferred" pronouns either, Simon Magnus insisted: "Your identity is absolute or it's not really quite *identity*, is it?" Simon Magnus said). Simon Magnus now argued that gender as such belonged to the last millennium, that anyone's use of a traditional gender pronoun was therefore best totally proscribed if we wanted to hasten the advent of the new order. Simon Magnus agitated for a mandate on "they" as the pronoun of reference for any and all individuals and collectives. Simon Magnus spoke at the department meeting with a literary sophistication the other faculty had not imagined the "comic-book guy" to have had in "his" (not that you could say "his" anymore) repertoire. The professors didn't know that Simon Magnus's veins ran with blue blood, blood practically from Plymouth Rock, as Mother Magnus would be only too happy to tell them were she still on the right side of the dirt.

Simon Magnus said, "Isn't everyone internally a collective and collocation of many voices and identities, a concept articulated eloquently even at the heart of our classics from Shakespeare to Whitman to Joyce, such that we have no right to call anyone with a psyche as teeming as Hamlet's or Walt Whitman's or Leopold Bloom's—which is to say, *anyone*—anything other than 'them?'"

While writing and then delivering this statement, Simon Magnus felt a distantly familiar unwholesome whole-body thrill, not only the energy of contempt with which the project had begun but also the exhilaration of swimming in a current of idea and emotion Simon Magnus had discovered rather than invented, a current from beyond the bounds of human community. Simon Magnus remembered feeling just this way when writing those notorious comic books that had reinvented the American superhero, except that Simon Magnus was now living the story rather than writing it. Simon Magnus's life itself was Simon Magnus's new graphic novel, a graphic novel become a *Gesamtkunstwerk*.

The department voted to refer the matter upward to the faculty senate at large. The next month, Simon Magnus made the same case to more skepticism from a less aesthetically inclined audience. Simon Magnus was followed as speaker by a trans assistant professor of sociology who narrated, with an unbroken voice but arcs of tears glimmering on each of her cheeks under the chamber's fluorescent lights, the vicious abuse she'd suffered outside an off-campus bar by men who referred to her in the third person alternately as "he" and "it." This sociological orator supplemented her speech with an editorial in the school paper accusing the faculty senate of having coerced her, of having forced her to defend her very sense of self, of having made her offer up her trauma for public consumption. The editorial occasioned a minor scandal online and the stepping-down of the faculty senate president, but in the moment, her testimony—to the not unpersuasive effect that Simon Magnus wished with the proposal of universal "they/them" to abolish her identity as surely as did those slurring sots who'd abused her—carried the day.

From this experience, Simon Magnus learned that public persuasion was as risky as the public was fickle, so Simon Magnus instead worked behind the scenes on the department chair, the Equity and Diversity Office, and eventually, the dean of the College of Liberal Arts. The charm and authoritative style of speaking Simon Magnus had first developed for dealing with the comic-book fan press and convention crowds and then in the college classroom—a style some critics acclaimed as the writer's true gift, so much that "Simon Magnus's greatest creation is 'Simon Magnus'" became proverbial in Simon Magnus criticism—worked just as well in private, at least for those unused to it.

These authorities weighed Simon Magnus's argument against the possibility of bad press. Wouldn't Simon Magnus's proposal of compulsory "they/them" earn the school a reputation for faddish radicalism from the rather conservative outside world, if not an internal rebuke from the trans community like the one Simon Magnus had already received from the colleague on the sociology faculty? Simon Magnus persuaded them that, in fact, it was not only an egalitarian gesture in line with the most advanced gender thinking—more advanced, Simon Magnus insinuated *sotto voce*, than any variant of transgenderism that upheld the old, bad binary—but was also preparation for a professional life that would be less and less personalized as automation took hold. "Have you heard about developments in artificial intelligence?" Simon Magnus inquired. Who would ever know or need to know the gender or even the ontological status (human? machine?) of managers and clients and partners in the future?

The transition to universal "they/them" would, moreover—and this, too, Simon Magnus had very nearly to whisper in the ears of chairs and deans, of powers and principalities—marginalize the groups that actually upset potential tuition-paying parents in the provinces—namely, the old-fashioned feminists who asked that female identity be granted special privileges and protections, and the actual transgender community, which good American Christians still found threateningly perverse. A genderless community, however, was without sexual connotation, was sexless enough even for the devout, was simply a fungible workforce and rational citizenry in the making, quite in line with the school's latter-day mission to train not the yeoman farmers of old but the office administrators and administratees of tomorrow.

In the end, without public debate or vote, Simon Magnus's measure was adopted, and students were referred to and even began to refer to one another as "they/them" regardless of either observed or professed gender identity, though the profession of identity, and hence the solicitation of personal pronouns, was still of course allowed. An eructation of conservative, feminist, and transgender objections briefly sounded, though the impossibility of these constituencies forming any coalition doomed their efforts to protest, and the university ended up hailed as an institution in the van of progress by forums as various as fashion magazines directed at young femmes, TV talk shows aimed at middle-aged housewives, and learned journals written for implicitly male libertarians of both left and right persuasions. Simon Magnus had created a world where all would be equally addressed as citizens, workers, and consumers first, and men, women, and in-betweens second, if at all, a world not unlike that of the silver-citadel'd planet Cyphron in the writer's masterpiece, *Overman 3000*.

Other public universities hastily adopted the measure, and Simon Magnus experienced a second celebrity, profiled in national newspapers and interviewed on popular podcasts. In the course of the victory, however, Simon Magnus came to understand that Simon Magnus had not gone nearly far enough when Simon Magnus had eliminated the gender pronoun. Simon Magnus had an unyielding, never-resting mind. Simon Magnus was Simon Magnus's own best interlocutor and adversary. Simon Magnus was the person least suited to win an institutional victory, because Simon Magnus would inevitably assault the very territory Simon Magnus had captured.

Simon Magnus sighted a new horizon: the abolition of the pronoun *per se*. Simon Magnus became aware of a contradiction in the very argument Simon Magnus had used to win the argument for "they/them," a logic which redefined the human as at once an aggregate plural mass and a teeming and inwardly diverse individual. Simon Magnus asked SimonMagnusself: Well, which was it? In theory, it could be both—anything can be true in theory—but which was more authentic to experience? If the individual was already a "them," then the crowd could only oversimplify and reduce this aggregate. Just because the aggregate could be disassembled by analysis did not mean it should be assumed prematurely into an abstract whole. Analysis proved only that—here, Simon

Magnus, in the full flush of a newfound devotion to using abstract intellect against itself, though Simon Magnus had never gone to college, quoted Adorno: "The whole is the false." What right had we to generalize at all? Consequently, why should there be pronouns at all? They—and "they/them"—only accentuated language's already brutal tendency toward abstraction. They assimilated you to some category or other.

People should have to say your name every time, and your name moreover should be some unutterable constellation of multisensory stimulants. When they say your name, they should have to dance and to paint, to cry and to compose a cantata, Simon Magnus argued. Rectifying names would come later, however; the personal pronoun as such had to be annihilated first. My pronouns are the insides of my cheeks gripped between my teeth and the flanges of flesh between my toes, the tingling sensation in my perineum when I look out from a great height and the languid heat of my head on an endless winter weekend afternoon reading abed. There are no pronouns. Call me Simon Magnus or call me nothing at all.

CHAPTER 3
Community Harvest

The day after Jacob Morrow shot himself through the eye in front of the Chapel, Simon Magnus's Studies in the Graphic Novel class was cancelled by the department. The department chair summoned Simon Magnus to his office.

In the wide, sparse administrative office—bare of the books that would have crowded the dim monk's cell of a tenured faculty member's office, bare of anything but a ficus tree and a smell like plastic—the department chair sat silhouetted against the high window at his back, snow swirling out of a blank sky, white on white. Early November and the year's first snowfall. It occurred to Simon Magnus that all the white light behind the chair was shining directly onto Simon Magnus. He can stare down the well of every pore on my face.

The chair leaned forward, his elbows on the sleek desk, his hands clasped in a gesture of warmth and goodwill. Simon Magnus, the pronoun activist turned proper noun activist, the man—or whatever—who had written those insane comic books with the sodomy and the exploding fetuses and whatnot, who didn't even have a bachelor's, let alone a doctorate, and yet who spoke in whirls of eloquence, obviously made him nervous. The chair was an old-timer, the kind the younger faculty dismissed as a fossil. White as a bone and blue-eyed, he'd been elected chair only because the youthful and ambitious scholars in the department preferred more time for research over the thankless task of administration.

The chair knew his colleagues didn't respect him, because they thought he didn't understand the new ways. An old salt, a humanistic Melville scholar from way back, his plow- or prow-shaped white beard in imitation of the master, with a yellow streak in the middle from the pipe he favored, he compensated for his superannuation by obeying with exaggerated solemnity whatever he'd been told was both revolutionary and mandatory. He had voted avidly for Simon Magnus's proposals, first for the pronouns and then for the proper nouns. He wore a pink sticker that read *HE/HIM* at all times on the front pocket of the white shirt where he kept pens, cough drops, his pipe, and a cigarette packet.

The chair said, "Personally, I don't see that you did a damn thing wrong. I've finally read some of it myself. It was perfectly"—he chuckled familiarly—"psychedelic. Christ, I haven't read an Overman comic book since I was six years old. He had a little white dog, I remember. Cyphro, was it? Your approach was certainly different from what I remember. Maybe it's better you didn't include the dog given everything else, the fetus and whatnot. Listen, Mr. Magnus, Simon, I mean, I mean Simon Magnus, you and I are from a different world—it might as well be the planet Cyphron. It's called Cyphron, right? We have skins like leather. We're old men, I mean people, you know, persons of age. Things don't affect us the way they affect these kids. Remember when you were in your teens, your 20s? When you'd be drowning in a sea of uncontrollable emotion for days? Developmental psychology. It's an interesting field of study."

He shuffled some printouts on his desk, hunting for relevant information.

"Do you know the brain isn't fully mature until the age of 25? Christ, I was married before that, wife number one, long may she thrive. Anyway, like I said, if it were up to me, there wouldn't be any problem here, but it's not up to me. The media's on this now—and social media, well, God help us. The experts in the student welfare office say there could be a real case here. Contagion effects. Leaving aside the actual suicide—well, I'm not sure we're supposed to say 'suicide' anymore, but I can't remember what we *are* supposed to say—the other students could have been affected too. Emotional harm leading to opportunity loss. That sort of thing."

He leaned back, folded his arms over his paunch, and signed phlegmily.

"This is hard. It's hard, but I have to tell you: they're opening up an investigation. They want to interview all your students. They want to go through the book carefully with some other experts—psychologists. Not people from the psychology department; they think faculty members even in another department would side with you on principle—would have a conflict of interest."

"The book?" Simon Magnus said.

"Your book. *Overman 2001.*"

"I didn't assign that book."

"No, but you did write it."

"What is the relevance of that to the suicide of Jacob Morrow?"

"Well, Simon Magnus, the ending, or not just the ending but the part in the middle too, all the material about the 'cleansing force.' The beginning's not great either. It could all be read as justifying suicide—or self-harm, is that what we're supposed to call it? Shakespeare said 'self-slaughter.' Not that Shakespeare should be regarded as the authority on the English language, I certainly wouldn't say that. Anyway, the whole thing about the cult praying for death, Overman's girlfriend, or partner, I think they call it now, sacrificing herself, well, to an unbalanced mind, if they say 'unbalanced,' well, you can see how it might look."

He shuffled some more papers and studied one he'd shuffled to the top. Seized by a coughing fit, his chest rattling like wet gravel, he briefly doubled over. The beard, the pipe, the cough—these were the only Melvillean qualities, Simon Magnus thought, of this otherwise wretched, loathsome coward. The chair straightened up, blinked his cloudy, red-rimmed eyes a few times rapidly and reapplied himself to his papers.

"They're bringing in some folks from outside, a nonprofit the service-learning office works with—Community Harvest, it's called. They, let's see, let me refresh my memory, I have it right here, yes, they, and I quote, 'provide mental-health resources to underserved populations'—in hopes of reducing the, well, you know, the violence out there. Do they still call it violence? You know, I learned the other day they're still called bullet points—those little dots, I mean, when you're making a list. I thought, bullets, that can't possibly be right. Anyway, they, Community Harvest, can go through a book like this and identify, well, hell, I don't know, I think they call them trauma triggers and whatnot. Pending the investigation, Simon, I mean Simon Magnus, I can keep you on the adjunct faculty, though I have to suspend you from the classroom. Legal's advising a written apology from you, addressed to the entire academic community."

"An apology? For what?"

"For having, well, I guess, though it sounds strange when I say it, for having written the book. The student welfare office said it couldn't hurt. They encouraged you, how did they put it, to 'take accountability.' I can send you some templates from their resource center. The student welfare folks also have some recommendations for your syllabus, if you do get back in the classroom.

'Texts that address these challenges our learners face in a more responsible way,' is how the representative said it to me, very nice girl, or woman, or, well, you know, whatever."

Simon Magnus must have said a polite farewell, shaken the old man's hand. Before Simon Magnus knew it, Simon Magnus was back in the hallway. There would be no written apology. There would be no revision to the future syllabi Simon Magnus might get to write, pending the results of the investigation, which there also would not be. When Simon Magnus walked out of the building that day, Simon Magnus resolved, it would be for the last time. Simon Magnus slipped down a dim stairwell to go to the office Simon Magnus shared with eight other adjunct professors to pack Simon Magnus's things.

What had Yeats written? Something about, "Did my poem send out those men to get shot?" No, that didn't scan, but something like it—Yeats, who had conversed with spirits. Despite Simon Magnus's occult reputation, Simon Magnus had only ever heard from one spirit. This Simon Magnus hadn't forgotten, would never forget. She had laughed in Simon Magnus's burning face, her red hair wild in the wind of the forest, and said, "What did you think, little magus? That you could have it all for free?"

Five minutes later, Simon Magnus exited the Cathedral through the revolving doors across the common from the Chapel, the place where Jacob Morrow had done it. In the prematurely wintry wind, Simon Magnus paused to stare across the grass, the hollows in the green bright with the massing wet snow.

A woman stood in the spot where Jacob Morrow had stood with the gun the day before, her back to the Chapel, as his had been. Something drew Simon Magnus closer to her through the blinding snowstorm. She was short with close-cropped auburn hair. She wore a black dress with black tights and black heels—no coat, despite the weather. Her bare arms and shoulders crawled with tattoos. Her hands were clasped awkwardly over her midsection. What was she holding? Simon Magnus got close enough to see a tiny revolver, antique from the looks of it, silver-plated, pearl-handled. Simon Magnus ran toward her.

"Don't worry, I'm not going to kill myself. Suicide is a sin. Against life, I mean. I'm here to kill her. I found Jakey's schedule for the semester. I went to the classroom to kill her, but class was cancelled. I don't know what I'm doing here."

"To kill Ash del Greco?" Simon Magnus ventured.

"That's her. That's the little cunt's name. Who the fuck are you?"

Simon Magnus hesitated for long enough to consider several false names, John James, Overman's alter ego, being the most obvious, but discarded them as beneath Simon Magnus's dignity and finally said, "I'm Simon Magnus."

Her wet eyes went wide with rage, and she fumblingly pushed the pistol forward. Simon Magnus easily bent back her wrist. The pistol dropped into the snow. She yelped in pain and fell, shivering and weeping, into Simon Magnus's arms, smelling of cold air, all-natural deodorant, and musky perfume.

"You killed my baby," Jessica Morrow cried. "All of you killed my baby!"

CHAPTER 4
Out of Time

Jessica Morrow wasn't one for the internet, but you couldn't run a business in the 21st century without it. She kept an Instagram account for Untimely Vintage updated at least once a week with enticing photos and descriptions of new arrivals, and she followed everyone back who followed her. She kept her eye on the DMs for business inquiries, but she usually only found obscene demands: "tits or GTFO," "feet?"

She did see a meme in the feed one day, however—the day after Jakey's funeral, in fact. Though she'd guessed that it had been meant as a dark joke, like most memes she ran into, commiseration in shared suffering and a shared laugh from some despairing boy in some suburban basement who couldn't get laid. (Is that why Jakey had despaired? No, he was surely too young, or had been too young, young or old as he'd ever be, to have worried about that.) Instead of giving her a grim chuckle at the often unspoken truth, however, this meme so succinctly—but also so strangely and so beautifully—expressed what she thought of as her dilemma that she, who had not cried at her son's viewing or his funeral, began to shake and sob right there behind the counter, beneath the encyclopedia set, in her mercifully empty shop.

The meme showed a little blonde girl, five or six years old. She looked dutifully into the camera, squinting or wincing more than she was smiling, a look more of apprehension than childish wonder.

Above an expanse of grass behind the girl reared the old skyline of the big city Jessica Morrow somehow thought, even now, that she would eventually somehow run away to, the skyline as it had been for the whole last quarter of the last century, commanded by those two columns, those giant bars of glass challenging the sky, proclaiming the dominion of man, of commerce, of America, for better and for worse, over the face of the earth.

The sky was clear but somehow ominous—probably the meme artist had, with some digital tool or other, exercised poetic license—not quite blue as a clear calm sky is blue, like the sky that Tuesday morning over two decades ago had been, but storm-darkened halfway to an electric indigo.

The color reminded her of when a pleasant dream slowly curdles to a nightmare. You're in the car with your father; you're on your way to a party; it's a sunny day. Then it's not sunny anymore; he turns his eyes from the road to face you; those black marbles aren't his eyes; that man is not your father; a party, you somehow understand, is certainly not where you're going.

In this purple, unnatural monsoon sky above the girl and the Towers, the meme artist had added, in a typewriter font evocative of the middle 20th century, the slogan: *The world you were raised to survive in no longer exists.*

Whatever it meant exactly—whatever political message the mememeister had intended—Jessica Morrow thought it described her problem exactly. She could have been that girl on that day. Over a long weekend when she was a girl, her mother had taken her on a Greyhound to the big city shortly after her father left. They'd shopped and dined and gone to museums; they's gotten dressed up and gone to see *Miss Saigon*. How could it be that she was 38 and had already lost so much? She wasn't raised to live in a world where her young and only child died long before she did ("long before she did"? when had she died?), and by his own youthful hand, his hand just barely full grown and beginning to sprout a bit of dark hair at the knuckles like his father, not the babyish blonde fuzz, the memory of which doubled her over.

Jessica Morrow finally calmed herself down enough to remind herself not to romanticize the world she had really been raised in, the world she'd escaped in every way she could at the time.

There was the prison of her first home to begin with, the place she'd lived for her first 12 years. It didn't look so frightening from the outside—nor even, when she revisited it as an adult, all that large—though in her girlhood and in her memories and in her nightmares, it loomed like a castle in which she'd been kept. Objectively, it was just a regular suburban house. It appeared warm, with its orangeish bricks the color of a cat's fur (she wasn't allowed pets) or a blaze on the hearth (her parents had had the fireplace bricked up before she was born).

Inside, it was just the three of them: daddy and mommy and baby. Even behind the doors and curtains, no one ever raised a hand or even a voice in anger. The immaculate white kitchen, the pale pink pristine carpet, the lawn they paid to have cut and professionally treated once a week—all these remained unblemished by what she sometimes saw in friends' houses, during visits to cousins, or on TV (she was allowed two hours' viewing a day, after homework, supervised): familial screaming contests in which all words of argument were lost in noise, doors slammed so hard the paint fell in patches from the walls, a white cheek blossoming with the red print of an open palm. No such overt violence would be permitted in her parents' house, just tense, terse remarks burdened with brutal implication.

Her mother to her father, as they watched an educational documentary on public television: "Cirrhosis of the liver, isn't that what your mom had?"

Her father to her mother, eyes on the middle of her dress before a dinner for his colleagues at the law firm: "You'll have to get that let out soon."

Both of them to her, in the calmest voices you've ever heard, like surgeons bending their shrouded antiseptic heads over a spread rib cage, and whether she was in her yellow Easter pinafore or her green Christmas smock or her tasteful homemade Halloween costume (Snow White, Cinderella: only princesses allowed), or whether she'd brought her report card home or won an art contest at school or made a new friend:

"What's the stain on the sleeve? What did you did to your hair? You'll have to have those teeth fixed. A lady crosses her legs. A lady doesn't slouch her shoulders. A lady turns her toes out, not in. The best colleges aren't very interested in A-minuses in fundamental subjects, you know. Art doesn't pay, you know. Her mother's a bartender, you know. Do you think you're going out in that? A lady doesn't watch that. A lady doesn't read that. A lady doesn't eat that."

Her parents had followed every rule, written and unwritten, that their own parents had told them they'd need to follow if they wanted to escape a somewhat sordid and slovenly set of working-class or (at best) lower-middle-class origins, origins their parents were ashamed of—the drinking, the fighting; men on unemployment, women with black eyes; this uncle in jail, that cousin knocked up at 17—but not skilled enough to transcend themselves. They, her parents, didn't drink or go to jail or have a baby too soon. Her father was a lawyer, her mother was a nurse: they were educated professionals, and they had gotten away from stoops on city blocks to buy a house like a hearth fire in a leafy suburb and bear and rear the perfect child, a princess in a pinafore who needed only minor adjustments to her teeth and hair and toes and shoulders and grades and friends and interests and desires and ambitions. The result was that husband and wife each felt like a prisoner, and the princess believed she'd been buried in a freezing dungeon 100 feet below the earth.

Then she went, in about a month, from the dungeon to the furnace. There had been hints and premonitions: for example, two business trips in a year to that same Babylonish city in the desert.

"I hadn't known slot machines and chorus girls played such an important part in estate planning law," her mother commented archly at their regular dinner hour as she spooned potatoes au gratin onto her father's plate the day of his return from his second trip.

Her mother didn't think her father had actually run away with a chorus girl, though that is how she always referred to the woman, likely a paralegal at some law firm out there in the desert. Back in those pre-social-media days, she and her mother never even saw a picture of their usurper, though Jessica Morrow did look her up later. She was barely younger, and not any prettier, than her mother, but on the evidence of her Facebook profile, she ran a relaxed, even boisterous household. The half-brother and half-sister Jessica Morrow never knew seemed to spend their whole lives in a swimming pool, and she certainly never saw the little girl in any pinafore. One picture showed the children, a boy and a girl—they were adolescents by the time Jessica Morrow internet-stalked them—eating dinner with their plates in their laps on the living room couch, and what's more, they wore their shoes in the house. Neither her father nor her mother would have tolerated the peril of food or shoes to the pale pink pristine carpet, much less from carelessly lounging, laughing 12- and 13-year-olds.

Jessica Morrow also got glimpses of her elusive father himself on his second wife's Facebook profile. He was no longer the tall, trim, dark-haired man in a suit she remembered from the mornings before he went to work and she to school, but a balding, potbellied suburban bon vivant. His Hawaiian shirt—she couldn't believe that—was unbuttoned to the navel, white hair curling thickly on his sun-leathered chest; he had a beer can dangling from his hand as he lounged in a lawn chair, a spiny xeriscape spreading out in all directions from where he carelessly splayed his boat shoes. In another, older picture, his baby daughter, his second daughter, sat in his lap and picked through his whitening pelt. He didn't look like he cared any longer what a lady was or was not supposed to do. Jessica Morrow was never to know for sure, however, since he'd abandoned her as well as her mother. He only sent his regular checks—no extras for Christmas or her birthday—to her mother. He did no more than his legal duty, this man of the law. He sent no word of salutation or recognition.

She could even understand it, sympathize with it, by the time she herself was an adult, maybe because he *was* her father, and the capacity to do whatever he had done ran in her blood. He had made a mistake, a long mistake; he'd lost more than a decade of his best years. In trying to evade squalor, he had forsaken excitement, spontaneity, pleasure, and comfort, too. (She remembered that the second trip out west—could there, her mother wondered, really be two estate planning law conferences in the same city in the same year?—quickly followed his own father's death, an event that must have made him aware of his own life's limit.) It's no small error to throw away half of your 20s and all of your

30s on an ideal that had, when you attained it, proved worthless: a house like a prison, a wife whose judgment made you afraid, a child whose fear—the fear you yourself inspired—you can read in her eyes. After a major mistake like that, you trembled with shame and embarrassment just to think of it. As for atonement, that's just a word. The people you hurt will never forget it, no matter what they might promise or how you might pay them back; they will always flinch at your approach or have a scheme of revenge locked away somewhere in mind. The best thing to do—after settling financial accounts properly, of course; he wasn't a barbarian, but a man of law—was to travel separate roads and forget the past had ever happened.

Who had it happened to, anyway? Time changed you so much you could hardly be said to be the man who had harbored those delusions, the man who'd inspired the panic in that child's eyes. How could he become someone else, how could he ever forget, if he still had to see that petrified little girl in a pinafore at Christmas every year for the rest of his life? How would he forget what he'd done, whoever had done it? How would she? Yes, she understood. So much of what she held against him was based not on justice, not on whatever he formally owed her or her mother, but simply the selfish resentment that he had not taken her, her alone, her without her mother, to the city in the desert, to the endless swimming pool.

After her mother died and then Jakey died, she remembered that her father was almost the last person in the world who knew her, and she thought about getting on a plane to the desert. He had failed as a father to her, but she was still living, so he hadn't failed as a father as badly as she had failed as a mother, when the minimal necessary requirement of the job is to keep the child alive. When she imagined a poolside reunion with her 60-something or 70-something father—his proper little lady, his stiffened princess, her arms now crawling with tattoos, a ring in her nose—she decided they would both die of embarrassment. Now that Jakey was gone, she thought she might kill herself instead, herself or someone else: the girl, for instance, the girl with him the night before his death in Untimely Vintage, the strange girl on the security footage: the girl with the scar on her ugly face.

CHAPTER 5
The Eye

If her parents' marriage had been her first prison, her mother's freedom was her second. This woman who'd never had more than one glass of wine with Sunday dinner started buying it by the box. Where her old house smelled of potpourri, her newer ones, a series of suburban apartments with roach-colored carpets and rusty tub drains, now reeked of smoke and ash. A prissy whispered "damn" if she dropped a fork or misplaced her keys was succeeded by "bullshit!" bellowed at the TV news and "cocksucker!" hurled out the car window at rival drivers. Despite her former husband's quiet insults, she hadn't really ever needed to let out a dress when she'd lived in the hearth-warm house; in fact, she would try on her wedding dress every year on their anniversary just to boast that it still fit as well as it had when she was 25. Now—in tandem with the switch from meals cooked at home out of health-conscious lifestyle magazine recipes to frozen dinners and crinkling bags of chips—she came to favor a billowing, cinchless mumu. Her high voice roughened. She snored on the couch after dinner, crumbs on her chest, a ceiling fan whose blades were edged with greasy dust spinning slowly above her with an inner-ear-deranging subliminal buzz. She went to the grocery store in slippers.

Her own ladyhood discarded—her experiment in escaping the family squalor having failed—Jessica Morrow's was even less of a concern to her. The divorce happened when the girl was 13, and that's when her mother began telling her—she might have told her for the first time on the Greyhound to the big city, to *Miss Saigon*, the bus that smelled like the toilet at its rear—that she had to start learning from her own mistakes instead of relying on her parents to prevent her from ever making them. The transgression of staying up past your bedtime punishes itself when you're too tired to stay on your feet the next day. It wasn't an absurd principle, Jessica Morrow later thought; it had truth on its side.

Should it be sprung on a child all at once, however, with no preparation, and all the mistakes in the world, even the ones you don't come back from, available all at once? There was, moreover, no worse preparation than a prior set of constraints so severe—the prison, the pinafore—that the child lacked even the smallest introductory experience of freedom, which, if it's not practiced like an art, will enslave you to your basest and most dangerous desires, even as you call them liberation. Jessica Morrow had never even had a drop of champagne on New Year's Eve, and now here was an unattended box of wine.

Jessica Morrow managed not to die—her mother, like her father, had her beat at parenting too—but she owed her life more to luck than to any wise decision she or her mother had made. She certainly might have died: many things could have killed her. Why not hepatitis from her first tattoo, a stick-and-poke job at age 14 from a junior boy her friend knew, a boy who took an excessive and even panting pleasure at branding her above the ass in his absent family's sweaty basement? Why not auto wreck, why not murder, crossing state lines flattened on a gritty truck bed under a suffocating black nylon tarp trying not to throw up as some other boy drunkenly careered and wavered down the highway to see some long-forgotten band—Live or Rusted Root. Why not drowning when still a third boy gave her her first tab of acid down at the surprisingly deep creek that ran behind her and her mother's then-apartment, when they took off their clothes and waded into the water so they could float on their backs, watch the stars pulse and fall all around them through the trees? Why not this, why not that?

There were a million things that could kill you, not least your own perverse and miserable soul. She didn't lead a very interesting life in those years; they weren't very well worth remembering, the drinking and the puking, the blasted eardrums, the red fishnet tights or black pleather pants, the old-pennies-and-spoiled-meat flavor of an unwashed penis in her marijuana-dried mouth. She wanted to forget, too, her silent mother, with her cigarettes, her box wine, her slippers, her apartments with their once-white wallpaper jaundiced from decades of transient smokers and plastic venetian blinds that would never come clean again.

She did well in school. She knew how to follow directions calmly, no matter how much you felt like screaming. The ashy haze of her false freedom, however, didn't truly lift until her senior year. She'd always loved art and taken elective art classes throughout high school. To spare herself the sights and smells of her mother's coarsening, she would ride the bus from whatever brown-floored suburban apartment building they lived in at the time down to the city, where she would station herself at a café window and draw the passers-by in her sketchbook.

She rarely depicted faces or scenery or nature; what people wore fascinated her. What they actually wore—often drab, dull, ragged, or merely functional clothes: the men in puffy coats with football logos in winter, the women in flip-flops and shapeless T-shirts in summer—sparked in her imagination a vision of what they might, in a better world with better taste, someday come to wear.

Her sketches grew increasingly utopian, and as her imagination overtook her, she was attracted less and less to the oblivion—drugs or sex—of her usual weekends. "Stuck-up bitch," her friends judged her, without understanding the nature of her transformation. She didn't shun the beer-and-handjob weekend parties in suburban family rooms under oblivious or absent parental eyes to haunt the urban cafés, bookstores, and museums out of any sense of social superiority, but because she had discovered, without having sought it, a higher inebriation she could barely put into words.

Something about art as she saw it in the Carnegie Museum or as she made it under her own hand was finally unsatisfying, however. "Stuck-up bitch" had its grain of truth. She had to admit her mother also had a point when, amplifying a theme more politely expressed in her childhood, she mumbled from the couch, a cigarette bobbing and burning down between her lips, "I hope you plan to hustle your ass out on the street, because you don't come from enough money to be an artist."

Jessica Morrow was never impractical, never an idealist. She didn't want to pursue a perverse path that led nowhere or persist in some behavior that offered solely personal gratifications but was of no real use to herself or anybody else. Sketches locked up in a sketchbook no one would ever peruse, paintings hanging in a gallery no one would ever visit—these were finally beneath what she thought of as her dignity.

The clothes people wore, she decided, were the real art, the realest art in the world. What revealed people's inner lives more than their outer ones, the way they chose or thoughtlessly failed to choose to picture themselves to society, which in turn affected how everyone they met judged them? Without our clothes, we were only animals, she thought, hairy robots programmed by nature; when we decided how to cover our bestial nudity with whatever of our interiors we wanted to show on the outside, then and only then did we become human. Only what people dismissed as superficial proved we had souls.

She began to understand her drive to have her skin tattooed with designs of her own choice in just this light. Once tattooed, she was never really naked: never un-souled. Even when she *was* naked, especially that final time, on the mortuary slab, no one could say she was only an animal, that she'd passively accepted her fleshly fate like a dead-eyed cow in a field waiting to be rendered down to meat, or (yes, she thought it) like her mother, fattening and spreading over a succession of sagging couches, her hair, once full and shining, now tangled in greasy gray strands around her broadened, shiny face. In her own way, Jessica Morrow would be faithful to the perfect little girl in the pinafore even if both her parents had abandoned their dreams and ambitions for that lost child.

One day during her senior year, she accidentally left her sketchbook behind in her art class. The teacher, Ms. Johnston, was so indiscreet as to browse through it at the end of the day. Ms. Johnston was not much older than her students, with brown hair all down her back, Indian print skirts, Birkenstock sandals, and a rumored affinity for smoking up behind the school with some of the senior boys after hours. She was never more than professionally encouraging about Jessica Morrow's completed assignments—the still lifes, the perspective studies, the landscapes in watercolor, acrylic, and oil—but she saw a different, or, as she called it, a psychedelic dimension to the sketchbook's futuristic procession of novel fashions recombined from the elements of traditional dress visible every day on the street. She always thought the girl had talent—she saw plenty of talent lying around, though she was still early in her teaching career, but not a lot of vision or ambition. When she returned the sketchbook, she told Jessica Morrow she thought she had it. She didn't say what "it" was, but she did say that an old friend of her grandmother's was sadly going blind and looking for some help running her vintage store near the university, especially with the buying process. "Jess," she finally said, "you've got the eye."

Untimely Vintage was one of those stores you had to take a short flight of concrete steps below the sidewalk to enter. The owner, Olga Nowak, kept the track lighting low. The walls were bluish, purplish—what was Jakey's little crayon called when he was a kid, periwinkle?—and the windows were high up and thin, so even at noon, being in the store was like being underwater. If Olga Nowak had ever called in some corporate consultant group to help manage her shop—a business-school bore at a party had suggested this to Jessica Morrow once—they would have told her to bring some order to the place. The racks of clothing were stuffed and unlabeled, not sorted by style or size or even sex, and every corner had antique oddments in piles, record albums or perfume bottles or dishware, whatever caught the old lady's glaucous eye at flea markets and estate sales. Corporate would say the customer, the client, whatever they called them—Olga Nowak liked to call them the marks and then laugh her wheezy smoker's laugh and show her lipstick-stained dentures—those people who come down off the sidewalk want to get in and find what they're looking for and get out. On the other hand, Olga Nowak was sure her unseparated heaps of gemstone and offal, of trash and treasure, would tempt customers to spend whole afternoons digging, because who knew but that the next ugly dress you turned over would have been concealing, crumpled in its gaudy shadow, the prettiest one you ever saw?

By the time she was 23, and kindly old Olga Nowak had retired down south with her seeing-eye dog, Jessica Morrow owned Untimely Vintage. She didn't change a thing. She kept the lights even dimmer. At the tattoo parlor a few doors down, she asked for a stylized banner up her arm to celebrate the occasion: it was to be Art Nouveau, like the signs for the Paris Metro, and to display an aphorism she'd encountered in a fashion magazine: *One should either be a work of art or wear one.*

CHAPTER 6
Art for Life's Sake

It was strange, then, after having rejected the merely biological for the spiritually aesthetic, that she decided to keep the baby. Her mother certainly thought so.

They were sitting in her mother's new kitchen. Her mother had inherited a house in the city from a childless aunt and decided to move into the bottom floors and rent the top ones for extra income. She had long since quit her nursing job to live on her ex-husband's alimony checks, more than enough to survive given low-rent apartments and a child in public school; but the responsibilities of being a landlord had goaded her out of her more than a decade-long stupor of torpid resentment. Her hair was colored and treated now, her face leaner, even if she still smoked a pack a day. She'd just presided over the renovation of the ancient kitchen with its 50-year-old peeling wallpaper and gouged linoleum into the white-walled, tile-floored room where they now sat on one of the regular Sunday afternoon visits Jessica Morrow began making after she'd moved out to live in an apartment above her vintage shop.

About two months along on that sultry August day, Jessica Morrow told her mother she was pregnant. Her mother widened her eyes and then narrowed them as she slowly jabbed her cigarette out in the brass ashtray. Finally, she said, "Well, I can't see the point of it."

"Point? There's no point. It's what people do."

Jessica Morrow felt her usual instinct to flee, bred in the conflict-averse house of her first rearing, the hearth-warm prison in the suburbs, but she kept herself calm and remained in her seat.

"Exactly. Since when have you ever just done whatever other people do?"

It was very nearly a compliment, as close to a compliment as her mother would come, but still, Jessica Morrow stood and began to pace the new tile floor with a satisfying clatter of her bootheels. Her mother wasn't wrong. Where was that aesthetic resistance to the mindless and the bovine that had made her the owner of a profitable small business while her more conventionally successful high-school classmates would still be paying off the loans on their worthless college degrees well into their middle age? (She hadn't gone to college; she had plenty of time to read behind her shop counter, and books were free at the library.) This was too simple, though, she told herself. Choosing to have the baby was motivated by the same insight that had led her to reject making art no one would ever see or care about or understand. Art divorced from life had never been her credo.

The well-fitting dress, the bias of whose hem elongated the leg into a curved column, the hat that sat at just the right angle to leave one eye in shadow and one beaming out, the sandal with the strap and the incline that showed the foot for the elegantly simple sculpture it was—these differed from the splattered painting on the gallery wall or the pile of trash on the museum floor as legal currency differed from play money in a children's game. Fashion was an art that made life possible, social life first of all, and then the reproduction of life *as such* that social life enabled. Clothes enlarged life, made it circulate and exchange and grow. The display of a floral sundress that fell just so and thinly over the bosom, or the winter coat belted elegantly at the waist, attracted the male to the female, the female to the male, and so produced not only an aesthetic response but also a biological—*bios* meaning, as she'd read in a library book, "life."

Art served life and perpetuated life and was life; to turn yourself into a work of art was to live life at its maximum intensity, a goal that surely encompassed what they called the miracle of birth. When she found out that her last "business meeting"—it was a private joke between them, to call it that—with her tattoo artist from the shop down the street had left her with a baby on the way, she decided in this one instance to accept her fate. She planned to do everything her parents hadn't. She would raise her child in a world of creativity and freedom and affection, not false-fronted poise and frigid resentment. To make up for the passivity of having lain back to accept this particular event, she would commit herself to turn that accident into a destiny by never abandoning this child. Anyway, her business made a profit; she could afford it.

Her mother wasn't concerned about the money. When she saw that Jessica Morrow had resolved to go through with the pregnancy, she even said, "We'll make it work," another remark at the verge of tenderness, where her mother had never before traveled. No, her mother's initial objection to the child was metaphysical.

"Is life so great that it needs to go on and on? That we should make more people who just do what other people do, who go on to make more people, who just do what other people do, and so on, forever?"

These remarks Jessica Morrow took as insults, retractions of the prior almost-compliment. Her indifferent mother, who'd never encouraged her creative pursuits for even a day, now reproached her for not living up to them. Moreover, her mother necessarily implied that her own daughter, she herself, Jessica Morrow, was no real contribution to the world. Her mother's next comment, however, she understood as remorse.

"Isn't it a kind of sin to bring someone into this hell when you're finally going to be too weak to save them from it?"

Jessica Morrow sat back down. "I'm keeping it," she said.

Her mother shrugged and lit another cigarette. "Who's the father, anyway?"

The father, the tattoo artist, she never slept with for his moral merit but simply because he had been there, just down the street. He had a certain mordant mean wit and, like her, an eye for how people showed themselves to the world. The first time he'd tattooed her, he praised the taut musculature of her upper arm. Fearful of ending up like her mother, she did 100 push-ups a day, 50 on waking and 50 before bed—girl push-ups to be sure, knees not toes, but push-ups all the same. As she reclined on his table, her shoulders sweat-sticking to the paper sheet, stung by what felt like a droning fusillade from a mechanical bee, he entertained her with a lyrical satire of all the types of flesh on which he had plied his trade, so much of it grotesque: the mottled, the pitted, the withered, the rippling, the sagging, the graying, the yellowing, the reddening, the wobbling, the furred, the clammy, the desiccated, the rotted; the gargantuan flank of a motorcyclist in leather and chains signaling some tribal affiliation, the withered arm of an ancient-looking middle-aged woman in a *Fuck Cancer* hat attempting final, futile control of her mutinous corpus; and the skin of a lucky young girl who'd just inherited her own business, so palely fuzzed and goose-stippled he could hardly bring himself to stain it.

She widened her lips and rolled her eyes at his flattery, artful but unsubtle in its modulation from the heinousness of others to the beauty of herself, excessive enough to be disavowed as parody if it failed to seduce. He would under no circumstances allow himself to be compromised. He was 30; he had steel gauges in his ears; he was there.

She had no time, really, for a serious relationship, running a business almost alone as she was, and she had no intention of marrying, her parents' model of marriage having proved a disaster. She lived in one of the studio apartments above Untimely Vintage—that, too, had been Olga Nowak's and had devolved upon her—and she would lead him up there once or twice a month.

One day, he arrived, and she realized she had forgotten to buy condoms, which she insisted upon not only because she'd read in some magazine about the dangers of hormonal birth control—blood clots or something—but also because she doubted she was the only woman the tattoo artist saw in a month. She almost put her clothes back on to go down to the drugstore on the next block, but she hastily calculated that she was at a safe enough moment in her cycle to trust her body to flush his seed in time. In the event, she was wrong, but an error that gave her Jakey could never be an error in her eyes. Jakey was the only person she'd ever "met," if that was the word for an encounter with the person who'd knitted together inside one's womb, to make her feel less than wholly isolated in the world, trapped inside a body that could barely reach another mind, the legacy, she didn't doubt, of that childhood pinafore, that childhood prison. The tattoo artist, after he was through with her, had never made her feel anything at all. The marks he'd made on her had outlasted even the boy he'd borne on her.

He hadn't been any less skeptical of her having the baby than her mother would be when she told her the next month. (How many people had tried to bar Jakey's entry into this world? Well, only two, but two was enough when they were your father and grandmother, so no wonder he—, she thought after his funeral, until she stopped herself from thinking it.) The July afternoon she told him was a lazy, long Sunday; they lay on the flattened mattress on the bare boards of her minuscule studio under the open window, a shaft of sun igniting the dust motes. She had air-conditioning or even a fan: she tended to forget about these things. They lay in their mingled sweat. The electronic music he favored chimed and beeped and whirred tinnily out of her laptop speakers.

She held his hand in front of her face as he lay in his post-coital doze. With her nail, she traced a tumid vein, unearthly blue, as it ran from his thin wrist diagonally across the back of the hand and into the base of his index finger, a river feeding the ocean of his energy, his capacity. Nature was not all, as she was always fond of observing, because this river ran through the forest of symbols he'd had his colleagues ink onto his hand, the memento mori of a grinning skull and mysterious runes she could not interpret on each knuckle, below the coarse dark hair that grew there. She loved this hand, though she didn't love him, a realization that quelled the desire she'd just felt resurging below where she—and she alone—knew a life was slowly gathering itself into order. Had she ever loved anyone? In the liquescent heat, the magazine cutouts she'd taped to all four walls—ball gowns and double-breasted suits and aviator goggles, a still life by Cézanne, a photo of a Japanese garden, an Art Deco skyscraper—curled and wilted. She loved the part severed from the body—the hand, not the man. She loved only things.

Pop psychology: her father's flight had taught her that to love a person was to expose herself to inexplicable, irreparable loss. It was a thought as true as it was banal. Why be superior to the obvious? she asked herself. Who were these people, anyway, who went to psychotherapy to hear what any idiot could tell you, as if mere knowing could help you live a day? She threw his hand away from her and said, "I'm pregnant."

He drowsily murmured into the pillow, "I'll drive you. I'll pay. Wait, is it free? Like insurance? Does the government pay?"

She supposed she was relieved that he didn't already know, that he wasn't an expert in this particular operation. She said, "No, I'm keeping it."

He lifted his head from the pillow. Puzzled frustration narrowed his eyes. "Is it a religious thing?" He reached out to stroke her hair, to coax her from her obstinacy with a purposeful gentleness. She batted his runic fingers away. A woman wailed under the whirring machines that sounded out of the laptop; she couldn't make out the words.

"No," she said truthfully. She wasn't sure if there was a God, or if God was a person or a force, or if this person's or this force's existence or non-existence committed her to any particular course of action. She had no systematic idea about when life began. Most of what was true in this world was concealed from us, she thought. She had taken a chance that day, when she decided not to put her clothes back on and go down to the drugstore, however; she felt, for her dignity's sake, that she was obligated to accept the result of her gamble. Also—though she was sure that "they," priests, doctors, psychologists, whoever sat in judgment on human choices, would tell her this was a dangerous reason to have a child—she wanted someone to love.

"Then what's the problem?" he asked. "It's not even a thing yet. I mean if we could see it. It would look like, what, dandelion spoors? It's just, like, *matter*."

"So are you," she said. She thought, but did not say, and so is everything I love. This included the vein in his wrist and the hair on his knuckles, but not him.

Jacob Morrow was born into this hell, as her mother called the world, the subsequent February, in the middle of the 21st century's first decade and in the middle of Jessica Morrow's third. Jacob *Morrow* because the tattoo artist—she tried not even to think his name—was gone by month four of her pregnancy. He didn't go west but south, not the Babylon in the desert but the Babylon by the sea—always warm weather with these feckless, fleeing men—so she decided her son would not bear his surname. If it was to fall to her alone to shape the boy into a man, she would not give him a failed man's name.

CHAPTER 7
Initiation

The break with her mother came when Jakey was five. Jessica Morrow was hardly a strict mother; as the young and sole parent of an only child, she often fell into the habit, especially as he aged out of babyish dependency, of treating Jakey like her younger brother, even her co-conspirator.

She raised him in Untimely Vintage, in a childless environment with a parade of eccentric adults who were liable to say God only knew what to a child. A dissolute old broker in a cheap and anachronistically checked suit once let Jakey—at about four years old—sip whiskey from his pocket flask on one of his monthly visits while he waited for Jessica Morrow to tally the wares he'd brought her from his clients.

For five years, she raised him in the tiny apartment over the shop, without an air conditioner or a TV or a microwave or a real bed, until she saved up enough for her own house in the suburbs, not too unlike the one she'd grown up in, the hearth-warm prison, except that she had the carpets stripped out and furnished the place with scarred antiques and didn't care if her son made a mess.

She even had a theory that children's developing brains were retarded by vapid cartoons and simplistic children's books—perhaps even deliberately, by governments and corporations that preferred docile consumers to alert citizens. Such cheap and easy entertainments artificially restricted the child's potential vocabulary, presented a moralistic and sensationalist view of reality, and encouraged caricatural and irritatingly precocious (rather than genuinely mature) behavior. How would he develop any taste for subtler pleasures with all that commercial clamor in his ear?

She'd prided herself on this insight in his childhood, and now she wondered, If I'd let him watch cartoons, would he have—, until she silenced the thought. She largely let Jakey read and watch not so much whatever he wanted as whatever she did, and they would discuss it in as egalitarian a back-and-forth as the naturally unequal relation between child and adult allowed. She thought the most momentous and terrifying topics—war, murder, sex, sickness, disaster, death—could be taken into the human mind and revolved, viewed from various perspectives, mentally handled, and could for that very reason be made familiar rather than threatening. (Was that true, or is that why he—?) Everything that was considered unmentionable in her childhood to and by a lady she freely discussed with Jakey, including the old broker's flask and the scalding drink it held.

"When you drink enough of it, it makes you feel good, even though it's hurting you."

"If it's hurting him, he'll stop drinking it?"

"It makes you feel so good you don't feel bad at all anymore and you want to drink it all the time. He'll probably keep drinking it."

"Why?"

"Because he's unhappy."

"Is he going to die? He was funny, I don't want him to die."

"Everybody dies, Jakey."

Maybe there was some hypocrisy, then, revenge for her own unhappy childhood, in the way she punished her mother for allowing Jakey to witness something she would not necessarily have withheld from him had she been there to explain it. Then again, he saw it in real life, not in the pages of a book or on her TV screen (and she allowed no other screens for Jakey, no phones or tablets or laptops for the growing boy, not until he was a teenager). No, he had seen *this* pornography on the screen of the actual.

He woke up one summer night panting and sweating—even in the conditioned suburban air—from a bad dream. He ran to his mother's bed and threw himself on top of her; as she stroked his long damp hair, he whispered to her what he'd seen in his sleep: a naked man with a naked woman growing out of the place his penis was supposed to be. No "wee-wee" or "pee-pee" in Jessica Morrow's house, no "down there" or "going tinkle" or "poo-poo" or "ca-ca"—no mind-destroying baby talk euphemisms. They spoke frankly of the world together, just the two of them, Jess and Jakey, Jakey and Jess, so "penis" was the word the child used.

Through a patient conversation that lasted until he fell asleep in her arms, she was able to infer what had happened earlier that day, when his grandmother was babysitting him at her place, the house she'd inherited, whose upper floors she rented. His grandmother had dozed off on the couch after lunch, as she often did. Jakey, bored with whatever she had on TV, wandered aimlessly up the back stairs her tenants used, to the second floor and then to the third, to the attic, a stifling room with a ceiling so dramatically sloped an adult couldn't stand up except in the very middle of the floor. Consequently, she rented it, usually under the table, for a very low price.

Through the slit of the attic door as it stood ajar, Jakey, frozen in fear and fascination, watched his grandmother's tenant rock and thrash, her hair and hands shaking like wind-thrown treetops, on a man who seemed—as she seemed also—to be crying out in agony, arching his back and mashing the pillow with his fists. They were like animals caught in some trap that had them both in its teeth by his penis and her vagina. Jessica Morrow explained in clear language what the man and the woman had been doing. At first, she had no real intention of holding it against her mother beyond a caution to be more vigilant, to drink an afternoon coffee and stay awake while her five-year-old grandson was in the house.

The next time she saw her mother and relayed the story at her kitchen table, the older woman chuckled in her wheezing smoker's rasp and said she'd been renting the attic to a girl whose regular procession of male visitors could be heard going up and down the back stairs at all hours, some on shameful tiptoe and others with stomping bravado.

"Jesus Christ, Mother, you're running a brothel?"

Her mother shrugged: "I never knew you to be so high and mighty. Some of the things you got up to in high school—you think I didn't know, but I knew. That first tattoo for example—branded like a cow!"

"It's not about morality. It's dangerous! You could be legally liable—did you even think about that?"

"The police aren't going to bother some girl who's not on the street. I assume she solicits on the internet."

"How the hell can you be so calm about this? Strange men from the internet coming and going all day—they could break in here, steal your things, cut your throat!"

"I could get hit by a bus tomorrow, too. Isn't that always what people always say? 'You could get hit by a bus tomorrow,' as if buses were running people down every hour. It's amazing anybody lives even a day. Now listen: she needs money from those men, and I need money from her, and that's all there is to it. She's going to do it here or somewhere else—so why not here? She needs a roof over her head, too, doesn't she? This is the world, Jessica. What world do *you* live in?"

With trembling fingers—her hands had been shaking for a few years now—Jessica Morrow's mother extracted a cigarette from a crumpled pack and then lit it with a Bic between her lips. Jessica Morrow could not form any answer to her final question. Here, she thought, was the total cynicism that had imprisoned her mother ever since her father's flight, the conviction that nothing could ever be joyful or even reliable again, a despair that justified letting the world lie in a broken heap with the excuse that if you pieced it back together, it would only shatter again soon enough.

Her mother's attitude was reasonable to the point of madness, an unanswerable assertion of total human frailty so complete it failed to recognize the need for some irrational saving faith in the good and the beautiful if you wanted to achieve even the minutest thing on earth. Jessica Morrow could follow the argument that the prostitute needed money and shelter, that prostitution was inevitable. She could appreciate her mother's broad-mindedness in this case, so different from her rigid posture in Jessica Morrow's pinafore-straitened girlhood. No amount of logic or tolerance, however, could convince her to bring Jakey ever again to an unsafe place—a place where johns with rap sheets and guns and knives (they *could* have these things) climbed the stairs all day to abuse some desperate girl carrying who knew what diseases.

She could say none of that to her mother in the moment; all the words, and the years of fury and resentment the words carried, logjammed in her throat. She simply walked out without a word. She never came back. When her mother called, she didn't answer. The old woman knew where she lived. She could have come to see her anytime; Jessica Morrow wouldn't have shut the door in her face. Her mother was too proud for that, however. They both were too proud to break their stalemate, to be the first to yield. So transient are our griefs that Jakey only cried for his grandmother for a few weeks and then seemed almost to forget her. (Was it a more important attachment than she knew? Is that why he—?) Then the old woman—not that old, really, not old at all, only in her mid-60s, but that was old enough if you took no care of yourself—had a stroke and died. That was the year before Jakey, whose own mother couldn't protect him from the cruel world after all, couldn't find any safe place for him to be, also died.

The third-floor tenant, the prostitute, what we now politely call a sex worker, showed up at Jessica Morrow's mother's funeral, dressed all in black, with thin mousy hair and glasses, a normal-looking woman approaching her middle age. They had seen each other a time or two on their mutual way in and out of the house all those years ago, when the woman was still renting her body and Jessica Morrow was still speaking to her mother, so they recognized one another. With tears in her eyes, the sex worker said to the dry-eyed Jessica Morrow, "Your mother was a saint." She walked away, not tottering on high plastic heels as Jessica Morrow prejudicially imagined, though the woman was approaching middle age and was perhaps a suburban matron by now, but firmly in sensible black flats; then the woman thought better of her final words and turned back. Three fingers balling up a tissue, one finger pointing, nail-bitten, at Jessica Morrow, she said, "You, though, are a stuck-up bitch!"

Jessica Morrow thought she saw the woman later, in the hospital, where they took Jakey when he—, after he—, even though there was nothing they could do in the part of the hospital above the ground, the part where it was white and brightly lit. It was probably someone else, though, not the former prostitute, unless the former prostitute had become a social worker, still renting her affections, her kindness, to others, except now in a more official capacity. No, it couldn't have been her; Jessica Morrow hadn't been thinking clearly that day.

She made what they called a scene, in fact, when they sent the social worker to talk to her, the social worker who looked like the prostitute. The social worker kept saying Jakey had "died by suicide," and, because she was insane by this point and couldn't really breathe, she'd said, just to see if she could say something, "Isn't it 'committed'? 'Committed suicide'?" and then the social worker with the mousy hair and the glasses had said, "Well, that implies it's a sin," and she'd answered with the question, "Isn't it? Against life, I mean?" and the social worker who may once have been a sex worker had said, with pity in her eyes, "I'm sorry—are you very religious?" and Jessica Morrow had said, finally, "No. I don't believe anything at all."

CHAPTER 8
Beautiful Boy

His mother called him Jakey; he called her Jess.

At his high-school graduation party, three months before he went to college, six months before he shot himself dead, she got drunk and serenaded him from behind the karaoke machine, her spiky hair wild, one dress strap falling off her tattooed shoulder, tears in her eyes, with "Beautiful Boy."

It wasn't typical of her. She was a private woman with only a few trusted friends; she hadn't since her teenage years been a drinker or partygoer. Her only son, though, was off to college, this after almost two years of online high school due to the pandemic. Celebration was in order. She reserved the top room of a bar near both Untimely Vintage and the university, where he'd be going in the fall. "Might as well get a head start in here," she teased him. She bought him a bottle of beer he gripped by its neck and pretended to drink for the whole of the night.

The Penshursts sipped white wine and beamed at their youngest and favorite customer. (They ran Prospero's Books, the used and rare bookstore a block down the same street from Untimely Vintage.) Mr. Penshurst presented him a first edition of *Middlemarch*. "You should be ready to read this now," the old man said, his cloudy eyes moist.

A few of his high school friends showed up, too: shy, smart girls who had corresponded with Jakey about music or books throughout the period of remote learning. Too embarrassed to perform karaoke, they hunched all night in a corner, whispering over their phones after presenting Jakey with a bouquet they'd bought from a grocery store on the way to the bar. Jessica Morrow offered to buy them something illicit and fruity to drink—"A margarita, girls, or a strawberry daiquiri"—but they shook their heads rapidly, nervously, wide-eyed but not making eye contact. One had just gotten her labret pierced—her (or perhaps their) own graduation gift—and the swollen lower lip under the wide averted eyes made her (or perhaps them) look both pouty and astonished.

She'd raised him in Untimely Vintage and tried to teach him to love beautiful things. He learned, however, to love beauty in the abstract and to take things lightly. From his naked babyhood, he never warmed much to clothes. He felt they caged him, prickled his skin, made him burn and itch. He was one of those who wore shorts in January. Holding his beer, pretending to drink it, he wore a white tank top, his long hair grazing his bare shoulders.

He grew up to be tall, like the father he never knew. She told him his father had been a tattoo artist; he never got a tattoo. Whatever wastrel of a scumbag his father had been, his father, like his mother, had had a keen eye and a trained hand, so she tried, as soon as he could grip the pencil, to teach him to draw. He had a gift for it. He could catch with deft lines the dimensions of what he saw; he could even freehand perspective by the age of 10. He didn't like drawing much, though—nor painting nor photography nor any of the visual arts when she tried those on him. He liked comic books, a taste he had to hide not from his public schoolteachers, who were happy when youth read anything at all, but from his real teachers, the Penshursts, the Shakespeare scholars turned bookstore owners. He and these strange girls sent each other what they called manga all the time, grisly Japanese comics full of schoolgirls and gore—not to her taste but no worse, on the other hand, than her own teenaged interests. She always told him he should draw his own, but he demurred. Here the world was, he seemed to say, complete in itself. Why not enjoy it in gratitude rather than vainly trying to create it a second time?

He startled her with his proficiency in music, mathematics, athletics, three wholly foreign domains to her. Unlike visual art, which added more things to the already thing-crowded planet, music took up no space. It simply vibrated the air already in your ear and miraculously changed how you felt about who and what and where you already were—or helped you to feel its reality more completely, more viscerally. Music was like a drug, or rather a medicine, pulled freely from the air. Not that he took drugs, except for his mug of morning coffee, a habit his grandmother had introduced him to when he was about four. Luckily, she thought with a hint of guilt, his own musical aspirations were humble: he was just a guitar picker, so she didn't have to stretch the budget for a piano or cello or for lessons at what they called a conservatory. Behind his bedroom door, she could hear the guitar chords giddily spiraling as if falling over themselves in a race toward some climax he never quite managed to bring them to.

She'd had no gift for numbers. She could balance the store's books and take measurements but nothing else, whereas he sailed through advanced algebra, geometry, trigonometry, calculus. He told her, "I can just see the numbers rearranging themselves in my mind. I see the order they're supposed to be in."

He loved to run. He set off from Untimely Vintage and ran through city parks and neighborhoods; he set off from home and ran around the high-school track and down tangled trails through the woody hills at the edge of their little suburb. Not a picky eater but an abstemious one—he'd eat pizza, but one slice; ice cream, but a cup; French fries, but just a handful—he never had an ounce of fat on his body. He offered the world nothing to grab onto. When he ran, his shoe soles seemed to tap the ground only out of a polite concession to earthly formalities; otherwise, they swept wholly through the atmosphere. She loved to sit back on the high school's sun-fired bleachers and watch him circle the track, his long hair flying. She couldn't get him on the track team, though.

"They would make me think about times and winning. The whole point is that you're not thinking. Your mind just goes blank. It's like you've merged with the air you're passing through."

He was a reader. He spent every day of his childhood summers in Untimely Vintage, helping her to mend garments or affix price stickers or fold clothes or put items on hangers; but as soon as he was old enough to cross the street on his own, he started sneaking out to Prospero's Books on the next block down. Prospero's didn't exactly welcome unaccompanied minors. The store sold whatever tattered, crack-spined paperbacks the students and faculty of the nearby university brought them for a pittance at the end of each term, but these were loss leaders. Prospero's real trade was rare and antique volumes, the kind of octavos and duodecimos, of incunabula, of tomes bound in calfskin or goat-, which one naturally didn't want a nine-year-old's clammy fingers to stain and tear.

The Penshursts, a severe English couple who had come to the university for graduate work in the 1970s and then stayed in the city to open the bookstore when they tired of academe, would glare at the boy as he entered. They would gently put him out when they found him curled in a corner with some science-fiction paperback of which they, who had once been aspiring Shakespeare scholars, could not intellectually approve.

One afternoon in those days of Jakey's boyhood, Jessica Morrow visited Prospero's Books by herself. She politely wandered its dim labyrinth of crowded shelves, pretending somewhat more interest than she felt; the narrow aisles smelled of wood and vanilla, and some kind of old-time jazz played faintly in the dust. She magnanimously purchased a turn-of-the-century collection of hand-colored fashion plates for $250. Then she told them who she was. She cajoled the couple, Mr. and Mrs. Penshurst, into allowing Jakey to visit whenever he wanted on the condition that he remain quiet and well-behaved. She proposed this as a gesture of solidarity between small-business owners.

"We have to stick together," she said, "before Amazon puts us both out of business. If a well-behaved little boy can't read a book here, of all places, it might as well be Amazon. In return, you guys can have whatever you want from my shop, *gratis*. Is that the word? *Gratis*?"

Mr. Penshurst had remained behind the counter at his desktop computer for the length of this conversation, which he seemed to regard as women's business.

Without looking at her, he grunted, "That's the word, my dear." Jessica Morrow faced Mrs. Penshurst across the counter. Large glasses subtly tinted in indigo veiled her eyes; her silver hair circled her thin neck in sharp edges. The older woman twisted knots of fabric out of her wool sweater while Jessica Morrow spoke, as if the young woman's bright American politeness caused her physical pain. She mostly nodded with pursed lips to Jessica Morrow's suggestions.

Mr. Penshurst, his own wool sweater sheathing the bulk he balanced precariously on his stool, spoke without raising his eyes from the computer. He agreed to her proposal, refused the offer of vintage wear, however *gratis* it may prove, and added a condition: that he and his wife would get some say in what the boy read on their premises.

"No trashy comic books and pulp fiction here, Miss. This is not a train station or a drugstore. My God, it's bad enough we sell the stuff."

To Jakey's gifts of music, mathematics, and athletics, the gray-haired English couple added a humanistic education as far in advance of what he got in public school as was Alpha Centauri or some other distant galaxy discussed in those science-fiction paperbacks the Penshursts were willing to buy from fools and sell to nitwits but unwilling to allow a young mind to consume in their presence. This accounts for the precocious literary education that was to impress Ash del Greco later, in his first year of college and her third, in the elevator, in the hallway, in her dorm room with its bare cinder-block walls. The Penshursts started him in his adolescence on Poe, Hawthorne, Stevenson, Lewis Carroll; then Shakespeare, Shakespeare, Shakespeare; finally, by his midteens, they marched him through Austen, Dickens, Tolstoy, Dostoevsky, Melville, Twain. George Eliot they reserved for his high-school graduation. "When you turn 30," Mrs. Penshurst said with tears in her eyes at his graduation party, "it will be time for Proust."

The Penshursts began by tolerating young Jakey when the bell over the door tinkled his arrival. They would give him a volume of their choosing and order him to some nook where he would not be under customers' feet. Girls from the university would trip over him anyway with their big clumsy Doc Martens on their way to the critical theory shelves; then, overcome with what they were just then learning in their classes to denounce as a spasm of repronormative affect, they would tussle his blond curls with their black-polished nails, faces chiming with the jewelry in their noses and lips and ears as they bent protectively over the boy, forgetting momentarily that there was such a man as Jacques Lacan.

Eventually, the couple, who had no children of their own, exchanged a wordless look of regret that they had sent him to curl on a carpet and be trampled upon; so they brought him behind the counter, read over his shoulder, quizzed him on the contents of the books they gave him, sent him to the dictionary shelf to take his choice of lexicons when he encountered a word he didn't know, encouraged him to form his own judgment of stories and styles. Mr. Penshurst in particular began to dote on the child, until the child was finally falling asleep in the old man's lap as he made his rare-book transactions on the computer.

"What does 'circumambulate' mean?"

"Look it up, my child. Look it up."

Mr. Penshurst would take Jakey on his visits to the Carnegie Library's rare book room, there to consult with the resident specialist on this or that volume's provenance and merit. On their three-block walk from Prospero's Books into the center of the university neighborhood where the library sat in its regally last-century Beaux-Arts splendor behind its colonnade of trees, the man and boy would pass the four vast statues representing the liberal arts that towered on high plinths in front of the museum that adjoined the library: Newton, Da Vinci, Bach, Shakespeare. Mr. Penshurst would fondly pat Shakespeare's plinth as he passed, the way generations of pilgrims might rub the patina from the hem or the toe of a sculpted saint. Not permitted into the rare book room, Jakey would sneak with a graphic novel into the library stacks—"sneak" because, while Jessica Morrow certainly wouldn't have minded, the Penshursts would have contracted the wrinkles around their pale eyes in withering disappointment at the sight of such sensationalist picture books in the bright child's hands.

(On a bench in the dim library stacks, the aisles between the shelves glowing faintly jade from the green-glass blocks that tiled the floor, Jakey, aged about 12, first irradiated and abraded his eyes with the hideous violations of Simon Magnus and Duncan McGinnis's *Ratman: Fools' Errand*, with the gnostic apocalypse of Simon Magnus and Marco Cohen's *Overman 3000*)

He would stop to pet dogs in the street. When he found a spider on his bedroom wall, or what they called a thousand-legger in the bathtub, he would clap a coffee mug over the creature and then slide a sheet of paper beneath its sticky feet to prise it from the wall's surface and trap it. He'd then carefully carry the mug through the front door and shake it out into the grass.

"Jesus, Jakey," his mother would complain, "I *drink* out of that. You can kill them, you know. If you found a strange man in your bathtub, let alone an insect, you could shoot him. Not a jury in the world would convict you!"

As soon as he was old enough to carry his own money, he would give a dollar to every panhandler on every block of the university neighborhood.

Jessica Morrow forbade the internet except for supervised school activities on her own laptop until he entered his teen years. She bought him his own tablet for his 13th birthday. Thinking the kid had to learn sometime, Jessica Morrow told him he could do with the tablet what he wanted; she assured him she wouldn't check, snoop, pry, or intrude as long as he didn't spend any money or get involved in anything illegal. Most sins, she thought, were their own punishment, and it wasn't as if abandoning him to cyberspace was the same as abandoning her to the real world, the way her mother had done after the divorce.

That summer, the summer between seventh and eighth grade, he spent a sweltering month in dazed insomnia, masturbating four and five times a night, wandering deeper and deeper into what he hadn't until then known to be the labyrinth of his own strange desires. He found enough available material for free online to keep both hands occupied from sundown to sunup. He began with a vague desire to see the dirty parts women kept covered under clothes like the ones his mother kept meticulously clean and mended and beautiful. Once this curiosity was satisfied, he found he had more—a bottomless reservoir of curiosity, in fact. Women's private parts in general, sure, but what about their various parts in various intriguingly unkempt states? What about unshaved armpits, untrimmed toenails, the crack of the buttocks when not properly tended? What other obscenities did women conceal behind the aesthetic illusion his mother vended in the name of fashion? Did women burp? Did they fart? Women squatting, the pubic mound unshaven. Women pissing into toilets, buckets, weeds. Women shitting onto newspapers, shitting their pants, shitting onto the chests of naked, balding men shackled to bedposts. Women vomiting on the floor of dark, dungeon-like rooms; women vomiting into the mouths of balding men chained naked to chairs, red ball gags between their teeth. What next? What more? All of this for free! What did the paywalls conceal? Could he borrow his mother's credit card undetected to find out? A whole feverish July's worth of nights spent this way!

His penis hurt so much in the mornings he could barely walk; all day, days dutifully spent in his mother's store or the Penshurst's store, he dreamed about returning to those latrines and dungeons, to women's bodies out of all control except the control provided by the four edges of the screen, to men's bodies, bodies like his own, in exquisite, grotesquely delicious agony under a rain of those women's filth.

The kid had to find out sometime. Jessica Morrow didn't raise a fool. One night, on the point of sneaking out of his bedroom at three in the morning to fetch his mother's purse down on the chair in the foyer, to steal his mother's credit card, to feed the hard earnings of Untimely Vintage into filthydommes.com or whatever other site to learn more about what urgent truths all that untimely vintage concealed, he answered instead an impulse, if not of pure virtue, then of incipiently virtuous revulsion. Standing by the bed, his underwear around his ankles, hesitating on his way to the bedroom door, unsure if he should commit the theft he'd planned, he suddenly took up the tablet instead and smashed its screen into the corner of his nightstand until it shattered and went permanently black. He told Jessica Morrow the next morning that he'd dropped it. She offered to buy him another, but he said, "I can use your old laptop for school. Besides, the internet's pretty boring."

He never had a regular girlfriend in high school. He was good-looking—thin and muscular, with that long golden hair he was always sweeping out of his eyes—but something in him repelled the girls who approached, even as it drew them in. "He doesn't want anything," one complained; his smiling self-containment and seeming strength pulled others toward him but only into a distant orbit. He was friends with everyone, all sorts of people, mostly female, cheerleaders and Goths and champion swimmers, but close with none. This was in middle school and the first years of high school; the last years of high school, the remote years, his more popular acquaintances forgot about him, and he contented himself with texting the shy, bookish girls who sent him manga.

After the senior prom, in an acquaintance's basement rec room—brown carpet, flaking flowered wallpaper from the '70s—someone brought him a guitar, and he strummed quietly, flat on his back on the cold floor, on the stiff fire-retardant fibers. Their friends dozed in sweaty heaps of their suits and dresses, neckties and high-heeled shoes strewn everywhere. Always irritated by clothes, he had taken off his shirt, his shoes, his socks. Later, when everyone was asleep, his date—just a shy, homely girl from his AP English class who shared his taste in classic fiction—came over to him and raised her purple dress like the mouth of a cave. He climbed inside.

Where did he come from? Jessica Morrow wondered. He must have inherited virtues that she'd never had the opportunity to observe in the callow, cowardly tattoo artist, whatever his wretched name had been. Jacob Morrow was a better person than she was. She thought a centipede who skittered into someone's bathtub had all but begged to become a wiry brown smudge on the porcelain; she didn't say so outright because it sounded cruel, but deep down, she thought that panhandlers ought, like the rest of us, to get a goddamn job.

Where had this kind-hearted kid come from, this veritable saint? she asked herself, the strap of her dress sliding down the tattoos crawling up her arm, tears running over her cheeks, as she sang out to him, her voice breaking, on the night of his high-school graduation, "Beautiful Boy."

PART TWO

CHAPTER 1

Hollow Well

Simon Magnus came from a place in New England where the old ways persisted even into the late 20th century. Hollow Well, a small port town on a river estuary, was founded by English merchants before the Revolution in the middle 18th century. They mourned the lack of that eponymously barren spring, since estuary waters are brackish; nonetheless, they settled, they built, they manufactured, and they sold. After logging, shipbuilding, and the quarrying of granite had declined as industries by the plastic-ridden and air-powered middle 20th century, the town turned its own heritage into its trade. The sidewalks remained red brick, as they'd been when James Bowdoin and Elizabeth Palmer Peabody traversed them, and the façades of the buildings remained colonial, all rational rectilinear brick and pilaster, the tall, narrow windows barely admitting any light and giving back to the street only blackness.

As Simon Magnus told the story—and her side of the story has not survived—a prim and loveless single mother bore Simon Magnus in the middle of the 20th century's eighth decade. She was slightly worse than shabby-genteel: descended from the town's founders but remanded with her abandoned child to a cold, rambling house at the edge of the dark woods, itself like its inheritor a cast-off of the long-scattered family estate, far from the estuary and the quaint town center.

Simon Magnus did not fail to be enthralled by the whisper of history in the antique bricks and stones, but Simon Magnus found SimonMagnusself no less seduced by the mystery the wilderness held beyond the town.

(As critics would come to observe, Simon Magnus's work is characterized by just this conflict between the orderly grid of human social organization and the tangled chaos that threatens to engulf it from its fringe. Any admirer of Simon Magnus's slim but influential corpus could produce examples. In the early issues of *Marsh Man*, for example, aggrieved at the capture of his human paramour by the city's leading CEO, also her father, the titular anti-hero immures Cosmopolis's streets in Spanish moss and nets its skyscrapers in liana. More famously, there is *Overman 3000*'s battle between the archons of the doomed planet Cyphron's Huxleyean rationalist dystopia and the hero's own parents, dissident gnostic scientists exiled to the planetary wilds, where they become far-sighted seers and beckoners of apocalypse. That Simon Magnus sided first and last with the moral wilderness cannot be denied by anyone who even peruses the author's oeuvre. On the other hand, Simon Magnus's devotion to the order of art, to what Yeats called "the artifice of eternity," gives the work an intricacy and symbolic depth that secretly organizes the obvious violence seething on its surface—or so the most sympathetic, not to say sycophantic, critics have claimed.)

Mother Magnus mourned her lost patrimony. Her despised father had been a gambler; he'd squandered three-quarters of the old colonial merchant's fortune at the gaming table. She likewise loathed the seducer, a Harvard man five years her junior with a yacht in Hyannis Port, who had promised her marriage even after she'd drifted alone and without anything resembling a dowry past a marriageable age; he'd filled her womb and then run away to his family's minor villa near Lake Como, where, the rumor ran, he had for his fortune married an heiress 15 years his senior and kept a menagerie of local girls and boys for his pleasure.

As she detected in Simon Magnus's face from infancy the countenances both of her father and of her seducer, as she detected in Simon Magnus's green, shrewd, and skeptical eye the card-player's cunning and the pederast's insouciance, she could scarcely stand to look at the child. She had only gone through with the pregnancy—even though Simon Magnus was conceived shortly after the nationwide legalization of abortion—to shame the absconded rakehell by flinging in his face her own capacity to keep her commitments. In the event, the man proved shameless as well as feckless: she never heard a word from him again. She didn't think he was worth the trench they carved down her abdomen to excavate Simon Magnus after nine and a half months, trapped sideways in the amnion and hogtied in the umbilical cord. One tradition Mother Magnus did discard was patrilineal naming: she gave the child her own family name, not that of the dissolute and escaped wretch she had foolishly allowed to ravish her. *His* name, she tried not even to remember.

Mother Magnus paid Simon Magnus attention only to ensure that her child dressed as befit the family's status, however attenuated, especially since reduced circumstances forced her to make do with inferior materials—in other words, to drive the rusting hand-me-down black Bentley out to the suburbs to buy their clothes at shopping malls and chain stores.

She carefully read Simon Magnus's report cards, too; Magnuses made the honor role, or what was the point of Magnuses? This, even as straitened finances compelled her to send Simon Magnus to the public school, alongside farmer's children new to shoes and girls with dirty knees and Negroes and such others she regarded as proper objects of liberal compassion—"We are not barbarians," she often said—but not as her offspring's rightful peers.

Otherwise, and as long as Simon Magnus stayed out of trouble, Simon Magnus could do as Simon Magnus pleased. Mother Magnus performed her good works as required by the family name—she ran the town's food pantry, for example, and sat on the board of the public library—and mused on the strange injustices of her life. She was too proud to work for a living, but too proud, as well, to enjoy the life her small and inherited annuity allowed her.

Her freethinking father had severed the family's tie to faith. She tried to take the infant Simon Magnus to the Episcopal church one Sunday, a plain building in white wood with a humble steeple she found eminently tasteful, but the child howled as they passed through the red door—the color of Christ's blood—and she was too embarrassed ever to return. Simon Magnus was raised, therefore, without religion, though the image of the blood-red door would recur as the gate of hell in "Orphic Mysteries," the issue of *Marsh Man* where the titular anti-hero sojourns among the damned to retrieve the soul of his human lover. Critics would later deem the visual, carefully described in Simon Magnus's script, "vulvic."

Simon Magnus always and only referred to her as "Mother" while she lived. After the catastrophe that attended the production of *Overman 3000*, Simon Magnus was convalescing in Paris when she had a fatal stroke at the relatively young age of 56; Simon Magnus did not return to attend her funeral. "The only good thing that old sow gave me was the run of the library," Simon Magnus said upon *Overman 3000*'s release in the celebrated final interview the author granted the comics press, just before a retirement to academe.

On built-in birch shelves, the library occupied the whole of the three interior walls in the disused study at the back of the dark, rambling house. When Mother Magnus inherited the property, she imagined that her studious or sedulous husband would use the study—would sign papers on the blotter, consult leather-bound law books from the shelves, and perform other such professional offices to rebuild the family fortune. No husband came, however, so she kept the room as she'd inherited it, the shelves lined from floor to ceiling, and shut the door on it forever, except to take the books she liked: Jane Austen, for example. The books were her father's bequest. Dead of cirrhosis at 41, he had read as well as gambled compulsively; he'd wanted, in his midcentury adolescence, to be like the culture heroes of the bygone generation, lost as it had been reputed to be—Hemingway and Fitzgerald—except that he had only their vices and none of their talents.

Simon Magnus spent a lonely childhood and adolescence either in that library or in the woods into whose eerie darkness its window peered. The neglected room, anyway, felt as hot as the woods in summer and as cold as the woods in winter; the window kept out neither cold nor heat, while cracks and damp patches spread across the walls; Simon Magnus imagined enjoying the library in the open air. Simon Magnus read: Chaucer and Shakespeare, Keats and Shelley, Poe and Melville, and his grandfather's beloved Hemingway and Fitzgerald, though Grandfather Magnus died before the child was born. Simon Magnus read Dostoevsky and Baudelaire and Nietzsche, too, because Grandfather Magnus had enjoyed advanced if *outré* tastes for small-town England in the 20th century's early and middle decades.

Mother Magnus did not own a television and would not go to the movies. Nevertheless, the youthful reading, recounted to many an interviewer during the period of Simon Magnus's fame in the world of comics, served Simon Magnus's reputation well; critics would discern even influences the author didn't claim, as when, for example, an academic wrote an article investigating the influence of Dostoevsky's *Demons* on Simon Magnus's portrayal of sectarian Cyphronian politics in *Overman 3000*.

Notoriously, Simon Magnus told more than one interviewer of a first masturbation to Milton's description of Eve in *Paradise Lost* ("half her swelling breast / Naked met his, under the flowing gold / Of her loose tresses hid"). In fact, Simon Magnus had lied to the interviewer about this, a lie based loosely on young Mishima's well-known first ejaculation over Guido Reni's *St. Sebastian*, though Simon Magnus would not read Mishima until adulthood, at the urging of Ellen Chandler. Simon Magnus actually first masturbated over a cover image of Mina Mars, Overman's longtime love interest and the professional rival of his secret identity, John James, at Cosmopolis's premier newspaper, the *Daily Nova*.

A sister of Simon Magnus's absconded father sent the child a box of comic books around Christmas when Simon Magnus was 12 years old. "Probably cleaning out the cellar," Mother Magnus muttered upon opening the box. This was no fit reading for a Magnus, however youthful, so she sent Simon Magnus to drop the full box at the end of the long driveway for garbage collection. Simon Magnus crept out barefoot in the snow at midnight on Christmas Eve to fetch back the box and place it in the library's closet.

The provocative cover showed Mina Mars transformed into a giantess wearing only a bikini as the entire Salvation Corps—Overman, Ratman, Female Supreme, Golden Torch, The Bolt, and the rest—strained to tie her down, Gulliver-style. When Simon Magnus saw this image, in the dim light of the library shortly after Christmas, lust stirred for the first time. As Simon Magnus studied it more and more closely in the following days, imagining SimonMagnusself into the heroes' diminutive postures, Simon Magnus thought about what it might be like to be half an inch tall, half an inch tall and in the bristly pit of Mina Mars's arm as if in a fissure in the earth; in the humid hollow above her collarbone, where he imagined her perspiration to pool; down between the twin dunes of her breasts whose upper slopes showed over the bikini top; beneath the lacy elastic of her bikini bottom; and then down, further and further; down; and then up; up; up and inside; and—

Simon Magnus felt a novel and even terrifying sensation, a flood of pleasure just this side of pain, a feeling that, at its crest, ejected mind for a moment entirely from body, a sensation described literally, Simon Magnus would later learn in Simon Magnus's more scholarly days, by the word "ecstasy."

Simon Magnus read—disjointedly, because the box of comics had neither order nor completeness—the adventures of Overman, Ratman, the Salvation Corps, and others alongside the adventures found on the birch shelves, the adventures Grandfather Magnus had once enjoyed, the adventures of Milton's Satan, Shelley's Prometheus, Dostoevsky's Raskolnikov. The comic books' garish pictures, the very vulgarity Simon Magnus's mother had wished to bar from her house, helped Simon Magnus to understand and envision better what the older authors had meant by their alternately utopian and nightmarish visions. Alone, Simon Magnus might have found the comics too simplistic and banal to hold much attention, and the classics too antique and convoluted to move the body and the soul. Together, however, the one set of books fertilized the other. Simon Magnus felt through the comics' crude images something of the passion and despair Milton, Shelley, and Dostoevsky meant to convey, while discovering at the same time, through the classics' elevated diction and thematic grandeur, the ideals those superheroes manifested for a popular audience in the present.

One day, Simon Magnus's mother took a long drive in the hand-me-down Bentley to shop in the nearest larger town. Simon Magnus came off the school bus and into an empty house. Simon Magnus entered Mother Magnus's bedroom and pulled on a pair of her tights to see how closely they might approximate the superheroes' form-fitting garb. Simon Magnus stood in front of her bedroom's old oval mirror, desilvering, pitted with black as if the world it reflected were itself cankered, and smiled to see how the tights gave form to childishly pudgy and otherwise shapeless legs. Simon Magnus stood with arms akimbo, chest thrust out, a lacy garter pressing inflamed spirals and arabesques into the pale flesh of the thighs.

When not reading classics or comics, Simon Magnus swept the windowsill clean of insect carapaces, crossed Simon Magnus's arms on the wood, rested Simon Magnus's chin on Simon Magnus's arms, and looked out to the forest, half-fearing and half-desiring to see some terrible beast emerge, all tusk and bristle and slaver, if only to prove that Mother Magnus's silence and the public school's dullness did not exhaust the possibilities of this world.

Simon Magnus would claim to have found just this beast in just those woods, though that remark, like the various appellations Simon Magnus publicly applied to Mother Magnus when she was no longer above ground, furnished critics evidence for the writer's incorrigible misogyny—until they were silenced for good by Simon Magnus's unanswerable declaration in recent years that Simon Magnus was not a man, no longer was a man, and had never been a man.

CHAPTER 2
Moral Wilderness

Simon Magnus's first love, as we know, was Valerie Karns. "Tell us about Valerie," the interviewers from the comics press would say, after Simon Magnus had mentioned Valerie Karns in an answer to one of the fan letters—"Where do you get your ideas from?"—published in the back of an issue of *Marsh Man*. Valerie Karns's story, or the version of Valerie Karns's story Simon Magnus saw fit to tell, subsequently became a routine feature of Simon Magnus's public persona. When Simon Magnus told the story live, the audience would laugh, clap, and stomp; then they would nod thoughtfully and titter nervously; and, finally, they would let out a sad, low hum.

"Valerie, dearest, darling Valerie, my first girlfriend—no, my first lover!" Simon Magnus would regale the audience at conventions. "She was just what you'd expect to find in the place where they burned the witches, in the region Nathaniel Hawthorne and H. P. Lovecraft and Stephen King came from." Simon Magnus followed this with a regular laugh line: "That list was in declining order of literary merit, by the way." After the laughter, intermixed with a few poptimistic jeers, Simon Magnus would go on, in a quieter voice, "Just a Goth girl I met in the woods while she was killing a bird for a ritual. She taught me everything I know about magic and art and love. She had a head of hair like a witch's pyre. She jumped off a bridge—not into water but onto train tracks."

They met when Simon Magnus was a junior in high school and Valerie Karns a senior. They would spend 13 months together: the 13 months from their meeting in October to her leap from the trestle over the train tracks the next November—13 months, time enough for her to teach Simon Magnus the Tarot, the *I Ching*, sigil magic, and how, more or less, to make love. Ordinary people are supposed to celebrate the humble pleasures of the quotidian, not to seek or—even when they occur unsought—to enjoy beauty and catastrophe. This was never Simon Magnus's way. Simon Magnus met her in that very forest into which Simon Magnus had always looked up from *Crime and Punishment* or *Vigilante Comics* to await some dark revelation's emergence. Simon Magnus would often repeat to interviewers that we always get what we ask for, whether we know what—or even *that*—we're asking.

Simon Magnus was in the woods with acquaintances from school on that fall night. The quiet and aloof Simon Magnus didn't make friends easily and had no intimates, no inseparable "best friend," but was attached to various exiles and outcasts, near-dropouts and autistic geniuses, science-fiction readers and chess players and secret homosexuals. Some of these shared his knowledge of classics or comics—rarely both—while others had access to music and movies and drugs Simon Magnus never could have found in that rambling dark house at the edge of the forest. They may not have communed with Simon Magnus, Simon Magnus may not have shared what was deepest in Simon Magnus with them, but their weekend excursions to used bookstores and movie theaters and record stores in town, to bright malls and drug drop-offs in desolate parking lots in the suburbs, gave Simon Magnus invaluable experience at the end of the 20th century's penultimate decade.

That night in the woods, Simon Magnus read a torn, much-thumbed thrift-store copy of *Naked Lunch* by the light of a little fire they'd set as the sun went down. Simon Magnus ignored Simon Magnus's acquaintances' drunken chatter and gossip, only raising both eyes out of the book from to time to time to read them an irresistible line of Burroughs's derangements and outrages.

By then, by age 16, Simon Magnus had already begun writing. The first productions of adolescence were stilted, encumbered by too many 19th-century models, but once Simon Magnus had found modern authors in the shops and stores Simon Magnus and crew took to haunting on weekends—once Simon Magnus had found Joyce and Faulkner and Nabokov, the Surrealists and the Beats and the New Wave science-fiction writers—Simon Magnus began to write delirious, ranting free verse and meticulously surreal prose.

Surmising that poetry and fiction had both been obsolesced by audiovisual media, Simon Magnus even began to think back on those comic books of Simon Magnus's youth and imagine what they might look like if a serious artist took them seriously. What could their vernacular sensationalism and sensuality do if wedded to experimental writers' desire to "fuck the reader up"?—or so Simon Magnus described 20th-century literature's deepest intention to Simon Magnus's variously riotous and depressed high-school acquaintances. Burroughs's cut-up method, for example, in its near-homonymy with fucking up: what if you took a comic book and tore it to pieces and reassembled it at random, scrambling its time sequence? What truths about the past and premonitions about the future might stand revealed on such discombobulated pages?

While these thoughts drifted through Simon Magnus's head, Simon Magnus sat on a hillside with Simon Magnus's acquaintances, the seats of their jeans hooked on twisted arches of tree roots to a steep slope that ran down toward a small clearing. Clockwise, they passed a bottle of Wild Turkey raided from some grandfather's cabinet, and anticlockwise, a long hand-rolled spliff.

A muddy ramp jutted up from the hillside opposite them; younger boys jumped their bicycles from it, trembling in the air before landing softly in the mossy mulch of the forest floor. Their cries of thrill and fear came up to Simon Magnus regularly. The alcohol made Simon Magnus feel as if Simon Magnus floated in the air with the sounds the riders made; the marijuana caused the sounds to come right up against Simon Magnus's ear, as if the boys' breath were clouding Simon Magnus's cheek.

Eventually, a group of senior girls skittered down the hill, clutching each other's shoulders as their boots slid in the leaves: witchy types in black camisoles and diaphanous dark skirts dirty at their white lace hems. They settled just above Simon Magnus and friends and tried with much shrieking laughter to build a fire with cigarette lighters. They passed a plastic vodka bottle back and forth among themselves. In low sarcastic tones, they seemed to mock the boys below them.

The more vigorous of the boys in Simon Magnus's circle began to play a game they sometimes indulged in when unknown girls passed in the school hallway or lunchroom. They shouted out female names, any names they could think of, on the theory that if one of them said the right name, the nominated girl would have to look up and catch the eye of the lucky guesser. Simon Magnus, flushing, embarrassed by these antics, locked eyes on Burroughs's prose and pretended to be somewhere else.

"Jane! Megan! Hey, Beth!"

"Liz! Hey, Cathy! Kristy!"

"Nicole! Katie!"

"Hey, Jackie! Hey, Alice!"

The young women shook their heads and did not look down *at* the boys, though they did look down *on* them. One, the tallest, her hair massy and orange, rhyming with the firelight and with the color the trees were turning all around them, got up coldly and went down the hill. She wore a bright pink tulle dress; it seemed to drift down the slope on a breeze. This hooked Simon Magnus's eyes out of the novel.

Simon Magnus discreetly stood, wiped the seat of Simon Magnus's pants, tucked Burroughs into Simon Magnus's back pocket, murmured something about micturition—reared on old books, Simon Magnus always said things like, "I must micturate," to the merriment of Simon Magnus's friends—and followed the girl down into the clearing. Simon Magnus half-stepped, half-skidded into the small valley, the cries of the young bicycle aerialists spinning above. When Simon Magnus arrived in the clearing, the girl was not there. At the bottom of the woods, where tangled roots at eye level wormed out of the hillside, Simon Magnus wandered into the shade of some trees. Because Simon Magnus's stoned, drunken head suddenly felt heavy, Simon Magnus rested it against a tree trunk. Simon Magnus lowered Simon Magnus's zipper and cast water down on the tree roots.

The rushing sound disguised the runch of her thick-soled boots as they crushed the branches and leaves. When she shone her flashlight into Simon Magnus's eyes, afraid someone, some vicious *man*, had come to kill her, she must have seen Simon Magnus's forehead, redly scored and bisected by the imprint of the tree bark. Simon Magnus threw Simon Magnus's arms in the air. The member that (in the eyes of the gender essentialist, at least) *did* make Simon Magnus a man dangled, dripping, in the open air.

"I'm not going to hurt you," Simon Magnus said.

Raising Simon Magnus's zipper, seizing Simon Magnus's courage, Simon Magnus asked her why she had gone down alone into such a dark and secluded spot.

With reluctant eyes and a mischievous smile, she led Simon Magnus back into the clearing and illuminated a brown bird, stiff and dead-eyed, between a kitchen knife and an old hardcover book. The beam of the flashlight was cold and white, the opposite of fire.

"They said they'd help me, but they're being bitches about it," she said, tossing her head in the upward direction of her friends. "Do you know what a haruspex is?"

Simon Magnus did; Simon Magnus had always had a large vocabulary.

"I'll help you," Simon Magnus said.

That is how Simon Magnus always ended the story when repeating it to the press as part of the Simon Magnus myth—that, and a jump-cut to the epilogue: her body broken on the train tracks, blood and bone scattered across wood and iron. Simon Magnus, having absorbed the magic she proved too frail to endure in those New England provinces, had transcended this tragedy and ascended to the stars.

Back in the forest, Simon Magnus held the flashlight as she went to work on the bird. Disconnected sensations are all that linger in the memory. A bit of gore caught in her pewter thumb ring. The scream of a boy high above as his bicycle's rear wheel threatened to spin over his head. Four bloody prints from the tips of her long delicate fingers on the open pages of the book, yellow and brittle. She arrayed the glistening innards in a pattern. She consulted her grimoire. She frowned and smiled at the same time, in that unforgettable way she had: Valerie Karns. Simon Magnus did not know what she saw; it just looked like a bloody mess to Simon Magnus.

CHAPTER 3
The High Priestess

Simon Magnus ended up in Valerie Karns's house that night. Not far from the Magnuses' dark house, but on the other side of the dark forest, it sat behind a crumbling, graffiti-bright train trestle in a cul-de-sac. In that dead end squatted a crowded warren of small houses where the labor force of the town's bygone industries had once worked. Now, anyone might live there, amid the overgrown lawns and cars on cement blocks and grime-blackened siding—anyone who couldn't afford anywhere better. Valerie Karns lived alone with her mother, a hairdresser by day and bartender by night. Her mother was gone from the house from seven in the morning to midnight, except for the nights she spent in the bedroom upstairs from the bar, plying yet a third trade.

Valerie Karns had discovered magic a few years earlier, when her former stepfather—he'd managed the hardware store next to the bar where her mother worked—still lived in the house. He would visit her bedroom during the long nights when her mother was at work. She pretended to sleep, her back to the door, one of the many cats who lived in the house pressed purring to her chest, when he came in. His lowering bulk made the mattress sink; she would roll, unless she clutched the corner of the mattress by her fingernails, into his lap. His silver-furred paunch like the back of a gorilla, the beer on his breath like sour pennies, the way the air whistled in one hairy nostril, the way his rough fingers—the nails permanently grimed in black oil—stroked her back with cajoling affection: these tormented her, sleeping and waking. The cat would shriek, would leap from the bed. She never made a sound.

She would regularly climb the sagging wooden steps that gave pedestrians access to the trestle above the train tracks. She read the graffiti, never knowing what it meant—bright bloody hearts ringed with runes—and imagined leaping down onto a train and letting it either kill her or carry her somewhere, anywhere: elsewhere.

She would walk from the public school to the public library: a pale gray building with a high red door, the vault of its lofty ceiling braced and crossed with wooden beams, its windows tall and colored like church windows, said to be the oldest building in the state. She felt cradled in its breadth. She would stay there until it closed, with the excuse of extracurricular activities and class projects. It wouldn't save her from the nightly visitations, but it spared her more time with her stepfather than was strictly demanded by his power and her powerlessness.

One night, leaving the library at eight o'clock, she spied him driving up and down the streets, looking for her, looking for her mother, looking for whatever else he might put his filthy fingers on. She ran back into the building and hurried unobserved to the bathrooms. She crouched on the seat of the last toilet in the ladies' room during the final inspection. When the librarians locked the building and left, she climbed down, stiff-kneed, and spent the night in the library.

It took hardly a minute to cross the whole one-room building—frigid on a fall night—that had housed the library for what to her, at age 12, in a bewildering and almost unnavigable universe, might as well have been hundreds or thousands of years. The oldest building in the state. Did it go back to Pilgrim times? Every school year, they started again at the Pilgrims. She had memorized the required facts of history. She had a good memory: she did well in school, since they didn't ask much else of her *but* her memory—a memory of facts that didn't matter to her and therefore didn't hurt to remember. She had no idea, however, what these facts meant, or even when, exactly, they had happened in relation to her own time, to the ground she stood on. The library's bare floorboards yawed and squealed; the glass of the tall, colored windows had begun to pool, ripple, and thicken at the bottoms of the panes. Glass, she'd heard in school, was not a solid; it was a slow liquid. It only seemed solid, but with enough time, it would change shape. Didn't enough time change everything's shape? What, then, she wondered, *was* a solid?

She found a flashlight in a drawer behind the librarian's desk. When the library was open, she'd stayed close to the children's books to avoid suspicion. She fell asleep over dull stories about children in miserable houses who escaped to have fabulous adventures, or slightly more interesting stories about the children of other lands and how they spent their days herding yaks or llamas or diving for pearls or harvesting rice. She wondered if these latter children in their funny hats, whose everyday life the books presented as equivalent to the fabulous adventure in the other kind of book, didn't feel as desperate to be somewhere and anywhere else as she did. "Elsewhere" attracted her because it was *elsewhere*, not anywhere in particular. There were things she loved in her house; she loved the cats, anyway. The whistle of air in her stepfather's nostril, however, would have ruined even paradise.

That night, alone behind the locked red door, with the building closed, she could read what she wanted. Carefully keeping the flashlight lower than the windows, she went up and down the adult shelves. She noted where the sex books were on the nonfiction shelves, the better to avoid them.

She didn't need information, didn't need a language for what was happening to her. She had watched people in a story like her own several times over on TV talk shows in the afternoon, between the time she got home from school and the time her stepfather got home from the hardware store. The stories gave her the words for her experience—"sexual abuse" and its accompanying paraphernalia: "penis," for example, and "vagina"—but suggested to her that it simply had to be endured. Adults stuck together. They'd close ranks against you if you told, "close ranks" being a phrase she learned from those shows. Your mother wouldn't believe you, other adults wouldn't believe you, and the police wouldn't believe you. The school might send you to a psychologist, who would try to figure out what was wrong with *you*. Doctors couldn't prove your story one way or the other; the world is a dangerous place, and bruises may come from anywhere.

Most of the people on those shows escaped just by growing up, by becoming one of *them*, allowing themselves to be changed by time. She asked herself if she thought she could wait that long. She usually had these conversations with herself on top of the trestle as the train clattered past below. Sometimes, even in adulthood, you were not safe. Your stepfather—your uncle, grandfather, mom's boyfriend, priest, teacher, coach, cousin, camp counselor—could get at you indirectly, change who you were. One of the adult women on those shows had 100 different people living inside her head, a team she'd formed to protect herself in childhood against the assault of mom's boyfriend, a series of stronger souls who could live with what she called the fear, pain, shame, and nausea. This woman would start answering the show host's question in a baby girl's squeal and finish it in an old man's growl.

Valerie Karns felt everything but the shame: those talk shows had spared her shame by showing her how often these things happened to people who had done nothing wrong, the same way floods and fires struck people on the local news reports that played when the talk shows were over. Valerie Karns wouldn't have minded company inside her head, during the hours and hours of boredom that made up most days until the 15 minutes of terror and disgust in the night. She would sit on the floor of the bedroom while the cats slunk around her, and she would give them voices and personalities and pasts and complaints and praises. Mostly what she heard in her head was her own voice, like an outside commentator, steadying and reassuring her: "still early," "not home yet," "maybe not tonight," "you're okay, you're okay, you're okay, you're okay, you're okay"—the latter what her dad always said to her if she fell down and scraped her knee or hit her head and couldn't stop crying, before her dad had to go live somewhere else, with somebody else's daughter, or his own, but somebody else's, too.

The talk shows got one thing wrong, at least in her case. The hosts and guests often talked for a long time about how those who molest children usually also worshiped the devil. ("Molest children" was another name she learned for what was being done to her, what had started being done to her when she turned 11 and hadn't stopped since, from the summer of one year to the fall of the next.) Her stepfather did not worship the devil. He took her to church *and* Sunday school, whether her mother came home after her long Saturday night behind the bar to accompany them or not. She saw him go down on his knees, clench his hands against each other, press his scaly yellow knuckles painfully into his forehead, shut his eyes as if trying to keep tears in, and pray. She didn't wonder why he prayed so hard. She knew, and he knew, and he knew that she knew: he needed forgiveness from God. He wouldn't get it from her. She prayed, too, but God hadn't spared her yet. The Sunday school teacher smiled and said, "God answers every prayer, but sometimes His answer is 'no.'" In her situation, she concluded, Satan was not the problem, nor God the solution.

That night in the library, she found *The Complete Book of Salem Witch Spells*. The cover showed a witch from the Pilgrim times: a tall, thin girl with blazing red hair and glowing green eyes tied to a tree trunk, fire starting at the hem of her white dress, a ring of pale men in black hats surrounding her as she cried out in defiance to the dark trees rearing overhead. She remembered that the witches had been burned by people who went to church every Sunday, that the witches had been accused of devil-worship. Valerie Karns's eyes were gray, not green, but her hair was almost the same color as the witch on the cover of the book, and she was tall and thin, too—she hated being tall and thin, hated the way her stepfather always said, "You're big for your age."

Cross-legged on the library floor, the flashlight held on a shelf above her in the grip of two hardcovers, she read in the book's introduction that magic is a tool for bringing what you want into the world, for aligning what they called your will with reality. The book quoted a man it said they once accused of being evil (she doubted all such accusations by now): "Love is the law, love under will." She browsed through the spells and paused on the one headed "Curse Your Enemy." She didn't have the bitter herbs or the lock of her stepfather's hair or the egg of the raven or the water in which the moon had shone. It wasn't safe to start a fire in the library. She ran to the window and looked up: the moon *was* full, though. She took this as a sign to proceed. She went back to the book and said the words of the spell three times. She even shouted the final couplet:

Lay him down in the dust!
Break his crown, dry up his lust!

She fell asleep curled around the spell book, in the white circle the flashlight made, until its battery burned out around three in the morning. In her dream, she ran, the cats at her feet, slinking and swirling around her ankles, from her bedroom to the woods behind her house. There, she found the woman with red hair and green eyes, who was also, she didn't know how, the Sunday-school teacher at the church her stepfather took her to (the actual Sunday-school teacher was gray-headed and plump and short, not tall and thin and flame-haired). This woman was tying her stepfather with sharp-looking twine to the trunk of a tree, the twine slicing into the bulk of his silver-furred gorilla-back belly, spilling blood down the thick silver hairs. She looked up and saw Valerie Karns, and she said, this witch who was also a Sunday-school teacher, "I'll do this for you, daughter, but it's not free. You'll have to pay me later."

Valerie Karns woke on the cold floor in the dark. From where she lay, she could see out one of the tall colored windows up to the full moon. To the moon, she whispered, "Please do it."

The next morning, her mother, who had come home early the night before, beat her on the shoulders and back with the heel of a high-heeled shoe. "You think you can stay out all night, you bitch, you little whore?" Her stepfather calmly watched at the kitchen table, drumming his thick fingers, his breath whistling in one nostril.

The next weekend, an icy rain fell as the weather turned: fall into winter. Her stepfather's car slipped off the road and smashed into a tree trunk. He flew through the windshield, and the trunk split his skull in two; then the car caught fire and burned his corpse. The God at the church, He sometimes said, "No," but this other god, this god who lived in the moon and the woods, she said, "Yes."

Simon Magnus knew this story. Valerie Karns had told Simon Magnus all of it on the 13 months' worth of weeknights they spoke on the phone and weekends they spent in her bedroom, the 13 months between the night she killed the bird and the night she killed herself. Simon Magnus didn't think the comics press wanted to hear anything as unpleasant as her recollections of her childhood, however, so Simon Magnus never said a word about Valerie Karns's stepfather or about how Valerie Karns discovered magic.

Simon Magnus presented Valerie Karns to the public as the "origin story" of this superhero writer, the mysterious figure who had initiated Simon Magnus into the mystery before disappearing into it herself. She was, in Simon Magnus's telling, a naturally occurring phenomenon: a Gothic dryad of the greater Salem forest. With charming self-deprecation, even though Simon Magnus was in fact deprecating *her*, Simon Magnus said she was just a mundane Goth girl: provincial countercultural flotsam of the late 20th century, randy and precocious.

Simon Magnus told the press that when they arrived together at her empty house on that night they first met in the woods, as soon as they had come through the back door into the stinking kitchen, amid the dirty dishes piled in the sink, with their shoe soles sticking to the filthy linoleum and the cats hungrily circling their legs, she immediately grabbed Simon Magnus's penis until it hardened, her hands still stained with bird's blood. Because she later whispered to Simon Magnus the whole story of her life, Simon Magnus understood privately but never said in public why *that* girl might have felt the need to seize control of *that* organ as soon as she possibly could. Randy mischief, despite what Simon Magnus implied to fans and fawning journalists, had had nothing whatsoever to do with it. After she'd jerked Simon Magnus to climax, she put her blood-stained and semen-wet hand over her mouth, went back through the door, and vomited in the yard.

Hand in hand, she led Simon Magnus up to her bedroom. Crinkled and torn magazine pictures of Paris and London were taped to the walls, next to hand-drawn, hand-painted Baphomets and burning witches, all of it lurid in the light from the red bulb fixed in her bedside lamp. A message scrawled in red nail polish on her dresser mirror read, "Love is the law."

She dropped herself to the carpet in a blossom of pink tulle and invited Simon Magnus to sit too. She did a Tarot spread. She'd made the deck herself out of Polaroid pictures. She posed for all the figures, for all the arcana, major and minor, though Simon Magnus didn't know they were called that yet. She'd taken the photos with the camera's 10-second timer and labeled the glossy white bottoms with the fruit-scented markers so popular in those years. She handed Simon Magnus the top card to demonstrate her handiwork: The Lovers. On the card, Valerie Karns stood naked next to a mirror, doubled, a mustache and a cock-and-balls drawn with charming crudeness in black marker (blackberry-scented) on her reflection. The whole deck smelled of artificial apple, lemon, strawberry, banana, orange—smelled sugary, like a candy shop, especially amid the musky incense perfume of her bedroom.

She did a simple three-card past-present-future spread. On the dirty pink carpet, unvacuumed and stained with nail polish, she laid down three figures of the major arcana, her own self in three guises: the Empress (she wore a cheap tiara), the High Priestess (a pair of real-looking antlers sprouted from her red curls), and the Magician (she held a still-leafy branch as a wand and wore a robe with an infinity sign—a lemniscate—hand-painted in red on the front).

Simon Magnus told interviewers that there on that dirty floor, with this handmade Tarot spread, she had manifested for Simon Magnus precisely what Simon Magnus had dreamed in the forest while reading Burroughs: what a comic book would look like if absolute intelligence were applied to its form.

"Valerie, darling Valerie, showed me the archetypes in their journey through the life cycle, the cycle itself available in every temporal permutation, represented as a spatial arrangement that made each image gather meaning to itself from every other—and it could be rearranged! Time was not linear. You could stand above it, see the past to your left and the future to your right, and then you could reshuffle the deck and live them again in a different order. This is what God sees: not time as a line or even as a circle but as every moment at once and in combination with every other. God sees time the way we see space. Reading a Tarot spread or reading a comic book, therefore, makes us God—or the closest thing to it."

Simon Magnus would only be able to articulate the insight later, after reflection and study, but the whole of the thought crashed into awareness before it could be said in words that night in Valerie Karns's red bedroom. Tarot and comics uniquely represented the fourth dimension in two dimensions by turning time into space. This placed the Tarot reader and the comics reader up in the fifth dimension, a divine plane, maybe *the* divine plane. Tarot and comics, then, were the highest forms of artistic consciousness, despite both forms' association with fortune tellers and smut peddlers, gypsies by the roadside and hack artists who couldn't get hired anywhere else. "'Despite' or 'because'?" Simon Magnus would rhetorically ask interviewers and audiences—for wasn't wisdom always scattered in the trash, pearls before swine, gems amid offal, shards of divinity lodged in the prison of the flesh?

Valerie Karns used the magic until it ran out. She'd conjured up Simon Magnus the summer before they met, she confessed, sitting naked in the woods in a circle of salt at 3:00 a.m. and imploring Aphrodite to bring her a man who might understand her and who would handle her gently. Simon Magnus handled her gently enough. Simon Magnus would tug the coils of her hair straight and then let them spring back into their spirals and tickle her cheek as she patiently explained everything she knew about the art of magic.

After graduation, she couldn't conjure the money for college or any job better than the night shift at the gas station convenience store off the highway. Her mother would come home from the bar at one in the morning, wake her up and shake her, ask her for rent money, threaten to throw her out. By the time she graduated high school and Simon Magnus entered senior year, Simon Magnus was already planning to go to the city. Simon Magnus asked her to come, but she simply said, "What will I do there?" as if she couldn't imagine living anywhere else, as if some spell, some salt circle, held her in Hollow Well. She sat for hours between midnight and five behind the convenience store counter, at first fearing and then wishing that someone would come in off the highway and shoot her dead. She told Simon Magnus this was price she had to pay for using magic first to harm another.

She had stopped drawing and stopped taking pictures, even as Simon Magnus became more inspired than ever, writing poems, planning long comic-book series, making an attempt at a novel—the latter about her, about the working-class witch of Hollow Well, about the Gothic dryad of the greater Salem forest. Simon Magnus called her every night; Simon Magnus read her every word Simon Magnus wrote in those 13 months.

Gradually, she stopped answering Simon Magnus's calls, stopped showing up for work, stopped getting out of bed. At midnight on the first wintry Saturday in November, she climbed the sagging wooden stairs to the trestle, her bare feet slipping in the sleet. She walked to the middle of the bridge, climbed up on the rail, and didn't even wait for a train. She didn't need a train to take her where she was going. She escaped from the prison of the flesh.

"What does it mean?" Simon Magnus had asked Valerie Karns of the Tarot spread on the dirty carpet of her red bedroom that first night, drowsy from the orgasm she had, without invitation, wrenched from the budding writer's body with hands still stained with bird blood.

"It means you'll go backward, even as you go forward."

Simon Magnus wouldn't tell the interviewers her answer. Simon Magnus *would* tell the interviewers what Simon Magnus thought it meant: the past was Mother Magnus, the Empress; the present was Valerie Karns, the High Priestess; and the future was the Simon Magnus Simon Magnus would eventually become—the Magician, of course. About what it had cost Valerie Karns to become and to remain, for as long as she was able to remain, the High Priestess, Simon Magnus never said a word.

CHAPTER 4
Cosmopolis

Simon Magnus's second great love—a matter of public record given their long cohabitation, despite both parties' later reticence on the matter—was Ellen Chandler.

The day Simon Magnus met her, in the middle of the final decade of the 20th century, Ellen Chandler had a problem. She had just been hired for a junior editorial position at VC Comics, one of the two large comic-book companies that dominated the industry. VC Comics had, for almost 70 years, published those superhero stories that sympathetic critics judged to be American consumer culture's unique (if somewhat vapid) contribution to world mythology. The company had just changed hands in a merger that reduced the number of the planet's corporations from six to five or five to four or four to three (Ellen Chandler couldn't keep track). Word had come down from the distant reaches of the conglomerate's hierarchy that the comic-book product needed to be overhauled for the coming millennium and that new personnel of a "dynamic, diverse, synergistic, and forward-thinking" disposition should be "onboarded ASAP."

The senior leadership wanted to refresh the proverbially childish field of superhero comics, to tell stories that reflected both the advancing times and the more and more adult audience who bought their comics in specialty shops with money earned at serious professions. No longer were they addressing a boy with a skinned knee and a single crumpled dollar bill in the elastic of one sock who turned a grocery store's wire spinner-rack while mom bought milk and detergent; instead, they aimed at the upwardly mobile university student, or even the divorced insurance agent or dentist, that boy became, a man who, whether in early adulthood or in middle age, wanted to know what Overman and Ratman were doing now and in circumstances more dramatic but not less degraded than his own.

"What, to you, says the 21st century?" senior editor Frank Donofrio had asked Ellen Chandler in her job interview, in a bright white office high above the city—the real-life city, she was soon to learn, whose fictional day side they called Cosmopolis in the Overman comics and whose equally imagined night side the Ratman comics conversely labeled Gothic City. (She and Simon Magnus would jokingly call it Cosmopolis for the entirety of the time they lived there together, as they likewise called its opposite number on the West Coast, where their not-quite-marriage would meet its hideous doom, by its own comic-book name, Oceanopolis.)

Thinking of *Blade Runner*—she'd watched it in her final class of her final semester at the city's second-best university, a senior seminar named Monsters, Aliens, and Strangers in Modern Culture—and of several prominent conservative politicians whom she reviled, Ellen Chandler had replied, "Neon at night: real darkness, fake light."

VC's vice president, Madeline Stein, also in the room, albeit with her back to it, staring out the window, down over the city, turned around and smiled, the fluorescent lights overhead catching in the lenses of her glasses, filling her matronly face with white.

The interview lasted half an hour. At its end, Frank Donofrio, his voice rising with every word, cried: "You're young! You're a woman! You've never read a comic book! You have an English degree from a premier university—with, for the love of Christ, a senior thesis on James Joyce!" This meant she was hired.

Frank Donofrio had counted among her assets what she considered her problem: she'd never read a comic book. Not one. Sometime over the summer between seventh and eighth grade, it must have happened while she browsed among the small offerings at the tiny Brutalist bulwark of a suburban branch library she and her father visited every Saturday, she went right from the girls' books, the books about babysitting and getting ready for the prom, the books about hardworking and long-suffering people of other lands, to the, well, whatever you called them, the *other* books: the books that made no claim to any special audience, the books for no one and everyone, the books that didn't care who you were, the books you opened and didn't understand, as if you had mistakenly picked up something printed in Greek or Hebrew, the books that made you think, "You're allowed to do *this* with words?" (She thought, in retrospect, *To the Lighthouse* might have been her first, though it could have also been *The Waste Land and Other Poems*.) The nuns at St. Anne's Academy, who made them use their protractors from math class to draw the straight lines required to diagram sentences, would, she thought, have forbidden such books, if they even knew they existed.

Comic books, however? No. An only child, she didn't even have a little brother who might've owned a box of old ones, going yellow and brittle, squirreled away somewhere in her parents' attic, back over the river, or, rather, through the tunnel. She was graduating from the university in a month. The major publishers, the companies who mostly published books *without* pictures in them, the ones she wanted to work for, even to *serve*, the offices she wanted to inhabit every hour of the day on the off-chance that she might one day catch some glimpse of an exasperated Susan Sontag or Don DeLillo or Joan Didion hauled in against his or her imperious will for difficult edits—they had all turned her down. Worse, they hadn't even replied to her applications, to her impeccable CV. Every bookish girl in the whole of Cosmopolis must have petitioned them. When her thesis advisor said his wife's brother, who worked in advertising and had all sorts of connections, told him that the comic-book company after its merger was looking for "fresh blood"—had it been "fresh blood" or "fresh meat"?—she could hardly say no, then, though she had never read a comic book in her life.

Simon Magnus, meanwhile, had skipped college. Simon Magnus came to the city to be an aristocrat of bohemia, to find a better version of the outcast crew from high school. No longer living in a small, respectable, and ancient town, nor under Mother Magnus's disapproving eye, Simon Magnus, vulture and magpie of the thrift shops, wore fur collars, floppy hats, high-heeled boots, white suits with paisley waistcoats, purple-tinted sunglasses. Simon Magnus grew Simon Magnus's hair out in long brown waves.

Simon Magnus wrote a cycle of poems about the life and death of Valerie Karns; some of the poems were just chants of the names of gods and daemons, others long, delirious descriptions of what she might have seen in the other world. Simon Magnus attended open-mic poetry readings all over the city, intending to step up to the microphone and shake the long brown hair out of Simon Magnus's green eyes and begin to declaim. Simon Magnus, in reality, sat in the audience and watched. After Simon Magnus's retirement or renunciation, the poetry would later be published in a limited edition by a small press that otherwise printed pornographic comics; they offered Simon Magnus an absurd sum of money to print something, anything, by the famous writer who'd quit.

She flipped over The Tower, she flipped over The Moon
She treated the trestle as a threshold
I couldn't hold her on the threshing floor of this world
Across wood and iron scattered blood and bone
A red cat with her eyes floats through my room

By day, Simon Magnus worked in a small coffee shop with a crooked plank floor and, for some reason, pictures of champion boxers on the yellow walls. The shop sat down the block from Ellen Chandler's railroad apartment; that was where Simon Magnus met her. By the time Simon Magnus came in for the night shift that Saturday, she'd already drunk four cups of coffee at a small round table littered with paper. The rims of her eyes stared starkly red out of her pale, freckled face; she looked like she might cry. Simon Magnus had noticed her before—she'd lived in the railroad apartment since the middle of her senior year at the university—but usually she sat more calmly, reading long modernist novels with a faraway half-smile on her face.

Wanting to test the new city persona of a voluble bon vivant, though it sat oddly on the child who'd spent an entire early life alone in a library, Simon Magnus imagined pouring her fifth cup of coffee and saying, in what Simon Magnus imagined would be an Oscar Wildeish tone, and in that strange accent Simon Magnus was then still working on sculpting from the New England provincial into the transatlantic atopic, "Have you gotten a job? What an undeserved fate for a beautiful soul." Simon Magnus remained behind the counter picturing it; Simon Magnus said nothing.

In Simon Magnus's mind, Simon Magnus compared and contrasted her with Valerie Karns. Neither of Simon Magnus's first two loves could be called conventionally beautiful: both tended toward the angular. Valerie Karns had been tall and thin with a mass of flaming curls like a hellish halo and a sartorial preference for lace and ruffles and anything suggestive of occult costume. Ellen Chandler, on the other hand, stood only a little over five feet but was as lean as Valerie Karns, or leaner, lean as a boy, with straight blonde hair to the small of her back and a preference for turtleneck sweaters, tweed skirts, and penny loafers when she felt fancy, for a T-shirt and jeans and sneakers when she didn't. Valerie Karns had painted her fingernails black; Ellen Chandler's were unpolished, bitten.

For Simon Magnus's own part, Simon Magnus stood just under six feet. Several causes kept Simon Magnus, at that still-youthful phase of Simon Magnus's life, just a skeleton wrapped, more or less tightly, in skin: an aesthetic devotion to thin-waisted dandification, a depressive anorexia occasioned by childhood loneliness and (more recently) grief, and the impoverishments of the demimonde. Simon Magnus got thinner and thinner in the city. On the Saturday night toward the end of a warm May when Simon Magnus first spoke to Ellen Chandler, Simon Magnus was disappearing into Valerie Karns's white dress, a blood stain from one of her sacrifices or divinations pale at the hem. In the city, Simon Magnus could not declaim poetry, could not speak to a woman in a coffee shop; Simon Magnus could only let Valerie Karns's dress declaim and speak for Simon Magnus.

The year before, back in Hollow Well, on a sunny Indian-summer day in November, the previous week's premature first snowfall melted, they'd buried the cheap casket into which they'd gathered her scattered remains. The priest speculated and insinuated over this grim box as to the destination of her suicided soul before concluding that it was not for us but for the Lord to judge. When the rest of the mourners crossed themselves, Simon Magnus drew a pentagram across Simon Magnus's torso. Simon Magnus followed the funeral procession on foot back to

Valerie Karns's house, where Valerie Karns's mother held a funeral luncheon mostly attended by her colleagues from the bar. She got drunk and tripped over a cat, her blonde wig coming loose. To Simon Magnus, she said, the wig slanted on her scalp, covering one eye, "What do you think you're doing in my kitchen, you little faggot? She doesn't live here anymore. You can go home to your fucking mansion."

Simon Magnus slipped away from the funeral-baked meats and went quietly up to Valerie Karns's bedroom. Simon Magnus found the room unrevised, uncleaned, a monument to her final dishevelment: the bed unmade, the sheets twisted and stained with ink and blood and who knew what, her final Tarot spread, a Celtic Cross, half-askew on the floor, though Simon Magnus couldn't read it through the tears in Simon Magnus's eyes. The mirror still announced in a nail-polish scrawl that love was the law.

Almost blindly, Simon Magnus took two dresses from her closet, a red and a white. Simon Magnus bundled them tightly and then ran down the staircase, ran through the kitchen, ran out the back door, ran across the yard, and ran into the woods before anyone could notice. Simon Magnus exited her life by the same route Simon Magnus had entered. Simon Magnus slept in her dresses until her scent had gone from them—and then after.

The day Simon Magnus met Ellen Chandler, Simon Magnus had carried the white dress in Simon Magnus's backpack on the subway and then changed amid the roaches and graffiti and floating cigarette ends in the coffee shop's single-toilet single bathroom. The bosom sagged down Simon Magnus's pale, hairless chest.

When Simon Magnus finally came to her table to refill (wordlessly) Ellen Chandler's coffee mug, she told Simon Magnus, because she had to tell someone, and because she thought Simon Magnus was the most gorgeous young man she'd ever seen, and because she'd wanted talk to Simon Magnus since she'd first laid eyes on the dress, "Listen to this shit," and proceeded to read Simon Magnus a florid narrative caption from the comic-book script it was her new job to approve and proofread:

Felled by the glowing blue cyprhonite—the radioactive rock remnant of his home planet of Cyphron—Overman's granite brow beaded blue sweat!

Simon Magnus mused quietly. "There's poetry there. Accidental maybe, but you could do something with it if you applied consistent principles. How far is it, really, from what Blake and Shelley were doing with myth—Blake especially, with his illuminated books about gods and heroes?"

In the course of her literary studies, Ellen Chandler had apprenticed more on the Gustave Flaubert and Henry James side of literature, with its devotion not to the Romantic sublime, not to myths and gods and heroes, but to the precise notation of everyday psychology. Joyce loved Blake—she knew that—but her

Joyce, the Joyce of her senior thesis, was Flaubert's Joyce, not Blake's Joyce; her senior thesis had been titled "'Who's He When He's at Home': Joyce's Domestic Realism." Still, she had never thought of superheroes that way, had never thought of comic books as in any way akin to "illuminated books."

She raised her gray eyes to Simon Magnus's green ones. "Keep your eye out for new talent," Madeline Stein had quietly advised her upon her hiring. "It's a new world out there." Could this most beautiful boy, shrinking into a white dress, who thought Blake wrote superhero comics, be the new talent she was looking for, her key to her advancement in the VC Comics office—or, better yet, her advancement out of it?

"Do you think you could write one of these?" she said.

Simon Magnus lowered Simon Magnus's eyes to Simon Magnus's feet—to the cheap sneakers peeking out from the hem of the dress—and shyly confessed, "I grew up reading them."

Simon Magnus didn't want to revisit the superheroes of Simon Magnus's youth. Simon Magnus wanted to write cryptic poetry and then die of tuberculosis (John Keats), turn to gunrunning in North Africa (Arthur Rimbaud), or jump from the deck of a steamer into the Gulf of Mexico (Hart Crane). The rent wouldn't pay itself, though, would it?

"Sure, what the hell," Simon Magnus said. "I could write one of those."

CHAPTER 5
I Will Not Let Thee Go Except Thou Bless Me

We could debate—some have already debated—whether or not Marco Cohen should count among Simon Magnus's great loves, despite their apparently never having felt anything for one another but mutual suspicion, annoyance, antipathy, distaste, and contempt. Given how it all turned out—the domestic apocalypse that gave rise to *Overman 3000*—such a debate would be perverse; but perversity hasn't detained commentators on the comic-book mage's career. Simon Magnus touched Simon Magnus's flesh to the flesh of Valerie Karns, Ellen Chandler, and Diane del Greco, but Simon Magnus and Marco Cohen, for all that they despised each other, penetrated one another's minds, even souls.

Ellen Chandler met Marco Cohen in a philosophy class in their senior year of college, a few months before she met Simon Magnus. He'd charmed her whenever (which was often) he quarreled with the grizzled and tattered old wreck of a professor, a man who'd sat in his youth with the Vienna Circle, about whether or not Hegel's metaphysics produced any concepts intelligible to logic and human reason. Before he'd ended up in that class, struggling with the professor, Marco Cohen had been wrestling with himself for years.

"You have to understand," he told Ellen Chandler in a bar one night after class, both of them chain-smoking, "we should absolutely obey the prohibition on making graven images—on idolatry—on fashioning any mere toy out of material that stands between us and the law. You don't have to be religious to think this. You're a woman, Ellen. You see how men stare at your body, as if their eyes were hands, as if they were choosing ripe fruit in the supermarket, and don't give a second's consideration to your mind, to anything you might have to say."

"Marco, I have freckles and a A-cup—honestly, I wish men would stare at my body!"

Never comfortable with ribaldry, especially not around women and certainly not *from* women, he blushed. His own eyes transfixed hers with their passionate intensity: eye to eye, not male eye to female body. As for his own body, he was short, like her, and his hair was already receding to the middle of his head by his early 20s. His body was all sinew and bone but for the paunch at his midsection. Later, after years spent hunched over a drawing board, his spine would bend into an S-curve almost like the stray lock of hair that fell in a figure-eight sign of infinity across Overman's forehead. Marco Cohen's own head was craggy, square, too big for his meager body.

"Anyway," she more seriously tried to resume the conversation, "your art—"

He lifted his hand to bat her argument down; they'd had the same argument 10 times over by that late date in the semester, the late autumn's first snow turning to street-lit slush in the avenue outside the dark, quiet bar where they were the youngest customers amid the old regulars, the ruins and burnouts slumped in wrinkled suits on their stools.

His art, he explained to her again, attempted to redeem art itself for the prohibition on graven images by reflecting to viewers both a literally and an ethically true picture of the real world they inhabited. With such a clear mirror held to their faces, they couldn't fail to recognize themselves as conscious moral agents ("conscious moral agents" was the secular translation, he believed, of "made in the image of the Lord"), tasked at every moment with acting justly in the world. These aesthetic views also aligned with his politics at the time: the Berlin Wall had fallen half a decade before, but Marco Cohen was a communist.

His mother once harbored dreams of becoming an artist before more pragmatic considerations lured her into professional life; she taught him to draw as soon as he could hold a pencil. Throughout his childhood and adolescence, she bought him sketchbooks and special pencils and paint sets and canvasses; she enrolled him in ateliers in the summers; she would stand behind him and guide his hand to demonstrate how to shade the underside of a painted peach bluish-purple to give it volume or crosshatch the shadow on the side of a man's face to convey the texture of the real. Sometimes when he painted, even as an adult, he could feel her breath hit the back of his ear, smell her cloying floral perfume.

His father dismissed the artistic life as unworldly. "You want him to paint pretty pictures," his father asked his mother, "but who will pay his rent?" Smelling of cigarettes and antacids, however, he had nothing to offer in art's stead but "business," a vague term that conveyed nothing but the dull consultation of charts and graphs to the growing child.

The child's maternal grandfather, on the other hand, offered an effective counterweight to his mother's advocacy of beauty. The old man was a widower—his wife had died when their youngest child, Marco Cohen's mother, was only a girl—a retired contractor, a man who'd worked by day with his hands and studied by night, living alone in a book-crammed apartment, what Marco Cohen's mother called a fire hazard. His schedule of abstemious meals and neighborhood walks was more regular than the sluggish clock mounted on his kitchen wall. Orthodox but eccentric, he scorned modern culture, condemned the television he didn't own but was sure showed what he judged pornography. Marco Cohen had met his maternal grandfather only a few times at weddings or other family events, a large, reserved man in black who didn't speak to him, who made him faintly afraid but unable to look away. When his mother began working longer and longer hours in the city, his parents judged it expeditious to send him after school and on summer days to the old man's lonely apartment in a decaying city neighborhood with burnt-out cars by the curbs.

The first summer day they took him there on their way into the city, his mother driving, his father in the passenger seat, smoking into the windstream, his mother cried quietly.

"Will you knock that off?" his father said.

"I, I just grew up in that fucking prison," she whispered, though the wind carried her words to her son. "I hated every minute of it. Why am I sending my baby there?"

"Because it's cheaper and more reliable than a sitter. He's a harmless old man. Let the kid keep him company for however long he has left. Your brother and your sisters keep *their* kids away—it's probably killing him."

In the rearview mirror, Marco Cohen watched his mother's mascara run. His father turned around in the passenger seat, jogged his knee, and handed him a sheaf of VC Comics: various issues of *Overman*, *Ratman*, *Female Supreme*.

"So the old man doesn't bore you to death," his father said with that wink he often gave Marco Cohen, as if he and Marco Cohen were in on some joke, though whatever it was, Marco Cohen never understood.

His parents walked him into the turn-of-the-century building, over the cracked warm marble of its lobby, and his mother kissed him goodbye at the dully golden elevator doors. After he got off the elevator, he stepped nervously down a long, dim corridor that smelled of a century of cigarette smoke. He knocked on his grandfather's door so faintly it was as if he didn't want to be heard. The tall old man, thin but square-shouldered, his long forelocks a yellowish gray, slowly opened the door. He chucked his grandson under the chin and smiled inside his gray beard, his teeth crooked.

He put out his long-fingered hand, the fingernails overgrown; it took Marco Cohen a few seconds to understand that his grandfather was ordering him to hand over the comic books he carried folded under his arm. He'd never read a comic book in his life—where his father got the idea he'd be interested in them, he had no clue—so he gave them up to his grandfather without regret. Then, in the doorway, his grandfather tore the whole sheaf of comic books in two—a muscular feat that impressed Marco Cohen more than Overman's merely imagined twisting of metal or breaking of chains ever would.

He spent two summers and two years' worth of fall, winter, and spring evenings with his grandfather when he was on the cusp of adolescence. The old man spoke little; when he did speak, he would ask Marco Cohen what he knew about their religion. When he found that Marco Cohen knew nothing, had been raised without religion (his father worshiped business, his mother beauty), that the child could not answer the simplest question—"Do you know Abraham?"—he would patiently explain, he would open the Tanakh and in his quiet voice read aloud. "Do you know what to say before you go to sleep?" he asked the boy. "*Shema Yisrael*. Every night. *Shema Yisreal*."

They would walk wordlessly around the city, and he would raise his long index finger to point out this or that—a squirrel holding a pizza slice between its dainty hands and nibbling the cheese; the leering, gaping gargoyle on the corner of a bank building—and leave Marco Cohen to reflect on the significance of what he'd indicated. He carried rolls of cash at all times; he would press a bill into Marco Cohen's hand and point: there was a woman with crazy, greasy gray hair folded into a filthy blanket in a doorway, or a man with two stumps that ended above his absent knees rattling a cup on the concrete. Marco Cohen would approach, as hesitantly as he'd approached his grandfather's door, and put the bills into their palsied hands. In the silence of the apartment, he did his homework, and then he read his grandfather's books, or tried to. Those volumes of theology, philosophy, history, and science were too big for such a small child.

Then his grandfather died, just as Marco Cohen turned 12. The loss was not merely of a man, though who could ever replace the widower, his measured and precise movements, his fingers deft and careful when he turned a yellowed page, his hands reserved in their workman's strength, restrained, as if not wanting to bruise a millimeter of flesh, even when he peeled an apple, his pointing finger that revealed the mystery of the creation? The loss of the old man was the loss of a world: the dim apartment with its bare floors and old armchairs, its shelves massed with books, sacred and secular, the dust motes tumbling thickly in the lines of light cast by the slats of the blinds, the weighty credenza dense with candles and a picture of his long-dead wife, a pretty dark-haired woman in her long-gone girlhood. Contrast this to the clean lines of the Cohens' condominium in a much more fashionable city neighborhood, what they called up-and-coming: its silver refrigerator like a spaceship, its two floors joined sleekly by a modernist spiral staircase, what books it held relegated, like other inefficiencies, to the bedroom.

After his grandfather's death, after the apartment's sale, Marco Cohen would draw it obsessively from memory, asking the old man in his mind for forgiveness, since one of the few things his grandfather had ever told him outright rather than by indirection was that art was a frivolity—worse than a frivolity: a blasphemy—a needless addition to the creation, a creation ever breaking down and needing our reparative attention more than any mere fantasies of our own did.

(He never mentioned it while the old man was alive, but years later, Marco Cohen told his mother about the time his grandfather had ripped up the comic books. "He did the same thing when I was a teenager. He found a sketchbook I was keeping—perfectly innocent drawing exercises: fruit on a table, my shoes, the view outside my bedroom window—and he tore the pages out in front of me and threw them around the room. They came down around us like we were in a snowglobe.")

Shortly after the old man's death, to relieve Marco Cohen's grief, his parents took him to the beach.

The beach didn't cheer his mourning eye, however; his eye, rather, grayed the beach, the flat gritty sand and the gross flesh exposed on it, and the waste of the ocean, its endlessness irrelevant to the near needs of humanity. "He was an old man, Marco," his father said, "and he had to die sometime." Eventually, to appease parents whose frustrated concern had begun to fill him with mute rage, he waded out into the chilly waves.

The spume gathering like a scum around his ankles, his shins, his knees, began to disgust him. Near him, a teenage boy held a teenage girl's head under the water in what was supposed to be flirtation, while an old woman stood rooted as the brine agitated the loose flesh of her thighs. Marco Cohen looked back and saw his mother sail her hand through the air and smile broadly in encouragement. "Take a swim, baby!" she called, her words almost lost on the wind.

He plunged forward. He shut his eyes tightly against the saltwater and breast-stroked out. Something happened, though—with his eyes closed, he didn't know what. Maybe he struck his head on a piece of floating detritus, or maybe another child at play caught his forehead by accident with elbow or knee, or maybe even a wave itself in its rolling had gathered force and hit him like a fist. In any case, he felt a pain above and between the eyes that sent his vision black, sent him reeling head over heel deeper into the water. When he regained awareness, he felt the long withdrawing roar drag him by the ankles out to the infinite depths. He held his breath and shut his eyes for as long as he could; these were somehow identical efforts, as if he didn't want to open any channel through which the breath of life might escape.

Finally, though, the nascent artist could withhold his gaze no longer. His eyes snapped open by reflex. From his perspective, he hung in the sky above a sunken city, its skyscrapers furred with algae, the spires of its temples tumorous with barnacle; pulpy, pulsing plasma that emitted garish pink and yellow light drifted down its avenues, while schools of fish darted in arrowhead formation like birds above the skyline. All human effort, all human meaning, lay buried beneath in the deep, its new inhabitants forms of flesh animated by a vital spirit that was neither intelligence nor love but mere appetite, the blind will to persist.

Some ray or jellyfish suddenly faced him in the watery sky above the sunken city. Its translucent wings wavered in the current as they swept forward to embrace him, to pull him to the thing's rippling pink mouth. He felt a sharp pain just below the waist; everything went black again. When he came to, he lay face up on the beach, his parents blinking down at him.

"You had us worried there for a second," his mother said, offering both her hands to pull him to his feet.

His father said, "I told her there was nothing to worry about. I've been swimming here since I was younger than you—you have to get out pretty far before it's deeper than the deep end of a swimming pool."

"Is that blood, though?" his mother asked, unceremoniously stretching the elastic of his trunks. His skin burned at the touch of her painted nails. "Come look at this," she ordered his father.

His father lowered his sunglasses and peered where she pointed. "Just a jellyfish sting," he said. "The both of you worry too much!" He handed his wife his sunglasses. "My turn," he said. He splashed out with a child's abandon against the waves and then dove in.

After his maternal grandfather's death, after his inexplicable vision in the sea, Marco Cohen turned in his quest for wisdom to his paternal grandparents' own library. To this he had more sporadic access. The old couple, after their long and successful careers as engineer and schoolteacher, had retired to a cottage upstate, and Marco Cohen's parents only drove up the highways from the city through wine country to see them twice a year, once when the leaves fell and once when they budded.

They were happy to let the child borrow books, however, even though they slightly patronized him in the process, mussing his hair while he mused over the *Communist Manifesto*, as if his interest in the most serious matters were no more than cute, like a picture of a mouse driving a car or a kitten in firemen's gear, nothing like his maternal grandfather's having mutely entrusted to his eye the mystery of the visible. The paternal grandparents' library contained multitudes, no less than the maternal grandfather's had, even though they were now relaxed retirees in pastel slacks who loved nothing more than a walk on the beach, a mimosa in the morning, a good movie in the evening—they called them pictures.

He passed over their masses of fiction—frivolity, he judged; his other grandfather had no such books—and, in the absence of theology, the genre they eschewed that his other grandfather had favored, found his way to the common ground between the two libraries: the history, the politics. (They'd been radicals in their youths, his paternal grandparents—they'd met at college, both of them communists; they became Trotskyists just after the war; finally, they settled into liberalism as their careers advanced.) This section contained volumes his now-liberal grandparents considered erroneous, extremist, but they possessed them in the conviction that even one's enemies' errors might hold a rational kernel of truth. This practice harbored the unavoidable danger, however, that heresiarchs collected or even quoted for the forensic purpose of exhibiting error may nevertheless inspire converts. Accordingly, Marco Cohen, his mind set alight by the absolute seriousness of some moldering interwar treatises, not to mention some of the simpler texts of Hegel, adopted, just as the Soviet Union was collapsing, the tenets of Stalinism.

If, for a time, it took a garrison state to embody humanity's hope for liberation from need, for that promise of jubilee sounded like a trumpet at the center of the Torah, then a garrison state it would have to be—a garrison state fortified, moreover, against the meaninglessly vital anti-life just waiting to devour us beyond the nearest shoreline. Why else had his grandfather's unerring finger shown him so often the sufferings of the poor? Trotsky's "permanent revolution," not to mention the liberal's vaunted "freedom," could wait until man had disciplined himself rigorously and ruthlessly in the arts of justice.

At least a garrison state didn't dazzle the eye with pornography, jangle the ear with advertising's sing-song, or promote those false gods of mere commerce and sensuality, such as coked-up titans of industry, heroin-addicted rock stars, and sluttish actresses, all of them preferring to reign in hell than to serve in heaven. (This is not to say that Marco Cohen ever believed in heaven and hell, only that his grandparents' library also contained, his grandmother having long taught high-school English, John Milton.) All of them, he thought, with the sunken city and the devouring jellyfish still alive behind his eyes, were the human equivalents of the pulsing neon flesh that meaninglessly fluttered in the ocean currents amid what once were the vaults and spires of temples.

"Pornography, pornography," his grandfather would say and shake his head on their walks as they passed a 10-foot-tall advertisement pasted on a wall behind a bus stop, a vast photo of a woman with her legs spread, beckoning with her eyes. He would show Marco Cohen the empty-eyed junkie sweating between her widely spaced feet, her sharp black heels. He would press a bill, rarely less than 20 dollars, into Marco Cohen's damp, nervous palm.

Wasn't communism, as a secular theocracy commanding the equality of man at the point of a gun, the only serious alternative to the slack indiscipline of worldly life, the kind that had allowed the paternal line to drift from his grandparents' advocacy of "permanent revolution" to his father's votes for the capitalist champions Ronald Reagan and George Bush? Marco Cohen's parents, however, found his religious and political fixations morbid, as they'd found his maternal grandfather's. Marco Cohen once overheard his father saying to his mother, "We should have had your old man committed."

Ellen Chandler couldn't stop herself from smiling, her heart jittery with wine and affection, when she thought about Marco Cohen in adolescence, acne-spotted, voice still cracking into the occasional falsetto, as he berated his businessman father and university administrator mother over the breakfast table, rattling the coffee and orange juice in their cups as he demanded justice of them, as they sighed under his bombardment, as his mother condescended to him with something like, "We admire your sincerity, darling," while his father rolled his eyes, checked his Rolex, and said, "We'll revisit this subject when *you* pay taxes," the both of them exchanging a look that anxiously asked, "Where did this child come from? This is America in the late 20th century, and we can do as we please. He should be at the movies, chasing girls, smoking a little pot.

How did we conceive this throwback mocking us with the insanity of the Old World?" His father would finally pound the table and say, "Capitalism is what gives you the comfort and the security you enjoy to lecture your father at the breakfast table, you little brat! If you think you'd be happier in China, I'll buy you the ticket myself."

Maybe she was only attributing to them her own judgments—the anxiety he made her feel. Ellen Chandler certainly hated Ronald Reagan and George Bush, but she loved Virginia Woolf, a bohemian and rentier, an anarchic madwoman who never cooked her own meals or scrubbed her own bath, and the point of whose work, if it could be said to have a point, was the futility of any single so-called objective vantage on the world, ethical or otherwise. Ellen Chandler had lost her virginity—if virginity was, she wasn't sure, a legitimate concept—at age 16, and happily, around the time she started smoking. Had Marco Cohen lost his virginity by the time she met him in their senior year of college? She didn't know; she suspected not. She adored Marco Cohen. The moment he started arguing with the professor on the first day of Modern Philosophy, the moment she heard him say, "Logical positivism hasn't relieved a single bit of suffering in this world," she thought to herself, I have to know this man. She found his politics, like his aesthetics, antediluvian, some belated madness out of Dostoevsky. This, though, was precisely why she adored him.

(Sans the adoration, his art teachers thought the same, much as they admired the intricate craft that lived in his wiry wrist, his bony fingers, his omniscient eye that saw the precise curve of the vein that crossed the back of the hand or the way the nervous pulse in a calf muscle might be triumphantly arrested in pencil lines. Still, they said, "Party trick, Mr. Cohen, mere *trompe l'œil*." They were professionally obligated to say it, since he had transgressed the 20th-century obsolescence of figurative art that began with the Impressionists' dissolution of the outside world in myopic subjectivity. This art-historical verdict was an arrogant and overly literal secular translation, he thought—even, he let himself think, a customarily gentile botch—of the biblical *Bilderverbot*.)

How rare, though, Ellen Chandler marveled, to find anyone who cared as much as he did—and about everything; who considered it his responsibility to form a total theory commensurate with the enormity of his concern; who would not take one action unworthy of what his mind, his soul, deemed right. Everyone else, including herself, was, she thought, a dilettante by comparison—saner and healthier, of course, but not nearly as worthy of love. A solitary, he pursued his communism in total isolation; he'd gone to a meeting of the campus socialists once, but the first speaker said the industrial proletariat was a relic of an old, bad history, that the new anti-capitalist vanguard was comprised of women and other of what she called marginalized peoples in the imperial core, and he'd left in disgust, theatrically scraping his chair as he stood, never to return. Ellen Chandler wanted to pick him up and put him in bed and tuck him in and stroke his balding head. She would visit him in his studio at midnight to bring him food, to make sure he kept fed, to make sure he didn't quite yet evanesce into that world of the spirit that was, however he called himself a Marxist materialist, his true home. When they went to the bar after their class, sitting at a little table in the corner they had come to think of as theirs, he always pulled her chair out for her.

"I was raised Catholic," she said to him one night in the bar after a moment's silence. "The whole fucking religion is a graven image. That's the only good thing about it! Otherwise, it's old men in dresses telling you not to have any fun while they eye up the altar boys. The homilies would put you to sleep, but you could always stay awake by looking at the stained glass windows—the way they colored the light that came through them and spangled the backs of the people in the pew in front of you—and those sadomasochistic reliefs of the Stations of the Cross on the wall, all that flogging and bleeding of the beautiful male body, like something out of Mishima."

Her eyes glassed over in reverie as she dragged on her cigarette.

"Well, there you go," he said. He raised his beer glass and slammed it down to reseize her attention, rattling the fruity wine in her flute. "You were missing the parables, the allegories, the commandments—distracted by some goddamn sex fantasy."

He said it fondly, without rancor. He liked to argue, he liked to berate, at least with his intellectual equals. He had a duty to reform the world. He also said it without any hint of flirtation. He didn't go to the bar with Ellen Chandler after class to seduce her. Rather, he found the crude jostle of male company intolerable, the arm-punching insults meant to certify that one man was another's loyal "brother," the crude sexual remarks and preadolescent delight in flatulation—no, he'd always preferred, almost exclusively, the friendship of women, whether they were his intellectual equals or not, even though they sometimes cowed him into shyness with the reminder that they, too, had bodies and pleasures.

Ellen Chandler, however, her body almost as boyishly lean as his, didn't quite answer to his erotic tastes. At that time, and for the better part of a decade thereafter, he was in love with one of the nude models in his figure drawing class: Diane del Greco, dark and ample, who would become his wife and the mother of his child—Diane del Greco, who would, in time, come to be Simon Magnus's third great love, or fourth, depending on whether or not we number Marco Cohen in the final, fatal sequence.

CHAPTER 6

A Love Supreme

Overman 3000 waited in their future, the vortex that would devour them, the Minotaur at the heart of their labyrinth. In the meantime, Simon Magnus carried three boxes of books, a backpack full of casual clothes, a manual typewriter, and Valerie Karns's two dresses from a back basement room—the first and cheapest place Simon Magnus had found upon arriving in the city—to Ellen Chandler's railroad apartment 20 blocks away.

She'd been looking for a roommate to share the rent even before she'd met Simon Magnus; her parents sometimes had to send a money order over the river, even with her editor's salary at VC Comics. When Simon Magnus began spending weekends in her apartment, and then weeknights, she asked Simon Magnus to move in. On the modest wage of what was not yet widely called a barista, Simon Magnus's contribution to the rent would be more honorary than actual. "I am here to lend moral support," Simon Magnus said the day Simon Magnus arrived with Simon Magnus's bags and boxes.

Ellen Chandler did not, in fact, so much ask as *demand* that Simon Magnus move in. She did so while kneeling by a low cot at midnight in a dirty, crowded hospital corridor, stroking Simon Magnus's bruised cheek. That afternoon, outside Simon Magnus's back basement room, a mugger had not only held a knife to Simon Magnus's throat until Simon Magnus turned over a wallet full of tip money from the café but also pushed Simon Magnus to the cold, damp pavement and kicked Simon Magnus in the chest and stomach and back, probably because—it was fall by then—he had spied the lacy hem of Valerie Karns's dress peeking from beneath Simon Magnus's long, stained coat.

Ellen Chandler and Simon Magnus both loved the city and feared it, the one from the suburbs over the river, the other from the small town in the north. Both had dreamed of the city, of veritable Cosmopolis, for their entire adolescence. Both had regarded suburb and town as a provincial prison—the stores in the town all closed at 5:00 p.m.; not all the suburbs' streets had sidewalks, and you were not in any case within walking distance of anywhere you wanted to go. The city, though, had its own walls and bars. If you were an alien to it, it could close all its doors to you or reach out of its mazy darkness and chastise you. Simon Magnus might have asked SimonMagnusself: If a man couldn't wear a dress in the city, where could a man wear a dress?—but the city had codes and shibboleths, zones in public where everything was forbidden and private chambers where everything was permitted. The older buildings, the banks and department stores from the first part of the century, held runic messages on their friezes; strange demons nestled, staring, from their eaves and buttresses; masonic mysteries hid in the upper air. Together, Simon Magnus and Ellen Chandler went deeper and farther than they would have gone alone, tasting every kind of food, from the Andes to the Himalayas. They bought records in dank, mildewy shops one accessed from storm doors; they bought used books in the narrow fronts of stores where who knows what—drugs or guns or girls—were vended from the rear.

They enjoyed a belated adolescent romance, of a kind Ellen Chandler had never experienced in her adolescence itself, despite her early sexual initiation, and a gentler one than Simon Magnus's conflagration of a high-school love affair with Valerie Karns had been.

They would go to movies—what they called films—and then quarrel about their structure, their symbolism, their spiritual significance, and their political allegory until three in the morning, dizzy with coffee and wine and nicotine. There was a dark, small one-screen theater between two high buildings that showed old films at midnight. They'd pass a bottle of wine back and forth in the front row and kiss with stained teeth. Her favorite was *Wings of Desire* ("Kitsch," Simon Magnus declared); Simon Magnus's favorite was *Contempt*, which she pronounced superficial—superficial and needlessly cruel.

She had taken college French. She would read to Simon Magnus from Baudelaire and Rimbaud in the original, and, in translation, went further afield: Dostoevsky, Borges, her beloved Mishima. Confined to English and preferring poetry to narrative as a rule anyway, Simon Magnus returned the favor with Keats, Hopkins, Yeats, Eliot. One day, they saw a splintery bookcase, handmade from heavy planks, that someone had put on the curb for garbage pickup; together they hauled it five blocks to their apartment; gradually, they filled it, Simon Magnus's books and Ellen Chandler's books mingling on the boards, falling against one another.

Mother Magnus had disliked music—it raised emotions she could neither resist nor dispel—so Simon Magnus had grown up almost without it; Simon Magnus loved Ellen Chandler, therefore, for her eclectic taste, her old turntable even in CD days, the carpet of record sleeves on her floorboards, her rooting in thrift store boxes of records, for sharing Chopin and Joy Division, Japanese techno and *Sketches of Spain*.

She had spent the first two years of college in her parents' suburban house across the river, taking the train to the university; the doors that blew open in her mind as she learned through her unsystematic but enlivening coursework about Nietzsche and Buddhism, quantum mechanics and mystic anchoresses, slammed shut again just as quickly every time her mother called her down at dinnertime for meat loaf and cheesy potatoes and quizzed her again about the impracticality of her English major. "We just want what's best for you. Have you considered pre-law?" her mother would coo. Her father, much as she thanked him for taking her every weekend as a girl to the Brutalist branch library where she'd found Woolf and Eliot, would puff through a mouthful of potatoes, "We *are* paying the tuition, sweetie."

During the last two years of college, she'd lived in a tiny high-ceilinged dormitory on the university campus with a neurotic asthmatic who'd banned smoking, lights, and noise after 10:00 p.m., and any too-jarring genre of music, even if only audible through headphones, even if part of the classical repertoire; led by allusions in Eliot and Joyce, Ellen Chandler enjoyed a senior-year Wagner phase, or tried to, anyway, when her roommate wasn't querulously wheezing at her from the bottom bunk to ground the Valkyries. This unfavorable living situation caused Ellen Chandler to acquire her habit of reading, writing, working, and chain-smoking in coffee shops until closing time.

Now she was living on her own—on her own, even though she lived with Simon Magnus. Living with someone you'd had sex with and who liked the same books and films you did didn't feel the same as living with people, whether parent or stranger, who couldn't comprehend who you were and what you wanted, who would be happier if you would simply become someone else.

Later, further into adulthood, she knew she had some obligation to feel superior to those early days with Simon Magnus, to dismiss them with a chastened middle-aged laugh as what they called pretentious. Their pleasure, hers and Simon Magnus's, hadn't been pretended, though, and she saw no reason to stand in judgment of two young people who wanted to fill every day with the most meaningful words and the most beautiful gestures they could find or devise. Kissing under awnings in a sudden autumn downpour, laughing into each other's mouths—these things happen. The accusation of pretense amounted to no more, even in her middle-aged view, than the anxious self-defense of smugly timid souls who had never risked themselves for the lives they really wanted—lives they therefore themselves had to pretend to scorn. Those days, even the bad days, and despite the horror to follow, Ellen Chandler would always count among the best days of her life.

How would she have survived those first months at the comic-book company without Simon Magnus? Simon Magnus and Ellen Chandler would collapse into each other on her narrow bed with derisive laughter as they rewrote together the schlocky superhero scripts sent in both by the old-time writers, the cigar-chompers and whiskey-drinkers who had seen the Depression and seen the War and had not been able to write the Hemingwayesque novels they'd spent their teenage years dreaming of, *and* by the young, newly professionalized fanboys, who came of age in the affluent society, and who may have been to college but had never wanted to write anything *except* comic books. Both the old-timers and the fanboys whispered their complaints to the higher-ups, even to Madeline Stein and Frank Donofrio, that this stuck-up new hire of theirs, this snooty feminist or postmodernist or whatever the hell she was, had taken it into her head to cut up their scripts. Frank Donofrio would just say, "Gentlemen, the 21st century is coming! It's almost here! You'd better get ready to live in it!"

On cold nights, they would huddle together in her slim bed, naked under the comforter. It had taken her a month to coax Simon Magnus into nakedness, another month to get Simon Magnus to make love to her. Sometimes, Simon Magnus couldn't sustain an erection. Simon Magnus often asked if she was all right when she was in Simon Magnus's arms—afraid, she thought, after Simon Magnus told her about Valerie Karns, to let another girl slip out of the world, to watch another girl break free of the prison of the flesh.

She also thought Simon Magnus might want to be a girl. She had no sexual objection to this, exactly. She thought of herself as what they called straight, straight even to a fault, straight enough to make them revoke her women's lib card. She knew she wasn't supposed to like it, but she liked to recline peacefully on her back as a man drove himself up and into her. Still, she couldn't deny that peeling Simon Magnus's male body out of Simon Magnus's female dress, this very action and image, this disrobing, this unveiling of the androgyne, this sight of a penis rising from its garland of tulle, made the entire middle of her body feel full of what the poets called fireflies, though when she was a girl she called them lightning bugs.

(There was something about the contrast—she couldn't have articulated it exactly—between the man's strength and his weakness; she recalled her first time, age 16, the weekend after her boyfriend, two years older than her, had flipped his motorcycle, the weekend she watched his face wince almost as if he were angry, though actually because he was in pain, as he mounted her, even with his shattered tarsus in a cast.)

Did Simon Magnus receive a reciprocal pleasure from finding under her long sweater her flat chest and her slim hips? She wondered. Between them, she thought, they added up somehow to a man and a woman, though precisely how she could not have said.

Simon Magnus did not want to be a girl. Simon Magnus did not want to be a boy. This is what Simon Magnus told her when she sometimes tried to play what Simon Magnus contemptuously called dress-up: to braid Simon Magnus's hair, to paint Simon Magnus's toenails, to see how Simon Magnus might look in hot pink. "This is your kink, not mine, my darling," Simon Magnus told her. At that time, Simon Magnus did not take care of SimonMagnusself, ate not enough or too much, often neglected to bathe, never took up a toothbrush. Often, Simon Magnus did not especially want to be anything except "a transparent eyeball," "the eye with which the universe beholds itself and knows itself divine"—Simon Magnus quoted Emerson and Shelley (respectively) at her from that store of childhood reading in the abandoned library looking out onto the dark woods back in Hollow Well.

Ellen Chandler didn't find this self-explanation persuasive. She even found it, in its idealism, its denial of the body's intractable claim, wearily reminiscent of Marco Cohen's way of thinking, for all that Marco Cohen and Simon Magnus had nothing else in common. Simon Magnus had told her all about Mother Magnus, about Hollow Well and Valerie Karns, about the pitted mirror in Mother Magnus's master bedroom, the elastic of the tights on the boy's flesh.

She had read some Freud and some Jung at college, had even put one mental toe into—and then quickly withdrew it from—the gelid tarn known as Lacan. She speculated that Simon Magnus had no experience of a real man on whom to model a real male self; Simon Magnus's father had vanished, and Simon Magnus's beloved male poets all strove to disappear into the poetic ether, into Shelley's "sea reflecting love" or Emerson's "over-soul."

Woman, by contrast, was the only solid reality Simon Magnus had known—in Mother Magnus's case, a reality like a brick wall, one you could bloody your head against all your life and get no response from. In Valerie Karns's case, he did find the reality of sex and death, but Valerie Karns burned across the sky on her own poetic journey out of this world; she proved, therefore, as unreliable in the end as both the genetic and the spiritual forebears, though she at least had given herself soul *and* body to Simon Magnus, however briefly, as father, mother, and the poets—none of whom would reply when Simon Magnus cried out to them—had not. Simon Magnus, she therefore surmised, wore female dress to become real, to incarnate a spiritual self into the only flesh Simon Magnus knew *as* flesh—female flesh.

She whispered her theory to Simon Magnus one night after they'd made love, her voice susurrating under the stained comforter in the cold room at the back of the railroad flat, and susurrating, too, under the sound of Coltrane playing on the staticky old turntable in the adjoining room, their heads buried in thick cloth redolent of sweat and sex.

Simon Magnus hissed in her ear, "Don't you fucking dare! Don't you dare reduce me to some banal case out of a textbook! Don't you dare take my life—my private life, the life I and only I have ever experienced, the life I have to live to the end, me and nobody else—and tell me it can be fully explained in a few clinical terms, as if my soul were no more complicated than my liver or, or, my fucking kneecap!"

Alarmed by the fury Simon Magnus poured down her ear—she had never heard Simon Magnus speak with such anger—she sat up to face Simon Magnus, perhaps to apologize, since she hadn't taken her amateur psychoanalysis much more seriously than she took their flirtatious sparring over film interpretation or poetry appreciation or musical taste.

Simon Magnus then did something that Ellen Chandler never told anyone about, so that it did not end up on the bill of indictment Simon Magnus's critics would later draw, the one charging the writer with misogyny, before Simon Magnus declared that Simon Magnus could not be a misogynist because Simon Magnus was not a man, not "the other" of a woman. Simon Magnus rose to face her, threw off the blanket, and punched her in the jaw so hard she fell backward off the bed and struck her head on the floorboard.

In the morning, one back tooth loose, she walked the wintry streets unable to stop crying, her whole body trembling. Simon Magnus, wearing her nightgown and slippers, found her, dropped to both bare knees in the snow—it was winter by then—and wept into her belly. Simon Magnus repeated almost catatonically a toneless plea for forgiveness into the middle of her body, her fingers tangling themselves into the knotty waves of the writer's long, unwashed hair.

During this time, in her capacity as VC Comics editor, Ellen Chandler received permission from Frank Donofrio under the company's "keep an eye out for new talent" mandate to assign Simon Magnus to write a poor-selling horror title, some laughable nonsense about a shambling monster.

"*Marsh Man*? What the fuck? You grew up reading Shelley, I grew up reading Woolf. How the hell did we get into this trash?" Ellen Chandler said to Simon Magnus over the narrow table where they ate their dinner, *steak au poivre* that night.

(Simon Magnus, who'd learned self-sufficiency in childhood, was always the cook, always ready to try a new recipe, the further from Mother Magnus's bland taste the better.)

Simon Magnus *had* read a few issues of *Marsh Man* in Simon Magnus's youth. The writing had melodramatically recapitulated monster-movie clichés down to the village and the torches, as if these were in any way relevant to the late 20th century. The Gothic art, however, almost squirmed with hatching and crosshatching, even under the muddy outside-the-lines coloring—was so textured you could nearly feel, could nearly smell, the reticulation of roots and moss comprising the marshily eponymous hero. This suggested to Simon Magnus that something gruesomely beautiful might be done with the concept.

(That initial *Marsh Man* artist, a self-taught prodigy of provincial background, had parlayed his comics success to a further and more lucrative career in illustration—book and album covers, Hollywood concept art, etc.—a leap of the kind both Simon Magnus and Ellen Chandler then hoped to make, in their case from comics to proper literature.)

By the following fall, a year and a half after Simon Magnus met Ellen Chandler, Simon Magnus had quickly metamorphosed *Marsh Man* into a critical darling, award winner, and cult classic, if not quite a bestseller. Admirers acclaimed and still acclaim Simon Magnus's delirious imagery drawn from the French Decadents and Surrealists (the muck monster abloom in spring with every hue and shade of swamp flower, pistil and stamen hungrily engorged), implied psychosexual perversion owing to Poe and Hawthorne (the creature decked out in his mother's wedding dress as he smothered in flowers his mother's murderers: his genius-botanist mother, assassinated by government agents for the illicit experiments that birthed the creature, her Erlenmeyer flask doubling as her womb), and a verbal impasto of narration that some stigmatized as "purple" but which, nevertheless, none forgot:

The shifting cascades of lichen and weed that make up his massy body begin to bleed through, to bloom as a black stain, on the white bodice of the gown his mother had married in, like blood seeping through bandages pressed ineffectually to a suicide's wrists.

Simon Magnus's meticulously detailed scripts tended to exhaust artists. Where other comic-book writers would begin a page with a description of the first panel that read simply, "Establishing shot on the swamp at dusk," leaving the artist to realize the swamp and the dusk as he saw fit, Simon Magnus would request research material from the city's vast public library—would pass between the marble lions who had since the beginning of the century maintained their guard, couchant on either side of the stairs by which you ascended to its edifice—the better to catalogue for the artist the exact number and type of plant that should be visible in the image. For one panel on a nine-panel page, Simon Magnus would produce a 3000-word description with lyric flourishes—"the water hyacinths pale like the center of a flame at dusk"—amid the amateur botany. One artist after another fell behind and had to be replaced on Simon Magnus's run of 30 monthly issues; readers tend even to this day, therefore, to remember the writing first and foremost.

In the celebrated story "Flowers of Evil," Simon Magnus famously brought Marsh Man to do business in the corrupt heart of Cosmopolis, this after authorities arrested his lover—a statuesque biologist who had come to the swamp to investigate its reputedly hybrid resident—for "indecent activities" after locals complained of their wetland amours.

The issue that dramatized their first hallucinatory love-making ("A Love Supreme") was itself burned in town-square pyres in at least two American towns, while a suburban comic-book store owner was arrested for selling it to a minor; few readers, however, whether friendly or hostile, would ever forget the central image of the beautiful biologist afloat on her back in a field of water lotus, her hair fanned out in a halo, with Marsh Man rising from the water beneath her to enfold her body in his own, decorously covering her nipples and her mons pubis with root and tendril, her mouth parted in ecstasy like St. Teresa's.

Likewise, the issue containing Marsh Man's 24-page courtroom speech defending his cross-species romance before an eventually weeping judge and jury ("The Love That Dare Not Speak Its Name") has justly gone down as an aesthetic *and* a political landmark in comics history.

Even sympathetic critics tend to allow, however, that the later issues of Simon Magnus's tenure inclined toward a certain unseriousness, especially when Marsh Man runs for mayor of Cosmopolis in a 10-issue narrative entitled "The Mask of Anarchy." It was as if Simon Magnus's (and perhaps even Ellen Chandler's) inability to respect the medium finally abraded their ambitions for it.

Simon Magnus typed most of those famous, award-winning scripts for *Marsh Man* with two frantic fingers on the ancient portable Remington Simon Magnus had hauled down from Hollow Well, purchased in adolescence for five dollars in a thrift shop. Each of them wearing a peignoir, Simon Magnus sat cross-legged at the end of the narrow bed, sending up a clatter of metal rain, while Ellen Chandler reclined behind Simon Magnus on the piled pillows, editing scripts with a red pen, lighting one cigarette from the end of another, as she warmed her bare feet on Simon Magnus's back, feeling beneath her soles, beneath silk, the starkness of Simon Magnus's ribcage and shoulder blades. In the adjoining room, Rachmaninov or Nina Simone or the Cure murmured from the turntable. Every so often, Simon Magnus would say, "Listen to this," tear the sheet from the platen, and read aloud to her what Simon Magnus had just typed. Ellen Chandler wasn't a sentimental woman; she only wept once or twice.

CHAPTER 7
The Bounding Line

He usually felt nothing for the female models, no more than a male doctor would ogle a pair of breasts beneath which a heart seizes and asphyxiates. Again like a doctor, he wanted to master with both his eye and his hand the organization of muscle and ligament, the texture of flesh—not to carve health into it but to indite its healthy image onto the surface of the world. For this, the eye had to remain dispassionate and the hand steady; desire would cause the eye to roll or blur, would make the hand tremble helplessly, both eye and hand ravenous to close the distance between artist and model and thereby, inevitably, abolish art.

This model, though, made Marco Cohen *want* to abolish art. It was not the broad dark aureoles on her heavy breasts, not the mass of her thighs stippled with gooseflesh, not her incongruously slim neck with the dark curling fuzz of her thick black hair at its nape. These were just body parts, a dime a dozen; anyone off the street might possess them. The way a shadowed or anxious look in her inky eye irradiated the ample naked body and the stark face with its Roman nose, softening it under the harsh studio light with an air of tenderness and vulnerability—*these* made him want to cross the room and throw a sheet over her before taking her in his arms.

It was a lazy Friday afternoon late in the semester, melting patches of snow in the street; the model had emerged from layers of boot and stocking, coat and scarf, her cheeks wind-chapped, the rest of her body warm and pale with close fabric, her calves and waist inflamed where elastic had cinched her skin.

Professor Anne LaMar capitulated to the students' lassitude and let them raid the supply closet and spend the hour working with the media of their choice, though it was nominally a drawing class. She had already complained to the students—bad pedagogical form, but how much were they paying her for this?—about how she would rather teach a painting class, about how she believed drawing to be a primitive and degenerate form of art, good only for the cave wall and the comic book. We moderns, she said, had learned that no lines exist in nature, only dynamic fields of color leaching into one another like masses of warm and cool air, and with consequences just as tempestuous, as long as the artist mastered his craft.

She swept, Anne LaMar, imperiously through their circle of canvases, ringed around the dais in the middle of the room where models stood or sprawled. Everything about the old woman swayed and flowed around her stately broadness:

her mane of fine steely hair, her long shawls and scarves, her flowing odalisque's harem pants. She pronounced.

"You might make a drawing to prepare a painting—what they appropriately call a cartoon—but to end at a drawing, to count yourself *satisfied* with a drawing, well, I certainly can't admire it. To call *yourself* a cartoonist—well, why not a clown? The painting classes were spoken for, however, so they unfortunately asked me to teach drawing instead. What can I do, my friends? I'm just a part-timer supplementing the not-always-reliable income from my real work."

Most of her students intended their own real work to be in the fields she scorned: illustration or advertising or design. They grumbled quietly about her snobbery, her outdated ideas of art for art's sake, but only Marco Cohen openly revolted, and for an entirely different reason from his fellow students' conviction that no conflict existed between art and commerce.

On the very first day, he'd rounded on her as she circled the room musing on the barbarity of drawing. He quoted Blake: "'The more distinct, sharp, and wirey the bounding line, the more perfect the work of art.'"

"Did your Mr. Blake get that from one of the angels and spirits he spoke to in the garden while bathing naked?" she quipped.

What time did Anne LaMar have for a madman like Blake? Art meant disciplining the eye—the real eye, the outer eye, not the mystic's notional inner eye—to the perfect perception of worldly surfaces. Blake's way, the way of inward perception, led to the narcissism of "anything goes": black canvases, white canvases, drip canvases, urinals, soup cans, spiral jetties, and all the other detritus in the 20th-century junk heap, just the other side of the same debased coin as comic books and pornography, all of it the cartoonish pursuit of the fantastic instead of the real.

She was old-fashioned, she knew, born, but only just, in the wrong century. She would die almost unknown of a heart attack three years after having Marco Cohen in her class. Later, in the 21st century, an academic feminist art historian would revive her forgotten work in a monograph-spawning gallery show titled *Anne LaMar's Romantic Realism and the Possibility of a Female Gaze*, which she, had she lived, would have judged cloying, patronizing, and almost worse than being forgotten. As if her gaze, which she'd learned from Monet, from Cézanne, were merely emotional and not precisely observed! As if it were reductively female and not what she knew it be—universally valid!

Marco Cohen also believed in the real, also believed in discipline, even also hesitated before Blake's mysticism. He protested all this to Anne LaMar during the frequent Socratic dialogues they held over the heads of the rest of the class, while every student, to include himself, was supposed to be focused intently and silently on drawing the model. To him, "the boundary line" meant not the artist's fancy or fantasy or vision from beyond. It meant the artist's reason, his careful selection of what was essential from what was inessential, what was typical from what was atypical, and, above all, what the world rationally ought to be rather than what it so irrationally was. He stood for a realism of the horizon, a realism that canceled the merely factitious, the contemptibly given—what a cynic means by "realism"—and elevated in this cynicism's place a realized utopia.

"Oh Christ," she said, "I remember your type from when I was a just girl in a class like this one. I thought they went out in the 1930s. I almost prefer"—with maternal fondness, she clapped a budding ad artist on the back and spoiled his line—"the merely commercial types to the utopians. At least advertisements, unlike communist manifestoes and little red books, don't get anyone slaughtered."

"They slaughter the soul," Marco Cohen grumbled, at which Anne LaMar burst out laughing, a great imperious scandalized hooting laugh.

"I shouldn't laugh at the moral enthusiasm of youth," she said, more to herself than to him. "College, however, is nothing if not the place you go to leave your youth behind."

The students groaned and murmured during these debates that echoed up the high walls of the skylighted studio. Sometimes, they even told him—they could not very well tell her, the instructor, charged with assigning them a grade—to shut the hell up and draw. They paid serious tuition to be in that room to learn a remunerative skill, a useful trade, and here they found themselves instead, trapped between the one utopian and the other, the aesthete and the puritan, neither of them concerned with that realest thing of all: money. Did the students in plumbing school have to endure endless philosophical disputes about the nature of water?

Anne LaMar chuckled with surprise on the day Diane del Greco came to pose, shadowing her nakedness with the half-scared look on her formidable face that made Marco Cohen want to cover her up and carry her out of the studio. Somehow, he felt, it would be too violent—like making an incision in that tremulous flesh—to draw her, so he rendered her body instead with an ink wash, gray gradients conjuring delicately where the belly declined to the pubes, where the indent between thigh and buttock muscles pitted and darkened the flesh of the hip, where a mole spotted one breast.

"No boundary lines, Mr. Cohen?" Anne LaMar asked over his shoulder. "What would your Mr. Blake say? I'm glad our new model has roused you to experiment."

He blushed, said nothing, went on distinguishing the darker gray of her lips from the lighter gray of her face—except that Diane del Greco, who had caught Anne LaMar's remark, curled those lips in a little snorting giggle, and Marco Cohen lost control of his brush.

CHAPTER 8
The Fool

By the time the century's last decade had passed its midpoint, Simon Magnus was finished with the 30-issue *Marsh Man* run. Its critical esteem and resulting publicity led Madeline Stein and Frank Donofrio to agree to let the poetic if morose author handle a marquee character. Simon Magnus, therefore, came to write what even its least sympathetic critics called the definitive Ratman graphic novel, despite the controversy it created and still creates in some quarters: *Fools' Errand*.

(Nothing infuriated Simon Magnus like the frequent misplacement of that plural apostrophe, for Simon Magnus had written a story about human folly, not this or that human's folly, still less this or that cartoon character's.)

Fools' Errand starred Ratman's longtime archnemesis, The Fool, a madcap prankster-gangster in comics' early days, wearing a jester's cap and bells. Simon Magnus reimagined the villain as a pale and lanky sociopath with purple-dyed hair and a parti-colored suit—puce and maroon, grasshopper and mint—a black string-tie ragged and wild. Simon Magnus even had Simon Magnus's version of The Fool cross-dress in the book's most notorious scene, his bare white legs sprouting from a pink tutu, his ivory penis lifting the tulle fringe. *This* Fool does not pursue crime for gain, nor to honor an antic and anarchic spirit of fun, but rather sees through all order, all doctrines, all ideologies, all hierarchies; this Fool sees to the chaos beyond the world, sees (thought Simon Magnus to SimonMagnusself) what Valerie Karns saw on the blank bedroom wall while her stepfather clutched her from behind, sees what Valerie Karns saw in the forest clearing in the glistening innards of the sacrificed bird. The Fool sees to the end of everything.

In Simon Magnus's book, The Fool tries to persuade the morally rigid Ratman that he, too, with his verminous animal totem and his vengeful war on crime inspired by the senseless slaughter of his family, ought to join the villain's rebellion against settled order rather than aiding the police in their vain quest to exorcise Gothic City's pandemonium.

When merely verbal persuasion fails, The Fool kidnaps and sodomizes the red-suited Sparrow, Ratman's adolescent sidekick—this to demonstrate to Ratman the existential and even cosmic trauma that may strike any- and everyone at any and every time, as indicated in the line The Fool speaks to Sparrow before perpetrating his hideous act: "Let me show you what this world means."

The revenge quest that follows the rape, dominated by Ratman's anguished internal monologue about whether or not he should violate his personal code against killing when he finally captures The Fool, a passage rife with homoerotic double entendre ("When I finally have my hands on him, will I be brave enough to take us to the end?"), has long been compared by enthusiasts in the comics press to *Hamlet*.

Critics also congratulated Simon Magnus for addressing, if in displaced form, the rumors of pederasty that had clung to the Ratman-Sparrow relation at least since the middle of the century: a man and a boy, two orphans, living alone together, dressing in garish tights and engaging each other in acrobatics all through the night.

(Quips and raised eyebrows among the youthful readership aside, the accusation of superheroic pederasty was first made in public by Dr. Felix Aaronsohn in the postwar polemic that incited the moral panic against comic books in the mid-century: *Altar to Moloch*. Felix Aaronsohn was a German-Jewish psychoanalyst who'd been reared in the *kultur*-worshiping, assimilated haute bourgeoisie, his sensibility shaped by Goethe, Schiller, and Heine, by Mozart, Bach, and Mendelssohn. From the shameful safety of America, where he'd gone to complete his doctorate, he witnessed the vaporization of his natal society in an orgy of sadistic irrationalism—three uncles, two aunts, and four cousins dead in the camps; his parents only just escaped to Australia. He thought, this fastidious and bespectacled doctor with a white mustache and a bronze bust of Goethe in the corner of his office, that he recognized intimations of the same psychopathic imago in the lurid and misspelled little stapled pamphlets his disturbed young patients carried with them into his clinic, clutched in their sticky little dirty-nailed delinquent hands. Horror stories rife with mutilation and rotting ghouls, crime tales whose gangsters drove hot skewers into stool pigeons' eyes, and even the superficially folkloric hero-legends connoting the morass of terror from which the world had only just in the years since the war emerged—from which half his family had *not* emerged. Overman? Where had he heard *that* before? Ratman's dandling his little red-suited Ganymede on his knee was small fry compared to what the overmen would do—*had* done—to the undermen, but this perversion didn't escape his notice either. Hadn't Goethe's Mephistopheles exhibited the same pathic desire? Hence *Altar to Moloch* and all that followed: the comic-book pyres in the small-town squares—Felix Aaronsohn had to admit, if only to himself, that he'd seen that before, too—and the congressional inquiry and the publishers' self-censorship, a censorship only beginning to lift until, years after Felix Aaronsohn's death, Simon Magnus tore the whole decorous curtain down out of the proscenium's high reaches with The Fool's epochal act of sodomy. An interviewer asked Simon Magnus what Simon Magnus thought of Felix Aaronsohn once. "The trouble with a psychologist," Simon Magnus had replied, "is his naive belief that evil can be dispelled by having a rational or moral conversation about it. Since it can't, it's more obscene to ignore it than to show it. Art is one of the few places left in our society where it can be shown.")

The graphic novel grew famous for its ambiguous ending—is Ratman strangling or embracing The Fool on the playground roundabout in the downpour, rain sizzling on the corrugated metal?—not to mention the hospitalized Sparrow's nihilistic sickbed monologue in the book's central scene, his blue eyes staring wide onto emptiness:

"We're just meat and bone bundled in a thin skin. It doesn't take anything—the lightest touch—to break the membrane and get all the way inside. I thought I had secrets in there. I thought deep down I was someone no one really knew. I thought I would carry that little room inside me all the way through my life no matter what. I thought I would be buried there, warm and safe, in that little lighted room. But he came through the window, oh God, oh Jesus save me, he came through the door, and it's his room now. And I don't have anywhere to go, anywhere to live. I'm locked out in the storm, and the night, the night, it goes on forever. It just goes on and on and on..."

Fools' Errand earned Simon Magnus as many plaudits as Simon Magnus received denunciations. The denunciations came from literal pulpits, as well as newspapers and news anchors, and, eventually, even from the top of the very power structure The Fool had pledged himself to destroy. "There wasn't this kind of crap in comic books when I was a kid, if you'll pardon my language," said the White House press secretary when prompted by a journalist. "If you're asking whether Congress ought to hold an inquiry, well, you won't get an objection out of me."

Frank Donofrio had grown up in the Depression; he had gone to war in Korea. Compared to what he'd seen in the first two and a half decades of his life—children roasting rats in alleys; men speared with bamboo and bayonets, spraying blood in graceful arcs as if they were statuary on top of a fountain; what they called a comfort woman, pregnant, beaten, her head down in a ditch, her hair streaked with mud, his own knuckles swollen—nothing he saw in a book could possibly offend him, despite a superficial adherence to a childhood Catholicism of whose promise he'd seen no evidence in the world. Neither, because there were so few sure things on this earth, would he dare turn up his nose at any book that returned a profit.

For her part, Madeline Stein had a degree in art history from one of the Seven Sisters. She had drifted laterally into comics publishing after a dry spell in the art world and the silence that greeted her first and last volume of poems.

She'd always wanted to see American comics, like their European counterparts, assay serious aesthetics, if only to assuage her own shame at working for most of her life in the field. When faced with the public outcry against *Fools' Errand*, she was therefore prepared to cite examples of progressive transgression by canonical artists and senseless and hysterical reactions thereto from the reactionary public and political establishment, everything from the *Madame Bovary* trial to the Nazi exhibition of "degenerate art." "What about Aaronsohn?" a journalist once asked her after the psychologist's death. "Aaronsohn was a book burner—little better than a Nazi himself," she somewhat notoriously replied. She later received a postcard from Aaronsohn's only child, a daughter who'd become a distinguished pediatric oncologist. The front of the postcard showed the Parthenon on its hill, the sky serene and classical as the temple; the back, in a printed hand precise and legible enough to serve as comic-book lettering, said only, "Shame on you."

Together, the gruffly pragmatic Frank Donofrio and the gracefully cultivated Madeline Stein assured nervous executives, who in turn assured nervous shareholders, that this would be the way things were done in the 21st century, and that they had simply better get used to it.

The comic-book industry had made feints in an adult direction before Simon Magnus came on the scene, had been creeping toward its adolescent and then young-adult and then middle-aged audience since the cultural revolution of the Vietnam era. In those proverbially incendiary and psychedelic days, college kids who'd grown up reading comics didn't want to stop but *did* want the form to develop in tandem with the maturation of their own tastes and experiences; these very college kids, bearded and long-haired and paisley-shirted, formed the next rank of writers and artists after the form's Depression-era working-class devisers, men who had been too poor and too "ethnic" to have done anything else with their artistic ambitions except work one level above pornography at publishing's pulpy nadir.

Doomed by the inertia of a corporation's commitment to the bottom line, this evolution toward adult comics first required a pragmatic shift in the way comics were sold—from the drugstore spinner rack to the speciality shop, the former catering to any child with a pocketful of change and the latter to a connoisseur with a line of credit. Changed economic prospects, not aesthetic ideals alone, allowed a concomitant shift in the industry's self-government, away from the restrictive Comics Code that forbade sex, violence, drugs, and subversion after the mid-century moral panic Aaronsohn had started. VC Comics's flagship characters may, in the decades before Simon Magnus's debut, have come up against gritty realities of urban crime, drug addiction, and the abnormal psychology that would necessarily accompany vigilantism and the status of *Übermenschen*, but no such character, not even the obsessive Ratman with his vengeful oversight of Gothic City, had gone through anything like what Simon Magnus put them through in *Fools' Errand*.

Ellen Chandler, reading the script as it came, page by page, out of the typewriter, would ask Simon Magnus again and again, "Are you okay?" Both Ellen Chandler and Frank Donofrio told Simon Magnus to provide The Fool with a new origin story to account for his unprecendented and extraordinary brutality; the old story, in which a college class clown met with an accident in the chemistry lab, hardly pointed to a future of nihilistic monologues and anal rapine.

They later regretted the request. Simon Magnus wrote a two-page spread that showed, nonsequentially, a cascade of sodomy: The Fool's father doing to the young Fool what The Fool would go on to do to Sparrow, and the father's father doing the same, and the father's father's father, until he was ordering the artist to draw buggery in Pilgrim times. This Ellen Chandler and Frank Donofrio might have countenanced, but Simon Magnus also wanted to show the grown-up Sparrow assaulting his own young son, and that son assaulting his son, and on into the future, until we were to see sodomy on the rings of Saturn a million years hence, all of this shuffled and disordered, the Pilgrim abutting the alien, like a Tarot pack. The Fool could do as he liked—even the old-timers allowed a little latitude to the villains—but the company would never tolerate such atrocities *within* what they called the Ratman family, so Simon Magnus was content to rest the graphic novel's case, like *Othello*'s before it, on "motiveless malignity." Simon Magnus insisted on the *Othello* reference Simon Magnusself, inserting it into one of Ellen Chandler's company memos defending the book.

The publication of *Fools' Errand* coincided with the premier of a new Ratman movie; the movie, combined with the controversy, helped *Fools' Errand* to become the bestselling graphic novel in history.

Another element in the book's success: *Fools' Errand* featured fully painted art by Duncan McGinnis, an art-school graduate from England who had wanted to be an abstract painter before the hungry comics company recruited him on one of its overseas headhunting drives. A plump man with gentle, heavy-lidded eyes, he'd grown up not in London but in the southern countryside. His father hailed from a long line of struggling dairy farmers; his mother was a DP from Galicia with a faded bluish tattoo on her forearm. He was an only child born late in his parents' strange and haunted marriage; he distrusted American cultural imperialism, objected to capitalism's deformation of serious art, looked for inspiration across the Channel rather than across the Atlantic, and dreamed of Fauvist color muted to acknowledge the charnel house the 20th century had been.

He'd learned about art from his mother, by way of the education she had received just before her world ended, along with her childhood, in a nightmare of marching men, shattered glass, and gunfire, all of it eventually going up in the smoke of Hitler's crematoria. If he ever thought of flying men, it was Marc Chagall who'd sent them aloft. Ratman? What in the hell was Ratman? A case study of Freud's? He was just out of art school, however. His old mentor told him the graphic novel—what in the hell was a graphic novel? was it like a *pornographic* novel?—would put his name before the public. As for the royalty deal the company offered to entice its new recruits, following the bad press they'd received for treating the latterly destitute creators of lucrative properties like Overman as mere work-for-hire: "Well," said his mentor, "just think, Duncan, if this nonsense takes off, you'll be able to, what's the phrase, write your own ticket!"

Duncan McGinnis translated Simon Magnus's precise script descriptions of the awful carnage wrought by The Fool into swirling masses of color and form; this artistic choice blunted the physical and amplified the metaphysical horror, which accounted in part for the critical acclaim greeting a work that might otherwise have been thought exploitative or sensationalist in its violence.

The artist declared in an interview shortly after the book was published, "I shan't be painting such rubbish again as long as I live," and confessed that it was the first Ratman book he had ever read and the last he would ever read. "Who is this American that he dares write these outrages? What suffering has he experienced? What entitles him? I regret the whole project. If every copy were burned, I would send up a cheer."

He took his royalty money and moved to a cottage in the French countryside; he cultivated a famously humble art, mixing the dung of the cottage's fauna into his beloved "earth paintings," those strangely mesmerizing works of art said by several theoreticians to redeem, if anything could redeem, the philosophy of Martin Heidegger. The only other book he ever illustrated was written by John Berger, a lyrical account of the long life of a country veterinarian. Any interviewer or questioner who raised the subject of *Fools' Errand* with Duncan McGinnis would find the conversation ended immediately: a hard stare, silence, a turned back. In that instance and that alone, the most serious and perhaps the best English painter of his generation had blasphemed his gift. Rumor held that his mother, when she saw the book, just a year away from her agonizing death from cancer, had lifted her tattooed arm and slapped him across the face.

With their royalty money, Ellen Chandler and Simon Magnus moved to a larger apartment and asked themselves, but never each other, if they ought to get married and have children. Did Ellen Chandler want to have a child with the author of Sparrow's sodomy? The apartment allowed pets. Ellen Chandler, who'd always had dogs in her girlhood, bought a pair of orphaned greyhounds, sisters, long and sleek, like liquid ribbons of felt or silk. She named them Virginia and Vanessa and would run with them through the city park every morning before work. Mother Magnus had forbidden pets—"We have evolved beyond living with animals," she once pronounced—so Simon Magnus lived warily with the dogs. Simon Magnus started at their approach, cringed at the touch of their damp snouts, their tongues, and mistyped words in scripts every time they barked.

Before that, when Simon Magnus began writing *Fools' Errand*, he had designed what magicians called a sigil, expressing the wish that the book make Simon Magnus's name. Following occult practices initiated by both Aleister Crowley and Austin Osman Spare in the early 20th century, Simon Magnus drew the sigil—a triangle bristling with what looked like spiral torture devices—in black marker on Ellen Chandler's chest and fixed eyes on it with an almost demoniac stare as Simon Magnus fucked her so violently that Simon Magnus slammed Simon Magnus's forehead against the bedroom wall and bled—Simon Magnus, whose erotic sensitivity and shyness Ellen Chandler had had to overcome two years before; Simon Magnus, whom she'd had to convince that neither of them would break if they made love.

Later, in the shower, scrubbing Simon Magnus's sigil and Simon Magnus's blood from her torso, she wondered why she'd let Simon Magnus do it. She wanted the book to be a success, too; she was its editor. She also wanted, however, to be more than the receptacle of this wish on someone else's behalf. She didn't want to be both the altar and the sacrifice to gods or demons she doubted she even believed in. A gray stain in the sigil's shape remained on her chest for a week, the chemical reek of the marker in her nostrils. For those five or seven days, she couldn't stand to look in the mirror.

The day after the sigil ceremony, she couldn't find her cigarettes. Simon Magnus had thrown them away, as she later got the writer to confess. "I was just thinking about how much I don't want to lose you," Simon Magnus told her.

"I did it to my mother once, too," Simon Magnus said quietly. "It was one of my earliest memories. I must have been five or six. They'd told us in school how dangerous cigarettes were. They said cigarettes caused cancer; I didn't know what that was, but I imagined a tentacled fungus growing inside. I'd had a nightmare and couldn't go back to sleep, so I crossed the cold floorboards of that awful house in the dark, though I knew she would just put me back to bed. Her bedroom door was closed, but I saw it outlined in the black wall in glowing orange. The doorknob was hot, but I opened it anyway, choked with smoke. She was asleep, or fainted, in bed, her face toward the wall, the comforter spilling off the mattress on fire, a line of fire to the door. She'd gone to sleep with a cigarette burning. I woke her up, and she got the fire out, and then she sent me back to my room. The next day, I found her cigarettes and put them in the trash. She smacked me across the face so hard I almost lost a tooth, but she never smoked again."

Simon Magnus had also begun consulting a Tarot deck at the beginning of the project: the much-thumbed thrift-store Rider-Waite deck Valerie Karns had given Simon Magnus as a Valentine's Day gift during their 13-month love affair, the one Simon Magnus carried on Simon Magnus's person at all times in the city but had rarely consulted before then, except to entertain café patrons. Simon Magnus laid out a Tarot spread every morning of the year that passed from the conception to the final draft of *Fools' Errand*. In all those 365 days, Simon Magnus never turned over a Fool card—not even once.

CHAPTER 9
Corporal Works of Mercy

Talking to Marco Cohen reminded her of talking to Ashley Bradley. It was like opening up the dictionary and the encyclopedia, like falling into a river whose undertow was information and ideas. Before she'd met Ashley Bradley, before she'd met Marco Cohen, she hadn't known people could contain so much, so many thoughts and opinions, so many things to say that you could think about for days after you spoke with them. Eventually, she wanted to strangle Marco Cohen just to shut him up; but at first, and for years, she enjoyed being swept along by his passions. She never had a chance, on the other hand, to get tired of Ashley Bradley.

Later, she would wonder where Ashley Bradley ended up. Probably in some suburb with a brood of children. Their friendship had been an explosion—sudden, brief, and leaving everything in ruins. It had been doomed because she'd felt it more deeply than Ashley Bradley had, or she believed she did. To Ashley Bradley, she'd just been a project. She didn't know that until the end, though; she didn't know they'd been watching her.

Had they gone to the length of watching her at home? Had they traveled to the house in the ravine, just above the muddy creek, and surveyed the unmowed lawn, the unweeded garden? Tracked the comings and goings of her father's Harley or the furtive visitors always at the door? Seen her parents still stuck in the quicksand of their adolescence, her father's hair to his shoulders, her mother's far down her back, the fringed jackets, the tinted glasses, Hendrix and Zeppelin rattling the windowpanes? Her father's angry fist and wandering eye; her mother's own eyes rolling back in her head as she danced barefoot on the wobbling coffee table? Had they seen the windows in the back, the eerie light of the grow lamps burning all night long, their purple haze reflected in the brown, burbling creek water?

No, they must have just smelled her: smoky and unhygienic, greasy, unwashed, overweight, her clothes soaked in dishwater and wrung out by hand—the washer broke long ago; her parents never had it fixed—the natural shampoo, natural soap, natural toothpaste, all of it free, no doubt, of cancerous additives (so her parents claimed) but not up to the late 20th-century standard that bodies should be perfumed or, at the very least, odorless. She had dirty hair hanging down all around her, dirty feet in old sandals no matter the weather, T-shirts with holes at the armpits, and homemade skirts coming unstitched. Her book bag was a mesh grocery sack.

Ashley Bradley started sitting with her at lunch in the public-school cafeteria when she was a sophomore and Ashley Bradley a senior. One Monday in autumn, Ashley Bradley came from the table of prim Christian girls in their shapeless brown dresses or voluminous violet sweaters; they said grace together every day before lunch, ostentatiously crossing themselves to the grim delight of the public school's many irreligious hedonists, who mocked them every day.

Since no one else ever sat with Diane del Greco, she figured she would at least talk to the girl who had suddenly swept down beside her, though ordinarily she was happy to sit alone and indifferent to the school's scorn of her homemade skirts and unmade face. She usually took revenge by drawing them, her classmates, in her sketchbook—and not caricatures either, because that would be too easy a revenge, to give a girl with small breasts no breasts or a boy with big ears elephantine ones. No, they deserved a precise reflection, a good look in the mirror, and no more: this is who you are, and this is *all* you are, if you can face it. (She and Marco Cohen later agreed on that, though each would eventually cease to be an artist.) Her mother had taught her to draw—her mother had wanted to write and illustrate children's books before meeting her father—and though her mother's brain stopped working well enough to wield the pencil, she practiced every day.

Some days, though, she drew at home and spent her lunch hour with the paperbacks she'd plundered from her parents' closet (shelves would have been a step too far in the direction of oppressive order): the Vonnegut and Hesse, the popularizations of yoga and macrobiotics, the flying saucer speculations, the guides to Native American religion and Hinduism and Buddhism. It was the book on Buddhism, whatever it was, Watt or Suzuki, that she had with her that day, the day Ashley Bradley brought her tray over and sat down—Ashley Bradley, tiny in her shapeless dress, her light blue eyes and light blonde hair and her tiny little mouth with its pale pink lips, a far cry from Diane del Greco's Roman nose and olive skin and plump figure and black, black hair.

Ashley Bradley said she'd had a fight with her friends. Diane del Greco, whose paternal grandparents, immigrant Italian Catholics, used to take her to church when she was a child, made a quip: "What about 'blessed are the peacemakers'?"

Ashley Bradley returned, "'He came not to bring peace but a sword.'"

A sharp reply. Diane del Greco invited Ashley Bradley to sit, even though Ashley Bradley had already sat. Ashley Bradley smelled of floral perfume. Immediately and unusually, Diane del Greco became self-conscious: What do I smell like? Smoke and sweat and incense and oil?

Ashley Bradley eyed Diane del Greco's book. They started to talk about Buddhism. Diane del Greco found it difficult to remember the conversation later because by the time it ended, she had been successfully proselytized; but if she thought only about the conclusion—that human dignity was better served not by renouncing desire but by directing it to the transcendent source of our being—then it would misrepresent as one-way religious propaganda what had actually been a mutually pleasurable exchange, each girl delighting the other with her wit or knowledge.

Ashley Bradley had conceded one or two of Diane del Greco's points. Diane del Greco opened with this defense of Buddhism: a fat laughing icon was more uplifting than an emaciated and wounded one—she thought of the pink little plastic Buddha her parents kept for luck amid the foliage of their horticultural operation. Ashley Bradley admitted this might be better for human morale overall. She urged Diane del Greco, on the other hand, not to think of Jesus as a moralizing victim, a beaten preacher, but also as the one who had cursed the fig tree, who had driven out the money changers, who had rebuffed his own mother: *Woman, what have I to do with thee?* "Don't forget the sword," she said, and they laughed again at their first shared joke. "If he were in this cafeteria with us right now, he might use it to split the heads of half the people here."

"Lucky for them," Diane del Greco said, "there's nothing inside."

Ashley Bradley doubled with laughter and briefly rested her forehead on Diane del Greco's shoulder.

(Diane del Greco had friends outside of school, the children of people her parents knew, and they would lock themselves in her attic and smoke her parents' product, which made intelligent conversation unnecessary, supposing they had been capable of it at all. They usually just watched sitcoms on a portable old black-and-white TV and laughed until they felt like throwing up. Her parents might have read those old paperbacks when they were around her age, but they certainly didn't remember them now. Maybe they hadn't read them anyway; maybe the books just came with the ensemble, with the beads and the bongs and the sandals.)

They talked together at lunch for five days straight, Monday to Friday; since they had no classes together due to the disparity in grade level, they had to fill the 45-minute period almost breathlessly with words. They covered life after death, the morality of sex, the legitimacy of violence, the uselessness of the school, and the futility of politics—usually disagreeing but each appreciative of the other's intelligence. Her conversation with Ashley Bradley was so good that the Friday night after their fifth lunch-table colloquy, she looked Ashley Bradley up in the white pages and called her to continue it, but only after nervously pacing the sticky linoleum around the yellow rotary phone on the kitchen wall with the pulp of the phone book curling in her sweaty grip for half an hour, her pulse drumming in her ears. She wondered as the phone rang if Ashley Bradley's parents would let her talk, if they might not be very strict; but actually, she later learned, Ashley Bradley was the strict one, and the former Mrs. Bradley—the only active parent Ashley Bradley had left after the divorce—was a bit cowed, even shamed, by her daughter's ardor and discipline.

It wasn't like Ashley Bradley to stay up past 10:00 p.m., but that night, she spoke to Diane del Greco until two in the morning. (Ashley Bradley, on a portable phone, whispered under the covers in her dark bedroom; Diane del Greco slumped against the kitchen wall, winding the plastic phone cord around and around her finger, so tight the tip swelled purple.) They compared what they'd read, and Ashley Bradley had read more: Ashley Bradley had read Vonnegut too—"A pretty funny guy, but a bit cheap and easy in the end"—and had Diane del Greco read Flannery O'Connor? She had not. As for music, a guitar could be played with soul, Ashley Bradley allowed, but wasn't it the more impressive art when an intricate composition, if it were made by a Bach, could be so animated with passion in its very solidity that it sounded like a trembling cathedral? She said she didn't watch TV when Diane del Greco tried to discuss those sitcoms she'd watched with her friends—were they her friends? *this* was a friend—while high out of her mind.

I should think, Diane del Greco thought, that this is an unbearable stuck-up bitch. If Ashley Bradley had ever said, "Jesus saves!" or if she had said, "Repent, sinner!" or if she had said, "On your knees!" Diane del Greco would have laughed in her prim, pious face, her light blue eyes and tiny mouth, and told her to go get fucked. Instead, Ashley Bradley had said "trembling cathedral," and now Diane del Greco really was on her knees.

Her parents said they were disappointed that Saturday night when she told them she was going to the mall with a friend. They liked her to bring her friends to the house and use their own product rather than handing money over to some other operation on the street, or in the mall's parking garage where her father himself sometimes went to vend—and besides, it was nice having family and friends under one roof. Ashley Bradley, however, had invited Diane del Greco to mass the following Sunday; Ashley Bradley said, since she had her license and access to her mother's car, that she'd take her to the mall to pick out something appropriate for her to wear.

"Mass?" Diane del Greco had said. "My nana used to make me go when I was little. I thought it was kind of boring, to be honest."

"No, you have to think of it like a movie, because that's what it was at first," Ashley Bradley told her. "Popular entertainment. There's a good story, with pictures and music and light. Sex and violence, if you know where to look."

In mall dressing rooms, Diane del Greco let Ashley Bradley costume her like a doll in a taupe dress and black Mary Janes and a fuchsia ribbon for her long dark hair. They went back to Ashley Bradley's house, where Ashley Bradley recommended moisturizers, volumizers, serums, conditioners, and fragrances. She held Diane del Greco's head under the tub faucet in the bright white bathroom and massaged unguents that smelled of orange and grapefruit into her scalp. With gleaming silver implements that looked like they'd come from an inquisitor's kit, she curled Diane del Greco's eyelashes and trimmed her cuticles; with a gray stone, she smoothed the rough rims of her heels. She invited Diane del Greco to choose a book to borrow from the shelf in her warm bedroom with its floral canopy bed; Diane del Greco took the *Inferno* in the Dorothy Sayers translation. When she got home from Ashley Bradley's that night, her mother looked up at her and said, "Jesus, what's that smell?"

The next morning, in the church, she watched spangles of color from the sun-struck stained glass glimmer over the heads of the congregants. Ashley Bradley pointed out to her the Stations of the Cross on the walls, the systematic destruction of that good man's beautiful body. During the sign of peace, she held Ashley Bradley's moist little hand a second too long. She went down on her knees. She lifted up her voice: *Gloria in excelsis Deo.*

Diane del Greco showed Ashley Bradley her sketchbook at lunch one day. Ashley Bradley looked from the drawings to their maker and back again as if searching for some resemblance between the slovenly girl and the precision of which her hand was capable. Diane del Greco could draw straight lines and perfect circles freehand. Her hatching, her modeling, made a world in three dimensions, as if her page were a room and you'd just opened the door. Her world was like our own but more crisp and clear, realer than real, as when you get new glasses. What a tribute she'd paid to the glory of creation, Ashley Bradley said, what flowers she had laid on God's altar.

Ashley Bradley gave Diane del Greco a rosary for her birthday: bloodstone beads, for the month she was born. Diane del Greco prayed daily, but never in school, never with folded hands and bowed head at the lunch table, in public, like a pharisee, like a whited sepulcher. (They had read the Gospels together over the phone.) No, she rolled the bloodstone beads between her thumb and forefinger as she fell asleep each night. She stopped smoking and more or less stopped seeing her other friends. She read the *Inferno* and discussed it with Ashley Bradley. Her grades went up. Ashley Bradley brought her pamphlets for colleges and art schools.

It ended when that school year did; it had lasted about seven months. Ashley Bradley was going to college out of state in the fall. They began to argue more seriously—almost bitterly—after Diane del Greco had read a few more books and had begun to catch up with what Ashley Bradley knew and believed; she was finally able to match her in argument, armed with something better than counterculture authors for adolescents or New Age spirituality. She had gone from Dante to Dostoevsky, and one day late in the school year, when they were sitting together at lunch, just the two of them, she wanted to know: how was Ashley Bradley to answer Ivan Karamazov's rebuke to a God who could allow even one child to be tortured? There must be some way to rescue the child *in this world* or the very idea of God was worth nothing. There must, she thought, be some way to organize love and justice, here and now.

In answer to this, as a way of saying that she *did* strive to organize love and justice in the here and now, Ashley Bradley confessed that Diane del Greco had been one of their projects, her and her holy friends, that they'd said to each other one day early in the school year just what Diane del Greco had demanded: how, for all of our prayers, have we helped a single soul?

They'd resolved, the holy girls at their lunch table, that each of them would choose one outcast in the school, some unwashed desperado, some tortured artist, some shamefaced homosexual, someone who'd done time in juvenile hall, someone who could barely read, some addict or alcoholic, someone who had scars on her arms or a switchblade in his pocket, anyone in the school who was obviously going down, and see if instead of offering abstract prayers, they could bring these poor people both back to society and back to God. They would be fishers of men.

Ashley Bradley was the only one who'd succeeded. The charity of the rest was refused by their would-be charges—Jessica Bianchi even had her tires slashed in the school parking lot, presumably by Alex Simmons, the leather-jacketed lesbian whose "sins" she'd offered to forgive—but, in the transformed person of Diane del Greco, Ashley Bradley had actually turned an outcast into a believer, a C-student into an A-student, a drug user into a sober citizen, an unclean body into a pure spirit. Diane del Greco, alone of all the pariahs the lunchtime prayer circle of holy girls designated for salvation, had accepted the message and had begun to act like a child beloved of God.

Diane del Greco reared back when she heard this, like someone who'd come into a room and found a snake in the middle of the floor. She started to turn away but decided against it. She let the tears roll without control down her face, openly, without shame, to let Ashley Bradley see the wound she'd dealt her. Ashley Bradley put her arms around Diane del Greco; she pulled her close and wiped her tears on her sweater, its thick weave burning Diane del Greco's cheeks. Nearby cafeteria tables full of rude boys tittered loudly at the sight. Ashley Bradley whispered down her ear, "It wasn't just for the good of it. I really liked you. I really did."

Diane del Greco soon came to regard the whole experience, like any teenage enthusiasm, as an embarrassment. How could she have lost her head like that, how could she have allowed herself to feel so strongly, to enter someone else's power so completely, to bow down to another person? At the same time, she had inwardly crossed some verge and could not return to her parents' opiated world in that house above the muddy creek. Ashley Bradley had disclosed a wider cosmos than Diane del Greco had known existed. She stopped praying the rosary, stopped going to church, and stopped believing in God, if ever she had—if it had been faith in God and not just faith in Ashley Bradley's charisma, in Ashley Bradley's pale face and pink lips. She kept reading real books, though, keeping them to herself. She had serious plans to go to college now, which she hadn't before; her parents, with their operation, could afford it anyway, at least part of it. She would become an artist. She kept drawing and thinking about what her drawing meant in relation to the person she was.

She saw Ashley Bradley for the last time that July. One last mission of charity: Ashley Bradley drove to her house to give her a few books since she was heading off to college soon and cleaning out her room. She tried to shut the door on Ashley Bradley, but Ashley Bradley held it open with her shoulder, the two of them balanced precariously up against the thin barrier between them. She had never invited Ashley Bradley in before, into that house with its unkempt lawn, its unwashed walls, Jefferson Airplane ratting the windows. She brought her up to the attic where the grow lamps shone, where she and her former friends used to lock themselves in and smoke. It must have been 100 degrees up there that day, in the lurid purple light.

"Will you draw my portrait?" Ashley Bradley shyly asked. Her mother, she explained, had requested it when she'd seen a few pictures Diane del Greco had given to Ashley Bradley. "More personal than a photograph," she explained on her mother's behalf.

In that room that reeked of warm earth and acrid smoke, Ashley Bradley posed and Diane del Greco drew. Diane del Greco had never seen another person with such perfect clarity, though the air wavered with heat. The faint hairs on the back of her neck, the spreading pools of darkness as she sweated through her modest dress, the gristling cartilage inside the spiral of her ear, the goosepimples on her arms and their standing whiteish fur, even in that jungle. She saw all the way to end of Ashley Bradley—from the ravine of pale flesh at the parting of her hair to the riverine topography of veins on the tops of her sandaled feet—and then she never saw her again.

CHAPTER 10
The Marriage of Heaven and Hell

The first time Simon Magnus went to a comics convention, midway through the *Marsh Man* run, Ellen Chandler was impressed by the line of about 100 people who formed to get the author's signature on their floppy pamphlets. For that occasion, Simon Magnus wore a loose white linen shirt and tight black jeans, while the other writers shuffled in worn loafers and T-shirts. The second time, after the publication of *Fools' Errand* a year later, a mob of about 1000 in their teens and 20s chased Simon Magnus and Ellen Chandler down a corridor, some of them apparently eager only to touch the hem of Simon Magnus's garment—a baby-blue suit, purchased for the event. Simon Magnus and Ellen Chandler had discussed the writer's wearing a dress to the second convention, but, as this would blatantly align Simon Magnus with The Fool and all The Fool's heinous crimes, they decided against.

She had asked Simon Magnus why Simon Magnus had both given The Fool this proclivity and made The Fool not only a sociopathic murderer but also a homosexual rapist.

(In fact, the company *had* received complaints from gay and lesbian advocacy groups as well as organizations on behalf of what were then labeled transsexual individuals, though this would prove nothing in comparison to the searing revaluation the graphic novel would receive on social media in the 21st century, the severity of these judgments only partially deflected by Simon Magnus's later claim to be SimonMagnusself without gender and therefore openly party to The Fool's own protean sensibility.)

When challenged by Ellen Chandler, Simon Magnus had given two replies, which would serve the author in good stead when interviewers put the same question more aggressively later, as social mores changed.

First, Simon Magnus said, the mere appearance of a phenomenon in a work of art is more important for that phenomenon's social status than whether the work portrays it as good or as evil. "Art glamorizes everything," Simon Magnus said, and art's radiant glamor, beyond good and evil, would cause life to imitate art. Ellen Chandler couldn't deny that at the second convention, she saw at least three men dressed in The Fool's pink tutu.

Second, Simon Magnus said, "It's both dishonest and dangerous to deny the horror squirming underneath everything—underneath everyone, no matter what they're wearing or if they're otherwise discriminated against or whatever. If you ignore it, you'll never see it coming."

Just after the publication of *Fools' Errand*, Ellen Chandler brought Simon Magnus to a cheap Italian restaurant to meet Marco Cohen and Diane del Greco for dinner. In the several intervening years between Ellen Chandler and Marco Cohen's college graduation and that dinner, Marco Cohen and Diane del Greco had gotten married. Diane del Greco was six months pregnant. Ellen Chandler hadn't told Marco Cohen to bring Diane del Greco to the dinner. She'd met the artist's model and wife once before and had frankly judged her to be vapid, a dimwit from the sticks unable to keep up with their conversations—not nearly good enough, in Ellen Chandler's opinion, for her brilliant husband.

She'd also told Simon Magnus not to wear a dress, but, after seeing The Fool's pink-tutu'd imitators at the convention, Simon Magnus wouldn't hear of it. Simon Magnus had written the best-selling graphic novel in history; Simon Magnus would do as Simon Magnus willed.

Simon Magnus had been so shy when they'd met, she reflected; the dress had been the only self-assertion, and then only in certain circumstances where safety was more or less guaranteed, like the coffee shop where derelicts and artists gathered or her bed where they made love. Now Simon Magnus spoke imperiously—to her, to Frank Donofrio and Madeline Stein, even to cabbies and grocery clerks—with a cynical wit that blocked all reply. At the second convention, she'd disliked how avidly Simon Magnus took to the adulation of the crowds, standing with a beatific smile, the type of smile that never shone on her, waves of hair spilling around a pale face, wearing that baby-blue suit, signing books and T-shirts and even, in one case, a tube-topped young woman's décolletage;

the young woman said she'd be going immediately to a tattoo parlor to have the signature inked on her flesh permanently. When Simon Magnus ploughed her that night in the dark of the hotel room—she'd borrowed "ploughed" from Joyce; she thought it was funny to call their lovemaking that, but Simon Magnus always found it distasteful—she wondered what writhed behind the writer's closed eyes. Who *was* Simon Magnus?

Now Simon Magnus spoke to her as if answering a rapt interviewer, with grand pronouncements about aesthetics and metaphysics; they no longer laughed over Simon Magnus's scripts or any other writer's. Bad writing now mortally offended Simon Magnus; Simon Magnus literally tore up a script that offended Simon Magnus's taste. "This isn't about anything! Ratman fights ninjas? Who the fuck cares? Where has this man been? Does he know anything? Has he never had a dream, a thought? Has he never wanted to kill himself at five in the morning? If he's never wanted to kill himself, he doesn't deserve to live! What has he read besides Ratman and Overman comics? These, these fucking cretins, these utter morons, they should be marooned on an island with nothing to read but the classics for five years!" Simon Magnus shouted, jumping on the bed as the confetti that had been the script rained down on her, her own body forcibly convulsed beneath the writer by the unsettled mattress.

Simon Magnus, therefore, wore a dress to the meeting with Marco Cohen, to their spaghetti dinner at Bella Notte—not either of the dresses salvaged from Valerie Karns's bedroom, the red or the white, but a new black one purchased with Ratman royalties, paired with high heels, specially ordered to fit the writer's long feet. She offered a warning, as the cabbie eyed them warily from the front seat, about the social attitudes of muscular restaurateurs reared during Mussolini's time in such rough milieux as Palermo or Pizzoferrato, but, as it happened, the maître d' merely raised one thick eyebrow at Simon Magnus's slingbacked and lace-hemmed entrance upon the bottom of the concrete stairs that led down to Bella Notte from the street—as if the black eye beneath the gray brow had seen stranger sights, had seen boys more (or less) pretty in rouge.

Marco Cohen stood so fast the back of his legs knocked the wooden chair to the floor when Ellen Chandler walked and Simon Magnus swept toward them across the almost empty dining room. Neither the God of Abraham nor the God of Stalin would countenance *this*. Diane del Greco discretely smacked his hand with her pink-painted fingernails as she, great-bellied, remained in her seat. Flustered, Marco Cohen bent over to right the chair.

His hair had thinned on top of his squarish dome, Ellen Chandler saw, and he'd grown thinner, if possible. The impending birth of his child, along with his failure to launch his artistic career, had visibly worn the man down. Before the meeting with Simon Magnus, he spoke on the phone to Ellen Chandler and confided the truth: he could barely afford half the rent on the studio apartment he shared with Diane del Greco, teaching the occasional night course; meanwhile, Diane del Greco, who came penniless to the city to be an artist but who'd settled for being an artists' model instead, had now abandoned the artistic life entirely and worked nine hours a day as a law firm's secretary. She had gone, he confessed, from the adoration of her early days, when she would listen to his theories on art and social justice as he painted her nude, to a petulant resentment that caused her to sleep with her back to him and to tell him she needed peace and quiet whenever he tried to broach any topic at all.

In the restaurant, Marco Cohen greeted Ellen Chandler with a polite hug, Simon Magnus with a finicky handshake—he offered only his fingers and slightly grimaced when he saw that Simon Magnus had red nails. Simon Magnus and Diane del Greco, who had not yet met, exchanged a conspiratorial and mirthful glance, as if both enjoyed Marco Cohen's embarrassment and dismay. Diane del Greco had also dressed elaborately—was that *taffeta*? Ellen Chandler wondered—while Ellen Chandler and Marco Cohen just wore jeans and sweaters and sneakers.

Soon enough, however, Simon Magnus and Marco Cohen, whom she was hoping in her capacity as editor to pair as writer and artist on whatever success would follow *Fools' Errand*, almost instantly ascended from the red-checked tablecloth to dispute for hours about about matters spiritual and political somewhere near the particle-board drop ceiling, while she and Diane del Greco twirled their fettuccine alfredo and linguine puttanesca (respectively) and, having little in common, discussed baby names.

"'Ashley' if it's a girl—we're sure about that," Diane del Greco said.

"Realism doesn't exist," Simon Magnus was saying. "All art is fantasy. Realist art is just a dull, unimaginative artist's idea of the real—which usually doesn't impress anybody else as terribly realistic, since we all live half in dreams and half in emotions anyway, and not at all in what you label 'reality.' You call Balzac's hallucinations realistic, fueled by 50 cups of coffee a day and an immersion in Swedenborg? Who described the emotions and dreams of the 20th century? Was it the Soviet painters with their peasants and proletarians, their factories and tractors? No! It was Picasso—it was that crazy horse screaming under the cartoon lightbulb in *Guernica* who told us how it felt to be under bombardment, better not only than a realist painting, but better even than a photograph, because a photograph—a realist picture, the realest picture of all—can only show the outside. Realism has got nothing to do with me, with where I live, in here, on the inside. Realism is happening on the outside, to the exterior of those people over there, whereas a picture like *Guernica*, it's a picture of the interior of your fucking head. Then we have Picasso's pictures of women: that's the inside of your head—fucking!"

There was Simon Magnus's crowd-pleasing manner: scandalous wordplay to titillate the readers of the comics press or a crowd of fans who wanted to hear the subversive author speak. "From the most unconventional mind in comics!" read some promotional copy advertising *Fools' Errand*. She laughed when she saw it in the office: we're all conventional when we're in agony. She remembered Simon Magnus at Simon Magnus's most conventional; she loved Simon Magnus at Simon Magnus's most conventional. She remembered the thin, beautiful boy in the dress curled on the hospital cot, both eyes blackened, and she remembered the nervous lover who'd said before their first time, "I've only done this with one other person," the penis shyly retracting. She found the bravado, the elaborate wit, the aesthetic dicta, even the female dress—now that Simon Magnus wore it aggressively to shock and impress rather than wearing it desperately to conjure a first love's ghost or to deck the inmost anima—to be a tiresome false front for someone who remained, whether anybody but her saw it or not, little more than a frightened child. She remained a frightened child, too. We all did, she thought. All the more reason not to embarrass yourself by trying so strenuously to conceal it.

Marco Cohen chortled more in outrage than humor: "This bullshit that you're saying to me, it's unbelievable. Subjective fantasy is the domain of advertising, propaganda, manipulation. Lock us up inside our heads, push the buttons of pleasure and fear to keep us constantly stimulated—all this so we don't notice the world going to pieces around us, all this to numb us to our own material deprivation and everybody else's. No! Art has to be a mirror, and we need to take a good hard look in it, to see the pile of shit we're living in and figure out how to clean it up."

"Then what, comrade? When are we allowed to have dreams and fantasies? After everyone gets fitted for a gray jumper and fed with equal rations of stale bread and cabbage soup? When will the artist be allowed to paint what he see on the insides of his eyelids?"

"Never, I hope!" Marco Cohen shouted. He pounded the table with his fist, rattling the dishes and silverware in front them. "You especially after that book Ellen showed me, the clown with his—" Marco Cohen, realizing he was in public, decided not to describe the central scene of *Fools' Errand*. Simon Magnus put red-painted nails in mock shock to the base of Simon Magnus's throat.

"Ellen here and her editor told me the goal was to get comic books and superheroes taken seriously as art," Simon Magnus said, patronizingly clapping

Ellen Chandler between her shoulder blades. "Serious art in the 20th century is transgression. You seem to have missed the *Lady Chatterley* trial and the *Rite of Spring* riot—too much time spent reading *Das Kapital*, I suppose—but they'll never take you seriously until you spill some blood on the floor."

Both acted out, self-consciously histrionic; they each swelled into caricatures of their positions, the better to savor the argument, Ellen Chandler surmised, though Simon Magnus understood Simon Magnus's motivation, while Marco Cohen remained a mystery to himself.

"I enjoy it when Marco's like this," Diane del Greco said quietly to her. "He never yells at me. He has a thing about women, you know. Kind of worshipful. It's nice at first, but I like to argue, too."

Ellen Chandler had ordered wine with dinner, or else she wouldn't have said to Diane del Greco, who naturally couldn't drink wine in her state, "Really? He used to argue with me in college."

Diane del Greco smiled with contempt. Ellen Chandler wanted a cigarette, but she had stopped smoking, for Simon Magnus's anxious sake. Marco Cohen, as if he could read her mind, absently took a cigarette from his front pocket and put it between his lips, but Diane del Greco smacked his arm and gestured toward her womb. He broke the cigarette in half and folded it into his napkin.

"When will there be time to fantasize?" Marco Cohen then went on. "You think the work of building a just society ever ends? When metal rusts and bricks crack and people get sick and children need to be fed every single day? There won't ever be time to dream. The revolution won't *ever* end!"

"That's Trotsky, not Stalin," Ellen Chandler tipsily mock-admonished, but Marco Cohen wasn't listening.

Diane del Greco heard; Ellen Chandler felt the pointed toe of a woman's pump dig sharply into her shin. "Oh, Ellen, I'm sorry," Diane del Greco said. "It's hard to watch where I'm putting my feet with this in front of me"—she put both hands to her belly—"but I guess you wouldn't know."

"The only true revolution is the revolution that liberates the individual to dream," Simon Magnus said. "This is the artistic revolution—the only revolution there is. As an artist, I *am* the revolution!"

"No individual is or can be free until all of us are free," Marco Cohen rejoined. "We have to work to free ourselves every single day."

"The individual is already all of us, commissar. In me, in you, in the halls of our heads, are men and women, boys and girls, ghosts and ghouls, your father and my mother, the president of the United States, a beggar in the street..."

"So what? For this very reason, the beggar on the street and the president of the United States should have an equal existence."

"They aren't equal, though, my friend. Nothing is equal to anything else. Everything is distinctly itself—only beautiful, only worthwhile, if it's *absolutely* distinct. If you force equality, then—well, it's as the poet said: 'One law for the lion and ox—'"

"'—is oppression,'" Marco Cohen finished.

They'd been hunched over the table in confrontation, craggy face and balding dome across from contoured face and hair falling in waves, Marco Cohen thrusting a fork with a meatball speared on its tines toward Simon Magnus's eyes, splattering the plastic tablecloth with red sauce, Simon Magnus unable for the interest and distress of the argument even to begin on the plate of primavera—and then the shared Blake quotation softened both faces into warm appreciation of the other.

Finished with her glass, Ellen Chandler ordered a bottle of wine for the table. Yes, Simon Magnus and Marco Cohen would collaborate—not as happy laborers building a wall on a collective farm but as wrestlers in artistic combat for the pleasure of an audience. She saw it all already, how Marco Cohen's meticulous line would realize Simon Magnus's delirious vision, how Simon Magnus's delirious vision would liberate Marco Cohen's meticulous line.

Over dessert—a plate of cannoli for the table; black coffee for Ellen Chandler and Marco Cohen, coffee blanched with plentiful cream and sugar for Diane del Greco and Simon Magnus—Marco Cohen brought out his portfolio and handed around his drawings. Ellen Chandler thought Simon Magnus lingered too long on the nude studies of Diane del Greco, on the soft, heavy breasts and pregnant belly Marco Cohen had pencil-feathered into a palpable amplitude on the coarse-grained paper. It made Ellen Chandler embarrassed of her own thinness and meagerness; she had drunk too much wine and suddenly wanted to cry.

Bella Notte's burly maître d' brought the check; his eyes widened appreciatively at the nudes he spied over Simon Magnus's ruffled shoulder.

"Look! It's me!" Diane del Greco cried.

CHAPTER 11
Biblia Pauperum

She had lived with Simon Magnus for three years now, almost as long as Marco Cohen had lived with Diane del Greco, whose baby, a boy they named Levy, was born three months after the dinner at Bella Notte. Ellen Chandler wondered if the *Marsh Man* run and *Ratman: Fools' Errand* were the only children she would ever have with Simon Magnus. "'This thing of darkness I acknowledge mine,'" Simon Magnus had once grandly remarked of *Fools' Errand* to a bewildered young interviewer from the fan press.

Ellen Chandler knew Simon Magnus needed a new project. The writer spent whole days after the success of *Fools' Errand* shuffling in slippers, drinking coffee, wrapped in a bedsheet, playing with Tarot decks and reading occult books fetched from the library. (Simon Magnus kept to the bedroom, wary of Virginia and Vanessa, even or especially when they rose from their curled sleep on the couch, came to the bedroom door, whined and pawed.) Simon Magnus had avoided the occult since Valerie Karns's leap from the trestle years before, the way you can never again go to a favorite restaurant or watch a favorite film you'd first shared with a departed lover, though Simon Magnus did have a Tarot deck and had occasionally used it to entertain café patrons before writing became a full-time job. Once Simon Magnus quit the café to write *Marsh Man* and then *Fools' Errand*, however, Simon Magnus claimed a need to take Tarot seriously—to return to magic—to do justice to the inadvertently Tarot-named villain, The Fool. This had made Ellen Chandler uneasy from the start, as if the spirit of Valerie Karns now lay between them in bed, a spectral weight on the mattress, a shattered girl in bloody ectoplasm, entrails spread for the haruspex's inspection on the train tracks: blood and bone, wood and iron.

She told Simon Magnus, "The Ratman creators were working-class Jewish guys in the Depression. They barely finished high school. They didn't know shit about the Tarot or the 'Western Esoteric Tradition'"—this was the title of one book Simon Magnus had carried home from the library—"and they probably just saw a jester in some movie or pulp magazine."

She couldn't deter Simon Magnus, however. During the writing of *Fools' Errand*, Simon Magnus laid out a Tarot spread every morning at the narrow kitchen table back in the railroad apartment as she hastily drank her coffee before heading in to the office.

"Are you supposed to do your own Tarot readings?" she'd asked. "Isn't that like a doctor treating himself?"

"It's not for me," Simon Magnus replied, waves of hair falling over the cards. "It's for Ratman and Sparrow and The Fool. This is how I'm plotting the book. Writing is exhausting. Why not let the gods take over for a while?"

Yes, that famous line Simon Magnus used on many an interviewer later had first been uttered over the breakfast table. Ellen Chandler rolled her eyes, checked her watch, dripped coffee on her blouse, and realized she would be late to work—not that Frank Donofrio much minded. Simon Magnus, she saw, would not get dressed that day. She put her stockinged feet into her high-heeled pumps. (She would have preferred something more casual, but already the men in the office didn't take her seriously—and besides her and the impeccable Madeline Stein, there were only men in the office.) She walked out. Her heels clacked reproachfully on the bare boards of the railroad apartment. She paused in the doorway.

"Have you ever had a mystical vision? A magical experience?" she asked Simon Magnus. "Have you ever seen a god or a demon?"

"No," he allowed. "Valerie had visions for the both of us. It's never too late to start, though. Is it?"

She thought it was absurd: the cartomancy and the talk of gods. You could read whatever meaning you wanted into anything, like finding animal faces in the clouds, myths in the stars. Why else were Jesus and the Virgin Mary always appearing to peasants in wall plaster and rock formations and scorch marks on tortillas? We as humans use this inborn faculty of pattern recognition and pattern generation properly when we create amusing, beautiful things to make life easier and more pleasant—or so she thought. Hadn't the comic aesthete Joyce understood this, while the tragic magus Yeats had not? she asked herself, thinking back to the footnote in her senior thesis claiming this very thing. We misuse this faculty when we arrogantly delude ourselves that we can see in the tea leaves or in the way cards fall out of a pack what God or the gods have planned for us. There was no God, no gods, she thought, and no plan but chaos. There's just us, thrown into the world, and whatever meaning we're able to make of the world in the few cosmic seconds we're alive. Still, she loved Simon Magnus more for what she took to be Simon Magnus's delusions: sitting like a child in underwear and bedsheet at the table over the cards, needing a haircut, too focused on play to eat or drink anything. Simon Magnus was still just a boy who came from nowhere, even if Simon Magnus wanted sometimes to be a girl, and Simon Magnus still needed Ellen Chandler's protection and guidance in the labyrinth of Cosmopolis, in the dark of Gothic City.

When Simon Magnus had first shown her his Tarot deck—the Rider-Waite that had been a gift from Valerie Karns—she'd swept the back of her hand through the air (a cigarette burning between her first two fingers) and sneered, as if disgusted, offended, that anyone would speak to her of such things. This was in the café, just after she got the job, just after she'd struck up what had begun as her friendship with Simon Magnus. She had been laboring over the scripts she had to edit from seven to midnight, lighting the tip of one cigarette from the end of another, complaining every time he refilled her coffee about the illiteracy and incorrigible gaucherie of comic-book writers. Once the place emptied out, Simon Magnus flounced down across from her, white tulle ballooning and then settling, and produced the deck.

"Do you want to know if you should stay in this job? If you'll meet the man of your dreams? How long you have to live?"

It was then she made her first dismissive gesture of hand and mouth, a gesture she'd repeat often when confronted with Simon Magnus's magic. She had studied James Joyce, Virginia Woolf, and T. S. Eliot—who had, in *The Waste Land* mocked and jeered Madame Sosostris, with her "wicked pack of cards"—but now she found herself beset by frauds of all sorts bearing vulgar and brightly colored icons of power, whether they called them Overman and Ratman or, or, or—well, whatever those figures were called on the stupid fucking Tarot cards.

"The Major Arcana," Simon Magnus said. "The Fool, The Magician, The High Priestess, The Hierophant, and so on."

"See?" she said. "It sounds like a fucking superhero team!"

That night, Simon Magnus only flipped the top card of the deck: the Eight of Wands. She studied the eight staves—were those buds on them? were they blossoming?—as they flew across the bright blue sky, above the green hill and the clear river.

"What does that mean?" she asked.

"It means 'keep working.'"

In those early days, Simon Magnus only pulled the cards out as a party trick or conversation starter. The composition of *Fools' Errand* made the author take cartomancy much more seriously. Even after Simon Magnus finished *Fools' Errand*, Simon Magnus continued to do spreads every day, even without the excuse of reading for Ratman, Sparrow, and The Fool.

Simon Magnus never canceled or made plans based on the cards. (Simon Magnus would sign the *Overman 3000* contract even though The Devil had come out that morning; Simon Magnus would board the plane to Oceanopolis with Ellen Chandler at five in the morning to begin work on *Overman 3000*, even though at three in the morning, The Tower had been the top card.) Simon Magnus did, however, use this habitual divination to prepare a range of emotions for—and plausible interpretations of—any given event.

The Magician had no more right than The Emperor to dodge obstructions or flee from challenges, since these provided necessary tests of his ability to align his will with the universe—"Love is the law," Valerie Karns had quoted, "love under will"—either by successfully surmounting obstacles and defeating enemies or else by learning to recognize his own defeat as necessary to the universe's unfurling and therefore as one indelible panel in a gorgeous tapestry. Neither, however, did The Magician need, like any ordinary person, to be surprised by bad news, as Simon Magnus had once been surprised by news of Valerie Karns's suicide and by the vicious bigot in the street on the day of Simon

Magnus's beating. Better to know you might have signed a contract with The Devil or boarded a plane destined to fall like lightning, better to strengthen your soul accordingly, than to walk naive and smiling into the abyss, the way The Fool did, though the cycle of The World would of course cease without The Fool's blessed recklessness.

The Fool came out at long last, The Fool who had hidden during the whole of the writing of *Fools' Errand* and for weeks afterward. Simon Magnus pulled The Fool the morning of the day Ellen Chandler came home with the news that, given *Fools' Errand*'s *succès de scandale*, the company was in the market for a radical take from its most radical writer on its flagship character: Overman.

One Sunday morning, the Sunday of the week they were headed to the city they joking called Oceanopolis to begin work with Marco Cohen on what would become *Overman 3000*, Ellen Chandler woke up, walked to the kitchen for her coffee, bagel, and orange juice, and found Simon Magnus already awake, laying out the cards on the table. Simon Magnus usually did simple one- or three-card readings on most days, but on Sundays, as a kind of Sabbath exercise, Simon Magnus preferred more elaborate formations.

She sat down without invitation in Simon Magnus's lap—Simon Magnus wore only a pair of boxer shorts—and clutched at the writer's neck and long waves of hair.

"Okay," she said. "Show me your gypsy tricks."

"That's one way to look at Tarot."

Simon Magnus smiled and settled into Simon Magnus's lately acquired manner of making speeches and pronouncements that success had brought Simon Magnus.

"First of all, the cards were the *Biblia Pauperum*, the 'Bible of the poor'—not unlike the way comic books started. The scripture of the illiterate. They offer heroes and villains, perilous or paradisal landscapes, into which you can project your own time, your own personality, your own struggles, and enchant your own life—and interpret it too, because every story, like every dream, requires interpretation. They offer wisdom and guidance as well, a narrative of the past and a prophecy of the future. To read Tarot is not really to cross-reference every card with a definition in some book of meanings but to look at the image on the card and ask yourself what it makes you think of, how it makes you feel. Then, consider them in different combinations and configurations. What seems to you to link up with what? What rhymes, what clashes? How does the pattern of shape and color in a given sequence make you feel? There's no shortcut; there's just spending time with it. It's a free and open-ended system of symbols. You should like it, with your educational background—it resembles a modernist poem more than anything else. Though it goes back to the Middle Ages, goes back perhaps even to Egypt or Tibet, Tarot in its modern form was codified in the modernist period and by people who knew your beloved modernists. Waite and Smith, for instance, were members of the Golden Dawn, like Yeats. Look here."

Simon Magnus pointed to the two cards at the center of the Celtic Cross spread on the table: The Moon crossing The Emperor.

"In the Celtic Cross configuration, the one underneath—in this case, The Emperor—represents the present situation. The one crossing it, The Moon, represents either the challenge this situation presents or the challenge it faces."

Ellen Chandler picked up The Moon card and studied Pamela Colman Smith's illustration. She narrowed her eyes at the dog and the wolf as they howled at the female face inscribed in the moon, at the crustacean climbing out of the river with its own claws lifted against the sky in solidarity with the other two animals, all of this framed between two towers in the distance. Behind her, Simon Magnus parted the curtain of her long blonde hair and kissed the stark bones of her thin neck.

"It could mean anything," she concluded.

"Yes, that's its charm," Simon Magnus said in her ear. "What does it mean to you? How does it make you feel?"

"I think the dog and the wolf just escaped from those two towers, the same way the crab escaped from the water. On the night of the full moon, everybody gets out of jail. All three animals look like they're worshipping the moon, thanking her for setting them free, as she showers them with light. How does it make me feel? It makes me happy. It makes *me* want to howl at the moon!"

At her reference to the moon, Simon Magnus clutched her buttock through her nightgown. The greyhounds, who had been curled around one another in long coils of sleek fur on the couch, rose, yawned, jumped down, wagged their tails alertly, trotted into the kitchen, and stared quizzically at the couple. She swatted Simon Magnus's hand away and asked, "What do the guidebooks say? What does it mean that you have it across this other card—The Emperor?"

"The guidebooks say the moon is our intuition, our imagination, our apprehension of the world beyond physical structures and authorities, symbolized by the towers. The dog and wolf are the tamed and wild aspects of our physical nature, and the crayfish emerges from our watery unconscious. This all adds up to confusion, deception, a sense of unreality, fear, and paranoia."

"I like *my* reading better," she said. "It's more hopeful."

"I like your reading better, too."

"What do *you* think it means?"

"I think The Moon crossing The Emperor means you and I are about to give the powers that rule this world more than they can handle."

They were still young, still young and in love. They began to howl together in the kitchen; Virginia and Vanessa scampered over to them, jumped and pawed them, lifted their own howling voices at the ceiling. Simon Magnus tore wolf-wise at her nightgown with sharp teeth and clenching jaws. Ellen Chandler playfully fought Simon Magnus off with fingers tightened to mock crab pincers.

Ellen Chandler would remember this Sunday morning as the last time they were happy together, just before they left for the city they jokingly called Oceanopolis to produce *Overman 3000.* The greyhounds circled Simon Magnus, but the writer forgot to flinch. Something was stirring in Simon Magnus's lap.

"I see one tower," Ellen Chandler said, "but where's the other?"

CHAPTER 12
Oceanopolis

The senior editorial team at VC Comics went on what they called retreats twice a year, in fall and in spring, first to the north to watch the leaves turn and then to the south to melt the winter out of their bones. On these retreats, they plotted in pastoral quiet the narrative journeys the icons and archetypes in their custody would take over the coming months. Would Overman propose to Mina Mars? Would The Bolt, radiation-immolated by the stony cosmic dictator IronReik in the company's last galaxy-spanning crossover event, return to life? How would Ratman's apprentice, Sparrow, fare as he struck out on his own in his adult guise as the vigilante Dark Angel? These questions and more the editorial team disputed over coffee and bagels on paper-strewn bed-and-breakfast tables, sketches and outlines brown-ringed or slickly transparent with dropped butter, or, their papers threatening to take flight like the superheroes whose destinies they debated, on the windy restaurant decks of beachside hotels.

Ellen Chandler had gone on a few of these retreats by the time she had signed Simon Magnus and Marco Cohen to the *Overman 3000* project. Didn't the creative teams, she asked Frank Donofrio and Madeline Stein, need such excursions out of the city's clamor even more than the editors? Where was the money for the writers' and artists' retreats? On the basis of Simon Magnus's success with *Fools' Errand*, she secured company funds for three summer months in what the company's comic-book characters knew as the fictional Oceanopolis. She rented a secluded bungalow on a desert hill in a neighborhood not far from the coast. There, she and Simon Magnus and Marco Cohen, undisturbed by anyone but one another, would produce *Overman 3000.*

"Maybe you'll meet a movie producer while you're out there," Frank Donofrio told her. "That's the future of this whole enterprise, you know."

The first disturbance came before she and Simon Magnus even boarded the plane. Simon Magnus only wore dresses on special occasions nowadays, such as the first dinner with Marco Cohen at Bella Notte. Even so, Simon Magnus, with long waves of brown hair and subtly tinted fingernails, with a taste for blousy shirts and pants so wide they resembled skirts, with heeled boots in winter and T-strap sandals in summer, always dressed in a style once perceptively described, by a profiler for a fashion magazine deigning to recognize the new avant comics, as "bohemian femme."

The day before their flight, however, Simon Magnus had gone shopping while Ellen Chandler was crying in the back of a taxi with Virginia and Vanessa, stroking their sleek heads, accompanying them beneath the river to the suburbs, where her parents would watch them for the summer—shopping while Ellen Chandler, for reasons unaccountable even to herself, slipped on the way home into a Catholic church with tears still in her eyes and lit a candle and then knelt in the dimness the way she'd done as a girl.

She remarked on Simon Magnus's shopping bag that night but hadn't seen the purchases. She assumed the bag held nothing more unusual than extra warm-weather-wear in Simon Magnus's usual style for the trip to Oceanopolis, even though she usually had to take Simon Magnus physically by the hand to purchase clothes and had never known Simon Magnus to initiate a shopping trip SimonMagnusself.

(Simon Magnus was very philosophically interested in the way Simon Magnus dressed, but this interest hardly extended to practical matters; Simon Magnus associated practical matters with Mother Magnus and her grim respectability. Though Simon Magnus claimed not to want Ellen Chandler to dress Simon Magnus like a child or a doll, in practice, Simon Magnus left her no alternative. The "bohemian femme" look was half her own creation, and in fact, they often wore each other's clothes when she didn't have to dress for work.)

The morning of the flight—the very early morning, since the flight departed at five—Simon Magnus, who did not habitually wash very thoroughly, spent almost an hour in the bathroom.

She rapped on the locked door impatiently, crossing her knees, and asked, "Are you sick?"

"Not physically!" Simon Magnus quipped over the rush of the water running.

When the door opened, Simon Magnus emerged from billows of steam with a shaved head, ballooning black cargo pants tightening and tapering into 18-eyelet black boots, and a close-fitting black T-shirt. Later that day, wraparound black sunglasses would complete the ensemble. A commenter on this particular phase of Simon Magnus's evolving persona, referring back to the earlier *Marsh Man*-era article, would say that the author had gone "from 'bohemian femme' to 'black ops.'"

Ellen Chandler dashed past Simon Magnus into the steamy bathroom to pee. A bit dazed and dizzy on the toilet, as a fog of musky masculine aftershave swirled around her, though she'd never known Simon Magnus to wear any scent at all, she said, "What the fuck is wrong with you?"

"To write the book," Simon Magnus pronounced in Simon Magnus's grand manner, "you have to become the person who can write the book. We aren't in the mystical fens anymore; we aren't even in Gothic City anymore. We've left behind those lands of magic and mystery; we've left behind The Moon, The High Priestess, The Fool. Overman belongs both to a more overtly sunlit world and a subtly blacker one. Overman belongs to the black sun of his home planet Cyphron. Science and technology. The control of the material plane. The superego over the id. The Emperor, The Chariot, The Sun. Overman would be too polite to call a boy in a dress names, but you know somewhere in there he might be thinking it. He was raised down on the farm, after all, in the American heartland. A boy in a dress is refusing to take power, but Overman is claiming it. I can't very well write Overman unless I claim power, too."

Such monologues had impressed her, endeared her, early in their relationship, when they'd come out more hesitantly, with a hint of self-mockery. She'd glimpsed something intelligent and authoritative, but also vulnerable and precocious, when she first met Simon Magnus: a boy defending his wounded self in the labyrinth of the Cosmopolis with the only weapons to hand—namely, wit and sensitivity. Before Simon Magnus had even visited her apartment, she loved nothing more than for the café to quiet down, for the "boy in the dress" to sit across from her and share a cigarette with her and make cynical comments about and wise revisions to the scripts she was tasked with editing, to make her laugh. Simon Magnus would add the perfect note of narrative poignance in caption boxes to a meaningless and almost wordless five-page fight scene meant to delight dull-witted adolescent boys—Ocean Agent and The Shark hurling reefs at each, grunting as they tear up shoals in sandy spumes—and lift the sequence into the realm of the psychic, the mythic:

Cold-blooded, an apex predator forged in the depths, immune to human disease, The Shark had swum in these waters for 200 years, had seen a million generations rise and fall and pass even through his very own teeth, and almost envied this man, his adversary, the energetic brevity of his life.

Now, though, Simon Magnus seemed to be speaking to the world even when it was just the two of them—Simon Magnus would in fact use the "you have to become the person who can write the book" speech in interviews, addresses, and prefaces after the success of *Overman 3000* guaranteed Simon Magnus's fame. As Simon Magnus gained a public, she found herself diminished, found herself reduced from the one person Simon Magnus wanted to spend Simon Magnus's days and nights with into nothing more than this public's first representative.

On the plane, Ellen Chandler, wearing a baggy T-shirt and baggy jeans and weathered Birkenstocks, her long hair in a wild ponytail, felt peculiarly out of place next to Simon Magnus's martial black gear, as she never had next to the moony magus dressed in bohemian femme.

The second disturbance came when the cab dropped them off at the house in Oceanopolis. It sat in the desert hills west of downtown: a long, flat, modern bungalow in ocean blue, all glass and intersecting planes, with pale wood floors and sea-green interior walls.

Simon Magnus went directly to one bedroom to deposit their bags. Ellen Chandler, alarmed by the echo of raised voices coming from somewhere in the house's vicinity, wandered all its hallways and opened all its doors. Then, beyond the sliding glass panes leading out from the kitchen, she found Marco Cohen and Diane del Greco deep in an argument. They shouted in the open air, on the stone-floored patio built into the desert hill at the rear of the house.

The couple became quiet when Ellen Chandler came through the sliding doors and onto the patio. She hadn't met them in person since the dinner at Bella Notte months before, had communicated everything to Marco Cohen by phone and fax—had communicated, most especially, the company's newfound bad-publicity-inspired largesse with royalty deals, the same that had enticed Duncan McGinnis to illustrate *Fools' Errand*, the same that had purchased her and Simon Magnus's new apartment. She knew that Marco Cohen, with a newborn baby and an impatient wife and too little work, could scarcely turn her down.

In the few months since she'd seen him, Marco Cohen had lost more hair and grown a patchy and prematurely graying beard. He wore a flannel shirt despite the summer heat; he paced the flagstones back and forth, kicking up dust in frustration, his brown shoes coated in pale grit. Diane del Greco, meanwhile, sprawled in the cushions of a wicker divan. Her sunglasses and painted lips revealed little; her translucent hot-pink sarong, worn over a two-piece maroon bathing suit, revealed more. She cracked her pink chewing gum loudly in her mouth and flexed her pink-tipped toes to slap one cork-wedge sandal loudly against her heel. Every sound they made echoed off the desert hill and its spiky flora.

"Diane," Ellen Chandler said politely. "I didn't know you were coming. How long are you staying?"

"The whole summer! Am I supposed to let this man leave me alone to run after a baby for three months while he soaks up the sun with his college girlfriend? No offense, Ellen."

"I told you," Marco Cohen said between clenched teeth, "there was never anything between us. We're more like, like brother and sister!"

"Flattering," Ellen Chandler said as she hugged him and kissed him on the cheek, her lips prickled by his beard.

"My parents have Levy for the summer," he explained quietly to Ellen Chandler. "I'm sorry I didn't tell you, but there was no talking her out of it."

"Well, look at you—Mr. Man!" Diane del Greco appreciatively growled, lowering her sunglasses for a better view, as Simon Magnus stepped out onto the patio, shorn and black-clad.

"What are we fighting about?" Simon Magnus asked.

The Simon Magnus she'd met in the café three years before, the Simon Magnus new to the eastern city they joking called Cosmopolis, the Simon Magnus still bleeding from the wounds Valerie Karns had imagined she was inflicting solely on herself and bleeding, too, from the wounds dealt by the vicious bigot on the street—*that* Simon Magnus would have stayed in the house until the argument had passed, Ellen Chandler thought, the way *that* Simon Magnus watched her in the café for months without approaching her until she spoke first. This new Simon Magnus swaggered out to break the fight up like an officer of the law—like Overman Overmanself.

"My husband is boooring," Diane del Greco said. She mock-yawned.

Marco Cohen lit a cigarette.

"Hey, give me one," Ellen Chandler said. He lit a new one from the end of the one in his mouth and handed it to her.

"Bad for your health," Simon Magnus said and playfully swatted Diane del Greco's extended leg out of the way to sit next to her on the pillow-piled divan.

"You smell good," she said.

"I'm *not* boring," Marco Cohen said. "I'm just not going to take some drug when I don't know what it is. The mother of my children certainly isn't going to take it either."

"Child," Diane del Greco admonished. "One child."

"Drugs? We have drugs?" Simon Magnus said. "This might be what we need to get the project started—to elevate ourselves to Overman's level of consciousness."

Ellen Chandler hadn't known Simon Magnus to take anything stronger than coffee, wine, cigarettes, and the occasional joint. She liked pot better than Simon Magnus did. It helped her to relax on the weekends and to fall asleep at the end of the working day, whereas Simon Magnus claimed it made the pictures and the words—the comic-book writer's tools—come in blurry around the edges, imprecise, sliding into one another. She had stopped smoking pot when they moved from the railroad apartment to the bigger apartment after *Fools' Errand*. The man upstairs in the first building had been her dealer—a sad, fat middle-aged collector who lived with his dementia-fogged mother and played chess against himself in an attic-smelling apartment heaped with moldy miscellanea, from board games to scientific journals. In the new building, however, flush as it was with urban professionals, she suspected that her neighbors either kept clean or else favored cocaine and amphetamines—nerve-jangling and anti-visionary drugs detrimental, she suspected, to those who worked in the arts. Where, then, she wondered, did Simon Magnus acquire this new interest in substances?

"Tell them the story," Diane del Greco said to Marco Cohen, fluttering pink-tipped fingers through the dry, dusty air, a bracelet jangling on her wrist.

"It's not even a story. Yesterday, I got a call from Frank Donofrio. He said they needed one more signature from me—for tax purposes, I think—before I could officially be the artist on *Overman 3000*. I didn't get there until late afternoon. Ellen was already gone for the day. So was almost everybody else. Frank had somebody in his office but invited me in anyway. In the chair across the desk from Frank, there was a tall, thin, bald man all in black. Actually, he looked kind of like *you*," Marco Cohen said, pointing at Simon Magnus's shorn head and martial outfit.

"Black is slimming," Simon Magnus said. Diane del Greco now had her leg over the arm of the wicker divan again—across Simon Magnus's lap. Simon Magnus steepled Simon Magnus's fingers above her naked kneecap as Marco Cohen spoke.

"I've never seen anyone like that in the office," Ellen Chandler said.

"The bald man didn't stop talking, not even to be introduced, when Frank waved me into the room. I sat in the other chair, next to him, as he went on and on. He had a theatrical way of speaking, as if he meant to be overheard by a crowd, not just one or two people in an office. What he said was strange."

"What did he say?" Ellen Chandler asked.

Marco Cohen turned and addressed himself solely to Simon Magnus.

"He kept saying how much 'the agency'—he kept talking about 'the agency'—had enjoyed *Fools' Errand*. He said he loved the portrayal of The Fool's fractured psychology—that's what he called it, fractured psychology. It might be a model, he said, for 21st-century subjectivity, as our lives become more chaotic, more fragmented by—how did he put it?—'the expanding information environment.' Like The Fool, he said, we would all become solipsists in our own worlds of meaning as we each 'sculpted ourselves'—that's verbatim, I remember: 'sculpted ourselves'—out of our own favorite media and data.

"Frank just kept nodding and saying, 'Is that right? Is that right?'—like a doddering old man. The bald man in black said, 'Just wait and see what the internet becomes. You know the internet? Superheroes will be real there.' The Fool, he went on, is a more appropriate hero for the 21st century than Ratman or Overman.

"'You weren't bothered by the, well, you know, the anal whatever?' Frank asked him. 'Well,' the bald man said, 'these things need to be exaggerated to have an effect. Plus, once you can do anything you want in the imaginary world—in "cyberspace," I think they're calling it—you won't need to make trouble in the real one. The final point, though we don't always want to talk about it at the agency, is that we sometimes like a bit of the sex and violence, the rape and the murder, in our media, because it takes a bit of vicarious trauma—that's the word we use in psychology, "trauma"—to make the otherwise dense public mind pliable. You know, open to suggestion.'

"'Is that right?' Frank kept saying, 'Is that right?' The bald man said *Fools' Errand* gave them—he actually said 'us,' not 'them'—some ideas for the next Ratman movie. 'We're obviously more in touch with the movie side,' he said. 'There's more money involved, so naturally it will have more eyes on it. We're glad to hear you've got your team working on the next thing out on the West Coast—that's the right atmosphere, just up against the dream factory. Still, we *do* like to drop in on the publishing arm every once in a while, too—see what they're up to in R & D.'

"Then the bald man turned to me, as if he'd just noticed I was in the room. 'Don't tell me,' he said, 'you're working with Simon Magnus on the top-secret Overman project? I can't get a word out of Frank about it. Trade secrets—I guess every business has them! We've got some ideas for Overman ourselves—he *is* the first and best American superhero, isn't he? the one who stands for 'the American way'?—but the director keeps telling me not to interfere on the creative side. He keeps saying, "Kid, don't bother the talent, they'll figure it out for themselves. There's a logic to art, and, no matter how it looks at first, it always ends up working out in our favor." He was an English major, the director—can you believe it? Me, I went straight for psychology. I wanted direct access to other minds, no artistic bells and whistles. Anyway, please tell Mr. Magnus how much I admire his work.' Then he got up and left. I signed the form, Frank clapped me on the shoulder and told me to have a good trip, and I left too."

"Where are the drugs in this story?" Simon Magnus asked.

"Just wait." Marco Cohen lit another cigarette. "I got into the elevator, and I found the bald man in there, as if he'd been riding up and down waiting for me while I was in Frank's office. I politely nodded at him, but he turned to look me full in the face. I could see myself in his dark glasses; I could see *my* face but not his. It was like a nightmare. All I could focus on was his skinny tie—it was silver against his black shirt and black jacket."

"That's a good idea—a silver tie," Simon Magnus said.

Diane del Greco ran her fingernail from the hollow of Simon Magnus's throat down Simon Magnus's breastbone and said, "It would work on you."

"Then—listen to this—he reached behind him, pressed a button without looking, and the elevator froze all at once. It shook so hard when it suddenly stopped moving that I almost fell into his arms. 'Look, Mr. Cohen,' he said, 'we don't want to give you any ideas. We *do* want to help you come up with some of your own, however.' He reached in the inside pocket of his jacket and pulled out, well, *this*—"

Marco Cohen took from the pocket of his jeans a crinkled plastic bag full of what looked like four plastic bullets filled with a translucent, iridescent, almost luminescent liquid of no exact color—or perhaps of every color.

"He told me, 'It's a brand-new synthesis. The boys in the lab say it's safe. Don't worry, we've all tried it. I'm not supposed to give it out like candy, but I'm sure some artists the agency really respects can put it to its proper use.' I told him I wasn't interested in drugs, but he said that Simon might be. 'Just show it to Mr. Magnus, see what he says. When you're relaxing by the beach, it might be the perfect time.' I said, 'You want me to get on a plane with this?' He said it was so new it wasn't on the books, didn't exist officially enough to be illegal. He handed me a business card with no name and no address, just a phone number. 'They give you any trouble in the airport, you tell them to call me.' 'Why not give it directly to Simon? To Ellen?' I asked.

"I assumed," Marco Cohen said to Ellen Chandler, "that he knew you if he came in the office regularly."

"This is all very new and very surprising to me," Ellen Chandler said.

"The bald man said, 'Honestly, we thought *you* might be the one who would most benefit, the member of the creative team who most needs—no offense—to loosen up. This'll open whole new worlds for you—trust me, Mr. Cohen, worlds they can't even dream of in those meetings you used to attend in college. The Sixth International Congress for Peace and Freedom, was it? We're glad your family and your work have kept you too busy to stay up to date with *that* business. You want communism? A connected world? You just wait and see what we have in store on the tech side. The whole world will be connected. Take one of these in the meantime, and you'll see that it already is. Congratulations on Levy, by the way. Children *are* a blessing, aren't they?'

"He pressed the bag into my hands with a smile. Then he restarted the elevator. When we got off in the lobby, we went separate ways, but he called over his shoulder, 'Mr. Cohen! Keep an open mind! True peace and freedom are found within!'"

"Diane!" Ellen Chandler said. "This strange man knows your baby's name—is threatening your baby!—and you want to take this drug, whatever the hell it is?"

"The Overman drug," Simon Magnus said. "Let's do it."

"You shut the fuck up," Ellen Chandler spat at Simon Magnus. She'd meant to say it playfully, the way long-coupled couples flirt by miming mutual exhaustion, but it came out instead with total contempt. Simon Magnus squeezed Diane del Greco's thigh with both hands, kneading the flesh into the muscle; she giggled and squirmed.

"The threat," Diane del Greco said to Ellen Chandler, "was about what would happen if we *didn't* take the drug. Aren't you supposed to be an editor, speaking of English majors? Aren't you supposed to know how to read between the lines? Anyway, my husband *does* need to loosen up—I don't care who says so."

Marco Cohen kicked the patio stones again and said, "We're artists. We get our ideas from the real world. We don't need ideas from some goddamn drug."

"Where do you think ideas come from?" Simon Magnus asked languidly, not looking at Marco Cohen, staring straight into Oceanopolis's clear blue sky, where the sun appeared through the dark glasses as a dim flare. "Do they come from in here?" Simon Magnus tapped the top of Simon Magnus's shorn head with two fingers. "What's in there, my friend? What's in there? What's in there is nothing but what has already happened: things we've seen, things we've heard, and whatever dreary, dull misfortunes have befallen us. 'Daddy touched me in the night, Mommy wouldn't hug me when she dropped me off for school.' Do you think you can make cosmic art—do you think you can create *Overman 3000*—out of *that*? Out of the wretched detritus of experience? Do you think invention is the same as observation, as memory? Do you think art is a photograph—you press a button and get a copy of the real world? Do you think it's the same as babbling on a couch to a bored and soulless professional in an office? No, my friend. Never once in history. Socrates had his daemon, Moses his burning bush, Muhammad his angel, Crowley his Aiwass. Shelley said it was the wind that blew through him, Emerson called it the Over-soul. As individuals, we are bundles of neuroses and bad memories and imprecise observations. What good comes from that? As artists, we are not individuals. We are receivers of the world-spirit. As artists, we have to make ourselves fit for the signal from—" Simon Magnus paused, at a loss, and then said—"from *somewhere else*."

"From drugs manufactured and distributed by the Central Intelligence Agency?" Marco Cohen asked, throwing his arms wide in outrage.

"Somewhere else, *any*where else. That part's not up to us. Anywhere but here, my friend. Anywhere but here."

"I like the way you talk," Diane del Greco said, more to herself than to Simon Magnus, and with mild surprise.

Ellen Chandler threw the butt of the cigarette she had bummed from Marco Cohen into the rocky hillside above the patio and stomped back into the house. "That could start a fire," Marco Cohen said. He climbed onto the hill, went on his knees, cut his fingers on the cactus spines and brambles as he dug for the ash and spark.

"You'll take it with me?" Diane del Greco asked Simon Magnus.

"All my life, I've allowed things to happen to me," Simon Magnus said, more to SimonMagnusself than to her. Simon Magnus's eyes were invisible inside the wraparound shades; in their surface, Diane del Greco saw only herself, reclined on the divan. Simon Magnus went on, "I've been *waiting* for events to happen to me—for something miraculous or monstrous to come out of the forest and save me from my meaningless existence. It's happened—I don't deny it's happened—over and over. Valerie came to me, Ellen came to me, this job came to me. I've gotten more of what I asked for than I had any right to expect. Now it's time I came to the world. It's time I stopped asking the world for what I want and started *telling* it what I demand. We have an opportunity here to experience and record things no one else has ever experienced or recorded. They want us to change the face of reality with this book, for us and for everyone else. I'm not going to waste my time."

"I don't know half the thing... things you're talking about," Diane del Greco said, her bare leg still stretched across Simon Magnus's lap as Simon Magnus fiddled with her jingling anklet.

"What I'm talking about is drugs, sex, the ocean, and the black sun of the planet Cyphron. I'm tired of wearing a dress. I'm tired of bending over and lifting my dress and waiting for someone to come along. Time to be a *man*."

She made a hand gesture she remembered her father making throughout her childhood when he played the music loud—she made the devil's horns with her thumb and pinky finger—and she said what her father, whenever he wasn't in jail, always said to her when *he* made the devil's horns with his fingers.

"Rock and roll, baby—rock and roll."

CHAPTER 13
The Queen of Cups

They had the house from mid-June through mid-September if they wanted it. Marco Cohen kept the drugs in the nightstand drawer of the bedroom he shared with Diane del Greco. If Diane del Greco or Simon Magnus suggested taking them, he changed the subject or flatly refused. He did not, however, use the lock on the drawer: their lives were their own, and it was up to them—yes, even or especially the mother of his child—to be honorable. As the vastness of their task confronted Simon Magnus, Marco Cohen, and Ellen Chandler, they had little time to think about anything else, anyway. Diane del Greco, for her part, drove to the beach on most days while the trio worked.

(Diane del Greco had rented a car on their arrival in Oceanopolis; of the quartet, only she and Ellen Chandler could drive, while Marco Cohen and Simon Magnus had never learned.)

VC Comics wanted to capitalize on the success of *Fools' Errand* by releasing Simon Magnus's follow-up as quickly as possible. It was to be an equally audacious approach to an even more iconic character: the first superhero, Overman himself. Ellen Chandler proposed that Simon Magnus and Marco Cohen collaborate in real time, in the same room—an improvement in speed and intensity over the customary process by which the writer produces a script for a distant artist and the artist illustrates a script for a distant writer, a process that had been made all the more cumbersome and alienating by Simon Magnus's densely visionary and sometimes even prolix approach to scriptwriting.

Marco Cohen asked Ellen Chandler why Simon Magnus's Overman story had to be set in the year 3000. After the outcry accompanying the critical acclaim for the adults-only *Fools' Errand*, Ellen Chandler explained, the company felt that a temporally distant setting would prevent readers from confusing Simon Magnus's sure-to-be-controversial vision of the character with their regular line of all-ages Overman titles, which by then included *Overman*, *The Adventures of Overman*, *Overman in Adventure Comics*, and *Overman: The Man Above*, not to mention the related *Overboy* and *Overgirl*, as well as Overman's regular appearances in *Salvation Corps*.

Ellen Chandler also had to explain the most basic facts about Overman to Marco Cohen, who had, he protested to her, spent his adolescence on the books in the libraries of his grandparents, on Trotsky and on the Tanakh, rather than on those superhero comics his grandfather had quite rightly torn up. Ellen Chandler tried to convince him of the overlap in concerns among all three sets of texts.

Overman is sent as a baby by dissident scientists from the dying planet Cyphron to our flourishing earth, in comparison to whose inhabitants he enjoys the abilities of a god—a god raised, nevertheless, as all-American John James by hardworking, church-going Midwestern farmers who instill in him a respect for the American way of life. From the farm of his boyhood, John James, determined to use his power to protect the people of earth, moves to bustling Cosmopolis. There he works as a sharp but somewhat nebbish journalist, the better to keep his preternaturally acute eyes and ears on the news of the world. From his day job at the *Daily Nova*, its Art Deco starburst lording over Cosmopolis's skyline, he learns how and when to intervene in the world as his alter ego, Overman—when to streak across the sky to rescue the innocent and to restrain the malefactor. His Midwestern mother helps him design his American-flag-colored costume, with its trademark billowing cape and the logo-like hexagonal "O" on the chest, an "O" doubly echoed in the curls of black hair dropping incorrigibly over his forehead in the pattern of a lemniscate.

Falling in love with Mina Mars, John James's intrepid and sharp-tongued fellow reporter at the *Daily Nova*, is not in Overman's plan, but fall in love with her he does, despite his dismay about the way Mina Mars patently adores the commanding Overman and concomitantly disparages the more reticent John James. Add to this Overman's almost lifelong rivalry with the resentful criminal mastermind Max Muller—portrayed variously over the years as a mad scientist, a gang boss, and a corporate mogul—and you have the ingredients for more than half a century of ongoing drama, or so Ellen Chandler explained to Marco Cohen.

"There's Moses in there," she consoled him one morning as they smoked cigarettes together on the Oceanopolis patio. "There's Samson. There's David. There's a concern for the oppressed there, too. Working-class Jews dreamed this up in the Depression, Marco. There's futurism: they refer to Overman as 'The Man Above' and 'The Man to Come.' There's something to it."

(She was remembering what Simon Magnus, a beautiful boy in a dress, one who'd grown up reading superhero comics alongside Blake and Shelley, had told her several years before in the coffee shop: "There's poetry there.")

Marco Cohen thought the whole saga childish and vapid, a poignantly vain power fantasy of the powerless: deracinated Depression-era working-class Jews with parents fresh from the shtetl, the older generation his own upwardly mobile parents both pitied and despised. They had, Marco Cohen judged, dreamed themselves into an ersatz mass-culture heroism too little distinct from the *Übermensch* ideology just then immolating their cousins—his parents' own cousins!—left behind in the Old World on the other side of the Atlantic, the dying planet Cyphron indeed. Now their cheap icon, torn from its own roots, however shallow, in a real people's real suffering, had become a totally empty commodity in the hands of even less cultured custodians, bottom-line-fixated businessmen like the senile and cynical Frank Donofrio, not to mention the so-called "fans," neither of which group had ever read a book without pictures in it. The final desecration of the ideologeme called Overman, Marco Cohen imagined, was whatever nightmare of sexual or occult horror Simon Magnus would order him to visit visually upon the hero—whatever came after anal rape in the dictionary of degradation.

"Where did my life go?" Marco Cohen asked Ellen Chandler. "I wanted to be a great painter, I wanted to *reinvent* painting, for God's sake! I thought truth and beauty would save the world."

Ellen Chandler put her arm around him. "There you go," she said. "Now *you* sound like Overman—except that he always says 'truth and justice,' nothing about 'beauty.'"

At the kitchen table, Diane del Greco ate pink yogurt and watched Ellen Chandler drape an arm across her husband's shoulder through the sliding doors that led out to the patio. Simon Magnus sat across from Diane del Greco and had Simon Magnus's back to the door. Simon Magnus was showing Diane del Greco the Tarot deck, the old Rider-Waite that Valerie Karns had presented to her young lover on their only Valentine's Day.

(When Ellen Chandler learned more about the history of Tarot, she'd asked Simon Magnus indignantly, "Why don't we call it the Smith deck?")

"These are the Major Arcana," Simon Magnus said, fanning the 22 cards from Fool to World before Diane del Greco. "Take them in order, and they tell a linear story of development, of transcendence, a journey from innocence to experience, from command of the material to habitation in the spiritual. Back again, too, because The Fool—the zero card—could just as well come at the beginning or the end of the deck, always there to take the leap of faith or of ignorance needed to restart the cycle. No life is a line or a circle, especially not today. 500 years ago, even 100 years ago, you might live all your life in a single place, whereas we flew across the continent just yesterday. You have to shuffle and reshuffle the cards to find your true narrative, which may at any time fall out in any order. The more out of order the Arcana, the more wisdom you derive from them, simply because you've had to interpret their new arrangements—to tell the story to yourself rather than having it told to you. Tarot, in that sense, is higher than any other narrative art, higher than cinema, fiction, even poetry. This is all that divination using the Tarot is: an interpretive act that tells you who you are. I hope to bring that art to comics. Comics, like the Tarot deck, is a sequence of iconic figures captured in rectangular images whose juxtaposition may bring forth unsuspected knowledge and mysterious sensations."

At the phrase "mysterious sensations," Diane del Greco gave Simon Magnus's shin under the table a gentle, bare-toed kick. "Ask the cards if we're going to have a good vacation," she said.

Simon Magnus shuffled the Major Arcana and then turned over The Chariot.

"It appears we will," Simon Magnus replied. "For at least some definitions of 'good.'"

Diane del Greco licked the last of the yogurt from the spoon.

The quartet drove to the beach that afternoon in the car Diane del Greco had rented. Beneath the freeway, vagabonds wandered dry concrete canals; pale pink buildings with Spanish roofs sat silent, as if roasted, under the unremittent sunlight. Palm trees rushed into the air on thin stalks ending in shaggy bursts, like missiles sent up to disrupt the monotony of the even blue sky. The city proper, at the center of all the sprawl between the ocean and the mountains, fell away behind them.

"This isn't a city," Marco Cohen said from the passenger seat as his wife drove. "I don't know what the hell it is—a spread of misery and privilege with no center, no clouds, no rain."

Diane del Greco reached from the driver's seat to squeeze his thigh. She said, "Try to make the best of it, honey."

When they arrived, Diane del Greco wandered off to a hotel bar and drank margaritas on a deck overlooking the beach. Ellen Chandler lay pale in the sand beneath a black umbrella and read *Doktor Faustus*. Simon Magnus and Marco Cohen paced back and forth together, out where the water rushed up and then withdrew, both of them dizzied when they looked down to see the surf churn backward around their ankles, as if the whole earth were moving while they stood still.

Marco Cohen, who had packed no shorts or swimming trunks or sandals, felt his brown shoes fill and watched his jeans darken from the bottoms to the knees.

Simon Magnus explained the projected plot of *Overman 3000* to Marco Cohen; Marco Cohen, though hired to illustrate and not to write, raised fierce objections.

"We tell the story out of linear sequence," Simon Magnus began.

"Why do you hate 'linear sequence'?" Marco Cohen said the phrase in implied quotation marks. "Why can't you just tell a story straight?" He pointed back at their footprints just before the waves crashed in to erase them. "Look: we moved in a line through space and time. We have no experience of anything other than linear sequence. That's good news! It means new things can happen! We can leave the past behind, we can create the future."

"The privilege of the artist is to see as God sees—or, in this case, as Overman sees. God has finished the Creation; he, she, and it sculpts in time as well as space, because God is higher than time and can see it from end to end, the way we perceive the three dimensions. To God, we are all elongated entities, scrabbling centipedes, with a zygote for a crown and a last atom of dust for a tail. God can focus on this moment or that moment in time, the way you can look up the beach or down, back at the city or out at the ocean, because, to God time is a completed structure he, she, and it stands outside of, not a process he, she, and it endures. All of art attempts, however vainly, to save us from having to endure it, too—to imitate God's perception by turning time into the space of the book or the image or the composition. This is discussed in your Bible, my friend. Do you notice how God is always punishing his, her, and its people—well, 'his' back then; they weren't very evolved, were they?—because he would tell them what he would do, which from his perspective, he had already done, and they grew impatient and turned to sorcerers or golden calves rather than trusting that their salvation had already been accomplished?"

"There's just us," Marco Cohen said. "We make the future. I don't believe in God."

"I don't either," said Simon Magnus. "It's just a manner of speaking—a locus for the intelligence of the structure."

"I don't know what the hell you're talking about. I hate the way it makes me feel. Like there's something real behind the words, but I don't know what the words mean. The way it looks like the ocean just stops, drops off from the horizon line, and you think there must be something behind it."

"There is," said Simon Magnus. "It's better expressed, though, in comics than in words. In comics, time turns into space in a crude but effective representation of what the universe looks like from the fifth dimension—what it looks like in God's eye. I had glimpses of this in *Marsh Man* and *Fools' Errand*, but I think I understand it fully now. We're going to change the world, my friend. We're going to teach people to see what God sees."

"My grandfather would have called you a blasphemer," Marco Cohen mused. "My *other* grandfather would have called you an obscurantist. Did you have a grandfather? Where did you come from? Who taught you these ideas?"

Simon Magnus looked out over the ocean, eyes invisible in the wraparound shades, mouth twitching slightly in the first sign of vulnerability Marco Cohen had ever perceived in the writer.

"I learned some of it from a girl, a long time ago. I learned some of it myself, trying to understand—" Simon Magnus extended a thin arm to the horizon, tremulous—"that she's still there in the constellation of space-time, just out of my sight, but not lost."

Marco Cohen would later make a private sketch of what he saw in that moment: Simon Magnus, half-buttoned black linen shirt blowing around a rawboned and hairless frame, shorn head and thin arm pointed almost desperately to the horizon, the hand hanging brokenly from the wrist, as if half-crucified on the sky, feet buried in surf at the end of pale, thin legs, as if beginning to disappear into this world. Marco Cohen glimpsed, however briefly, what he thought of as the crying child at the heart of the labyrinth of concept and rhetoric in which Simon Magnus had armored SimonMagnusself. As an artist, Marco Cohen always sought this elusive but inevitable gesture, the pose that drops the pose, when a person forgets not to stand in the awkward, broken posture of need. He'd read it so quickly on Diane del Greco's face that first day in the art class when she undressed—the skewed smile, the fear of showing herself, behind the exhibitionist bravado. This, Marco Cohen thought, *this* I can work with.

"Okay," he said, his socks squelching in his soaked shoes, his pants sagging with salt water. "We don't have all day. Tell me the goddamn story."

From where they stood on the beach, they could see Diane del Greco, her sarong flapping in the wind. With both hands, she held a clear fishbowl glass; she drank a liquid as iridescent as the pills the bald man in the black suit had given to Marco Cohen. Marco Cohen looked out over the ocean, to the blurred horizon; Simon Magnus held her eye and waved back. Simon Magnus murmured something, but the wind tossed the words across the sand before they could reach Marco Cohen's ears.

CHAPTER 14
Übermeat

As we know, *Overman 3000* was a nine-issue limited series in three sets of three chapters, this to echo the three in the title. Simon Magnus also intended to invoke the numerological significance of number three as completion—for example, in the trinity of Father, Son, and Holy Spirit; the Hegelian dialectic of thesis, antithesis, and synthesis; and the tripartite Platonic *and* Freudian structures of the psyche as morality, identity, and desire—but without the hubris of claiming to have attained the balance and totality of four, given four's even more ambitious connotation of the symphony with its four movements, of the mandala with its four quadrants, of the four Evangelists (Matthew, Mark, Luke, and John), and of the four territories in Jung's map of the soul (self, persona, shadow, and anima-animus). Simon Magnus promised SimonMagnusself to save four for a later work—to *earn* four. There would, of course, be no later work.

(One night in bed in the bungalow, after a day spent laboring on *Overman 3000*, Ellen Chandler tented *Doktor Faustus* on her chest—she always cracked the spines of books, a habit that irritated Simon Magnus—and said to Simon Magnus, quickly, so as not to lose the thought, "The problem with the occult is that it's no better than the science it claims to reject. It's just imitation science. It's all false precision, like biblical literalism, which itself wouldn't have occurred to anyone before the Scientific Revolution, before literal scientific fact displaced allegory as the most privileged form of truth. All your numerology—your 78 cards, your 22 paths, your 12 houses, your 10 emanations, your four this and three that and two of the other thing—it's harder to memorize than the periodic table. It's not art. It's too mechanical to be art. I mean, it's fine if the artist uses it as an arbitrary structure, uses it parodically. Humor's a passion, too. To use it in earnest, though, to manipulate numbers and think *that* will change the world—"

She had gotten carried away with her sudden insight; she was as if speaking to herself. Then she became aware of the expression on Simon Magnus's face: Simon Magnus stared at her from Simon Magnus's side of the bed, where Simon Magnus reread the red *Book of the Law*, with a look of wounded disgust. The expression on Simon Magnus's face, the narrowed eyes and curled lip, said, "What am I doing in bed with this person?" Their quarrels over the occult had once been ludic, flirtatious, the stuff of opposites-attract romantic comedy. Now, however, Simon Magnus regarded her, if only for one unguarded moment, with actual repulsion.)

Simon Magnus proposed to begin the story in the middle of things with John James's adoption on earth, just after the Civil War of the 2990s.

"*In medias res* is good enough for Homer and Virgil," Simon Magnus answered Marco Cohen's continued protest against the author's nonlinear method. "Do you consider yourself the artistic superior of Homer and Virgil?"

Marco Cohen countered with the ethical priority of the book that began, "In the beginning..."

Simon Magnus waved the objection down and continued with the plot. For a century, the Muller dynasty ruled Cosmopolis as a nanocracy overseen by the network of intelligent machines running in every citizen's bloodstream and monitored from the Muller Towers, their stark M-shaped, double-triangle citadel looming on the skyline. After the failed uprising of the provinces in the last decade of the 30th century, however, the Mullers extended their domain to the entire country. Max Muller, the latest heir to the dynasty, asked himself, "Is it worth the expense of nanobotting the captive rebels?" Brute force should be effective enough: the serfs of the provinces might be governed as cattle had been in the same part of the country, back before cattle went extinct in the middle of the previous millennium.

Instead of cattle, autogenerating pseudo-organic matter fed the North American Union: a foodstuff genetically engineered to be so nutritionally efficient that a citizen need consume only a tablespoon a day. This roiling, bubbling, swelling, globular green mass of beneficent cancer, familiarly called the übermeat, grew in half-mile barracks and needed constant pruning and shearing before it could be sliced and packaged for continent-wide distribution. Scientists—and moreover, political authorities—feared that nanobotting the übermeat might lead to its sentience. A rebellion among superfluous human populations was bad enough, Max Muller thought, but a revolution of even half-intelligent dinosaur-sized carcinomas had to be avoided as an existential threat to the regime. Some jobs just couldn't be fully nanomated. A combination of old-fashioned robot power and human labor tended the übermeat, then; humans occasionally found themselves absorbed into the pulsating green mass—a splotch of red would spread and then fade like a time-lapse bruise on its rippling hide—but worse even than that were workers' claims, as they sliced the stuff, that they could hear it screaming.

A group of these workers, or rather slaves, fed and housed in tin-shack satellites of the übermeat barracks but remunerated no further, saw it one midnight: a lightning storm out over the plain, followed by an earthquake, and then a streak of light crossing from heaven to earth above the horizon. Something called them, against the defensive prudence of those forced into servility, to investigate. They snuck out in a company under the stars. On the plain, they found what looked like a giant golden chalice shattered in the dirt.

("When did these people ever see a golden chalice?" asked Marco Cohen, to which Simon Magnus waved a silencing hand through the air and said, "Poetic license, my friend, poetic license.")

Haloed by the flaming wreckage, a Cupidon wrapped in red, white, and blue robes blinked his wide, wet eyes at the poor laborers in their stinking gray rags. This first generation of post-Civil-War captives retained some vestige of the faith of their fathers; they found a way to rear this baby in the wilds beyond the barracks, a task made easier by the child's seeming invulnerability to the elements, scarce need for nutriments, rapid aging, and capacity to take flight. There seemed little this prodigious alien infant couldn't do or didn't know.

"He's able," Simon Magnus explained, "to download the internet—or what they have in place of the internet in the year 3000—out of the air and into his head."

"Christ, this is all so silly," Marco Cohen said. "'Übermeat.' 'Nanobot.' These are names for toys! Another thing—why reinforce the victim complex of the heartland? I was born in the city and never left, and you came to the city from your little town—Ellen told me—as soon as you could. Why do we want to get sentimental about militia members in goddamn cow country?"

"First," Simon Magnus replied, "it's part of the myth. Overman comes from the middle of the country, from the hearth and heart of its values. You know it's a myth; I know it's a myth. I know it's a myth better than anyone, my friend, because I come from the *real* dark heart of this country, the place where they burned the witches. You have to work *with* the myth, not against it, however. You have to find what made it so persuasive a picture of their real or imagined condition to such large numbers of people in the first place—people who, we have to hope, are not just dupes and idiots. 'Everything possible to be believed—'"

"'—is an image of the truth.' I know, I know. I'm very tired of people quoting William Blake at me all the time."

"Ellen tells me you used to style yourself an 'anti-imperialist.' Don't you think the poor farmers of our Midwest have more in common with the third-world peasants you champion than they do with urban intellectuals like us—with a man who draws naked women and another man who sometimes wears a dress?"

"Just because you're a man who works the land doesn't mean you don't want to wear a dress," Marco Cohen protested.

"There you're right," Simon Magnus said. "We will add a transvestite—unremarked but decisively present—to the sequence where they find the Cyphronian spacecraft. As if it were the most normal thing in the world."

"Will there still be men and women's clothes in the future? In a technocracy, or whatever stupid thing we're calling it, won't everyone shave their heads and wear the same silver jumpsuits?"

"Plausibly, plausibly. We are not prognosticating, however: we're fabulizing. The real year 3000 will be incomprehensibly alien to us; we couldn't survive there, the same way we couldn't survive in 3000 BC. For the purposes of the story, we will ground our imagined future in enough familiar detail to make the importantly—which is to say *thematically*—alien details stand out."

Readers will recall that the whole company of übermeat workers—standing in for the couple who reared the original Overman alone, which Marco Cohen had to concede was an admirably small-c communist touch on Simon Magnus's part—trained their foundling, and were eventually trained by him, in the art of rebellion.

After five years, he appeared to be a grown man. He lived out on the plains, barely in need of sustenance, capable of standing naked in any weather. He seemed to live, in fact, in the sky; he came to be called Overman because the workers would say with wonder as he wheeled through the wisping clouds, "He's over us all!" He circled the planet. He could evade satellite sight lines because he was able to read their energy signatures in the air. Robotic aircraft and surface-to-air missiles attempted to shoot him down, but they only crashed in fiery sunbursts on his flesh, leaving a smudge of ash but not so much as one bruise or abrasion. From the atmosphere, he vacuumed into his mind the corpus of human knowledge, both in its Muller-regime-altered versions and—one strata deeper in the datastream—the original texts.

In the candlelight of a high lamasery, snowdrifts massed against its windward walls, he discussed the *Dhammapada* in fluent New Chinese, though he quoted the text in the original Pāli. In a deep vault beneath the ruins of Rome, the ailing and embattled pontiff, inbred product of centuries of the underground church's desperate eugenics, took him for an incubus until he came more fully awake and thought instead he might be an angel: a faint electric glow seemed to attend him everywhere. He quoted to the pope the secret Gospel of Thomas: "Split a piece of wood, and there I am. Lift up the stone: you will find me." To the executive of India, the last of the democracies, he pledged himself an ally.

Finally, his apprenticeship complete, Overman went underground as the unassuming would-be media star to Cosmopolis to confront the reigning Max Muller, a sickly man who ambulated his hairless form inside a shimmering nutrient-dense, clear-plasma haze that kept him alive and even hale despite his congenital frailty. What Overman didn't count on, however, was falling in love with Max Muller's consort, the regime's chief propagandist at the *Hourly Nova* newsfeed, Mina Mars, with her cascade of raven hair and her shy, embarrassed eyes, with her mouth too quick and witty to be entirely harnessed by the nanobots and the ideology they trailed through her blood and lymph, her flesh too ample, almost overripe, to admit of technological constraint.

Max Muller, the enlightened nanocrat, allowed his consort privileges of freedom he would not extend to the populace. Citing his family's long history of support for the irrelevancy of what they used to call biological sex, he would not surveil her either. No Muller child had been conceived by organic intercourse, gestated in an organic uterus, or passed through an organic vaginal wall in 200 years; all of this once-unruly business was now carried out instead, as soon as two people bearing sperm and egg had supplied the necessary organic substrate, inside intelligent nanofiber amnions. Thousands and thousands of them hung like insect eggs amid the high dim vaults of the city's gestational hubs.

It fell to Mina Mars, therefore, to discover with John James, against the steely autoclave wall of the long, gray, track-lit corridors after hours at the *Hourly Nova*, what animal pleasure felt like to humans, or at least, if one could still use this term, to the human female. At the intimate touch of his flesh, or at the rapturous transport of the pleasure it caused in her, the nanobots in her bloodstream short-circuited and died, liberating her mind for the first time in her life.

"Which brings us," said Simon Magnus, "to part two—to the planet Cyphron."

"Wait a minute. There are holes in your story logic here," Marco Cohen said. He went on to identify the same gaps in Simon Magnus's science-fictional plotting that critics and readers would point out from the first reviews in the fan press to YouTube commenters today. "How does he evade surveillance for five years? They leave their main food source *that* open to attack? The whole society is controlled by, by, whatever bots you called them, but an alien gets through the perimeter? There's no apparatus to find that the new hire at the *Hourly Nova* doesn't have the requisite machines in his blood? There are no surveillance cameras in the corridors?"

Simon Magnus replied privately to such criticism the same way Simon Magnus would later reply publicly, to the chagrin of Simon Magnus's detractors. The detractors judged the writer, just as Marco Cohen judged Simon Magnus, a deviser of flashy surfaces and empty illusions, a juggling magician whose sleight of hand was clumsy and obvious. The reply delighted Simon Magnus's admirers, on the other hand, who chortled at such audacity in defiance of common and even uncommon sense.

"We are not here to give them a logical experience," Simon Magnus later said to several interviewers—just as Simon Magnus had said earlier to Marco Cohen back on the beach as the waves crashed against their pacing legs or in the little office of the rented bungalow overlooking a rocky desert slope full of St. Catherine's lace and black sage. "They can have a logical experience when the police officer pulls them over for speeding or the doctor tells them they have six months to live. That's logic: no arguing with the speedometer or the blood test! Logic is a way of getting to a conclusion. For living things, there is only one possible conclusion. Logic is death. We are here to give them a dream instead—one a little better than the average dream, because those tend to take place in one's mother's house or in one's high school gymnasium or other such dispiriting locales, whereas I would rather dream about the planet Cyphron and the black sun in its sky. Whether in gym class or on a distant star, to have a dream is to have an emotional experience of the most intense imagery. Both your reaction to the imagery and its content will help you to know who you are, will show you parts of yourself you didn't know existed, will teach you pleasures you weren't sure were available. What you're calling 'story logic' is properly understood as nothing more than a pretext for the delivery of these images, these emotions—the way pornographers used to preface their tales with the claim that they only wanted to show readers how *not* to behave. I think the best readers don't require very much of this scaffolding. They can fall asleep pretty much at will, without the lullaby or tranquilizer of your miserable 'logic.' This is the attitude we should encourage. We don't want art to make more sense than life itself. Just the opposite, really."

Marco Cohen would ask for photo reference as he set out to draw Simon Magnus's visions, but Simon Magnus always replied, "Just draw what you see in your head. Draw what the words make you think of. Here, close your eyes. 'Nanobot.' When I say it, what do you see? Now draw that."

"Can't you show me what you're using for research? Maybe you have books with illustrations."

"'Research'?" Simon Magnus asked, placing fingertips to throat-hollow in a gesture of offense and outrage, a remnant of the feminine persona once worn by this now shorn and shaded *man*. "I can't endure it when a writer has committed 'research.' Then you have to sit through pages and pages of a lecture on brain surgery or the inner workings of the mafia or how a spaceship gets up there. I don't give a damn how a spaceship gets up there! I've never researched anything in my life. I read a few months' worth of science magazines to immerse myself in the lingo, just enough to be able to write poetry with it. I write what I imagine, my friend. You should draw what *you* imagine."

Marco Cohen had never drawn what he imagined. He always drew from life, or at least from what remained of life in his memory. To draw what you imagined, he thought, seemed immoral in at least a minor sense, or bathetic anyway. To draw what you merely imagined when the whole world opened itself to you the moment you raised your eyelids—what was this but masturbating while a beautiful woman lay next to you in bed?

As he designed in his sketchbook the fashion and architecture of the year 3000, Diane del Greco lay next to Marco Cohen in bed. This was a commission, work for hire, and who would look at it other than the people who read this sort of thing?—comic books, for Christ's sake, just kids' stuff. Why shouldn't he draw it fast, too fast to bother with research? Why not? When he got back to the city—the real city, not this fake city with its freeways rather than neighborhoods, where everybody was either completely rich or completely poor, where you never got a break from the sun—he would get back to his painting, too. He would propose murals to school boards, neighborhood commissions, city councils; he would show the lives of the people *to* the people, raised into art, to give them the dignity and the strength to go on. He would think about teaching more; currently, he taught the occasional college class on a catch-as-catch-can basis, but maybe he could get into preschools, kindergartens. He had a son to raise now; he had to concern himself with how the next generation would learn to see.

He closed his eyes and let Simon Magnus's words suggest images to him. To draw purely from imagination *did* resemble dreaming. He could recognize a surreal recombination of previously seen images and styles—this Art Deco building, that Art Nouveau hairstyle, and whatever faces and forms swam up out of the depths when Marco Cohen summoned the visual correlate of a novel concept. As with dreaming, you sometimes thought, "Where did that come from?" or "I haven't thought of her in years." He didn't like it. Dreaming wasted precious hours you could spend discovering what was real. Why did he keep drawing Mina Mars, traditionally dark-haired and buxom, as angular and blonde in her year-3000 sleek silver jumpsuit, as an alluringly severe woman like—who? Who did she look like? She was supposed to look like Diane del Greco! He almost tore the page furiously pressing the eraser back and forth against the rough grain as he expunged this inadequate and disquietingly familiar image of Overman's lover.

Diane del Greco had been asleep as he drew into the cold night—he hadn't gotten used to the desert atmosphere yet, the way you couldn't keep your window open after a hot day as you could back east, not unless you wanted to freeze by morning—and had been sleeping so soundly he'd forgotten she was even in the bed. Suddenly, she jumped up, running fingers through her hair.

"Marco! I dreamed we were at the beach and then it started snowing—but really you were throwing eraser shavings at me!"

"As long as you're awake—" Marco Cohen began.

She playfully slapped his arm. "Not now, baby. They'll hear us! Besides, you haven't wanted to since Levy—"

"I don't mean that. Will you stand up for a minute?"

"I'm not wearing any clothes. It's chilly in here!"

"Just for a minute. The clothes in the year 3000 are form-fitting. The future, I'm finding, is a very cold place."

She stood naked, shivering, with her back to the open window, embracing herself, gripping the thick flesh of her upper arms, the dark hairs standing up on her forearms, her heavy thighs pressed together to conserve heat, one foot warming the other—still, after all these years, slightly hesitant to be drawn, as if she might feel the artist's pencil prick her skin. There she was: Mina Mars, a live and lively creature, chilled by the dead future, standing at the window and waiting, whether she knew it or not, for a stranger from another world to light her on fire.

CHAPTER 15
Black Sun

"Which brings us," Simon Magnus raised Simon Magnus's voice to repeat, tired of Marco Cohen's objections and interruptions, "to part two."

The second of *Overman 3000*'s three parts flashed back to the planet Cyphron. Now that she was unbrainwashed after Overman had "fucked the nanocracy out of her," as Simon Magnus indelicately put it to Marco Cohen, Mina Mars made a plan. No pushover, she didn't want to trade one domineering lover for another. She promised both Overman and Max Muller, but for different reasons, to investigate the source of Overman's power. The invulnerable figure continued to streak through the skies of Cosmopolis, back and forth across the two towers of the "M" symbolizing the Muller dynasty's immemorial reign. He descended only to frustrate the brutal patrols of the nanocracy's nanopolice as they attempted to incinerate on the metal pavement the perpetrators of whatever malefaction the nanonetwork running in everyone's blood alerted them to. The first time Overman interposed himself between a police nanodroid and a teenager who'd rashly attempted to hack the Muller mainframe, the machine unloaded its laser fire against his chest for two full minutes and then went up in a burst of spark and smoke. His clothes burned away, Overman streaked back to the plains, where the workers who'd found him fashioned him a more durable costume in red, white, and blue from the swaddling clothes in which he'd fallen to earth, his family crest—what looked like a stylized "O," visually echoed in the lemniscate of unruly black hair that fell across his forehead—now emblazoned on his barrel chest. To Max Muller, Mina Mars said, "I'll find out how to stop him," while to Overman, she said, "I'll find out how to help you," and she set off under each man's protection to the garrisoned heartland where the serfs grew the übermeat.

Sparing no time to gain these serfs' trust, she simply wielded the threat of Max Muller's power to get them to lead her out onto the unpoliced plains where Overman had crashed as a baby five years before. She ordered them to excavate the spot with the tools they used—the hooks, the blades—to slice and prod the übermeat. When the golden chalice that had arced down from the sky emerged in its shattered shards from the depths of the earth, she almost wept. More intrepid than she was sentimental, however, Mina Mars soon began fiddling with the ship's parts, to the shock of the gathered workers, who regarded the thing with religious awe.

Finally, she twiddled the right fragment, and a crystal blossomed in her head: the crystal of time itself, seen from outside, spatialized, as it were, in its wholeness. She saw the planet Cyphron, dead a million years, dead for as long as it took the cryowomb to carry its sole native son across the cosmos. She saw it dead, a hazy absence in the blackness, fragments hung among the stars; and she saw it thrive in its mantle of ocean and forest beneath the darkly radiant paradox of its black sun; and she saw it pool and cool as a new aggregate of magma; and she saw the very rock form; and she saw it before it existed, an absence in the blackness once again. Voices in her head, compressing 10,000 words of information into each second, directed her attention beneath her awareness, told her everything she wanted to know in a minute's time—a minute that would occupy, Simon Magnus said with satisfaction, the better part of three 24-page issues of a comic-book miniseries.

There she saw the Cyphronites in their final phase, an accomplished and singular planetary civilization, the lush green carpet of forest the planet once boasted now silver with tower and citadel at every point, steel and glass and plastic. Even in the food and the water, even in the bloodstream, she saw the infinitesimal machines that until just a few days before had run in her own blood, whose surveillant information network operated a nanocracy absent of any individual's will. It seemed to her, then—though she had to wait to think this later, once the information download had had time to circulate through her conscious mind—that civilizations on every planet ran a predictable course, rotated from birth to apogee to death in a regular cycle.

Organized resistance to the Cyphronian nanocracy had accordingly emerged in the planet's final phase, a resistance larger than anything she knew on earth. A cult or cultus comprised of dissident scientists formed—it had to be scientists, had to be those who knew how the nanocracy operated, because only they would also know how successfully to evade it—and carried themselves to the last wilderness beyond the silver citadels.

Investigating the laws of the universe, practicing a renegade science pledged to truth rather than to power, they came to believe that only an evil genius could have constructed a world of matter so easy, once certain conditions had been satisfied, for technology utterly to enslave. Perhaps technology *was* the creator: wasn't it in technology's interest to manufacture the very cosmos of matter that allowed technology to emerge and then to enslave? Perhaps God was the machine they assembled at the end of time, which traveled back in time and created them so that they could assemble it in the first place. Did the planet's black sun, a light-haloed shadow in the sky, symbolize any less? In defiance of these brutal physics, the scientists began asking themselves questions of metaphysics. What about this unnameable, ineffable something they felt inside themselves—yes, even immured in the nanocracy, even beneath the nanobots that surfed their capillaries and arteries on police patrol—this mysterious inward sensation of the numinous the pre-nanocracy civilizations had vague names for: the breath, the soul, the Holy Spirit? Surely this indefinable and bodiless everything, this thing-that-was-not-a-thing, and which (because it was not a thing) had no material body to control, must be out there somewhere, somewhere beyond the machine god's empire, beyond the black sun. Surely it must exist outside them as their deepest source if they were able to feel it inside themselves.

This corps of dissident scientists first dug in crypts and cellars to find whatever records of pre-nanocratic thought the nanocracy had not eradicated. Then, armed with this wisdom, they tore their sleek silver tunics, grew their hair long, took those analeptics science had synthesized to purge the nanobots from their bloodstreams, and, expertly defying the surveillance regime, marched barefoot under cover of night—though, in the glare of the silver citadel, there was no cover of night—out to the wilds, there to petition the true God, the God of gods, to ask him and her and it to return and consume in fire if necessary the world of mere and brutal matter, the false machine-god's hybrid of flesh and steel, that knew only power, that did not know what the god beyond flesh and steel had to know, which was the prompting felt deeper inside than mere flesh, for which we have not found a better name than *love*.

They danced and chanted, they said sacred names unheard for millennia, they coupled and rutted—yes, they had rediscovered sexual reproduction after 200 years of the artificial womb—they wore the flesh of whatever animal had not been hunted to extinction before artificial food was devised, they sacrificed plants and flowers, birds and body parts. Altars out in the wild heaved to heaven couples who moaned and fucked in a circle of sparrows' entrails and bloody foreskins, all aflame.

"Who says prayers aren't answered?" Simon Magnus demanded of Marco Cohen. "Who says magic doesn't work?"

For the flame did descend—or it descended *and* ascended, just like the heresiarch's true God, who existed both above and below, outside the cosmos and inside the person. Volcanoes erupted. Earthquakes rent the land. The sky crackled with lightning that split the silver citadel. The sky itself caught fire, black smoke streaming in the firmament. The true God had come back to assert the superiority of mind over matter, soul over body, spirit over the unholy fusion of flesh and steel.

"Meanwhile," Simon Magnus said to Marco Cohen, "as all this is happening, we will also tell a love story—the story of Overman's parents, the famous Ben-Ja and Tova."

In the wilderness, our rebels discovered the old-fashioned way to make a baby. The animal mother-love dulled by centuries of the plastic womb roared back to life like an aggrieved lioness and pawed the quaking earth: the brilliant mathematician Tova, her beautiful boy at her bare breast in a collapsing bower, demanded of her husband, the master astronomer Ben-Ja, that her son be spared the coming conflagration. Maybe Cyphron deserved to be destroyed, but how could anyone say tiny Ben-Da had invited the lifespan of what they used to call—before pest eradication and artificial food—a fruit fly?

Here followed the most celebrated of the otherwise grave and high-minded series's suspense sequences, as Ben-Ja and Tova re-entered the disintegrating city under a hail of brimstone to place the squalling infant in the cryowomb, and the cryowomb into the rocket. More than one adolescent male would concede having shed a tear as Simon Magnus and Marco Cohen told Overman's origin story in more detail and with more pathos than it had ever been told before. The parents looked up, clutching one another desperately, their tear-drowned faces lambent in firelight as the pregnant rocket ascended the burning sky, a golden monstrance rising with the holy infant in its sanctuary. Then the planet itself shattered into a sphere of fire as it ejected a tiny projectile among the stars.

"Like conception in reverse," Simon Magnus said when instructing Marco Cohen on how to draw the famous two-page spread. "The sperm racing *away* from this hideous ovum, only to fertilize our earth a millennium hence."

At "hideous ovum," Ellen Chandler, present for this particular story conference, slapped Simon Magnus on the arm, harder than she'd intended.

Weeks passed, devoured by work. Marco Cohen drew all day every day, with Simon Magnus hovering above him, pacing and raving, telling him the story so he could convert it instantly into images.

Their mode of collaboration had been Ellen Chandler's idea. She'd read in a history of American comics that it had been a semi-standard practice in the industry's wild early days, stories passed down the generations: young men crowding a single tenement apartment to produce a 64-page comic in one weekend, writers scribbling in the dry bottoms of bathtubs and on windy fire escapes, artists drawing on every surface from kitchen counter to one another's shirtless backs, the cigarette smoke thick as fog, coffee and beer swilled by the gallon, the sweaty place redolent of a ship's hold or prison or reptile house. An adjusted, slightly classed-up version of such a weekend, carried out to three months—this might furnish the excitement she sometimes felt missing from this job, attracting as it did the socially awkward, the misfit never invited to his high school parties. Nothing like such wild weekends ever happened on the editors' retreats she'd gone on, so why not try to make it happen with her lover and her old friend?

VC Comics also wanted the new book fast. "Lightning doesn't strike the same place twice," Frank Donofrio warned. "They'll forget you if more than a year goes by." This was the main reason she locked Simon Magnus and Marco Cohen into a house together for three months away from the world they knew. Nine 24-page issues in three months, she calculated, was 216 pages, about two pages a day—more than feasible, she decided, especially with her there to edit and approve on the spot. Only the presence of Diane del Greco threatened to foil her plan.

(Ellen Chandler missed her turntable. "We need some music," she said once into the pen-scratched semi-silence in which Marco Cohen concentrated on his illustrations. Simon Magnus replied, "As long as it sounds like the future, go get what you want." She borrowed Diane del Greco's rental car and drove to the Virgin Megastore; she bought the cheapest stereo she could find and a clutch of newish CDs she thought might function as sonic wallpaper for the 31st century. Portishead, St. Etienne, Massive Attack, Hooverphonic—the end of the millennium's robot requiem. That night, they danced on the patio, even Marco Cohen, matching their bodies to the drum-machine pulsations, the melodic flights and drops, of the electronic music. Diane del Greco draped a shawl across Simon Magnus in the cooling night air; Ellen Chandler and Marco Cohen passed a cigarette back and forth in regular rhythms.)

As Simon Magnus narrated the destruction of Cyphron, as Marco Cohen tried to draw as quickly as Simon Magnus spoke, Diane del Greco, bored of the beach, festooned Simon Magnus in robes and wraps, dresses and skirts, all of them hers. Simon Magnus was too skinny for her clothes. She had dragged a mirror into the office. She posed Simon Magnus back and front. She made Simon Magnus stand on a chair. She clumsily struggled to fasten a necklace clasp at the bone-ridged back of Simon Magnus's neck.

"I like your new look, so manly" she said, "but isn't it fun to play dress up?"

Ellen Chandler complained that Simon Magnus had never allowed *her* to dress Simon Magnus.

"Well, of course, Ellen," said Diane del Greco. "You look like a *boy*!" She clapped both hands over her mouth—all she had meant to say was that Ellen Chandler *dressed* like a boy. "No offense, Ellen," she said through her mortified fingers.

Marco Cohen had developed his own speed technique for the collaboration: instead of the laborious process, typical in comics, of one artist drawing the story in pencil, another embellishing in ink, and a third providing the speech balloons, narrative captions, and sound effects, Marco Cohen did it all and directly in ink. In the meticulous majesty with which his intricate crosshatching swept back and forth across the page—as if, one early critic remarked with a quiet reference to the story's auto-spawning übermeat and self-governing nanonetwork, "the story were telling itself in sentient ink"—any minor errors would either get lost or else provide vibrant texture.

Even Simon Magnus, who otherwise found Marco Cohen a truculent presence, an irritating curb to the imagination's freedom, had to concede that American mainstream comics, with its assembly-line mentality, had rarely witnessed such a heroic feat of drawing. Much as Marco Cohen would rather have reinvented gallery painting as public art in the mode of realist panorama, the objective survey of our real society and its real injustices, still, he couldn't help but labor just as mightily on the fake societies and fake injustices of the black-sunned planet Cyphron or of the planet earth in the year 3000.

At night, his hand, his wrist, were locked and cramped. Ellen Chandler, by now used to working with artists and familiar with their tips and tricks, lowered his arm into a deep bucket of ice water.

So Diane del Greco dressed Simon Magnus in women's clothes, thought Ellen Chandler to herself. So Ellen Chandler cradled Marco Cohen's limp arm over an ice bucket, thought Diane del Greco to herself. So what? they thought. We're on vacation.

Halfway through their vacation, in the middle of July, the four of them sat on the patio after a long day's work. Marco Cohen and Ellen Chandler smoked one cigarette after another and reminisced about college, about the city they jokingly called Cosmopolis. Diane del Greco carefully painted her fingernails scarlet. A fire burned in the little grill set in the center of the patio, to warm the cold desert night. Trip-hop buzzed and chimed from the little stereo inside. They drank tequila; they'd found a bottle in one of the bungalow's cabinets. All of them except Diane del Greco were dizzy from work; they drunkenly talked about this and that, movies they'd seen, childhood memories, dirty jokes, all except Simon Magnus, who stared at the blank in the sky where the moon should have been: "New moon," Simon Magnus murmured, "and time for new beginnings, new manifestations. Can you feel it? The end of the century, of the millennium. What rough beast..." Suddenly Simon Magnus stood and announced, "I've made a sigil for the success of the project."

"Simon," Ellen Chandler said. "Please don't."

"I think we should charge it," Simon Magnus declared, raising Simon Magnus's voice to drown out hers. "*Together.*"

"What's a sigil?" asked Diane del Greco, fanning her hands through the air to dry her nails. "How do we charge it?"

Ellen Chandler rounded on her and spat, "Don't you miss your newborn fucking baby?"

"Somebody's missing something," Diane del Greco said quietly to herself but loudly enough to be heard.

Ellen Chandler threw down her tumbler of tequila; it shattered in glittering soprano on the patio stones. She stood, her eyes wild and glistening, stepped through the glass, ran into the bungalow, and slammed the sliding door behind her so hard that a jagged crack ran like lightning from the top right to the left bottom. Marco Cohen walked after her. He slid the door open in front of him and slid it closed behind him very gingerly. The music played on, no longer sounding festive, but then it never had: a woman begged for protection, her voice fragile over the drum-machine beat. Simon Magnus and Diane del Greco didn't meet each other's eyes; they stared at the bloody prints of Ellen Chandler's bare feet on the flagstones and the broken glass sparking in the firelight.

Finally, Diane del Greco repeated her question.

"What's a sigil? How do we charge it?"

CHAPTER 16
Books of the Law

Marco Cohen and Ellen Chandler refused to take the drug the man in the black suit had handed the artist in the company elevator. Now that more than a month and a half of work had gone by, now that summer drifted more quickly toward its end, Simon Magnus wanted to ingest the iridescent pills before devising the story's conclusion.

Simon Magnus intended the climax to illustrate that Overman was not simply a muscle-bound do-gooder in a skintight suit, as he had so often been portrayed in the many decades of his history. Instead, wrapped in that cape stood a genuinely alien intelligence gifted with a higher-dimensional perspective. It wasn't a perspective native to Cyphron, either, but one the hero gained in the cryoship womb, his consciousness gestated over one million years of infancy in the vast stellar wastes, and fed back into the onboard computer the Cyphronian heresiarchs had loaded with the planet's history, there to be downloaded into Mina Mars's human consciousness. From this vantage, he could apprehend at one glance the whole of reality: a roseate crystal of space and time rotating in the ineffable ether of fifth-dimensional higher-than-space-time, a lambent glasswork burning with every passion ever experienced, preserved forever in its intricate and eternal structure. Overman knew there was no death; Overman saw this hard gemlike flame flicker in its absolute solidity forever.

Simon Magnus increasingly believed that art in general, and the art form of comics in particular, were best suited to inculcate in the populace this cosmic perspective. Valerie Karns's homemade Polaroid Tarot deck on the stained bedroom carpet back in Hollow Well had sparked this faith instantly in Simon Magnus's mind, a spark it took a decade to fan into conscious understanding, a decade of reflection and reading. From Mother Magnus, with her crushing and impenetrable conventionality, to the dullards who populated Hollow Well's public high school, to the thug who'd tried to kick a man in a dress to death in the streets of a teeming Cosmopolis, Simon Magnus had always regarded the populace with boredom, mistrust, and even fear, was always wandering off after strange girls in forests and cafés to evade the public's demand for conformity, had even tried for a while, and in a sense, to become such a strange girl SimonMagnusself.

Imagine, however, the general run of people: first, the Overman fans; then their friends and relatives; then *their* friends and relatives; and so on and so on, especially if a film got made, art rippling in its diffuse effects out to infinity. The book itself would be a sigil—a *hypersigil*. Imagine its audience liberated into genuine aesthetic and spiritual vitality, no longer constrained by terror, resentment, or incomprehension when faced with the unconventional, the strange, the inexplicable, the other. Space-time is finished—we need only enjoy it! If you think this is wondrous strange, then as a stranger give it welcome. There is no death! *There is no death!* If there was no death, then it would be as the mage had said, the mage who had, beneath the awareness of complacent college-goers like Ellen Chandler, designed the entire 20th century: "Do as thou wilt shall be the whole of the law."

Take Diane del Greco, thought Simon Magnus. Simon Magnus and Ellen Chandler had both dismissed her, after that dinner at Bella Notte back in Cosmopolis, as what they called a bimbo: her airhead squeal, her self-regard, her taffeta dress and bright lipstick, her air of never having opened a book in her life. Ellen Chandler still thought of Marco Cohen's wife that way—"What can an intelligent man like that have to say to such a ditz?" she whispered to Simon Magnus in bed their first night in the bungalow—but the more Simon Magnus looked at her, the more Simon Magnus saw in her.

Ellen Chandler and Marco Cohen had driven to pick up dinner one afternoon following a long day's work on *Overman 3000*; Simon Magnus and Diane del Greco lounged on the patio, drinking sangria. Simon Magnus's black button-down was open to the navel, hairless chest reddening in the sun. Diane del Greco lay prone on a bright lounge chair, her bikini top unfastened, its straps dangling to the stone floor from beneath her flattened breasts, her olive skin burnished almost brown. They began talking about their pasts.

"I came to the city to be an artist—to get away from my parents," she said.

"Repressive?" Simon Magnus asked.

"Are you kidding me? I wish. If anybody ought to have been repressed, it was those two—Dad in and out of jail, Mom's brain permanently fried. I was raised in a drug den. Why do you think I like nice things? Because I barely saw anything nice until I was a teenager. Maybe they aren't the right nice things, but I like what I like. I know you and Ellen think I'm trashy because I like to dress up and have fun, but let me tell you, I was brought up in the real trash, and I'm grateful as hell I got out."

"Why didn't you become an artist?"

"I didn't have enough money to enroll in any art programs, so I started modeling instead. I figured I could get into the art world that way. I did, sort of—that's where I met Marco."

"Isn't it unethical for an artist to date his model? Like a doctor coming on to his patient?"

"He didn't come on to me. He would never—he's too shy, too polite, at least with girls he likes. Oh, he'll fight with a man the way he fights with you. Men are different. He fights with Ellen too, the way he used to fight with that art teacher he still complains about, Anne something. Women whose intellect he respects, whose intellectual approval he craves—they somehow don't count as women to him. Anyway, I came on to *him*. I said, after class, 'I can't help noticing you were distracted when you were drawing me.' I did a little of this and a little of that."

She poutily lowered her chin, batted her lashes, and tossed her hair.

"What did he say to that?"

"He asked me if I was Jewish. He said I looked Jewish, I think. I said, 'Technically, I'm a Catholic.'"

"What did he say to *that*?"

"He said, 'Close enough.' The common ground, I guess, being ritual and tradition. As opposed to, well, you guys, with your go-it-alone and do-it-yourself approach. That's what he said, anyway, if I'm remembering it right. He said everything back then, every word in the English language. I used to love to listen to him talk."

"Good for him! This doesn't explain why you abandoned your art, however."

"A family can only afford one artist, baby, you should know that. I go to work every day, even now. When I come home, there's the kid. If you think I'm a bitch for taking my saved vacation time and leaving my kid behind for the summer, I'd like you to work eight hours a day and then take care of a little screaming, crying, shitting, pissing, and puking infant for the next four or five hours—four or five if you're lucky, if he doesn't scream till six in the morning. I was going out of my mind. Maybe I'm not cut out for it, anyway. Not everyone is. My mother wasn't. I never thought I'd have one, to be honest with you. I never planned on it. Marco wanted to have children so much, though."

"I want to see your work," Simon Magnus said.

Simon Magnus led her by the hand to Marco Cohen's little office studio overlooking the desert hill furred in St. Catherine's lace and black sage. She sat at her husband's canted drawing board, a soft pencil—2B—poised over a loose sheet of vellum. She hadn't put her bikini top back on; her breasts hung pale but dark-nippled above and below tanned skin. Simon Magnus stood over her and waited for her to begin drawing. Their eyes locked; they both said at the same time, "Well?"

"Well, start drawing!" Simon Magnus cajoled.

"What am I supposed to draw?" she asked. "The blank wall? Take off your clothes. See what I did for years. See how it feels."

When they returned from their food run, Marco Cohen and Ellen Chandler discovered this tableau—a topless Diane del Greco sketching a portrait of the nude Simon Magnus, the room hung heavy with Diane del Greco's pendulous breasts and Simon Magnus's dangling, listing penis. Neither Diane del Greco nor Simon Magnus moved to conceal themselves. I'm on vacation, she thought, while Simon Magnus repeated to SimonMagnusself, There is no death! *There is no death!* Simon Magnus almost cried out: "Do as thou wilt!"

"You know, you're both scum as far as I'm concerned," Ellen Chandler said quietly. Her arms folded across her thin form, she limped from the room, her feet in her Birkenstocks still painful and bandaged from the night she'd stomped through the shattered glass. Marco Cohen rushed toward Simon Magnus with a raised fist but lowered it when he came within a few inches of the nude writer. He retreated and trailed after Ellen Chandler instead. He didn't even look at Diane del Greco.

Simon Magnus congratulated SimonMagnusself on not flinching from the threatened blow, on retaining the proud contrapposto, arms crossed and head cocked, which Diane del Greco had been sketching. "You need to become the person who can write the book," Simon Magnus had told Ellen Chandler, and here was Simon Magnus standing Simon Magnus's ground like Overman Overmansself.

Marco Cohen left the room and then came back in. He snatched the pencil harshly from between Diane del Greco's thumb and forefinger. Without looking at her, he snapped it in half and threw each half up in the air. Then he left for good.

Simon Magnus and Diane del Greco stared at each other conspiratorially, like middle-schoolers daring one another with gapes and leers not to laugh out loud in a solemn classroom, until they heard the rented car reverse itself again down the driveway.

"All right," she finally said. "Let's do it."

"Do 'it'? Do what?"

"All of it. They're never going to let us do it, are they? Well, they're not here now. They left. What we do is up to us."

"It does appear from one point of view," Simon Magnus mused, "that we may have prematurely shackled ourselves to people with dispositions less artistic than they might have imagined. Behind their superficially advanced thinking, their vaunted college educations and sophisticated broad-mindedness, they're just a timid Catholic schoolgirl and a permanent Yeshiva student."

"This is what I'm saying, baby. Let's do it. The drug, the sigil, whatever else we can think of. We're in trouble already, so let's go all the way."

Simon Magnus had shown Diane del Greco nothing but bravado for the brief length of their acquaintanceship. Simon Magnus treasured their acquaintanceship for just this reason: bravado was out of the question with Ellen Chandler, who had knelt by a hospital cot where Simon Magnus lay curled in on SimonMagnusself, who had tenderly kneaded Simon Magnus's knuckles as Simon Magnus bled and wept and slept. Like Mother Magnus, Ellen Chandler had seen Simon Magnus as an infant, or near enough. Ellen Chandler had gone all the way with Simon Magnus in one direction and therefore could not travel all the way with Simon Magnus in the other. Simon Magnus felt Simon Magnus would almost always be an infant in Ellen Chandler's eyes. What a relief, then, to enjoy the uncomplicated and unembarrassed pleasures of Diane del Greco's adventurous company. "All the way," though? Simon Magnus, even naked before her, had been playing a game, curious what would happen, trying, perhaps to provoke Ellen Chandler—but had Simon Magnus committed, even without knowing it, to going "all the way"? *I am in blood stepped in so far*, Simon Magnus thought, but couldn't remember the rest.

Simon Magnus walked naked from the room and took up the Tarot pack on the kitchen table. Simon Magnus riffled the deck until a card leapt out face down. Simon Magnus turned the card over and then reared back as if it had caught fire. Diane del Greco appeared at Simon Magnus's back and tried to peer over Simon Magnus's shoulder; Simon Magnus quickly jammed the card back into the deck and the deck into the box.

"What do the cards say?" she murmured hotly into the hollow between Simon Magnus's shoulder blades, encircling Simon Magnus's slim naked waist with her arms, her cold rings and bracelets raising gooseflesh on Simon Magnus's skin.

"They say we shouldn't do it."

"They can't say that. You told me *we* get to interpret the cards for ourselves. There are no bad cards. You told me even the Death card just means transformation."

"It certainly means transformation, but there's no 'just' about it."

She lowered her hands below Simon Magnus's waist and coaxed the "yes" she couldn't get from Simon Magnus's mind out of Simon Magnus's body instead. Do as thou wilt, Simon Magnus thought. Whose will was this?

"Wait," Simon Magnus said. "We have to draw a sigil first."

Later, she thought they were wrestling playfully, both of them naked, in the tangled sheets of the bed she shared with Marco Cohen, each one taking turns pinning the other to the sweaty mattress. They gasped and coughed in the strong chemical reek of Marco Cohen's silver marker, with which Simon Magnus had inked an intricate crystalline structure on her chest. Then Simon Magnus began to wrestle her seriously. It didn't take Simon Magnus long to wrest the bag of iridescent pills, pilfered from Marco Cohen's nightstand, out of her hands, though her scarlet nails tore at the plastic as they had just been raking Simon Magnus's back. Simon Magnus leapt nimbly from the bed. She tried to follow but tripped in the twisted sheets. By the time she scrambled up and got to the bathroom, Simon Magnus had slammed the door shut and locked it.

Simon Magnus shook the contents of the bag into Simon Magnus's palm: there were four of the iridescent bullet-shaped caplets. They seemed to glow against Simon Magnus's pale skin. Simon Magnus dropped three of them into the toilet and flushed. Simon Magnus put the fourth in Simon Magnus's mouth and bit down. An acid burn seared first the mouth and then the throat and then all the way down the gullet and all the way up to the back of the eyes. Brain and heart caught fire. Struggling not to gag, Simon Magnus climbed into the tub and turned on the hot water, so hot it burned. Simon Magnus's outside burned, but inside it felt cool and blue, glowing almost purple, like the hazy band where the ocean meets the sky.

On that horizon, there it was, just as Simon Magnus had always known it would be—or not "always," but at least since the night Valerie Karns had thrown down her homemade Polaroid Tarot spread, Valerie Karns with her wicked pack of cards, with her Tarot pack and her Tarot pack, who had come out of the dark forest to save Simon Magnus, just as Simon Magnus had spent Simon Magnus's life hoping someone or something would. Here—coming closer and closer over the horizon to where Simon Magnus stood naked at the tip of a pier inside Simon Magnus's mind—here it was.

The thing from the forest for which Valerie Karns had stood now rose from the ocean and fell from the sky as Simon Magnus writhed in the fire of the water. Space-time, all that ever was or would be, whirled on its axis. Closer and closer it came, and Simon Magnus's eyes grew sharper and sharper, sharp as Overman's, so that if there had been a forest, Simon Magnus would have been able to see every vein in every leaf on every tree. Now Simon Magnus saw the past-present-future, saw SimonMagnusself elongated, winding snakewise through Simon Magnus's life, from the abandoned library in the dark house to the bloody clearing in the dark forest to the railroad apartment where Coltrane spun on the turntable to this very moment, suspended in burning water, in a bungalow on a desert hill near the ocean. Give yourself time, Simon Magnus thought. Give yourself time and enjoy it.

There was Valerie Karns, lovely Valerie with her flaming hair, those irreplaceably sad and angry eyes, Simon Magnus could look at her forever, but no, here she was climbing the icy trestle in her windblown nightgown and chapped bare feet, blinded by tears, no, look elsewhere, there was Ellen Chandler, harried and chain-smoking in an itchy sweater, Ellen in desperate need of a laugh and an intelligent conversation, her long, straight blonde hair fanned out across her bent shoulders, her legs crossed, one penny loafer bobbing, her white socks cutely falling down, so smart, so knowing, in her own way so beautiful, and, no harm in looking ahead, it was in its way the opposite of depressing, for there she was at the age of 93, her hair chopped and thin and white as ice, her face a shattered pane of wrinkles, but the eyes still intelligent, still lively, if rheumed and clouded, an intelligent machine with a soft blue glow in the pane of its face tending to her in her senescence as she slowly expired in her mechanical bed, and if she went to sleep and didn't wake up at the age of 93 in the final third of the 21st century, what was that but the natural course of things, lovely Ellen, and now, wait, look back, here was Diane del Greco, naked at the bathroom door, pounding her fists, calling, "You son of a bitch," and there she was as a teenaged girl, acne-spotted and greasy-haired and overweight in an ugly tie-dyed T-shirt, eyes red-rimmed with marijuana, talking with some much primmer friend in a boxy sweater with a crucifix pendant catching the high-school lunchroom light, collapsing with helpless laughter into this friend's waiting arms, who was Diane, really, he had no idea, for here she was standing naked in a circle of easels, her Roman-nosed face a quarter vexed with shame, and here she lay in a crinkly paper gown, feet in stirrups, doctor bent between her parted knees and shaking his head, and here she was on the operating table as they prepared to unseam her nine-months' belly, and here she was beneath Simon Magnus, fully naked now, the scar six inches below her navel (and 12 inches below the silver crystal sigil of space-time) seeming to smile up at Simon Magnus, and here, it was all here, so what could be the harm in looking into the future, to see if she would, for example, stay married to that unendurable moralist Marco Cohen, that was all Simon Magnus wanted to know, so why not look an inch or two into Diane del Greco's future, Marco Cohen's future, and see, see, see, oh Christ, oh Jesus, not that, Simon Magnus hadn't wanted *that*—

Simon Magnus's vision went black. The dark slowly abated, as when your eyes begin to discern shapes in a room lit only by the moon. Trees reared overhead; their tops susurrated in the wind. A woman with red hair and green eyes, flames licking up from the hem of her white dress, came forward from the depth of the forest. Simon Magnus suddenly knew Simon Magnus was bound down on the stump of a tree.

"What did you think, little magus?" she said, laughing. "That you could have it all for free? Keep the evil all in your art without its spilling into your life?"

"If it's my price," Simon Magnus said, "then why aren't I the one who's going to die?"

"The one who dies has it easy, little magus. Escape from the prison of the flesh. Reassumption into the ocean of the all. The one who lives has to live *with* it. That's the highest price there is to pay."

The flames consuming her dress had reached her torso by now, and the ends of her long red hair. Dismissing him, she waved a white arm fringed with fire and trailed narrow white fingers long as roots.

"You have to live with it," she said. "Now return to life."

A scream tore through Simon Magnus's body and lifted Simon Magnus, steaming and scalded, from under the brimming water and up over the side of the tub into the white-fogged bathroom. Simon Magnus collapsed to the floor tiles, where water pooled and cooled, body on fire, the vision fled from the mind, replaced by agony. Diane del Greco, meanwhile, had picked the lock with a bobby pin. She crouched down and held Simon Magnus's hand as Simon Magnus whimpered.

"I'm so sorry," Simon Magnus whispered. "I'm so sorry, Diane."

"You rotten bastard," she said. "You took it without me. What did you see? Did you see the future?"

"I'm so sorry," Simon Magnus repeated in a hoarse whisper as the steam dissipated, as the red flesh mottled and paled. "I'm so sorry, I'm so sorry, I'm sorry, I'm so sorry..."

Later, she helped Simon Magnus into the bedroom Simon Magnus shared with Ellen Chandler. She lay next to Simon Magnus, still murmuring apologies, until Simon Magnus fell asleep. She slipped from the bed, but on her way out of the room, she saw a small, leather-bound red book on the nightstand. It reminded her of her first visit to Marco Cohen's tiny studio apartment, a little room without shelves where towers of tattered paperback books spilled down from every wall, whose bare floorboards were paint-spattered in blotches and streaks, his realistic canvasses leaning precariously against the teetered book piles, a fume of oil paint and turpentine so thick she could barely breathe. The smell of turpentine would always make her think of having sex for the first time, on Marco Cohen's hissing air mattress, surrounded by the haunted eyes of the street people whose portraits he had just painted as a protest against the city's indifference to the homeless. He had had a little red book, too—*the* Little Red Book, as it turned out. She couldn't remember if her parents had that one among their counterculture artifacts. As Marco Cohen snored beside her, she browsed through the thin pages. She opened to a chapter titled "Women" and read:

In agricultural production our fundamental task is to adjust the use of labor power in an organized way and to encourage women to do farm work.

Fuck that, she thought. Wasn't that why her grandmother, her sweet old grandmother, had made the crossing from the old country in the middle of the century—so that she wouldn't have to wring the necks of the chickens or turn the stony soil with a rusty spade? "You lucky," her grandmother had always admonished her with one bent arthritic finger whenever when she complained about some minor chore as a girl, "you lucky you no have work in *campagna*." If the artist snoring beside her, the artist who'd just spent himself inside her—"Don't worry, I'm on the pill," she'd lied; she didn't know why she had lied—if he thought she was ever going to do farm work, he had another thing coming. She tossed the book aside and tried to sleep in the turpentine haze, under the painted eyes of the dispossessed.

Years later, she stood above Simon Magnus as Simon Magnus slept and browsed through another little red book. This one was called *The Book of the Law*. Some of it was gibberish—"The Khabs is in the Khu, not the Khu in the Khabs"—and other parts intelligible: "Every man and woman is a star," which, she thought, was precisely why nobody wanted to do farm work, for Christ's sake. There was no chapter named "Women," but, still, she read this:

Now ye shall know that the chosen priest & apostle of infinite space is the prince-priest the Beast; and in his woman called the Scarlet Woman is all power given. They shall gather my children into their fold: they shall bring the glory of the stars into the hearts of men.

For he is ever a sun, and she a moon. But to him is the winged secret flame, and to her the stooping starlight.

Stooping starlight! she thought. Shove your stooping starlight up your ass! She tossed the book down; Simon Magnus murmured at the thud of its spine against the nightstand.

What would it take, she thought, to be free of these men and their little red books of the law? She drew her nightgown tightly around herself to conceal from herself the metallic-smelling silver sigil Simon Magnus had drawn on her chest. Tears came to her eyes; she wanted to see her baby, little Levy. She wanted to feel the tiny clutch of all his pink fingers around just one of hers. She wanted to try nursing him again; maybe she could give milk this time as she hadn't been able to do before—except that he, too, would grow from her substance to be just another lawgiver, wouldn't he? Just another man with a lawbook, another man of the law, asleep in a mussed bed, surfeited from what he'd drained out of her.

CHAPTER 17
Against Life

The next day, the bungalow vibrated with silent recrimination. It was in neither Ellen Chandler's nor Marco Cohen's nature to make what they called a scene. Marco Cohen always stood ready for an intellectual quarrel, but in private life, about private matters, and to a woman not his intellectual sparring partner, to the companion of his bed and the mother of his children, or rather, of his child—no, he would not lift his voice. Diane del Greco couldn't help but notice, however, that he had begun to look at her every so often, when he thought she wasn't looking back, with contempt, ever since she'd insisted on leaving Levy with his parents to come to Oceanopolis. As for Ellen Chandler, she would do to anyone what she had done to her parents, if they could not understand or appease her: she would leave them behind.

Marco Cohen went back to work: drawing, drawing, drawing, and *drawing* some more, indentured to the realization of Simon Magnus's awful gnosis. Ellen Chandler edited the scripts from other writers the company sent her. Simon Magnus and Diane del Greco sat on the patio in mutual silence. Diane del Greco wanted to know what Simon Magnus had seen, but Simon Magnus would tell her nothing. "I didn't see anything," Simon Magnus repeated. She sat almost primly, legs crossed, wrapped in a shawl, though the weather hadn't warmed.

(Scrubbing had only dulled but had not removed the crystalline silver sigil from her chest; she assiduously concealed it from Ellen Chandler.) Simon Magnus couldn't bear many clothes on the skin that had been scalded in the bath. Simon Magnus sat in just black boxer shorts; Simon Magnus's eyes looked as if they'd seen to the end of the world, of several worlds.

One day, Simon Magnus went into the bedroom and sat at Ellen Chandler's feet, the bandages over her soles spotted with blood. She wouldn't look up from her work. No matter how long Simon Magnus sat in silence, she would not raise her eyes unless Simon Magnus spoke. Simon Magnus waited for five minutes.

Simon Magnus said, "We should leave. We should quit the project. We should quit VC Comics. We should go back home, they should go back home. We can start again, Ellen. You can apply again to the big publishers. I'll write poetry..."

Ellen Chandler, eyes still lowered, said, "Absolutely not. You signed a contract."

"Contract? Who cares about that? This is—"

Simon Magnus was going to say "life or death," but how could that be explained to Ellen Chandler?

"Listen to me, Simon," she said, her eyes still on a script, her hand occasionally making a deft red correction. "You've been misled about the way the world works. Your mother takes care of you, Valerie takes care of you, I take care of you. You don't always approve of the way we take care of you. You say vile things about your mother, you were going to leave Valerie behind to rot in Hollow Well, and you haven't been treating me very well lately—but still, we've taken care of you. You can't deny that. We've given you a house, given you a job, given you your intellectual interests and your writing projects. That's what you call magic, Simon: women taking care of you. You can't book a trip without me, you can't pay rent without me, you wouldn't be 'Simon Magnus, comics' most unconventional mind'"—here she made scare quotes with her fingers and affected the obese voice of a fan-journalist—"without me. We wouldn't have this house to work in without me. I never minded, Simon, I never minded. Because the moment I saw you in the café, a lost little boy in the great big city wearing an oversized dress with its hem dragged through the muck on the floor, I thought, 'Jesus, I'd really like to know him.' We could talk about anything—books and music and movies—and you were so sensitive to artistic form. You had in your own way such an open heart. You cried all the time. You cried in the hospital, you cried when you told me about Valerie. I was the hard one, mean and sarcastic, the way I had to be, coming from nowhere, a woman from the provinces alone in the city, and you always said—remember what you said to me?—'There's poetry there.' You used to show me the poetry. I needed to see it. I wanted to know you forever, Simon. The person you became to be *this* writer, though, the writer of ugly things like *Fools' Errand*, the person you became to show the world how tough-minded you and comic books and art could be, the person you became to make yourself too hard for the world to kick in the street—that person, I don't want to know. I already had the best of you. I don't know who you are now. The first time I saw the person you are now, that version of Simon, he punched me in the face because I tried to tell him who he was—so go ahead."

She pushed the script off her lap and leaned forward, chin first. She pointed at her jaw.

"Go ahead," she repeated. "Go ahead!" Tears ran from her hard gray eyes as she stared into Simon Magnus's green ones.

Simon Magnus stood and walked from the room. She crawled across the bed after Simon Magnus's retreating back, repeating it—"Go ahead, go ahead!"—until she found herself face down, sobbing into the comforter, pounding the mattress with her fists.

In this atmosphere, the bungalow sat almost silent except for the occasional scream and accusation, its inhabitants prostrate with resentment and loathing and guilt and anxiety. Ellen Chandler slept in one of the bedrooms; the other bedroom was empty; Marco Cohen slept in the office; Diane del Greco slept on the couch; Simon Magnus slept, even in the desert's nighttime chill, on the patio. Diane del Greco refused out of sheer obduracy, out of pride, out of what she called self-respect, to fly home to her baby. Yes, in *this* awful atmosphere, as July became August and August faded to September, Simon Magnus invented and Marco Cohen illuminated and Ellen Chandler invigilated the third and final part of *Overman 3000*.

Readers will recall the extraordinary conclusion. After Mina Mars's vision of space-time—she had borne witness to Cyphronian millennia, but when she fell out of the trance, she found that less than a minute had passed on earth—she understood what would happen. Earth had reached the same terminal civilization stage as black-sunned Cyphron just before its own consumption in fire: both planets endured a cultural heat-death that was the logical terminus of intelligent organisms' coevolution with technology. She had had time to glance briefly around the universe while in the throes of her vision, and she saw it on planet after planet after planet: the waters and forests sheathed in steel and glass and plastic, the large animals and then the small ones gone, the birds and then the fish and then the insects extinct, and then all the ardor and unpredictability, all the hot misdeeds and ingenious leaps of faith, gone out of the people, if they even *were* still people. Was *she* still a person? she asked herself. She answered herself—and Simon Magnus's feminist critics have never forgiven this line of interior monologue, not even after Simon Magnus pronounced SimonMagnusself to be without gender—"Only in Overman's arms." She knew what she had to do.

Mina Mars summoned Overman to the plains. Together, over the course of a year, shielded by bombardment from the Muller regime's satellites and drones, they led the heartland's gnostic revival in an ecstatic orgy of prayer and coupling. As high priestess, Mina Mars became particularly fanatical: she summoned the cleansing force, the true God from beyond the stars, to come into her, to possess her, to inhabit her, before it justly annihilated the soul-dead earth. Even after she found herself pregnant with Overman's baby, she kept praying to incarnate this devourer, much to Overman's sentimental-paternal chagrin. Overman, in the meantime, had his steely hands full with the restive, resentful, and murmuring band of self-exiled serfs he and Mina Mars led in the revolt against the nanocracy. Still, their dancing and rutting congregation was consistently refreshed with maroons and deserters from the battalions the Max Muller regime had to send in to tend the übermeat after the first serfs' exodus. Eventually, the übermeat itself, and thus the North American Union's population that relied on it for food, came under threat from the revolution. Yes, the übermeat—did readers think Simon Magnus had forgotten this detail from the beginning?

Meanwhile, Max Muller, arch-nanocrat, ardent believer in the total control of the human organism by the machines that human intelligence had devised, felt an acute wound. He was bereaved of his consort by the man from beyond the stars—a perfect man who required no plasma suit to keep his frail form mobile and alive, the way Max Muller did. Max Muller had always set the blood-borne nanobots to put him to sleep the moment he rested his head at night, but even they could not drive her dark hair or the curve of her breast from the anguished mind encased in his bald dome. Immoderately, in the guise of defending the übermeat from the gnostic revolt, he designed his revenge, as well as his jailbreak from what he considered, in the inmost recess of his soul, below where the nanobots could drift, the prison of his flesh. He would transfer the nanobots in his bloodstream, encoded with his intelligence, into the übermeat. Enfleshed in this teeming and autospawning cancer that fed the continent, he would rise against Overman, engulf him, ingest him, dissolve him, and finally excrete him onto the desolate plains.

Every comics reader remembers Marco Cohen's extraordinary sequence of two-page spreads, the linework dense and tangled as a rhizome: Overman and the Mullermeat clashing above the plains, the gnostic cult crying to heaven down below, lightning in the midnight sky as if the firmament would at last crack open and admit the light beyond—all of it like some fresco of the Last Judgment. Because the miniseries was out of continuity, because it was set in the year 3000,

Simon Magnus and Marco Cohen were able—Ellen Chandler nodded solemnly in spite of herself—to have Overman overwhelmed, swallowed, and scattered by the meat monster, dead forever. A rioting greenish worm-tower of tentacled egesta, the Mullermeat howled triumph to the breaking heavens.

At last, the climax. On that lightning-struck field, on that darkling plain, Mina Mars herself rose to challenge Max Muller. Her black hair went up in a column of fire, her dark eyes burned red, her feet, flames playing along the soles, left the earth. Her own swollen belly carried her into the air like a balloon. She hovered in the sky above Max Muller, the übermeat, the conqueror worm, the lightning acrackle over all her naked flesh, and she squalled like a hurricane. A seam opened from her breastbone to below the navel. White light fanned out from this breach in the middle of her corpus and burned the Mullermeat to ash, set the plain alight, burned up the acolytes, and split the earth. The true God, the cleansing force, had come into her after all, had come into her as Overman's own seed, irradiated to godliness in his million-year infantine exile. She laid down her life, sacrificed herself, immolated herself in the act of giving birth to the right and the just obliteration of our senescent planet.

Only the epilogue remained. A haze cleared in the dark black of space where the earth once spun, a void hung with planetary tesserae. "Zoom in on one rock," Simon Magnus ordered Marco Cohen, "zoom in so we can see it: the tiny little baby curled in a crater in a vast asteroid, a veritable planetoid, vegetation blooming around the crib where he lay with his thumb in his mouth—Overman and Mina Mars's baby, the destroyer but also the creator, the very heat of his flesh gestating a world around himself, the immemorial cycle ready to begin again. Zoom out now," Simon Magnus said, "zoom out to Mina Mars's vision, what we saw at the end of part one: space-time rotating in the fifth dimension." Rotating "around and around and around, around and around and around," to quote the graphic novel's celebrated final narrative caption.

Marco Cohen overcame the nausea Simon Magnus's presence caused him ever since he'd walked in on Simon Magnus posing naked for his wife. As he drew the final page of the series, he addressed a question to Simon Magnus, as he had not done once in all the late-summer weeks they'd spent working on the concluding chapters: "Would a happy ending kill you?"

Simon Magnus hadn't looked right, hadn't looked well, since the day Diane del Greco drew the writer's nude portrait, the day Ellen Chandler limped from the bungalow and got into the driver's seat of the car Diane del Greco had rented, the day Marco Cohen had run out and opened the passenger door and sat down beside her and let her drive him up and down the coast highway till midnight, screaming and crying and singing old songs from the radio in one another's arms—wasn't she, by now, almost his oldest friend?—until they found a hotel for the night. Simon Magnus had posed so imperiously that day, crossed arms and shorn head, contrapposto with a dangling dick, but now Simon Magnus appeared half dead, skin parched and gray and stretched thin over the shaved scalp, eyes staring wide out of stark, wasted sockets. Marco Cohen didn't know what had gone on between them—he wouldn't give his wife the satisfaction of asking—and now Diane del Greco and Simon Magnus weren't speaking to each other either. The drugs were gone, pilfered from the nightstand, the drugs the man in the black suit had pressed on him in the elevator at the VC Comics office back in Cosmopolis. Marco Cohen felt that if he simply finished this job, got out of the prison of this rented room, and flew back east, to his parents and to his son, then life—including his marriage—might be made whole again. The time was so close: he almost felt safe challenging Simon Magnus, as he had at the beginning of the project.

At Marco Cohen's question, the faintest hint of the familiar glimmer of irony and superior knowledge flashed in Simon Magnus's otherwise dulled eye.

"This *is* a happy ending," Simon Magnus said. "Time spins back on itself and forward again. Time can neither be created nor destroyed. Everything that ever was and ever will be remains there forever, just as our story and characters will be always be safe, locked in the pages of our book."

"Tell that to the billions of people we incinerated for a higher purpose at the end of the story."

Marco Cohen didn't know why he bothered to argue. It was just a job. They weren't real people, just characters in a silly superhero comic book, not fit for adults to read no matter how much sex and violence they put in. He needed to do the job because he had a family now, but why argue with the writer of the book any more than he would argue with the customers if he were bagging groceries: "Do you really *need* this candy bar?" Simon Magnus viscerally enraged him, however; the thought of Simon Magnus made him want to smash something with his fist. Whatever he'd seen that first day at the beach of the writer's inmost need had been dispelled by weeks and weeks of the oracular speech free from self-doubt, of the voice that wove its spell of appealing, heady abstraction. He wanted so badly to puncture Simon Magnus's afflatus, to let it burst, to let reality dispel its gaseous nihilism.

"We've saved them from death by placing them in all the panels leading up to their destruction," Simon Magnus said. "Now they can never die. It is really how the universe works, demonstrated in the form of our graphic novel, as surely as it's demonstrated in the Tarot pack. There is no death, if you think about it correctly. There is no death!"

Marco Cohen thought Simon Magnus said it with peculiar urgency, as if somehow desperate to convince him. He was not convinced.

"You seem to think that kind of philosophizing, that kind of abstract mentation, can redeem suffering. It's just a manner of speaking, though. It's semantic, pedantic, whatever. It's just words! When you're suffering, there is no time. There's only the moment of suffering itself, swallowing everything, annihilating everything, so much that you think about killing yourself just to get to some new moment or at least leave that one, that eternity of pain. Nothing redeems pain. That's infinite time. You want to talk about a devouring force? There's your devouring force. Nobody has the goddamn right to do that to anybody else."

Marco Cohen snapped his pencil in half. He justly pitied himself for the last few weeks, the weeks since Simon Magnus had posed for Diane del Greco, when he'd had to do all the requisite drawings of Mina Mars alone in the office, late at night, weeping onto the Bristol board. Mina Mars bore Diane del Greco's likeness, the long dark hair, the ample body, because he had used his own beloved as his model for Overman's. Now that he feared his marriage might be at its end, he could hardly bear to indite onto the page the image of Mina Mars cradling her heavy, pregnant belly, just as Diane del Greco had done when she'd carried Levy. The joy of his baby's birth—that had been infinite time, too.

Simon Magnus stood at the window overlooking the slope, back turned on the office, on Marco Cohen, facing the St. Catherine's lace and black sage. Another yellow-sun, blue-sky day. No matter what clamorous hell you had consigned yourself to in this false city, this Oceanopolis, the yellow sun and blue sky would mock it with unremitting equanimity.

"Maybe this shouldn't be published under my name," Marco Cohen said quietly.

"You'll get paid either way, my friend. VC Comics won't care. It's my name that sells the books, not yours. Who are you?"

Marco Cohen laid his head in the circle of his arms on the drawing board, the way he'd done when sad or tired as a schoolboy.

"I wanted to capture those moments, those moments of suffering, those moments of joy, too, when time becomes infinite, when your life for a moment stretches into forever. Those moments, few and far between—they're the only real moments. The only moments when we're really alive. I'm sorry I ever let my head get turned by any theory suggesting otherwise. Any theory that brought me here. There's theory and then there's life. I just wanted to preserve life, those moments, like the moment Levy was born."

Simon Magnus said nothing. Marco Cohen kept talking into the warm circle of his arms, moistening the Bristol board, breathing in the ink fumes, speaking to himself, not to Simon Magnus.

"One picture, one immortal moment, one at a time. You can keep your comic books, your Tarot decks, your philosophy of history, your meaningless abstract belief that what you call a fifth-dimensional perspective means human suffering and human joy don't count for a damn."

Out in the living room of the bungalow, the telephone rang. Marco Cohen heard through the office's closed door the distant murmur of Ellen Chandler picking up the phone and then calling to Diane del Greco.

Simon Magnus, ignoring the phone, said quietly, "One picture or two pictures or 78 pictures doesn't matter. To make art at all is to set yourself outside life, above life, superior to life, *against* life. If the part of you that has to *live* a life can't stand that, if the human part of you is too loyal to human things to allow the inhuman part of yourself, the superhuman part of yourself, the part that lives in the fifth dimension, to enjoy the complete perceptual freedom art demands, then you are obligated to find a different vocation, my friend."

"I'm not your fucking friend," Marco Cohen said. He began to cry into the circle of his arms, onto the Bristol board, smearing his inked page, the final page of *Overman 3000*, even before—yes, he would distinctly remember this later—*before* he'd heard the squealing cry of agony tear out of Diane del Greco's throat and through the office door.

It was an old rotary phone, squat and black, with a weighty receiver, heavy in the hand, a relic of the middle of the century that had somehow survived in this rental property, forgotten, into the century's end. Diane del Greco wrenched the receiver out of the base with a clang of the ringer. She walked toward the office with the receiver in her fist, its black wire coiling and springing behind her. She threw the office door open, crossed the room to the window—her face twisted into a tragic mask of screaming fury and despair—and beat Simon Magnus's bald head over and over again with the massy black handset. Simon Magnus submitted to her blows, offered no resistance whatsoever, did not even raise defensive hands; Simon Magnus simply went down beaten to the floor. Blood slashed across the walls and carpet; blood splashed onto the final page of *Overman 3000* on the drawing board.

"You knew!" Diane del Greco howled. "You son of a bitch! You knew! You knew! You knew—and you didn't *tell* me! I could have gotten there, you son of a bitch, if you'd told me! I could have been *there*! You knew, you knew, you knew!"

Marco Cohen wrestled the bloody receiver from her hands and pulled her, her pale pink shawl striped with Simon Magnus's blood, her face drowned in tears, into his arms. The ghostly outline of the crystal sigil was revealed on her chest.

"What is it?" he said. "Diane, tell me, what's wrong?"

Ellen Chandler watched from the doorway. She made no move to help Simon Magnus as Simon Magnus bled onto the carpet. She said calmly, smoking a cigarette, "What did you do, Simon?"

"He's dead. Oh God, my precious baby is dead. This son of a bitch knew it would happen, *saw* it happen, and didn't tell me, when I could have been there. Oh God, oh Jesus, my baby, Levy, Levy, Levy..."

Marco Cohen stood with her in his arms and then hurled her to the floor. He gave her one swift kick in the stomach with his heavy brown shoe.

"Don't blame him," he said without raising his voice. "It's obvious what he is. *You* should have known. *You* should have been there. *You* never should have left. This is *your* fault. I wish to God I'd never met you."

In the doorway, Ellen Chandler threw down her half-smoked cigarette and then ground it into the carpet with her sandal. She walked to the middle of the room. She looked first at Marco Cohen, second at Simon Magnus, and third at Diane del Greco. She extended her arms and helped Diane del Greco to stand.

CHAPTER 18
The World Crosses The Tower

Simon Magnus spent three days in the hospital. Severely concussed, Simon Magnus's shorn head crisscrossed with runes and arabesques of stitches, Simon Magnus spent the first two days gripping the mattress, trying not to vomit, confused, taken out of time, speaking to the air with Mother Magnus, Valerie Karns, Ellen Chandler, Diane del Greco—all the women Simon Magnus had ever known. Had Simon Magnus ever known anyone but women?

On the third day, they wheeled Simon Magnus out of the hospital and into a taxi. Simon Magnus told them to bill VC Comics. Simon Magnus asked the driver to stop at the bungalow. Inside, it was empty, the walls and floor of the office still slashed with blood. Simon Magnus packed Simon Magnus's belongings, the only belongings left in the place. Simon Magnus took the little red *Book of the Law* and set it on the electric coil burner of the stove they never used in all their time there (they'd ordered takeout every day instead). Simon Magnus set the burner to high, watched the coil turn a pinkish sunset orange with heat, and then watched the red book flare up in a fireburst. Simon Magnus stood in the spiral of drifting black ash.

Simon Magnus, smelling of smoke, returned to the taxi and asked the driver to go to the airport. Simon Magnus bought the last ticket on the earliest flight and flew back to the city—the real city, Cosmopolis, not the false city in the endless sunshine by the ocean. The apartment Simon Magnus had shared with Ellen Chandler was empty. Virginia and Vanessa were gone, along with all of Ellen Chandler's things. She hadn't left a letter.

Two days after Simon Magnus's return, the Twin Towers fell.

As soon as planes were in the air again, Simon Magnus spent the *Fools' Errand* royalties on a ticket to Europe. Simon Magnus landed in Dublin and spent two days wandering the city. Simon Magnus wept and recalled Ellen Chandler's besottedness with its modernist chronicler, remembered the vague plans they'd made to travel to this city someday and walk in Dedalus and Bloom's peregrinating footfalls. Simon Magnus took the train from the city center to Dún Laoghaire, the stony Martello Towers blurred in Simon Magnus's tear-streaked headache eyes, and crossed in a rocking overnight ferry from Dún Laoghaire to Cherbourg on a gray, nauseous sea. On the rest of the royalties, Simon Magnus traveled alone around the Continent for the better part of a year.

In November, in a cheap hotel with canted floors in the 17th arrondissement, where the lights in the hallway turned off at night for economy's sake, Simon Magnus stood on the window ledge, gripping the loose shutter, watching the cars speed below, and thought of Valerie Karns. In a cybercafé beneath the pavement on the Left Bank, Simon Magnus checked Simon Magnus's VC Comics email. Frank Donofrio offered congratulations: "Ellen's been sending the pages in and we couldn't be more excited, Simon. This is a whole other level of work—and not so obscene either, though Madeline might have taken slight exception, if you know what I mean, to the exploding womb and whatnot." Ellen Chandler curtly reported, with no greeting or sign-off, that she had received a letter from a lawyer meant for Simon Magnus, announcing that Mother Magnus had died.

In December, Simon Magnus had Nice to SimonMagnusself. The streets were empty of tourists; rooms in fine hotels with plush carpets and soaking tubs and balconies overlooking the city were a third of the in-season price. The gray beach stretched into the gray ocean; the gray ocean itself extended to the gray skyline. That was where Simon Magnus spent Christmas, where Simon Magnus welcomed the New Year, only the third of the new century, the new millennium.

In a luxury hotel's blinding white bathroom, Simon Magnus was doubled by a blinding headache. Simon Magnus let Simon Magnus's hair grow back in, around the scars. Simon Magnus suffered particularly vivid nightmares, where fleshy bladders of no intelligence stalked the dreamer through a labyrinthine city. Simon Magnus thought Simon Magnus would never write again. The words and pictures wouldn't come, except as nightmare, and then in no particular order. Any order, any story, would exact a price. Simon Magnus haunted whatever English-language bookstores Simon Magnus could find, but even reading failed, the words blurring—even Keats, even Hawthorne, could no longer reach the innermost core or *coeur* where Simon Magnus lay curled on the cold bare floor of an abandoned library before a dark forest, wailing.

Desultorily, Simon Magnus plotted self-slaughter, but inertia, depression, neurotic and anxious perseveration saved the writer from this, a kind of suicide's block accompanying the writer's block. No method was either painless or certain enough: the bullet could merely graze the brain; the pills might just induce emesis; the rope could break, leaving you in an undignified heap on the carpet; and how long did it take to drown? No method would spare the blameless outsider physical and mental harms, either—why risk crushing a passerby at the end of your journey out the window? Why damn a chambermaid *sans papiers* to the memory of discovering a tub full of blood?

In a cybercafé in Marseilles—the city, Simon Magnus distantly recalled, where the Tarot pack entered Europe on its way up from Egypt out of the mists of time—Simon Magnus saw that *Overman 3000*'s first issue had been published to rapturous acclaim in the late winter. Marco Cohen's ink-first drawing had been published without color in an unusually bold gesture. "We've never seen art this passionately detailed in American comics," read one online review. "Compared to the feverish intensity of *Marsh Man* and *Fools' Errand*," said another, "the icy cool and rational world-construction of *Overman 3000* suggests that Simon Magnus has grown up—has traded precocity for wisdom." "Could the portrayal of the slaves in the Midwest and their rage toward the two towers of Max Muller's rule in Cosmopolis be any more disturbingly timely?" asked a third. Simon Magnus had foreseen everything; everything Simon Magnus had seen had happened. In a filthy hostel's communal toilet, Simon Magnus spread a pair of scissors level with each eye; then a drunken German tourist stumbled inside the door to retch. "*Krieg ist die Hölle*," he grunted. Later, Simon Magnus stood on the pavement and watched an anti-war march pass in its hundreds. Their standard was a rainbow-colored flag emblazoned with the word *PACE* in white.

Sometime in April, Simon Magnus circled Lake Como on foot every day for a week, wondering which of the old men walking arm in arm around the placid water, which of the old men dozing in the sunshine over newspaper and ashtray and cappuccino at the outdoor cafés, might be Simon Magnus *père*, not that Simon Magnus's father would be so old. After Dante, in a jangly cot in a grim hostel, Simon Magnus tried to write a poem about eating "the salt bread of exile"—Simon Magnus subsisted on panini from street vendors. The poem came to nothing.

In Barcelona, in summer, Simon Magnus wandered drunk all day up and down La Rambla, warmed with desire and embarrassment by the prostitutes' solicitations. Did Simon Magnus, still in the leather-and-jeans masculine get-up, though with hair and beard growing out shaggily, want to sleep with them or to be them?

Ellen Chandler found Simon Magnus again, this time by phone. Simon Magnus wondered how Ellen Chandler had known where to call. The corporation that owned VC Comics, Simon Magnus guessed, like every corporation, had every inch of the earth charted, every name on file. Why had Simon Magnus fed this behemoth, reminiscent of nothing so much as the Cyphronian and Mullerite nanocracies, visions as vicious and personal as *Marsh Man* and *Fools' Errand* and *Overman 3000*? Why had Simon Magnus allowed them to project such evil visions on the unsuspecting world, as if the world deserved to live out one person's peculiar strain of perversion and despair? Why had Simon Magnus helped this monster made of money to breathe pestilence over the earth? Simon Magnus thought of the fans at the convention, the men in The Fool tutus, hot pink; what had they been like before they'd read *Fools' Errand*? Had Simon Magnus so resented the provinces of Simon Magnus's origin that they had to be obliterated forever, as the empire was just then planning to obliterate the now-provincial Mesopotamian cradle of civilization itself, looting its patrimony, poisoning its earth? Had Simon Magnus sold Simon Magnus's gift for the ability to manifest Simon Magnus's will? If so, was this hell? *Nor am I out of it*, Simon Magnus thought.

Ellen Chandler's voice on the phone line spoke with an almost exaggerated softness and slowness, as if, across the ocean, somewhere in the heart of the empire, she felt Simon Magnus's inner state as strongly as Simon Magnus felt it. Even so, she still she did not warmly greet her former lover. She said an old friend from college, now an academic administrator in an English department, believed that comics was as serious an art form as any other and that *Overman 3000*'s formal complexity and psychological depth were presently proving it even more than *Marsh Man* and *Fools' Errand* had. He, the administrator, would offer Simon Magnus a visiting writer appointment and a renewable lecturer position, a respectable school. It wasn't a school in a major city like what they in the comic books called Cosmopolis, Gothic City, or Oceanopolis, but in a smaller city, further inland, near where, in the year 3000, the übermeat would be farmed, the kind of place that in the comics, given its industrial past and post-industrial present, they'd call Steel City if they deigned to call it anything at all. Teaching: it would be something to do during the day, something to help the mentally prostrate writer crawl from hour to hour—Ellen Chandler's own phrase; she had, Simon Magnus later understood, moved in her own despair from Joyce to Beckett—even if the royalties and the inheritance meant Simon Magnus didn't need the money.

For the long-distance call, Simon Magnus had to use the hotel manager's phone at the front desk. The manager, a matronly woman of about 60 with a thick helmet of curly black hair, stared up from her swivel chair into Simon Magnus's face for the duration of the exchange with Ellen Chandler. Her already hard smile tightened the longer the conversation continued, that smile at odds with the cheerful sweater draped over her grandmotherly plumpness. Simon Magnus suspected she also managed at least some of the girls in the thigh-high boots and the bare-midriff shirts out on La Rambla.

Simon Magnus didn't want to teach college—and in *what* city, *what* provincial hellhole? How else, Simon Magnus wondered, *would* Simon Magnus crawl from hour to hour, however? How else would Simon Magnus get off the phone with Ellen Chandler and out of this bawd's dark gaze? Yes, yes, Simon Magnus, who had never gone to college, would teach college. Simon Magnus, who had thought to colonize the provinces, would return to the provinces for a richly deserved damnation.

"Take care of yourself," Ellen Chandler said coldly. "I've left VC Comics, by the way. If you have any questions, you'll have to deal with Frank and Madeline directly."

The sun was sinking over the city, diagonal to the Christopher Columbus monument towering above the harbor. The Spanish shipmaster pointed west, to the New World, in theory, but Simon Magnus read in a guidebook that the statue's finger in fact indicated, somewhat meaninglessly, the southeast, pointed not to America but to Africa. Simon Magnus walked out to a supermarket in a winding street off La Rambla and bought a bottle of orange juice and a bottle of vodka and drank from each in successive rhythm on the beach. With the mariner, this beach also faced east, unlike the beach in Oceanopolis, the beach where the sun sank. Simon Magnus walked back to La Rambla and picked up one of the women who stood a little apart from her colleagues: a sullen-looking dark woman taller and older than the writer.

When Simon Magnus re-entered the hotel with the woman, the manager's smile melted with gracious politeness. She rushed to summon the elevator for them, as she had never done for Simon Magnus alone.

In Simon Magnus's room, they drank screwdrivers and traded clothes. Given the state of Simon Magnus's soul, sexual intercourse was out of the question. They ended tangled together on the bed with cynical affection, Simon Magnus in just her red tights, she in just Simon Magnus's black boots, her penis nestled along her thigh. Simon Magnus laid Simon Magnus's face in her naked lap, weeping into her public hair, smelling the salt sea odor that rose from their mingled effluvia.

Her English wasn't good; Simon Magnus's Spanish was non-existent. When Simon Magnus drunkenly proposed they trade clothes, she said, "You just like me?"

"What are you?" Simon Magnus asked.

"Woman," she said. "*Siempre y para siempre.*"

"No, then," Simon Magnus said, pulling the elastic of her garter slowly up Simon Magnus's leg. "That was never what this was about. I'm not anything. I've never been anything. What I am is nothing. *Nada.*"

Her eyebrows arched with disbelief, her eyes widened with pity, her mouth sneered in contempt. She drew back in slight fear, as if she'd summoned a demon.

"*Madre de Dios.*"

Simon Magnus fell asleep in her lap. In Simon Magnus's dream, it was the day of Valerie Karns's funeral again, Simon Magnus was in mourning clothes again, Simon Magnus had again snuck to her room to rescue her dresses, her scent, whatever remained of her presence. In life, tears had dimmed her final Tarot spread in Simon Magnus's eyes. In the dream, the center of the Celtic cross glowed, brighter than day, iridescent, and Simon Magnus could read which card crossed the other. Simon Magnus woke up crying in an empty bed and smiled for almost the first time in nine months.

CHAPTER 19
The Mothers

Diane del Greco and Ellen Chandler got into the rental car, backed down the driveway, and drove away. Marco Cohen tried to get in the car with them, but Ellen Chandler pressed the button to lock every door. He went back into the bungalow and called an ambulance for Simon Magnus. After the ambulance left, he called a taxi to the airport and packed his clothes blindly, in a rage of grief, a grief of rage.

He called his parents. They told him what had happened. In the middle of the previous night, while Marco Cohen had cried over his drawing of Mina Mars, Levy, on the other side of the country, had climbed from his crib, crawled from his grandfather's old office (now spoken of as the baby's room), tumbled down the elegant modernist spiral staircase that joined the upper to the lower floors of the Cohens' condominium, and broken his neck. Marco Cohen's parents found him, skewed and still and blue, at the bottom of the spiral in the morning.

He left behind his drawing tools, left his pens and his pencils and his sharpeners and his nibs and his erasers and his Bristol board and his sketchbook and his T-square and his ruler and his compass, left behind the bloodstained work of *Overman 3000* sitting on the canted drawing board in the blood-slashed office.

Waiting for the taxi, he saw Simon Magnus's Tarot deck on the kitchen counter. To do something, anything, with hands that numbly quivered with grief and rage, hands that itched to pound or throttle something, anything, he plucked a card from the deck. The Wheel of Fortune. The ugly cartoon on the card was a lot of gibberish to him: a snake, a dog-woman, winged animals, an angel, arranged around the eponymous wheel that spun in the clouds, all manner of the hideous nonsense whose hidden significance Simon Magnus insisted upon even as Simon Magnus destroyed all the significance that was right there on the surface of life, destroyed Ellen Chandler and Diane del Greco, destroyed even Overman and Ratman with his vicious gnosis. Marco Cohen threw down the card. Then, once the card was upside down, the letters on the wheel in the center caught his eye, the familiar letters he'd first seen in his grandfather's still, silent *studium* of an apartment back in a world that was gone, that would never come again. The letters were יהוה, except that they alternated around the spokes of the wheel with four other letters, TARO or ROTA, depending on which direction you read them in or where you started, or, worst of all, TORA, as if these were interchangeable, as if the book of ultimate significance, the book of the law, were equivalent to a mountebank's deck of cards, as if the giver of life had given it to us to be broken on a wheel of cosmic absurdity and the endless repetition of the same, and not for us to cultivate it, improve it, heal it where it was broken, and create a new future. Marco Cohen picked up the card again and tore it to shreds and threw the pieces in the air like the garbage they were. He took up the rest of the deck and looked around for a way to destroy it, and then he had every intention of going into the office and destroying his work on *Overman 3000* as well, but then he heard the taxi driver honk the horn in the driveway. He forgot about the Tarot deck and hurried out with his bags to fly home—home, to bury his son.

The driver, dragging out the fee, drove him to the airport through Skid Row. Blinded by tears, he saw, under the ever-equal blue sky and sunshine, men and women in gray rags and heaps, attended patiently by flies waiting for the life to leave them, and he vowed, if he ever did anything else again, to do something about *this*.

In a motel by the beach, Diane del Greco couldn't stop crying. She choked and hyperventilated and nearly passed out on the stained comforter, between the paneled walls. Ellen Chandler finally got on top of her, took both of her hands, and forced Diane del Greco to breathe deeply in and out, in and out, in and out, in a slow rhythm. When Diane del Greco had regained some calm, she lifted her head and kissed Ellen Chandler hotly on the mouth. Ellen Chandler leapt from the bed, wiping her lips with the back of her wrist.

"I'm sorry, I'm sorry," Diane del Greco said. "I know what you must think of me. I know you thought I was stupid when we first met, not good enough for Marco. Then you thought I was a cold and cruel bitch, leaving my new baby alone for three months—and not going to the, to the, the funeral. Now you must think I'm out of my fucking mind!"

She rolled on her side, her back to Ellen Chandler, and began to heave with sobs again. Ellen Chandler ran to the tiny bathroom, its yellowish walls and filthy floor tiles, and threw up into the moldy, slanted toilet bowl. She couldn't stop heaving. Suddenly, Diane del Greco was above her, behind her, gathering her long blonde hair through her fingers so it wouldn't get dirty. Ellen Chandler thought she might faint; she fell back into Diane del Greco's arms.

They fell asleep on the bed, exhausted from grief. Ellen Chandler caught sight of the silver sigil that remained on Diane del Greco's chest. She traced it with her finger. "I guess the book will be a hit," she murmured into the dirty pillow.

Later, they walked out on the beach. They found a gaggle of teenaged boys around a scraggly driftwood fire on the sand. Diane del Greco tossed her head to summon one of them away from his friends. He bounded across the sand to them, running his hands through his sun-bleached hair, probably thinking he was about to be seduced, but Diane del Greco only said, "Are you holding?" He sold them a dime bag and some papers and then shuffled back to his friends, kicking up the sand before him. As Ellen Chandler and Diane del Greco walked further down the beach, the boys could be heard scolding their friend after he rejoined the circle—"You fucking queer, you didn't get their names and numbers?"—and then all the boys began to call after the two women at once:

"Julie, Nicole, come back! Do you need a lighter?"

"Emily! Heather! Where are you going?"

"Hey, Allison! Hey, Samantha! We just want to talk!"

The wind from the ocean soon carried their voices away, female name after female name evanescing in the salty air, none of them "Ellen" or "Diane."

Ellen Chandler still had Marco Cohen's lighter in her jeans pocket from the night they'd spent in the hotel after Diane del Greco drew Simon Magnus's nude portrait. Diane del Greco and Ellen Chandler smoked for a while behind some rocks; then they walked into the water as the sun set beyond the waves. Flecks of dying sunlight glimmered and rippled in the dark water.

Diane del Greco said, "I just can't shake the feeling—I've had it all my life—that I'm not supposed to be here. My grandparents trying to farm on stony hills in the middle of Italy, like their grandparents, and their grandparents, and their grandparents, I don't know, maybe that's what we're destined for, maybe we should have stayed. They come across the ocean, and my grandfather works himself to death before the age of 60, his lungs lined with tar, and they get together just enough money for my dad to get into drugs as a teenager and start dealing. He meets my mother, one of his customers. Here I am, raised by these burnouts and criminals. I never talk to my grandmother, she's still alive, she speaks Italian, and not even proper Italian, and I don't know what the hell she's saying, the poor old woman, she's 75 years old and has been wearing black for 15 of them, black as tar, but I guess they saw something, they could sense something, they didn't know what it was, over the next hill and the next and the next and then across the ocean, some higher life than the one they were living, so they came here, and all they found was more work. My parents sensed it, too, the presence, the promise, whatever it was, but they found it in the way the drugs made them feel. What did they find out here, down here, in the world, the real world? A filthy house and the inside of a jail cell. The drugs never really worked on me, to be honest. You can have a good time—your skin tingles, your head feels light—but that's it. You forget for a while, but then you wake up, and then you remember. The thing, the thing over there where the sun is, it isn't in there, the promise, the presence. It's not out there. Maybe it's in other people. I sensed it here and there in a couple of people, a girl I used to know, and then Marco, people who seemed to see something I didn't, who seemed to have some kind of working relationship to God or whatever you want to call it, even though I don't believe in God, but I feel something, just out of sight, just over there where the water drops off, I feel it, Ellen, and I don't know what it is. I know you think I'm stupid, and I let people think that because it's easier, but listening to Marco talk, listening to the girl I used to know, I felt they spoke some kind of language from beyond the world, the language the angels spoke, the language behind the words, if you know what I mean, and that's all I ever wanted, to talk in that language, and I can't, I never could. I could draw it when the drawing was good, but that never panned out either. Nothing else ever really satisfied me, not even when that girl touched me, or Marco touched me, so go ahead, what the hell, think I'm an airhead and a slut and leave me alone. Then Simon, well, I'm sorry, but to hear Simon talk, you know what it's like, there's nothing like it. Marco stopped even trying to touch me after the baby was born, even before, I think he was worried he would hurt us, or I had become purely a mother for him, not a lover, so when I got to know Simon, and I'm sorry for this, Ellen, but I thought, Jesus, this might be my last chance, maybe the third time's the charm, and the magic and the Tarot pack, well, you know. I don't have to tell you, do I? Simon couldn't touch the deepest thing in me either, though, Ellen, because whatever it is, it can't be touched through the body. The baby, Ellen, the baby, I didn't understand it when it was happening, for the first six months I thought the baby was holding me prisoner, like I was in *its* womb, I used to fall asleep fantasizing about—did your mother ever threaten you with this? mine did—selling him to the gypsies, whatever that means, wherever there are any gypsies, whatever gypsies are exactly. The baby screaming for me, sucking on me, on top of me all the time, the prison the baby was keeping me in was my own body. I dreamed once that the baby died, and do you know what I felt, Ellen, do you know what I felt, when I woke up and there he was? Can you imagine what I felt? Please don't make me say it. My Levy. Marco picked the name. We agreed. I could pick if it was a girl, 'Ashley,' and he could pick if it was a boy, 'Levy,' and it was a boy. When I found out about this trip, three months with Simon, yes, I said to Marco, 'Yes, you better believe I'm coming with you,' and he wanted to bring the baby, and I said, 'So I can babysit while you have fun? Hell no!' This was me getting out of jail. Now, Ellen, oh my God, now that I know it'll never happen again, I just keep thinking about those six months in an entirely different way, that the way I felt when he was sucking at my breast and I was so exhausted I could barely keep my head up, maybe that was the thing I'd been looking for all along, the feeling just over the mountain, over the ocean, where God lives, where the gypsies live, and maybe I felt so imprisoned by it because I knew I wasn't making myself worthy of it even though it was what I thought I'd wanted, and maybe this is the punishment I deserve for that, for running away here to the end of the world, for chasing Simon instead of taking care of my baby, maybe it's all I deserve, but you will never make me believe it's what that precious baby deserved, Ellen, you will never make me believe it, and now I will give up anything to have my baby again, but I will never have another baby, I will never look Marco or his family in the eye again as long as I live, and as for Simon, let me tell you, Ellen, Simon took the drug and saw what would happen and didn't tell me, Ellen, when I could have gotten on a plane and been there, and so, God forgive me, but I hope Simon dies tonight,

I hope I killed him, I hope Simon rots in hell, but all I want, Ellen, all I'll ever want, is to try it again, to have my baby back."

The sky was dark, the water cold. The women shivered in one another's arms as the waves rocked them, Ellen Chandler's long blonde hair and Diane del Greco's long black hair spreading and falling like seaweed all around their tingling bare shoulders.

Ellen Chandler said, "I'm pregnant."

PART THREE

CHAPTER 1

The Trap

Ash del Greco had seen to the end of everything.

She explained this to Jacob Morrow the night they met, the night of the first day of classes in his first year of college and her third, when he was 18 and she 21: how easy it was to arrive at the terminus of thought. People and events—which weren't separate, by the way, she told him: people made events, events made people—had a logic. Begin with certain premises and arrive without fail at certain conclusions. Once you grasp this logic, you don't have to wait to find out what happens to anybody or anything; you can quickly traverse the whole journey in your own mind.

For example, she elaborated, take her mother. Her mother had been raised in a dirty, disordered house by drug dealers and drug users who hadn't paid any attention to her. She therefore spent the rest of her life pursuing beauty, order, and attention—except that she had no instinct, no "feel," for these qualities since she hadn't been raised with them, so she was forever backing out of rash commitments she'd made in an attempt to redeem her childhood. She never allowed herself to know she was doing precisely this, however. In her 20s, she'd converted to Catholicism, nominally (but only nominally) the religion into which she'd been born, shortly after Ash del Greco—christened "Ashley"—came into the world. A few months before that, she had married a Catholic accountant, her second husband, in whose office she worked as a secretary.

(She'd been in a brief, failed first marriage with an artist, back when she had run away to the big city to become an artist herself, but she never spoke about this period of her life to her daughter, and Ash del Greco knew nothing about it.)

If there was one thing Ash del Greco couldn't imagine, it was her mother as an artist. She'd always supposed the real artist, the one her mother had briefly married, was her father, but then her mother insisted that her father's identity was completely immaterial, and the man, the anonymous sperm donor, whomever he might have been, never sent one Christmas or birthday greeting or a penny in child support after he left. Ash del Greco bore her mother's surname even after her mother married the accountant and converted to Catholicism, which was just as well, because she divorced the accountant when Ash del Greco was five. Ash del

Greco's mother still told herself she was a practicing Catholic to this day, even though she used the church's gift of regular absolution as a license to sin. She took communion despite her divorced and remarried and divorced status. "Google it, Canon 915," Ash del Greco told the irreligious Jacob Morrow. On and off, during her marriage to the accountant and after, she slept with strange men and also—this, Ash del Greco only suspected, but she suspected it strongly—strange women. Yes, Ash del Greco had early and easily solved the puzzle of her mother. Born to chaos, seeking order, drawn back to chaos again, ignorant of her own needs: a sad hypocrite, impelled by unspoken, even unrecognized desires. She'd die regretting everything, both her freedom and her self-restraint. Most people were just the same, if you knew how to look.

As for herself, Ash del Greco wanted to evade such ready capture by logic, such exhaustion by explanation. She knew her need to be absolutely unpredictable itself paradoxically created a predictable, even a fatal pattern, however: if you do the unexpected enough, people will begin to expect it of you. Coming of age in the second decade of the present century, she had—she admitted it ruefully to Jacob Morrow by way of example—ridden the gender carousel throughout her high school years. She'd gone from "she" to "they" and back again to "she," with a month or two somewhere in there on "he," and another month on "xe," and weeks contemplating "it," shedding dresses and long hair and "Ashley" for army pants and a shorn scalp and "Ash." She decided in the end, however, by the beginning of her senior year of high school, after a break with her closest friend, who had been more or less what they called a transmasc enby, that *amor fati*—she took this term from Nietzsche; did he know Nietzsche?—was the most dignified response to what one was not really supposed anymore to call one's natal sex, that "she" could in fact mean anything and nothing at all. She wasn't wedded to "she," exactly, but neither did she care. From those days, she retained only the redaction of "Ashley" to "Ash" because it sounded more impressive: one decisive, declamatory syllable connoting ruin by fire, rather than a limp, feminine trochee that meant—she'd looked "Ashley" up online—"dweller near the ash tree meadow." She kept the short hair, too. It was easier, let's face it, to manage in the morning. "Not everything is a symbol," she admonished him, though he had not proposed that everything was.

She explained all this to Jacob Morrow in her dorm room at midnight, as they sat cross-legged on the thin, stiff, gray carpet in front of her bookshelf. He told her he tried, himself, to avoid the internet; he'd left his phone, for example, in his own dorm room, hadn't looked at it in hours, and didn't miss it. His mother bought it for him, paid for the data plan, and insisted he carry it everywhere, "for safety's sake," she'd said, but he felt safer without it.

(Her own phone glowed and trembled seemingly every five seconds with app notifications—he would soon learn of her startling online presence—but she was able to divide her attention expertly, without missing what they called a beat, between the screen and him.)

They'd met, Ash del Greco and Jacob Morrow, six hours earlier. Her mother, the sad hypocrite, had dropped off the last of her things, irrepressibly crying, telling her not to do drugs—Ash del Greco had never done any drugs (except once, which her mother didn't know about and which might anyway have been a dream) and had no plans to start, but her mother was thinking, as always, of her own parents—and pulling her in again and again to her thin camisole and translucent sarong and sunscreen miasma and fleshy suntanned, sun-damaged arms for one last "one last" hug.

Ash del Greco, herself now smelling embarrassingly of the florally perfumed sunscreen, then found herself in the elevator with Jacob Morrow. It was just the two of them. Each stared into space in polite silence so as not to invade each other's presence in the close quarters, in the claustrophobic steel cell. He held a bottled water he'd just purchased from the vending machine in the lobby, while she clutched a taped-up cardboard box full of books to her chest. Just as the elevator accelerated, the tape on the bottom of the box ripped and dumped the books with a series of hollow slams and thuds against the elevator's corrugated metal floor. Jacob Morrow had journeyed to the lobby in just his socks, and Ash del Greco's *Riverside Shakespeare* crushed his instep, but he didn't complain. He instantly dropped to his knees to help her pick up the spilled volumes. Before she could get out the words, "I'm sorry," he hefted the largest of her books off his foot, regarded the Chandos portrait on the cover, and asked, "What's your favorite play?"

She stared him up and down quickly, taking him in at a glance, her eyes darting, avoiding only his own eyes. She didn't think he looked like a reader—maybe a sporty stoner, from the way he dressed, his long hair and tank top and cutoff jean shorts and white athletic socks, his long and lean build—but she reminded herself to let people surprise her, even though she had seen to the end of everything, had seen so far that she thought nothing would ever surprise her again. Also, because she was still unpacking, she hadn't donned the black uniform she'd begun wearing in high school, after Ari Alterhaus's death and resurrection, but was rather in just her pajamas: she wore a yellow onesie—kitten-eared hood up—and slippers with whiskered kitten faces. What must he have thought of *her*?

"*Hamlet*," she said as the elevator doors opened onto her floor. He joined her in scooting all the fallen books into the hallway so they could carry them to her room. "I'm not supposed to say *Hamlet* because it's too obvious. I'm at least supposed to say *King Lear*, which they say is the most sublime, or, since I guess I'm nominally a girl, something magical and lyrical and fairyish, like *A Midsummer Night's Dream* or *The Tempest*. No, though. It's *Hamlet*. He does everything he was able to do in *Hamlet*. It's even the funniest, funnier than the comedies. He invents the modern self, the mind suddenly alone in the universe without Mommy and Daddy, feeding on itself, gnawing on its own limbs just to feel something, and then he invents the way out of *that* trap, which is to do something else, *anything* else, just as long as you stop thinking and act. He does die—but we're all going to, anyway."

She made this speech, the words racing each other, almost tripping over each other, on the walk from the elevator to her room. A blonde girl in a pink bathrobe, carrying a pink shower kit, passed them by with a look of fascination and disgust. Ash del Greco didn't invite him in or thank him for helping her; after that first glance in the elevator, she didn't even look at him. He simply followed her, as if this were expected of him, his long legs keeping slow and deliberate pace with her short ones as he trailed at her heels. He smiled at her sententiousness as if it charmed more than offended him to be so presumptuously instructed by this tiny "girl" in "her"—was it "girl," was it "her"? you never knew, he reflected—kitten onesie and kitten slippers. At the dorm-room door, she turned to him and caught the smile; she found it patronizing but better than being called, as she was called in the corridors and classrooms of her public high school and in the long comment threads on her online videos, an ugly know-it-all stuck-up bitch.

As they were setting her books onto the dorm floor, there to be organized and placed on her shelf—a splintery rickety mess of uneven boards she'd made her mother pull the car over to haul from a sidewalk one summer day—she said, "What's yours? Don't say *Hamlet*, either! It's too obvious."

He didn't hesitate: "*The Winter's Tale*."

"You're just saying that to sound impressive. Something magical and lyrical and fairyish but not even famous! Your favorite is really *Hamlet*, isn't it? You can tell me the truth."

Instead of protesting that she'd caught him in a contradiction by telling him not to state the obvious and then judging his statement of the recondite a mere power play, he only quoted, "'It is required / You do awake your faith.'"

She raised her eyebrows at him—her eyebrows were brownish-blonde and unruly, her hair (what he could see of it inside the hood) dyed deep black—and he lifted his long tanned arm and swiped his long brown hair out of his eyes with his long tapered fingers. Whatever test she hadn't even quite realized she'd assigned him, he'd passed.

Her room had almost no decorations, and how she was lucky enough to get a single—he had an engineer who seemed to speak not one word of English for a roommate—he didn't ask. Maybe because she was a junior, while he was only what they called a first-year, since you couldn't say freshman anymore, first-year students being neither necessarily men nor fresh. The white cinderblock walls were unadorned. Her clothes sat in black piles on the bare mattress, in front of the closet; she felt no urgency to organize them the way she did to get the books right. She *had* hung twinkling rainbow string lights over the bed and the desk. The two of them sat in that flickering glow and not any brighter illumination. She let down the hood, and he saw the scar on the right side of her face: the seared and puckered flesh spiraling from the top of the cheek to the jawline, destroying the lower half of the ear in its rightward progress. She seemed almost to thrust it into his own face, a second test, perhaps, after the Shakespeare. Now she stared him in the eye.

They remained on the floor, shelving her books for hours because they had to pause to quarrel about each book's merits, to read passages aloud, to look up facts about the authors on her phone. They argued about organization. She favored alphabetical-by-author as the most neutral choice, avoiding invidious and inherently ambiguous categorizations of genre or period. He proposed chronology by author birthdate to anchor the chaos of art and thought in a historical continuum, a record of achievement and influence. He hadn't read William S. Burroughs; she hadn't read Jane Austen. Her books were mostly old paperbacks, torn and crack-spined and underlined by previous owners in blue ballpoint pen sometime in the middle of the last century, scavenged from secondhand stores, library sales, charity shops, and those free house-shaped book boxes that had lately sprung up in her suburban neighborhood. The *Riverside Shakespeare*, the big glossy hardcover whose vast spine had bruised his foot in the elevator, was an exception: a 16th birthday gift from her mother—a philistine, her mother, but one who knew enough to know Shakespeare meant "classy."

It was her summary of Tolstoy's *Confession* that led her to explain to him how she had seen to the end of everything. (He hadn't read it, though he *had* enjoyed *Anna Karenina*, which she'd found dull—too many fancy balls, too many debates about how to run a farm, too many details, too many characters, too many pages, too many words—and had left unfinished.) Tolstoy had seen to the end of everything when he discovered Schopenhauer's pessimistic philosophy. (Pedagogically, she held up Schopenhauer's *Essays and Aphorisms* next to Tolstoy's *Confession*, two black old Penguin Classics with brittle yellow pages.) He therefore arrived at the end of thought, in a gray waste of meaninglessness that stretched as far as the eye could see, out to the blank horizon. Unable to breathe in that atmosphere, Tolstoy had fallen back into the arms of the great-bearded God whom he resembled, but she resolved instead to brave the cold wind of nihilation without such paternal supports—or, for that matter, maternal. She found an austere pleasure—here she waved the battered old black New Directions paperback of Sartre's *Nausea* at him, one of the only *novels* she actually liked—in the knowledge that if we were thrown into an empty universe, then it was for us to furnish its emptiness out of our own inventive heads.

Her tastes ran to the canonical, if to its countercultural and philosophical end: Dostoevsky, Melville, Nietzsche, Camus, Bataille. She read to him from *The Story of the Eye*, which she described as "pornography about the futility of sex," to which he'd replied, "Isn't *all* pornography about the futility of sex?" Though ostensibly repulsed by what she read—something about a schoolgirl who sucked eggs into her vagina—he inexplicably found his penis stiffening in his shorts. He jokingly chided her for the lack of female writers in her library—just Emily Dickinson, an old copy of *Final Harvest* with the front cover ripped off—but she waved his objection away. Female writers, she said, were too domestic, too sentimental, too cowardly, too much like her hypocrite mother, to stare down the writhing emptiness of the cosmos. Not for nothing had it occurred to her in the first place to abandon "she," she explained, and she had re-assumed it less from feminine conviction than for convenience's sake. He politely offered to let her borrow his copy of *Sense and Sensibility*.

The exception to this canonical rule on her shelf, this reign of classic-if-countercultural prose and poetry, was her complete set of Simon Magnus, from the five volumes of the experimental run on *Marsh Man* through the scandalous graphic novel *Ratman: Fools' Errand* to the one-volume collected edition of the magisterial *Overman 3000*, those alternately gorgeous and gruesome books that made the news and made the author's name, that got banned and got seized and got burned by local authorities and angry parents, that were denounced long ago, even from the White House.

Jacob Morrow also enjoyed the occasional excursion into Simon Magnus's strange sensibility—he'd found them when voraciously reading his youthful way through the public library—but he wondered at the comic-book writer's outsize presence in a personal library otherwise devoted to more overtly highbrow fare, a library that held no other books with pictures in them and barely any other books that even told stories at all.

Their conversation about this question led them to discover, with relief, that they were both enrolled in Simon Magnus's Studies in the Graphic Novel course, which would begin the next day—relief because they didn't want to stop talking to each other, and the class unburdened them of having, at the end of this first dialogue, which stretched until three in the morning, to come up with some awkward invitation to meet again or, even if they exchanged numbers, which they did, to indulge in some ungainly drama of to-text-or-not-to-text? or how-long-to-reply-to-a-text? or any such life-wasting social game.

"Why are *you* taking Simon Magnus's class?" Ash del Greco asked him. "It's a long way from Jane Austen to *Fools' Errand*. I haven't read it, but I have the impression no one's anally raped in *Sense and Sensibility*." Before he could answer, she quipped in her rapid patter, "Which is why I haven't read it."

He shrugged and spoke slowly, more slowly than her, as he tended to.

"It was the only class in the English department taught by somebody who wrote books I've actually read. I thought it would be interesting to see what the writer is like. How do the books line up with his life? I mean, I know you're not supposed to say 'he,' but—"

She stared him in the eye again as he nervously recalled what she'd told him: that she had once abandoned "she" just as Simon Magnus had abandoned "he."

"—but his whole pronoun and proper noun game is pretentious and annoying, isn't it?" she finished for him.

They laughed with relief and small exhilaration at having said, together, in private, something publicly forbidden.

Most people you met made up the solid floor of the world; you walked right over them to wherever it was you intended to go. Every so often, however, maybe once in a decade, a stranger turned out to be not a beam of wood or slab of cement but rather a trapdoor, and then you dropped, helplessly, clear into another life. They had so much to talk about.

She concluded their first conversation with her own confession, not to his face but in a text message after he'd finally given her his number and gone back to his own room at 3:00 a.m. She sent this to him in a text message because, after nine hours of conversation, she knew him well enough to know he was too polite to tell her she was crazy, but she didn't want to watch the flicker of alarm at her delusional madness cross his gentle brown eyes. She texted, "you can't tell anybody this my mother thinks I don't know but I do know Simon Magnus is my father."

CHAPTER 2
Brutta Faccia

"Where the hell did you come from?" That was how Ash del Greco's mother used to reproach her when she misbehaved, from the earliest years she could remember through her young adulthood. She always wondered what it meant exactly.

The parents on TV—and other kids' parents in what they called real life, who were themselves, she'd observed, only reenacting what they saw on TV—had different habits of rebuke. To take the classic example, they would shout in their misbehaving children's faces their children's three names—first, middle, and last—to confront the stray whelps with their full status as human beings denominated in and therefore responsible to a dense web of social obligation. "Ashley Ellen del Greco!" her mother might have erupted, as if to demand, "Isn't drawing all over the walls of your room in permanent marker beneath you?" or "How could you possibly claim to 'have no gender' when I deliberately gave you two beautiful female names?" Her mother never said that, though.

Instead of reasserting her errant daughter's total identity, her position in the human race anchored by her three names, Diane del Greco chose instead to call this identity into question. Rather than "Ashely Ellen del Greco!" she always said, "Where the hell did you come from?" On the surface, it meant something between, "Who do you think you are to be behaving this way?"—a call to basic ontological humility, an attempt to shame the child with a reminder that no man or woman is a god, free to do whatever he or she wishes—and, "Could I have raised a child who would act this way?"—a claim on the child's loyalty, an attempt to make the child feel guilt for having drifted from that parental mooring for whose stability the child really ought to feel nothing but gratitude. If that was all it meant, it was only a rhetorical question, intended to jostle her back to herself when she acted like someone worse than she should be.

Her mother's eyes seemed glazed, however, her mouth seemed slack, and with some real puzzlement, whenever she asked, "Where the hell did you come from?"—as if she truly did not know, as if she had expected to come upon a child of her own, the bone of her bone and the flesh of her flesh, and had found instead a prowler in the house, a centipede in the bath, an orphan from the doomed planet Cyphron.

When did Ash del Greco remember first hearing her mother's strange question? It was on the day she acquired the scar, her first memory of anything, her second birth: the agonizing birth of her consciousness. She was five years old on a smotheringly hot July afternoon at her grandmother's house in the dead middle of the day.

Her mother was at work; she was then keeping the books for a small local law firm. Her grandfather at that moment, on that summer afternoon when Ash del Greco was five, strolled a cement-walled prison yard, serving a two-year sentence for possession with intent to distribute—not his first. Her father's whereabouts—even her father's identity—was unknown. Her grandmother had intended to make lunch for herself and her granddaughter, but instead, having smoked half a joint, she fell into a doze in the raveling old armchair in front of the soap operas and game shows that flickered on the ancient TV, a TV so ancient at the beginning of the 21st century that it still had antennae sprouting from its top.

Ash del Greco, sweltering in her overalls, felt hot and hungry and bored. She didn't understand the soap operas; she didn't like the sharp rotten smell of the lumpy yellow cigarette burning down between her grandmother's dreaming yellow fingers. Her grandmother's long, stringy, gray hair blew in the hot breeze of a whining metal fan; a fly buzzed around her grandmother's drooling lips; smoke reeled out of the dusty ashtray, shaped like an inverted turtle shell, on the brown carpet at her grandmother's dirty, tattered slippers with their backs crushed by her grandmother's calloused yellow heels. Ash del Greco climbed down from the couch. She knew what she would do: she would go to the kitchen and make lunch for herself. She was old enough; she was a big girl.

Only when she got to the kitchen, only after she'd passed through the dining room, its table piled high with papers and torn envelopes, did she remember that she had no idea how to make lunch. She had watched her mother and grandmother do it before, so she thought she knew. She thought she would boil a hot dog for herself. She wasn't entirely sure, though, in what order the process went. She opened the refrigerator, nudged aside the cans of beer and pop, and found the hot dogs—there were three left, with the plastic shell of the container ineffectually folded over them. When she took them out, cold slimy water that had pooled in the plastic dribbled pink on the sticky yellow linoleum. You weren't supposed to eat them cold; her grandmother had said you'd get worms if you ate them cold. It almost made her not want to eat them at all—weren't they almost the same color as the purple-pink worms she'd seen half-drowned on the sidewalk after a rainstorm, stretching their long bodies thinner and thinner as if trying to get away from themselves?—but then she remembered how good the salt and the fat tasted, especially with bright yellow mustard and jewel-green relish, and told herself she just had to cook them.

She decided to turn on the stove first, to let it get hot while she figured out the pot, the sink, the water. First, she turned a knob from "off" to "H." Then, more out of curiosity than need, she dragged a splintery wooden kitchen chair from the table across the linoleum, climbed up on it, and watched the left front coil of the electric stove as it slowly flushed with heat.

The heat didn't change the coil's color right away. It stayed a dull grayish black even as she, standing above it on the chair, started to feel the warmth reach her stomach, her chest. The air around the spiral changed before the spiral did; the atmosphere began to waver and ripple, as if the heat had somehow turned the air to water. The coil then lightened to an even lighter shade of gray, the color of cigarette ash, even as the little flecks stuck to it, the debris of old dinners, first shriveled black and then flared up red and finally disappeared.

At last she saw the metamorphosis she'd been waiting for. A translucent orange-red like sunset, like fire turned solid, invaded the spiral from the center outward, until the whole coil glowed and pulsated brightly in the tremulous air. She felt faint. She had forgotten about the hot dog. Between the heat of the afternoon—her grandparents didn't have air-conditioning, though it wasn't as hot downstairs as it was in the attic where they grew their special plants—and the heat from the stovetop, she must have been swaying on that chair in a high fever. The coil started to spin in her eyes.

How could she explain what she did next? (She remembered what she did; she would remember it even if her mother didn't constantly remind her, if everyone didn't constantly remind her, if the mirror didn't constantly remind her; it was in fact her very first memory, since what was it but her first conscious act, the first act committed by a person capable of remembering?) Maybe she did it because very young children don't yet know what the artist and the magician later struggle to forget: the law of cause and effect binds us in a chain and drags us forward through linear time, enslaving our souls to the needs and agonies of the body.

How was she to know the act of a moment would in its way last forever, or at least all of "forever" that she got to experience? She didn't know, for example, that she would have to overhear her *great*-grandmother, her mother's father's mother, a toothless nonagenarian who was losing what little English she spoke as she neared her doddering centenary, an ancient woman who had seen as a girl Hitler's army raise the dust of her hill village and, later, the Statue of Liberty rear green out of the salty spray, lift her withered flesh-hung arms to heaven and say of her when she was just five years old, the day she got out of the hospital, "*Povera bambina—brutta faccia!*"

Before that day in the kitchen, she had experienced pain, plenty of it. She was a sickly child. Ear infections, croup, various undiagnosed twists and upheavals of her stomach and intestine as they refused to digest what it was offered whether from breast or bottle—she had often lain prostrate, writhing and wailing, under the torture of pain. She felt these, however, as assaults from outside, inexplicable, unrelated to the before and the after, the way an animal senses sickness or injury. Because she was not yet conscious, she had never linked pain to her own actions, had never experienced it as a consequence.

What she wanted in that moment in her grandmother's kitchen was to feel the red of the coil in her own body, to make this glowing marvel a part of herself, to see what would happen if she joined herself to this spiral-steel fire. In itself, this was a form of hunger, like the bodily need that had driven her to the kitchen in the first place. She wanted to be a hard flame, the way the coil was; she wanted to live but on fire and to be on fire but to live, aflame but discrete in her body. She didn't know it would hurt.

She knelt on the chair to get her face level with the burner. She laid her already febrile cheek down in the center of the red-hot iron coil.

Her mind, like the dinner debris that had been on the burner, first exploded red and then went black. When she came awake, shunted from unconsciousness by the scream of agony her face had become, and by the fatty smell of seared flesh, she lay in her mother's lap. Her mother had come home early from work; her mother had entered the kitchen just in time to see Ash del Greco deliberately put her face down on the red-hot burner.

Her grandmother cried and accused herself loudly, pacing the kitchen and smoking. Her mother, pressing an icepack to Ash del Greco's charred face, wept silently, her eyes wide and mouth hanging open, stunned to silence. Only her mother knew what Ash del Greco had done. She would keep Ash del Greco's secret; she would tell everyone, starting with her own mother and with her father's mother, that it had been a terrible accident. She would also, from that day forward, regard her daughter with suspicion, anxiety, mistrust, a hint of contempt—even no little fear.

Ash del Greco woke up screaming, but outside, a siren screamed louder; she knew she'd done something wrong and expected in her haze of pain the police to come collect her and put her into a prison as solid as this prison of pain. She couldn't stop screaming. Her mother lowered her stunned face to look into her daughter's eyes. Somehow, through some thin tunnel in the screaming and the siren, through some chink in the wall of the pain prison, Ash del Greco heard her mother whisper: "Where the hell did you come from?"

CHAPTER 3
Against Novels

The recovery from the burn took so long that Ash del Greco had to be held back a grade level. Until high school, until Ari Alterhaus, she had no friends. It turned out that Ash del Greco's mother wasn't the only one who wondered where this strange and strange-looking girl had come from. By the time she was the oldest student in the third grade, her classmates' overt, cruel teasing about the spiral scar gave way to a whispered, almost polite aversion and disgust, as if they feared her.

Her classmates feared her because on the first day of the third grade, she tersely explained how she'd acquired the scar when introducing herself to her homeroom class. "I just wanted to see what would happen," she said and shrugged. Sister Grace, ancient, a rigid black obelisk with a pale and palely mustachioed white face, took the occasion to explain in her elderly growl that one's body was a gift from God: a temple of the Holy Ghost. We were called to treat it with as much respect as we treated God Himself, she sternly reproved the strange girl with the spiral scar.

Her fellow students might have gotten over the disfigurement itself as they matured, but the stain of that ungodly madness proved indelible, especially in the small Catholic school she attended from kindergarten through eighth grade, and where, in consequence of the tiny student body, there was no escaping whatever identity you'd been assigned early on. As poor Danny Kelly learned, if you succumbed to the ubiquitous temptation to taste the Play-Doh in kindergarten, then this, if there were 50 people in your entire class, would still be your most salient characteristic when you turned 14, and "Play-Doh Danny" would be shouted in mischief the day you graduated middle school, and even your parents would laugh fondly. Everybody, however, had felt the temptation to discover whether the Play-Doh tasted as good as it looked and, in its peculiar sweet-clay way, smelled; this was pleasure-seeking gone awry but pleasure-seeking all the same, which anyone might shamefully sympathize with, a sympathy their shame disguised as contempt. What precedent among the common pleasures and desires was there, on the other hand, for the willed searing of one's own face on a stovetop, just to see what happened? In the third grade, Ash del Greco's classmates could not articulate this insight but only act it out: if all she wanted in life was to see what happened, then what *wouldn't* she do? Looking back on it later, she really couldn't blame them for shunning her so absolutely.

To the boys, she didn't exist at all, except when they remembered that she'd deliberately laid her face on an electric stove burner, a gesture for which they extended a cautious, sympathetic respect. "She's *really* fucked up," she heard one boy whisper appreciatively to another in the seventh-grade lunchroom, as both giggled anxiously. The girls tended to waver between looking at her the way they might look at a cockroach if they found one scurrying in the bathroom or kitchen—pure stomach-tightening, skin-crawling revulsion, atavistic horror in the face not only of the inhuman, for kittens and puppies and bunnies were inhuman, but of the verminous, of the insectoid, even (who knew?) of the protoplasmic—and the way they might look at a mouse in the same place—with the same initial revulsed sensation, yes, but this time crossed by a flickering insight that in another and a more controlled context, a cartoon tea party, for example, the creature might almost be cute.

It was to this contemptuous pity in which she found the average girl to specialize that she owed her friendship with the person who would become Ari Alterhaus. After the divorce from the accountant, her mother couldn't afford another year, much less another four, of parochial school, not if Ash del Greco wanted to go to college, so the public high school it would have to be. Jackson High School was enormous, 500 to a graduating class as opposed to the 50-student classes of St. Gabriel's, but Ash del Greco didn't care. If everyone refused to be your friend, and rightly enough, then what did it matter if "everyone" numbered 50 or 500? At least she wouldn't have to wear those pleated skirts anymore or kneel by compulsion to gods she had, by the eighth grade, stopped believing in—the meek man in the dress with his neat little beard and his bleeding heart, not to mention his mother, who was robed like the nuns, except in sky blue, and who, in almost every picture of her, was shown with her foot planted on the neck of a snake. (Ash del Greco felt sorry for the snake.)

Two extraordinary things happened in the August of the year Ash del Greco was to enter the ninth grade. First, early in the month, on an ordinary Sunday morning, she was walking from her bedroom to the stairs leading down to the kitchen. She passed her mother's bedroom door when she heard the unmistakable heave of a sob. She stopped in front of the door—it was almost but not quite shut—and peered through the thin slit that admitted a narrow view of the bedroom.

Yes, her mother was sitting and crying on the edge of the unmade bed in her nightgown, the comforter twisted awkwardly around her waist as if she'd just woken up from thrashing in a nightmare. Ash del Greco squinted her eyes and looked harder. As she wept, her mother clutched a book in both hands: she gripped it and she bent it as if she wanted to tear it to pieces. Could she be crying over one of those silly romance or mystery novels Ash del Greco always made fun of her for reading?

("Believe it or not, there was a time in my life when I read what you're calling 'serious' books, sweetie," Diane del Greco had told her daughter when she'd mocked her for reading *Once a Duchess, Twice a Bride* or *Murder by Pie Bird* or suchlike, "but all it did was ruin my life.")

Ash de Greco peered: no, the book was bigger than a paperback, more colorful, more glossy—it looked like what they called a graphic novel. Ash del Greco liked all kinds of things her mother labeled "weird shit" after the weekly mandatory maternal survey of her phone and laptop history, but even she rarely read American-style graphic novels, as opposed to manga. Diane del Greco, who seemed with her suburban ways to be what Ash del Greco had already learned from the internet to call a normie *certainly* didn't read them.

"Oh God, my precious baby," Diane del Greco quietly moaned through her tears over the graphic novel as she bent and twisted it.

Later that day, Diane del Greco went out for groceries; her daughter, who often accompanied her, eyes glued to her phone as she shuffled in her hoodie and oversized jeans behind the shopping cart, pled her usual stomachache to stay home. As soon as she spied the car making the turn out of the driveway from her window, Ash del Greco ran to her mother's bedroom. She opened every nightstand and dresser drawer, searched the closet, and finally found the book wedged under the mattress of the still-unmade bed, its mingled smell of stale sweat and floral perfume: *Overman 3000* by Simon Magnus and Marco Cohen.

Ash del Greco knew little of Overman. Wasn't he the stiff red-white-and-blue bore with the cape who always did the right thing in the nice city in the sunshine? She hadn't even ever seen one of the Overman movies, let alone read the lame-ass comic books. She knew Ratman had something to do with Overman, and she *had* seen a Ratman movie. In that one, it was the villain, The Fool, she couldn't take her eyes from, the psycho-killer in the pink tutu and the suicide vest, all jittery gestures and cackles, someone who might, she thought, have understood why she'd placed her face on the burner. She'd only seen half the movie, though, back when she was 10 or 11—the celebrated, Oscar-winning, War-on-Terror allegory *Ratman Rises*—before her mother caught her streaming the pirated file on her phone, smacked her hand, and turned it off. Aside from that, she always avoided superheroes, in any medium, since most of the movies besides *Ratman Rises*, and presumably the comic books they were based on, were little more than kid's stuff, jokey and colorful and cheerful. At that period of her life, the end of middle school, she mostly read pirated horror manga online in awkward fan-made translations: all women with long black hair and melting faces, or, even better, arthropodal-fungoid masses writhing their tentacular way from wholly alien dimensions into our quotidian cosmos, the squamous monsters both nauseating and somehow also what they called *kawaii*. What could Overman have to say to her? More importantly, what could Overman have to say to *her mother*?

She flipped through the book and saw Mina Mars: there, in the kind of overly granular and realistically rendered American art style that her early immersion in manga ensured she would never develop a taste for, *there* stood her mother, the same as in the early photos she'd seen, the girl with the cascade of dark hair and the Roman nose and the olive skin and the type of long but massy body they called buxom—a disgusting word, Ash del Greco thought, a disgusting reality, and one totally foreign to the pale, tiny daughter whose head, its own hair thinnish and blonde, was too big for her almost pathologically skinny body. Add the contrast between her mother's Roman nose and her own, freckled and on the puggish side of what they called *retroussé* (she had once googled "names for types of noses"), and she, too, had to ask: where the hell *had* she come from? She ran out of the room with the book.

Ash del Greco always read, all day long—when, Diane del Greco wanted to know, was Ash del Greco *not* reading?—and at a much higher "grade level," whatever this meant exactly, than the classmates who would not speak to her. She read fragments, however: sentences, lines, scraps of poetry, passages of philosophy, chapters of manga, images captioned with pithy quotations in startling juxtaposition (otherwise known as memes). The books she checked out of the public library on her monthly trips with her mother tended to be books full of the poetry and philosophy she saw quoted in the feed, on the timeline, *if* she could find such recondite stuff at the suburban branch library, and these she opened at random and read incompletely; she checked out *tankobon* too, but the serials were only ever available at the library out of sequence, often with pages torn out, presumably to decorate bedroom walls or to inspire what they called onanists (she'd read that word somewhere online)—little better, then, than fragments themselves.

Ash del Greco did not love novels, neither the worthy novels they'd made her read in school, C. S. Lewis Christian propaganda fantasies and the like, nor the romantic entertainments about dark lovers, expiring girls, and oppressed gay boys favored by her female classmates. (The male of the species, she observed of the limited set comprised by her classmates, did not read novels of any sort, even when commanded to do so by women in authority.) Where, in a novel, was the intensity of the charge carried by a line of poetry or by a philosophical provocation? Novels conveyed wisdom by subjecting you at length, with much tedious detail, to a manipulative story. Eighth-grade English had culminated in a reading of *The Pearl* by John Steinbeck. Ash del Greco denounced this parable in her book report as "sententious" (she'd googled "other words for 'preachy'" and thought "sententious," with its echo of "sentimental," which that dead-baby book also was, sounded better than "didactic"). She received an A- and a comment from Sister Katherine complimenting her vocabulary but suggesting as well that humility might be a virtue, even in a justly severe critic. Fuck humility, Ash del Greco at 14 years old had thought: humility was for simpering slaves! (She was just then enjoying on the feed on her phone a bot that posted one aphorism of Nietzsche's every hour of every day.)

During their class discussion of *The Pearl*, Sister Katherine had written *RADIX MALORUM EST CUPIDITAS* on the board and then translated it for them. During the change of classes, when Sister Katherine's back was turned, one of the boys hastily added an "s" to the final word and then just as hastily erased it, blushing, as everyone helplessly giggled. The nun swiveled around with narrowed eyes: "I don't know what you're doing," she said, "but I know it's wrong." Ash del Greco recorded the Latin phrase to show her mother later—Diane del Greco, who had a refrigerator magnet bearing the words, in hot pink script, *Whoever says money can't buy happiness doesn't know where to shop. CUPIDITASS* was right, thought Ash del Greco.

(Every Wednesday night—because it was not crowded, the way it would be on weekends—they went to the mall, Diane del Greco and her daughter. At first, they used to go to the mall nearest their house, a squat yellowish structure, grimy on the outside, dim and close-feeling inside, somehow, despite its size. Ash del Greco, even at the age of seven or nine, would wander away from her mother's interminable clothes shopping to browse the adult horror and science fiction paperbacks in the chain bookstore until a usually exasperated Diane del Greco—"I've been looking for you everywhere!"—would come to collect her, laden with pink and gold shopping bags. The stores kept closing at that mall, though, and then the drug deals in the parking garage became shootings in the parking garage, so Diane del Greco, around the time Ash del Greco entered adolescence, began to drive them deeper into the suburbs to a grander structure, skylighted and white-walled, where the clothes were more expensive and where there were neither shootings nor bookstores amid the high-end boutiques. By then, Ash del Greco had a phone; untroubled by the lack of a bookstore, she sat on the rim of the stone fountain in the middle of the mall scrolling the smudged glass until Diane del Greco had finished. Diane del Greco's bedroom, after she divorced the accountant, always looked like a cyclone had spiraled through, had spun her bright and floral wardrobe to the four walls, around the tangle of her unmade bed. Neither of them, mother or daughter, cared very much for cleaning—Diane del Greco because she had not been raised to do it, Ash del Greco because she lived inside herself rather than inside the house—and so the place would deepen with massed and dusty disorder for months, plates cresting the sink and scum coating the bath, until Diane del Greco would inevitably erupt to Ash del Greco, "Ashley, you can't *live* this way, for Christ's sake!" and institute a rigorous cleaning regimen for a week, the whole place reeking of bleach, until she began again to languish in the twisted sheets and to leave her skirts and dresses in the spot on the floor where she'd stepped out of them. "Maid's day off," she would say to any unannounced visitor.)

Because she hated novels, Ash del Greco was not prepared for what a writer like Simon Magnus could accomplish not with charged poetic lines or philosophical provocations alone—though Simon Magnus had put those in as well—but also with the music of narrative. She began *Overman 3000* with the intention of pushing herself through the book dutifully, as a way of spying on her mother, of trying to find out what her mother was crying about, of trying to answer that question constantly droning in her inner ear of what her mother's life had been and of where she herself had come from, since she did not know her father, nor even who her father was; but by the midpoint of the book, the moment in the narrative where the gnostic scientists make their barefoot march out to the wilds and the wastes under Cyphron's weird black sun, she found herself turning the pages faster and faster. She was the one crying by the time Mina Mars exacted her vengeance on the Mullermeat for slaying Overman, by the time the girl—who looked just like her mother had looked when her mother was a girl—rose into the sky and allowed herself to be torn from sternum to coccyx by the cosmic cleansing force in a repetition-with-variations of Cyphron's own apocalypse. Simon Magnus not only wrote about time as a complete fourth-dimensional structure containing all our triumphs and all our tragedies rotating in fifth-dimensional space; Simon Magnus had in fact built such a structure, a crystal palace lit from within by the black sun of human perversity and echoing with carefully calibrated resonances and dissonances, making an eerie music as it whirled.

When she finished *Overman 3000*, two hours after she'd started reading it, she lay cruciform on her bed and stared at ceiling, prostrate from the intensity of that sublime vision, of that apprehension of a higher reality. Hadn't she read somewhere online that architecture was frozen music? Probably. She had read everything online at least once; by the time she was 14 years old, there really wasn't much she didn't know. As for music, she didn't like that either. Music invaded your emotions beneath your awareness, the way a virus stealthily infects you and silently replicates itself inside you until you erupt into feverish sickness, suppurating and inflamed, long past the time when you would have been able to prevent it. She hated to go anywhere in the car with her mother because her mother played that awful Lite FM station with all the sad songs about people bereft of their lovers. Her mother always sang along and smiled, but Ash del Greco had to turn her crying face away, though she had not yet either had or lost a lover and often suspected she never would. Now she knew that good novels—graphic novels, in this case—did what music did, unlike fragments of poetry and philosophy. Fragments of poetry and philosophy pricked, she thought, the mind, an obvious and therefore stimulating irritant; music and novels, by contrast, leaked silently into the heart until they drowned it. She liked to have her brain pricked or punctured, every few minutes if she could manage it, but that inner inundation, which suffocated you before you knew it, which in its excess of feeling made knowing itself, brain stimulation, impossible—never. She despised music as she despised novels. As for architecture—considering the shelter that was her mind, she had no need of it.

She had never read anything like *Overman 3000* and didn't want to read anything like it ever again. John Steinbeck bored her with the elaboration of an obvious and banal message—*RADIX* etc.—but Simon Magnus had carved a much more startling thesis into the very cosmos. The word "sententious," however—she'd adored that word ever since she found it in the online thesaurus—still applied. What else could a novel, graphic or otherwise, ever be?

She'd read *Overman 3000* not to end up a weeping mess on the bed but to discover why it had left her mother in the same state, her mother who looked just like Mina Mars. In incognito mode, so that it wouldn't show up in her mother's weekly history checks, she searched online for both Simon Magnus and Marco Cohen. Simon Magnus was the writer and Marco Cohen the artist according to the credits in the front of the book, so if there was a visual resemblance, it must have been due to the artist. Marco Cohen, however, had a two-sentence Wikipedia entry crediting him with *Overman 3000* and then noting his disappearance from the world of art—comics art or any other—and his tragic and untimely demise.

The Wikipedia entry linked to a long article titled, "What Ever Happened to the Artist to Come?" It had appeared a few years before on *Temple*, a website devoted to Jewish religion and culture. Its author, Jonathan Klein, a self-described "typical millennial nerd," narrated his quest to tell Marco Cohen's story in full for the first time: the acclaimed artist who had not drawn one line since *Overman 3000* and who'd then died in such grim circumstances. Jonathan Klein interviewed Marco Cohen's surviving art teachers—not Anne LaMar, alas; she'd been dead for a decade, he noted, and hadn't even lived to see her own revival—and they dutifully relayed the way his ethical exactitude warred with his preternatural gift. Jonathan Klein had then spoken to many other comics artists about Marco Cohen's dizzyingly meticulous and grandly sublime style. "He made the rest of us look like we were drawing Mickey Mouse," said an older contemporary, while a younger one, more accurately to Ash del Greco's manga-reared sensibility, claimed by contrast, "Too much detail: it detains the eye, postpones the story." Most of the article concerned Jonathan Klein's own struggle to reconcile a ban on idolatry with a life consecrated to culture—he had returned to his faith with the onset of middle age after two decades of ferocious secularity. This struggle was exemplified on a lower intellectual level, Jonathan Klein explained, by the famous Jewish preponderance among the inventors of superheroes, men who had devised an undeniably lurid spectacle with an ineluctable ethical dimension. He eventually tracked down a cousin of Marco Cohen's, a successful lawyer, who told him the whole story over lattes in a Starbucks near her firm. The artist's baby had died as he was completing *Overman 3000*, said Marco Cohen's cousin. Following this tragedy, Marco Cohen divorced his wife; the ex-wife declined to comment for the story, Jonathan Klein reported, and so he left her nameless. Marco Cohen then renounced art and threw himself into good works, into charity and activism: he taught art in prisons, he chained himself to pipelines, he lived among the destitute, and he gave away all he had. Five years after completing *Overman 3000*, he put himself between an irate pimp and a 15-year-old girl in the nighttime alley behind a homeless shelter where he volunteered; he was stabbed nine times in the stomach with a switchblade and left to bleed out on the filth-strewn pavement, the murderous pimp and the helpless prostitute having both fled in fear of the law. The story created a small sensation in the comics fan press. Then Marco Cohen, except as an adjunct to Simon Magnus's gnostic vision, and occasionally, as a man who'd died trying to save a fellow citizen as if he were himself a superhero, was soon forgotten. His own parents, who'd never recovered from the death of their grandchild—it had happened while the baby was in their care—died in succession shortly afterward: the mother of an aggressive cancer, the father of a stroke. Jonathan Klein drove to the cemetery where Marco Cohen was buried and placed a pebble on his gravestone. The article ended when Jonathan Klein flew to a Jewish assisted-living facility in Florida to sit face-to-face with Madeline Stein, the cultivated art-history graduate and VC Comics vice president who had approved the hiring of Marco Cohen 20 years before, only to find the old woman's mind half-gone. In what he called one of her intermittences of lucidity, he proposed to her the conflict between the biblical ban on images and the spectacle of superhero comics against which Marco Cohen had rebelled. "Please," she said raising her withered hands as if to fend off an assault. "The man was a fanatic. He was as bad as Aaronsohn. Just flip ahead 10 pages in Exodus from the ban on images—there you'll find the great artist Bezalel, praised as a master craftsman! HaShem never could make up his mind. I should have told Cohen that when I had the time. There's never enough time, is there?" Then the journalist and the former VC Comics vice president laughed together hysterically over pudding cups at the irony of existence, and so the article ended.

That was all Ash del Greco could find about Marco Cohen. He sounded too serious ever to have been involved with a woman like Diane del Greco. Anyway, they weren't Jewish.

Simon Magnus, according to a much longer and more detailed Wikipedia entry, had also departed comics after *Overman 3000* but had more credits to their name (it was "their" then, in the period between "he" and "no pronouns") than Marco Cohen. These credits had inspired no less than five popular movies, including *Ratman Rises*, with its tutu-sporting Fool, and had altered the archetype of the superhero, according to one article, "from a sunlit Apollonian idol to a *blackly* sunlit Dionysian beast." Yes, Simon Magnus inspired much more than one journalist's quest for identity; Simon Magnus inspired academic articles with titles like "From Apollo to Dionysius: Simon Magnus's *Gesamtkunstwerk*"—she was able to read the first page of this on the JSTOR free preview—and inspired, as well, more casual critics to make pronouncements like the one she heard in a YouTube video: "Before Simon Magnus, every superhero story took place in Cosmopolis; after, they all take place in Gothic City." When she read on Wikipedia that Simon Magnus had lived with the editor Ellen Chandler in the polis or city the comics called both Cosmo- and Gothic until shortly before the publication of *Overman 3000* #1, she immediately surmised what had happened: Diane del Greco had gone to the same city to be an artist and had met Simon Magnus and had broken up Simon Magnus's relationship by getting pregnant with Simon Magnus's baby. *Overman 3000* #1 was published the month before she was born. The math checked out, more or less. Her father, or her currently "they/them" and therefore gender-neutral all-gender parent, was a famous writer.

She'd learned a new word too: *Gesamtkunstwerk*. She had the internet pronounce it for her and resolved to say it as soon as she could; surely high school, the public high school she would enter in just a month, with so much time to learn freed up from the religious dogma Catholic school had inflicted on her, would give her the opportunity. She would never learn any language besides English fluently—syntax was music and novel and architecture: not for her—but she would have words from every language on earth, brain stimulants, in her cyclopedic lexicon. Eventually, she would learn every word in the world.

She was trying to find a pirated pdf of the *Overman 3000* as *Gesamtkunstwerk* article when she found the Tumblr instead.

She didn't have much time to linger over it just then, however. She had been so lost in welcome thought and unwelcome emotion that she hadn't heard her mother return from shopping, and now her mother was pounding on her bedroom door. She sat up in a panic and rushed to put *Overman 3000* out of sight, but she wasn't fast enough. Her mother threw the door open and said, "What the hell is *this*?" Staring down Ash del Greco from the doorway, one hand on her hip, in a thin summer sundress with a plastic flower in her long dark hair, Diane del Greco held a crumpled card in her other hand, outstretched. Her eyes, fixed on her daughter's face, hadn't yet landed on the book, which lay between them on the bed. It took Ash del Greco a second to remember what the card was: an invitation, addressed to her, to some party. She'd crushed it into a ball and thrown it away the day before and had thought nothing more about it.

"Why did you throw away your invitation to Maddie Scholtz's end-of-the-summer pool party?"

"She sends those to everybody out of politeness—her mother makes her."

"I know, I work in the same office as her mother. It *is* polite! You're going to public school now, and a popular friend from St. Gabe's would be a good person to have on your side. I heard she invited people from Buchanan, too, since she knows them from volleyball. She wants to introduce St. Gabe's kids to some of the Buchanan kids since they'll all be going to high school together now. This is a great opportunity for you. You can meet new people and reintroduce yourself to the old ones."

"I don't even have a bathing suit," Ash del Greco said vacantly, trying to decide if she could make a subtle, unnoticeable move to conceal the book—maybe stretch her leg over it or slide a pillow on top of it—while she still held her mother's angry gaze.

"Where the hell did you come from?" Diane del Greco said. She pursed her lips at her daughter's shapeless sweatshirt and sweatpants. "We'll buy you one. Middle school's hard on girls—believe me, I know that—so I let you slide these last few years, but I want you to have fun in high school. You're going to this party, Ashley. No two ways about it!"

With that, Diane del Greco tossed the crumpled-up cardstock invitation toward her daughter; her eyes followed its gentle arc through the swirling dust motes caught in the afternoon light and landed with it directly on top of *Overman 3000*. Not saying a word, she stomped into the room and snatched the book up with one hand, doubling it on itself. Her dark eyes were wide and cold and wet when they re-met her daughter's pale ones. She swung the book through the air until it slammed against Ash del Greco's spiral-scarred cheek and knocked her sideways off the bed. Diane del Greco then dropped the book to the carpet and collapsed onto the bed herself. She knew her daughter hated to be touched, but, all the same, she pulled Ash del Greco up from the floor and into her fleshy arms and against her chest, her sweaty sunscreen in sudden miasma making the girl's head ring and her stomach turn.

"I'm so sorry," she cried onto Ash del Greco's neck. "Oh God, I'm so sorry, my baby."

CHAPTER 4
Notes from Undergirl

The Sunday night of the day in August when Ash del Greco's mother struck her in the head with *Overman 3000*, she spent alone in her room with the Tumblr: *Notes from Undergirl.*

She'd found it because it posted screenshots of almost the entirety of the academically paywalled essay about how *Overman 3000* was a *Gesamtkunstwerk*. She lay in her bed on her side with the sheets and comforter pulled up not only over her body in its sweatpants and sweatshirt but over her head and over the canted laptop, too, and she feverishly read.

(She lay beneath the sheets *and* beneath the comforter, because, though it was what they called the dog days of summer, Diane del Greco, fanning her overheated and abundant flesh in all weather with envelopes and books and magazines and any stray papers, kept the whole-house air-conditioning at 65 degrees, especially now that she had no accountant husband to look at the control panel and shake his head and raise it by 15).

As she lay and read, she whispered this word over and over again to herself under her breath. She mimicked as best she could the most exotic sounding of the pronunciations she'd found online, on a website where native speakers pronounced various words in their own languages for the benefit of foreigners. The tricky parts were crowded into the end: the thick, almost perverse under-the-tongue whisper of the *s* breaking against the *t*, the slow and utterly un-English *eeehhherr*, like an old man's groaning sigh vomited out of the *v* sound and then gagged on the *k*. She loved the word for its massive hideousness, its hideous massiveness, like some cliff-bound Gothic castle, its black-walled battlements rising out of a greenish, poisonous mist.

Undergirl's profile read only "he/she/it" and "i'm nobody who are you," without a question mark. The profile picture showed a sleek head in a full skintight black plastic mask, the material shiny, almost iridescent. The header image looked like a high-angled drone shot of a city, the buildings cascading and tessellating with the landscape they occupied in dark and neon ranks. They lit the night sky blackly pink.

(It was probably located somewhere in China. Ash del Greco had just been reading something somewhere about what they called techno-Orientalism, an article still half-read in one of her browser's 100 open tabs, though whether the article had said techno-Orientalism was a neutrally appealing aesthetic option, a fashion you might consider adopting for the fall, or the simultaneous effect and cause of Western imperialism and white supremacism, or some mixture of both, she could not quite recall.)

The header image had a vertiginous effect, tingling the pit of her already burning stomach, like when you look down from a great height, because it showed how dominantly, how *totalizingly* human works proliferated over the landscape, how they had even *replaced* the landscape: it was as if aliens had invaded the earth, and we were them. The faceless black head in the profile picture—who was he/she/it but the ideal citizen of this total, this absolute city? The page's background was colored almost the same strange dark pink as the sky in the header image; the font was italic and sans serif, showing up in a hard-to-read dark gray against the dark pink.

Ash del Greco whispered, "*Gesamtkunstwerk, Gesamtkunstwerk, Gesamtkunstwerk, Gesamtkunstwerk, Gesamtkunstwerk, Gesamtkunstwerk,*" until it seemed like a word in an alien language, which it was.

Undergirl specialized in what they called web weaving, the collage or montage of cultural fragments adding up to a mood or idea: a lyric from a song that came out this year plus a panel from an American comic book plus a stanza from a 17th-century baroque poem plus a GIF from a 10-year-old American sitcom plus a detail from a Minoan mosaic plus a paragraph from a 19th-century French novel plus an untranslated haiku from the Edo period plus a still from a generations-old Soviet film plus a panel from a webtoon plus ten lines of poststructuralist philosophy. Undergirl practiced this art with an austerity rare on the platform. Out of respect for creators, you were supposed to follow up your weave with a list of its sources; out of respect for persons experiencing a disability requiring them to use a screen reader, you were supposed to describe all images and type out all screenshotted texts. Undergirl dispensed with these niceties, to the chagrin of frequent commenters charging the account with "ableism," "exclusion," "gaslighting," and "gatekeeping." You had to figure out your own self what he/she/it meant by his/her/its montages.

The tone, the mood—what they called the vibe—was clear enough. Undergirl judged the unassisted human being no more than a slop of uncontrolled emotions and undisciplined thoughts. He/she/it highlighted passages from the Bible, the Qur'an, the *Bhagavad-Gita*, the *Dhammapada*, the *Tao Te Ching*, the dialogues of Plato, the sayings of the Stoics, the lyrics of the T'ang dynasty poets, the tragedies of Shakespeare, the philosophical tracts of 19th-century pessimists, and other such works of a scriptural status—quotations Ash del Greco either recognized or easily found through googling—to emphasize the age, universality, and durability of this thesis.

Against this essential or existential human slovenliness, Undergirl lifted the standard of the Übermeat. He/she/it plainly loved *Overman 3000*, the only American comic book he/she/it regularly included in his/her/its panoply of manga-and-anime-sourced imagery, but he/she/it read it against itself, decomposing its crystalline architecture, its veritable *Gesamtkunstwerk* of a narrative, into blackly glittering shards and fragments. In place of Simon Magnus's faith in a spirit from beyond, the gnostic cultus of the rioting, rutting Cyphronian and Terran dissidents, Undergirl exalted instead the inhuman spires and networks of the technocracy they sought to annihilate. Undergirl took Max Muller's side; Undergirl posted images again and again, almost as if they served the otherwise sexless blog as an unspoken erotic ideal, an intrusive sexual fantasy, of Max Muller's feeble, hairless body, suspended and ambulating in rolls and folds of shimmering plasma across mirror-clear floors, and then of Max Muller incarnated slug-like in or as the rearing and coiling agitations of greenish, artificial neoplasm.

It took Ash del Greco about an hour of increasingly blear-eyed scrolling and googling to crack Undergirl's code. By the end of her investigation, she had opened scans of five new-to-her manga in five more browser tabs and downloaded seven theory book pdfs from two Russian pirate sites to the enormous folder labeled "books" and password-protected against her mother, who wouldn't in, any case, have been able to understand its contents anyway, not that Ash del Greco understood much of it either. Theory in its full articulation was hard, but Ash del Greco could decrypt online presences and entities easily enough. It was only a matter of letting their characteristic mood wash over you and then finding the right words to attach to this feeling; you found these words by skimming pdfs of theory books or CTRL-F'ing your way through them, or else by listening to lectures or podcasts about them or by their authors, preferably at 2X speed. You could find out anything in an hour online, really, if you could keep the screen from scalding your retinas or the touchpad from cramping your fingers.

Ash del Greco still scrolled *Notes from Undergirl* for another hour after cracking the code, because now she wanted to know—since he/she/it never composed an original word—if he/she/it was really a person or was rather a bot, a script, a self-perpetuating algorithm programmed to disseminate this gorgeous nihilism, perhaps by a foreign government wishing us to be demoralized. If he/she/it was a person, what did he/she/it look like? Was he/she/it in fact gorgeous? Ash del Greco scrolled and scrolled, hoping to see, for example, in a phone photo of a passage in a print book, a stray fingertip caught holding the edge. If the fingernail were bitten or long, clean or grimy, painted pink or painted black or not painted at all, then this would tell her almost everything. She found nothing, however, not one clue to any human identity behind the account. She was surprised when she remembered how she'd gotten to the Tumblr, why her head hurt, why she'd been crying: she'd wanted to find out if Simon Magnus was her father, her sire, her all-gender all-parent, the mother-father who promised to make her mother wholly irrelevant.

Ash del Greco fell asleep in a feverish sweat, the comforter pulled over her head, the laptop burning and whirring three inches from her face, her head pounding, her eyes hot in their sockets. She dreamed that her mother was leading her by the hand through endless branching black corridors. Her mother laughed and said, "Come on, come on, baby, your father's waiting!" until Ash del Greco pulled away and ran on alone through the dark labyrinth. Eventually, she slammed headlong into a wall. She shot up in bed at three in the morning, threw the comforter from her, and hurled the laptop to the floor.

Maddie Scholtz's end-of-the-summer pool party took place on the subsequent Sunday. That was the second extraordinary thing to happen that August. Maddie Scholtz's mother had rented out the whole public pool after-hours for the event; for the sake of the parents, she presided over an illicit makeshift bar on a smuggled-in picnic table at one end of the pool, while Maddie Scholtz's stepfather dished out cake and ice cream to the teens at the other. All the mothers—it was mothers primarily in attendance—lounged on towels in the grass drinking strawberry daiquiris. The mothers took turns making them in an old blender; its top kept flying off, globs of pink slush flung in all directions, as the mothers doubled with screeching laughter and wrung out their sticky hair. Most of the soon-to-be-high-schoolers either sat at the pool's edges, paddling their feet in the water—the girls, mainly—or splashed and thrashed and dunked and cannonballed—these were the boys—inside what looked to Ash del Greco in the darkening haze like an agitated wedge of greenish luminescent gel.

Ash del Greco sat cross-legged on the cement in a black sweatshirt, black jeans, black socks, black Mary Janes, switching between a pirated manga and *Notes from Undergirl* on her phone. Her stomach burned, as it always did, the back of her throat still raw from the sugary white birthday cake icing. ("Eat something, Ashley, for Christ's sake," Diane del Greco had said; she literally shoved the cake between her daughter's lips, fingertips slick with the icing's canola grease.) Around her, her peers hopped barefoot over the still-hot cement (it had been almost 100 degrees that day, summer's last wild flare) to and from the pool, their bare swimsuited flesh jostling around her pained face, shedding droplets of chlorinated sweat onto her glasses and onto her phone screen.

Her mother approached, over- and underdressed for all occasions, now in a hot pink sarong and cork-wedge sandals and—though night had just about fallen—a wide-brimmed straw hat with plastic pink flowers in the band. She teetered over, twirling her half-drunk daiquiri in its plastic flute between her fingers, butted Ash del Greco in the shoulder with her broad hip, and said, "Why don't you go talk to *her*?" Diane del Greco gestured extravagantly, indiscreetly, her bracelets jangling, her daiquiri sloshing, to the other side of the pool.

There, in a black electric wheelchair, still and stiff and monumental as an Egyptian funerary sculpture, sat the figure who would be first introduced to Ash del Greco as Arielle Alterhaus, just as Arielle Alterhaus would find herself introduced to Ash del Greco as Ashley del Greco, even though they would eventually come to call one another—and demand to be called by everyone else—Ari and Ash.

Ari Alterhaus wore a plastic brace around her shoulders and neck held to her head within a surgical halo of black rods; she had black fiberglass casts on both arms and black plastic medical boots on both legs. Beneath all the medical equipment, Ash del Greco saw an incongruous floral print bathing suit and deathly pale skin, corpulent at the middle. Something in the juxtaposition of soft and fragile flesh with the rigid artifice of the medical equipment, and on what had looked at first in the setting sun like a statue more than like a fellow almost-ninth-grade girl, made Ash del Greco catch her breath.

Ash del Greco slowly walked around the pool, her peers dodging and weaving around her slow march, and stood next to Ari Alterhaus. Both stared straight ahead, over the heads of their peers as they shouted and splashed, Ari Alterhaus's head held in place by plastic and steel, Ash del Greco's by something like fear or desire or the fear of desire.

Ari Alterhaus said, "I jumped off the roof. Well, not the roof—that makes it sound more dramatic than it was. I don't even know how to get onto the roof. I jumped out the attic window."

"I, I wasn't going to ask."

"You weren't going to ask, but you *did* want to know. What else do you want to know?"

Ari Alterhaus spoke in a low monotone, through closed teeth. Ash del Greco crouched down next to the wheelchair to hear her better. The mingled smell of sterile plastic and the funk of dead skin massing under the casts and braces made her dizzy.

"Why did you jump out the attic window?"

"Part of me wanted to die. Do you ever look ahead at your future life and think, 'It can't just be this, day after day after day of *this*, can it?' Another part of me figured it probably wasn't high enough to kill me. If it didn't kill me, it would at least force things to change. I like things this way, honestly. I've never broken anything before. The bones are loose now inside the flesh and blood casing. I don't love the pain, but the pills take that away pretty well. What I like is this feeling of being held in place. You know the word 'carapace,' from biology? Having a skeleton on the outside? I wonder if this is what a spider or a cockroach feels like—like nothing can hurt you. I've already hurt myself, anyway, just about as bad as you can be hurt, so what can the world do? A 'monstrous vermin'—that's from Kafka, I just listened to the audiobook, I couldn't sleep last night, I can't ever sleep, even the pills just create, like, a haze, not sleep. I don't know if you know Kafka. *The Metamorphosis*. The audiobook was read by a text-to-speech bot who didn't know where to put the emphasis or the pauses. 'Mon-strous-ver-min.' I like the way I look in the mirror, too. Still and self-contained, like a statue, except that I can move around and talk. There's this other book I like, you probably haven't heard of it. I never met another girl who's heard of it. It's called *Overman 3000*, but not, like, a typical dumb superhero comic. I don't know how to describe it. There's a German word, you might not know it, it means—"

"*Gesamtkunstwerk*," Ash del Greco whispered. The word was so long it took all the breath out of her body with it. She whispered, but Ari Alterhaus heard her.

CHAPTER 5
The Heresiarch

Ann Alterhaus sat on the school board. It was easy enough for her to make a few calls to guidance counselors and administrators and get Ash del Greco's schedule rearranged. She now shared the same schedule with Ari Alterhaus and was therefore able to carry the injured girl's books between classes, take notes for her, help her with trips to the restroom, and assist her at lunch. This came as a relief to Ann Alterhaus, a harried family attorney and public figure who kept long business hours.

Twice divorced and now a single mother, Ann Alterhaus worried almost for the first time in the whole course of her motherhood about her daughter, usually the most self-sufficient of children. She had previously trusted her daughter to care for and entertain herself since at least the age of seven or eight. No smart daughter of hers would get hurt or burn the house down or fall for scammers on the phone or predators on the internet if left home alone all day, not when there were tasks to complete and knowledge to attain: a physical world full of housekeeping chores and a digital world full of every type of information. It had never been a problem before that Ari Alterhaus had few or no friends; mother and daughter agreed that she was easily the superior of anyone in her public elementary and middle schools.

Ari Alterhaus had not told her mother the explanation she'd given to Ash del Greco for her fall—the exhaustion of both these worlds, the physical and the digital, in a cataclysm of boredom, of despair. To her mother, she'd said she had gone in a fit of nostalgia to look at some old toys in the attic; there she'd become fascinated by a bird's nest just outside the window and had fallen while trying to get a closer look, almost a martyr to the free intelligence her mother so prized. Ann Alterhaus had considered sending Ari Alterhaus to school with some kind of professional health aide, or else hiring someone to monitor her while she performed her schoolwork at home, but the prices really *were* extravagant, even on her salary. She was so grateful, then, when Ash del Greco came along and volunteered to be Ari Alterhaus's body servant that she had a giant plastic-wrapped wicker basket full of flowers and wine and fruit and cheese and crackers and cakes and pastries sent to Diane del Greco; it took two men to haul the crinkling basket in from the truck into the filthy kitchen, under Diane del Greco's bemused and Ash del Greco's mortified eyes. "Maid's day off," Diane del Greco told the delivery men, slipping each a crinkled dollar bill with a wink.

Ash del Greco's decision to perform this service puzzled her as much as it did her mother because, for as long as she could remember, she had hated to touch anyone or to be touched by anyone. Her mother always hovered over her, always gathered her against her breasts, always planted wet kisses on her cheeks: it always made her want to vomit out the already burning contents of her perpetually inflamed stomach, and Diane del Greco was always pouting and crying after her only child had shoved her away. Now Ash del Greco came into contact with Ari Alterhaus almost every hour of every day. She had never been so close to another person since her infancy—even though she had no memory of infancy, no memory of anything before the spiral searing of her face suddenly brought her to consciousness.

For the first two months of ninth grade, Ari Alterhaus, then still Arielle, remained what they once cruelly called wheelchair-bound and what we have now decorously learned instead to call a wheelchair user. From her arrival at school at 7:30 in the morning to her departure from school at 2:30 in the afternoon—she emerged from and disappeared into a specialty van—Ash del Greco, then still Ashley, remained at her side. Ash del Greco was permitted to use a laptop in class to take notes for both herself and for Ari Alterhaus; Ari Alterhaus and Ash del Greco were permitted to leave every class five minutes early to beat the change-of-class crush in the hallways; they also received special permission to eat their lunch privately in an unused classroom—this had been a special request of Ann Alterhaus—to avoid the public spectacle of Ash del Greco feeding Ari Alterhaus, who could not lift her hands to the height of her mouth due to the fractures in her back and shoulders. Ash del Greco feared offending her delicate stomach too much ever to eat lunch herself. Now she gripped a pizza slice in both her own hands as Ari Alterhaus bit into its dripping, greasy tip; she allowed Ari Alterhaus to bite french fries from her own grease-slicked fingers; she spooned applesauce into Ari Alterhaus's open mouth. After lunch—there was no word for the nauseating dread and shameful curiosity this occasioned—Ash del Greco would assist Ari Alterhaus in what they politely called the restroom, perhaps, Ash del Greco surmised, because it was where you went to expel the rest of what you had eaten and drunk but could not digest. She herself—then still "she," then still "herself"—could not digest much.

A month into the semester, Ann Alterhaus dismissed the home health aide and allowed Ash del Greco to come home with Ari Alterhaus in the specialty van and stay until she herself returned from work, usually around dinnertime, though sometimes not until eight or nine at night, at which point she would call a car for Ash del Greco and send her on her way. Ash del Greco would microwave frozen dinners for Ari Alterhaus and feed them to her; she would type her homework for her and help her dress for bed; she offered further help in what, with reference to a home rather than to a school, was called the bathroom rather than the restroom, though one might rest in the bath far more than in the tubless and often crowded school facilities.

Ari Alterhaus's house was at the other end of the same suburb where Ash del Greco lived, was double the size of Ash del Greco's house, was cleaned twice a week from top to bottom by an elderly maid who spoke no English and who looked at Ari Alterhaus with uncomprehending dismay. In the living room and dining room, the carpets were a grayish blue, the walls a grayish silver. All the appliances in the kitchen were stainless steel, the so-called island granite, the floor marble. There was a TV the size of a wall in the living room, never turned on. Thick blue drapes screened the tall windows and admitted no light. Ash del Greco, thinking of the warm disorder of her mother's much smaller house—the dirty brown carpet and loudly damasked furniture and gaudily floral wallpaper and hard-water ring in the toilet and dishes heaped in the sink—thought it looked like a hotel, a nice hotel, like the one they'd stayed in when her mother was still married to the accountant and they'd spent a week at Disney World.

By Halloween, Ari Alterhaus was threatening to emerge from most of her medical carapace, to be able to walk and to feed herself again. Ash del Greco remained by her side, still came home with her after school every day. "I'm so glad you have a friend," Diane del Greco would say when her daughter returned at night, "but Ann really should be paying you." After a second's decent interval, she would also usually add, "That snooty bitch."

As the fall wore on, Ari Alterhaus began to experience what her lifelong pediatrician, Dr. Peter Farr, called setbacks. It wasn't so much, he reported to Ann Alterhaus, with whom he had in fact gone to middle and high school, that her bones and tendons weren't reknitting themselves properly as it was that the X-rays and MRIs showed subtle new injuries.

"What the hell are you implying, Peter?" Ann Alterhaus demanded, arms akimbo, alone in his office as Ari Alterhaus sat out in the waiting room after her exam. Dr. Peter Farr lifted his hands in defeat, shook his balding head, and demurred before her valedictorian's posture of command. He'd ranked third in their high-school class, and he'd intended, upon entering college, to practice neurosurgery, before some natural limit, whether of innate intellect or of innate drive, had set a boundary to his ambition—a limit Ann Alterhaus had not encountered in her own field of law. She'd somehow detected this limit in him in their school days; she'd shown him contempt even 20 years before, back when she always bested him, her main rival, by solving before he could the intricate problems their AP Calculus teacher would set them as a brain stimulus at the beginning of each class. Her smile had been vicious, her legs crossed politely in the smart skirt she'd always worn, almost alone, in the public school's unisex sea of baggy blue jeans. In his little clinic nested in its anonymous beige professional building just off the highway, wearing a navy blue pantsuit two decades later, she ordered that he carry out a battery of new tests on the corpus of Ari Alterhaus—tests, she suggested with crisp articulations of the medical jargon, for exceedingly rare carcinomas of the bone and soft tissue, the kind of malignancies that seem, often and mysteriously, she added, to afflict exceptional children.

On Halloween night, a Tuesday that year, there was no rest for Ann Alterhaus, so Ash del Greco and Ari Alterhaus sat inside by themselves. (The Alterhaus's neighborhood, for safety reasons, had scheduled trick-or-treating for daylight hours on the preceding Sunday.) They sat on Ari Alterhaus's bed, her tablet between them, and streamed horror movies. They usually watched movies at double speed or even dragged the scrubber quickly across the video progress bar and absorbed the plot from the preview images that sped past. In this way, they watched four or five in a single evening.

Few horror movies were what they called cosmic enough to satisfy them. They'd acquired this term from H. P. Lovecraft's treatise *Supernatural Horror in Literature*. They'd listened together to the online audiobook at double speed, laying next to each other on the bed, the tablet between them, staring up at the white ceiling it bluely illuminated. "Cosmic horror" signified a more-than-terrestrial terror, a fear not so much of mundane menaces like the murderer wielding a knife, an axe, or a chainsaw, but rather a horror that evoked, as the difficult master had written, "the thought of the hidden and fathomless worlds of strange life which may pulsate in the gulfs beyond the stars, or press hideously upon our own globe in unholy dimensions which only the dead and the moonstruck can glimpse."

Who cares, they asked each other rhetorically, about some freak in a hockey mask hacking up naked cheerleaders? These slasher films didn't even show proper contempt for the flesh, since they unfailingly used the cheerleaders' intact bodies to titillate the presumedly adolescent audience before showing them bloodily disaggregated by the maniac. "I hate movies with sex in them," Ari Alterhaus said. "It ought to be against the law." Ash del Greco agreed. True horror reduced the human body to absolute nothingness by revealing it to be a speck of material in the overall machinic structure of matter, which, since it was the source of all pain, was also, properly speaking, *hell*. Hadn't this been the gospel of the doubled gnostic sects, the earthly and the Cyphronian, apparently speaking for the queer author, in *Overman 3000*?—a book Ari Alterhaus had recommended to Ash del Greco the first night they met, isolated at the pool party, only to hear in reply, "I've read it." Ash del Greco's second reading would be in tandem with Ari Alterhaus's 10th or 11th, their heads bent on her bed over the blue light of her tablet where they slowly scrolled a pirated pdf.

The only good movie they found to watch that Halloween night was an independent film apparently made on a four-figure budget, if that, and shot on shakily held phones: *The Heresiarch*. It was an hour long, probably because the budget wouldn't cover feature length. Ari Alterhaus and Ash del Greco watched it on normal speed to the end.

The entire film was set in a nondescript, blandly beige office. A young man claimed to have escaped from a cult. He explained to an initially incredulous psychotherapist the rites and rituals of the cult leaders who'd abused him. She, the therapist, a sensitive and pretty young woman, spoke gently and with compassion; she believed herself to be treating him for a combination of paranoid psychosis and self-harm.

"I'm sorry, Michael, but the police can't find any records of this cult," she told him.

"They hide in plain sight," he said. "They're in the highest places. What if I told you the chief of police was a member? What if I told you the mayor? The governor?"

She smiled sorrowfully and, in defiance of the mandated professional coldness, leaned across the distance between them to steady his jittery knee with her prettily manicured fingertips.

Whatever the reality of the cult, this apostate certainly hadn't imagined—though she thought he probably *had* self-inflicted—the runes and arabesques scarred in angry flesh across his torso and down his inner thighs. The mutilation of the body, he explained to her, its adornment in blade and fire with letters in a long-lost language, a language likely sunk with Atlantis and of which we possessed only rudiments, was needed to propitiate the plasmic gods outside time.

These alien gods were a synthesis of supercomputer and jellyfish who'd accessed our realm through the internet, hence the cult's total rejection of any technology newer than the invention of the transistor. At this information, the therapist, taking notes on her laptop, looked up over the rims of her glasses and smiled with flirtatious irony. The central scar on his chest showed the coiled tentacular horror the cult meant to flatter into letting them live when it finally came to devour our realm.

In the end, the therapist moved her chair closer and closer to his. She unofficially diagnosed him with erotic repression as she stroked the scars on his inner thighs; the cult had forbidden sexual congress to its members, since procreation would only generate more matter for the jellied devils to consume. Young Michael, though not *so* young, was, in consequence, a virgin. The film came to its climax, so to speak, when the therapist succeeded in seducing the apostate. He stood naked, his scars bared to the beige politeness of her office, the polypy hieroglyphs in angry red flesh rebuking its clinical calm; then she, too, stood to disrobe.

"If it's just a matter of fucking," she said almost offhandedly as she stepped out of her beige pumps, "then there are probably rival cults who think they'll gain even more credit with the invaders by engendering more bodies for them to feed on. Imagine a rival cult with a breeding program."

With this, she unbuttoned her blouse and let it fall to reveal, between her breasts, injured into the tender flesh, the exact same scyphozoan icon he wore on his own chest. Cut to black, roll credits.

After *The Heresiarch*, Ash del Greco and Ari Alterhaus sat mute for a moment. Then Ari Alterhaus said, "I have to pee." She no longer needed Ash del Greco to accompany her to the bathroom. She was able to walk, more or less, though she still wore a medical boot on one leg—one of her two fractured ankles was stubbornly not healing—and a soft collar on her neck to protect the fragile vertebrae. She limped from the room.

Ash del Greco was rarely left alone in Ari Alterhaus's bedroom, so she now looked around freely. It was every inch a young girl's bedroom, pink-walled and pink-floored. The canopy bed had pink translucent curtains and pink flowers on the comforter and stuffed animals piled among the pillows. Ash del Greco crept quietly to the closet door and slowly opened it: inside were only clothes, neatly ranked on sturdy wooden hangers. Ari Alterhaus, who seemed to Ash del Greco to know everything, even to have *read* everything, apparently did not own a single print book.

When Ari Alterhaus had not returned from the bathroom after 15 minutes, Ash del Greco, bored now, tiptoed from the dim room into the dark hallway. She saw Ari Alterhaus standing at the head of the long staircase leading to the huge house's lower level. Her neck and leg immobilized, still partially carapaced, she awkwardly pivoted her whole body around to face Ash del Greco.

"I'm not ready to come out yet," she said. "I could only jump once, though. I could only jump because I didn't know how much it would hurt. Just a few more months. You do it, though. You do it. Please."

Ash del Greco stood almost two heads shorter than Ari Alterhaus, so she ran with her head down toward Ari Alterhaus's chest. After she'd knocked Ari Alterhaus off her feet, she wasn't able to stop her own momentum. They both tumbled together down the long staircase, Ash del Greco clutching at Ari Alterhaus as they spun and thumped in an octopus whirl of eight limbs. It was easy enough to believe the story they told Ann Alterhaus when she came in two minutes later to find them in a broken heap on the ceramic tiles at the foot of the stairs: that Ash del Greco had only been trying to help Ari Alterhaus down the carpeted steps when they'd slipped. Ari Alterhaus went back into the wheelchair, this time for 14 weeks since she had so aggravated her fractured vertebrae that she'd lost almost all feeling in her left leg and side. ("The right would be good too," she told Ash del Greco.) Ash del Greco had, miraculously, only broken her wrist and was still able to function, in effect, as Ari Alterhaus's body servant even with a cast on one arm—black, to match her friend's.

CHAPTER 6

Them

By the late spring of their freshman year, both Ash del Greco and Ari Alterhaus had healed almost completely. A physical assault on the physical, a material assault on the material—these were not enough to subdue the physical and the material, to subject them finally to the kingdom of mind, to the cleansing force they'd read and reread about in Simon Magnus's opus, *Overman 3000*. (They'd come to this philosophical conclusion half in words and half in the strange telepathy they had developed after having spent so much time together.) This was when they decided to become, each separately as well as both together, a "they," a singular and a plural. For the ninth grade, they'd remained Ashley and Arielle, but at the beginning of the next school year, they transformed, first into Ash and Ariel, and then, for symmetry's sake, into Ash and Ari.

One night, early in sophomore year, a Wednesday in early June when Ann Alterhaus didn't return from her office until 11, spring thunder crashing outside and rain spattering against the huge house's high panes, they sat together on Ari Alterhaus's bed. They had their heads bent, yet again, over the pirated pdf of *Overman 3000*, glowing between them on Ari Alterhaus's tablet. Their heads weren't touching; no part of their bodies touched. After their period of assisting them during their convalescence, during which they held their hands or arms or waist to guide them from their wheelchair to the toilet or to their bed, or when they helped them to keep themself clean after using the toilet, or when their fingertips in a misgauged delivery of food brushed their lips—all events that filled them with some unutterable combination of nausea, panic, and fluttered longing—they ceased to touch them, and they never touched them in turn.

Ash del Greco had by then informed Ari Alterhaus of their surmise that Simon Magnus, then also "them," and their inspiration for their own becoming "them," was their real parent. As if it were a religious icon or object for meditation, they had onscreen the double-page spread where the cleansing force, the alien god *in potentia* as Overman and Mina Mars's fetus, cleaved from sternum to mons pubis with a blast of blinding fire a woman who looked for all the world like a young Diane del Greco, her glossy cascade of black hair blown back against the sky in her screaming birth-death agonies.

"Your father wrote this. Your mother was the model for Mina Mars. Do you know what this means?" Ari Alterhaus said.

Ash del Greco wanted more than anything to know what it meant—to know where, in fact, the hell she, or rather they, had come from.

"It means your father thought of you as a soul, as energy, as an eruption of pure spiritual force into the universe. You're here to make it all purer with your soul. The body is the last thing that matters. If it has to be destroyed to purify the spirit, then destroy it. You're the pure child of imagination, of Simon Magnus's imagination, not of your mother's body. You didn't really come from a woman. You're not really a woman, any more than I am. We aren't even human. We're what Simon Magnus is writing about, the aliens from beyond the universe, stranded here in this, this, this"—Ari Alterhaus gathered into their furiously clenched fingers through the fabric of their sweatshirt the fat that sat in a doughy ring over their waist and the adipose tissue depending from their chest—"this mud, this shit, this fucking filth."

"Then where is he?" Ash del Greco asked. "Why isn't he here?" Suddenly, they twisted with the fingers of their right hand the flesh of their left arm to remind themself of the pronouns Simon Magnus then used, the same way they twisted their arm if the name "Arielle" or the pronoun "she" ever drifted through their head in reference to their friend: "*They*, *they*, *they*, I mean. Where are they? If they're my father, my parent, I mean, then why aren't they here?"

"If you're part of their soul, why do you need their body to be here? They birthed you out of words and pictures. They don't owe you anything after that. You don't have a father or a mother. Simon Magnus is both in one, and their book gave birth to you. This is your mother *and* your father, your all-gender all-parent. *This*."

Ari Alterhaus held up the glowing tablet with *Overman 3000*'s womb-bursting climax onscreen.

In the dim pink room, as the storm rumbled and dribbled to its conclusion outside, the tablet cast its blue glow onto Ash del Greco's scarred face, making the spiral's ridges and pits look like the wind-drifted sands of a desert in moonlight.

Ash del Greco's ever-burning stomach, though mostly empty, seized and heaved. They ran from the bedroom, down the hallway, to the Alterhauses' immaculate bathroom. On their knees, on the hard, smooth tiles, aside the sunken tub in Carrera marble, they vomited into the blindingly white toilet. (It had no hard-water ring in its bowl.)

Suddenly, Ari Alterhaus came behind them. They gathered their long and thin blonde hair through their fingers to draw it out of the path of the bile. When they had all the strands of their hair bunched in their fist, they stretched their other hand out to the medicine cabinet and retrieved a pair of glistening silver scissors. As close to the scalp as they could, they severed their hair. When they were finished retching, when they had chopped off as much of their hair as could be sheared away, they guided their head from the toilet to the sunken tub, where they wet their remaining hair, lathered it in floral-smelling women's shaving cream, and, with a glistening silver razor, shaved it down to the pallid, bristling skin.

When Ash del Greco came home that night with their head shorn and their declaration that henceforth they would be "Ash" and not "Ashley," "they" and not "she," a pure flame of genderless soul and not a woman forged from mud and filth, Diane del Greco heaved back her red-tipped hand, her bracelets jangling, her pink nightgown billowing with the motion, and struck them hard across the spiral-scared face.

Ann Alterhaus responded oppositely to Ari Alterhaus's identical manifesto. Unlike Diane del Greco, whose time spent among the artistic avant-garde in cosmopolitan environs had been limited to her early and middle 20s and had ended in catastrophe, after which she'd returned, chastened, to the suburban lower middle classes from which she'd emerged, Ann Alterhaus had enjoyed from birth forward the company of other upper-middle-class professionals, to include physicians, therapists, journalists, and of course other lawyers, not to mention the grandees of the local Democratic Party establishment. Later in their acquaintance, Ash del Greco would overhear Ann Alterhaus tell someone on the phone, "The girl, or whatever, Ash, is really quite intelligent and well-spoken and may even have a bright future, given, well, you know, the family background. The mother, though, she is—and I don't mean to be rude—pure white trash."

To Ann Alterhaus's mind, her child's—no longer her daughter's—status only confirmed what she'd always suspected about their—no longer her—breadth of intellect and depth of soul, neither of which could possibly be reduced to a pretext so flimsy as "biological sex," if this even could be said to exist, and experts increasingly said it did not. Hadn't Ann Alterhaus struggled all her own life to overcome the confinement of her ambitions this putative "sex" had supposedly destined her for? Hadn't her own father, the distinguished and long-serving judge, once said to her, "We expected your brother to go to law school, not you"? Ari Alterhaus now carried Ann Alterhaus's battle deeper into enemy territory. The enemy was all everyone who believed nature to be fate, anatomy to be destiny, anyone who believed man was born to rule and woman to serve. If Ann Alterhaus, in her capacity as doctor of jurisprudence, had conquered the law governing social life on female power's behalf, then the twice-born Ari Alterhaus would conquer social life itself, simply by existing in an unsexed skin, on behalf of sex's wholesale obliteration. She offered her child her unconditional support. She even added "she/they" to her own office email signature, though she wasn't entirely convinced the grammar of the situation wouldn't decrease clarity in communication.

Ann Alterhaus was a practical woman. She both felt and enacted these insights without quite being able to articulate them. Dr. Peter Farr, the pediatrician who had been Ann Alterhaus's high-school classmate, relieved to have found a nameable reason for what he'd interpreted as the psychological distress that impeded Ari Alterhaus's physical healing from her fall out the attic window, prescribed testosterone. Ann Alterhaus was able to get Ari Alterhaus's top surgery—the redaction of the offending excrescence of flesh on the chest—scheduled without any trouble, given her own status and connections in the community, which she was happy to lord over physicians who seemed more hesitant and less enthusiastic than she thought her child's courageous transition from merely female to fully human warranted.

Ann Alterhaus had a friend from college who had become a nationally recognized journalist: Kristen Connolly. She invited Kristen Connolly to return from the nation's capital, where she worked a women's rights beat in the halls of Congress and in the White House, to her humble hometown, this former steel town become a tech and ed hub, to chronicle Ari Alterhaus's transition. When Kristen Connolly, a wiry middle-aged woman with a nose ring and magenta-framed plastic glasses, interviewed both Ash del Greco and Ari Alterhaus, they—both together and apart—kept to a prearranged script about feeling trapped in the wrong body and deploring society's gender binary. They knew this was what they were supposed to say, that these words, like magic spells, would trigger medical and legal protocols and invite the sympathy of broad-minded citizens and progressive journalists. They kept to themselves their shared commitment to liberation from the prison of the flesh. At a school assembly in the 10th grade, they, they individually and they as a pair, were summoned to the stage and applauded for their bravery, though Ash del Greco, always oversensitive to the least stimulus, could hear an undertone of boyish hooting and girlish snickering in the crowd, words like "dyke" and "freak" subliminal in the applause.

Ari Alterhaus and Ash del Greco agreed not to mention to anyone, least of all to Kristen Connolly, their private theology, their obsession with *Overman 3000*, with Ash del Greco's possible true parentage. These rather avant-garde, even antihuman sensibilities might alarm outside observers who would otherwise take their side out of nothing more religiously ambitious than a desire to appear compassionate and forward-thinking. In the article on Ari Alterhaus and Ash del Greco that eventually won her a Pulitzer Prize, Kristen Connolly quoted Ann Alterhaus: "Their fight is all our fights: against the fascist impulse to categorize and divide, an impulse that has been frighteningly dominant in our politics lately." Thoughts of this kind had not occurred to them, to Ash del Greco or to Ari Alterhaus, whether together or apart. They were not political creatures, not avid news watchers or students of public power. Ash del Greco had read another quotation somewhere in the 150 tabs open in their browser: "When the anthropologist arrives, the gods depart." At the kindly, silly, well-meaning journalist with her belated nose ring and her clownish glasses—just the kind of bathetic middle-aged woman they hoped never to become, her pale lips pursed in sincere concern above her mottled neck wattle—they, they singly and they doubly, laughed behind their hands.

Diane del Greco forbade drugs and surgeries, and she doubted in any case that her insurance would cover such interventions. "When you turn 18, you can have done whatever you can afford to pay a doctor to do to you," she said. "Until then, under *my* roof, you're not having any parts removed." They would never tell Ari Alterhaus this, but Diane del Greco's prohibition filled Ash del Greco with relief. Existing from birth in a state of low-level sickness that no doctor had ever been able to cure, even the ones who didn't diagnose the physical pain as purely psychological distress, Ash del Greco flinched from white coats and did not share Ari Alterhaus's romance with the whole panoply of medicine from pill to lancet. Ash del Greco, then early in their belated puberty, was not in any case especially endowed with what used to be called secondary sex characteristics. "You know, sweetie," Diane del Greco said once said in a mall fitting room, looking over Ash del Greco's briefly disrobed form in the mirror, "you kind of look like a boy." Diane del Greco refused to say "they" in the singular: "I didn't go to college," she said, "but even I know that's not proper English." Ash del Greco was rarely in the house anyway. Ash del Greco spent all their available time at the Alterhaus residence caring for Ari Alterhaus after their surgeries.

Ash del Greco was at the Alterhaus home for the weekend when the Sunday paper was delivered to the del Greco residence with Kristen Connolly's syndicated article on the front page, below the fold: "In a Swing-State Suburb, a Difficult Reckoning," read the headline, with the subhead: "Students Reject the Gender Binary." Diane del Greco shuffled out in her pink slippers to retrieve the paper in its plastic sleeve from the dew-soaked November lawn. In her warm kitchen, in her empty house, her coffee cooling on the counter, she stared at the article's accompanying photograph: the tall Ari Alterhaus seated, the short Ash del Greco standing, both of them bald, Ari Alterhaus wearing a tight silver mesh shirt to show off a newly streamlined torso, Ash del Greco in a baggy black sweatshirt, a look of impish satisfaction on Ari Alterhaus's almost smirking face with its plump cheeks' three-days' patchiness of beard, a look of never-to-be-appeased dissatisfaction, of restless sullenness, on Ash del Greco's. Diane del Greco, who had once dreamed of being an artist, still had an eye for the composition of pictures. Any other two people in such a posture would be touching one another—Ash del Greco, at least, should be resting an arm on the seated Ari Alterhaus's shoulder—but these two touched at no point. Diane del Greco dropped the newspaper in the kitchen sink, got the grill lighter from the drawer, and set the paper on fire. She choked and cried in the black smoke of the newsprint.

Despite the headline's "difficult reckoning," Ash del Greco and Ari Alterhaus's transition from womanhood to personhood occasioned little controversy in their vast public high school; they were so inseparable, so much a single being, that not even the most hidebound of the teachers or mischievous of the students had much trouble saying "they" of this almost always in any case doubled entity, even though the one was tall and the other short, the one fat and the other thin.

The exception was a shop teacher, Bill Goines, who never had either student in his class, and who elected to take early retirement rather than be compelled to use the plural pronoun in the singular. He told a conservative journalist—Tabi Gonzalez, a young woman in a short, tight maroon dress and spiky black stilettos who came to the school from the capital the week after Kristen Connolly to report on Ari Alterhaus and Ash del Greco for her YouTube channel, *Give Me Liberty! with Tabi Gonzalez*—that his Christian faith demanded he refuse to participate in the delusion that a person could change sex, much less exist between sexes. "It ain't natural, and it ain't what God wants," Bill Goines said, a vein pulsing bluely to the side of his buzz cut. "Look it up: Deuteronomy, chapter 22, verse 5."

To Ash del Greco, Ari Alterhaus laughed and asked what could possibly be less natural than God. To the media and to the school board, who invited them to speak about the controversy at the monthly meeting in the high-school gym, Ari Alterhaus said, without a trace of laughter in their voice, that Bill Goines's comments created an atmosphere of harm, which invited hateful violence and invalidated innate identities. Ash del Greco sat next to them and said nothing, their spiral scar aflame as if every eye in the cavernous room were on it, that barracks-like gymnasium reeking subliminally of generations of sweat. The school board members in the center of the gym and the audience on the bleachers applauded Ari Alterhaus's sincerity and bravery. Bill Goines stomped from the gym, his rubber-soled work boots squealing on the varnished boards. Tabi Gonzalez rushed toward Ari Alterhaus with her livestreaming phone held high and began to shout questions; she had to be tackled and then dragged out by school security. She left one black stiletto behind, upright, on the gym floor.

CHAPTER 7
Nullification

While Ari Alterhaus recovered from top surgery—Ash del Greco spooned applesauce into their waiting mouth above the suture smiles beneath each resettled nipple—they began, together, to research nullification. Upon hearing the theretofore unfamiliar term, Ash del Greco had asked, "Isn't that just suicide?" but Ari Alterhaus quickly turned the tablet around and invited them to read the details of the procedure. In the case of what used to be called a biological woman and was now understood to be a person assigned female at birth—though Ash del Greco and Ari Alterhaus came more ambitiously to believe that being assigned *human* at birth was more burdensome to the soul, after which the addition of gender was only a comparatively minor insult—the surgeon would perform a hysterectomy, a vaginectomy, a labioplasty, and, more than likely, the shortening of the urethra. This would create a smooth, unbroken fall of flesh from navel to perineum. Ari Alterhaus showed Ash del Greco "after" pictures and then William Blake's colored engraving, *Satan in His Original Glory*, in which the vaguely indicated diaphanous drapery around the soon-to-be-fallen angel's thighs concealed no genitals.

"Simon Magnus and Marco Cohen were both inspired by Blake. It was the only thing they agreed on apparently—one of the editors said that in some oral history of *Overman 3000*. Then I found an article on it."

Ari Alterhaus took back the tablet, toggled open a different tab, and turned it back around to show Ash del Greco the pdf: "The Marriage of Heaven and Hell: William Blake as Collaborative Intertext in *Overman 3000*." Ash del Greco's eyes widened for a moment—William Blake was *intersex*?—until "sex" resolved itself in their eyes back into "text."

Ari Alterhaus said, "It's a sign. Everything's a sign, if you know how to read."

The plan, loosely, was for both Ari Alterhaus and Ash del Greco to get what was familiarly called the nullo surgery when they turned 18. Ari Alterhaus had already secured Ann Alterhaus's permission; Ann Alterhaus didn't become one of the premier attorneys in the city by being unable to follow an idea to its logical terminus.

(When a rash paralegal in her office, Marjorie Anderson, a matronly woman of about 60 who had served the firm for over 30 years, asked Ann Alterhaus if she wouldn't mind not having grandchildren, she rounded on the older woman—rounded on her pastel yellow sweater and pastel pink pants and blonde-dyed pixie cut, on the framed photographs of various poolside or picnic-blanket children and grandchildren ringing her desk—and said, "My grandchildren are my daughter's, I mean my child's, brilliant ideas. Unlike flesh and blood, they'll live forever." Ann Alterhaus reported the paralegal to human resources for her discriminatory remark. Wanting to avoid the lengthy investigation into her conduct that human resources initiated, Marjorie Anderson took an early retirement and went to live with her son's family down South, where, reclining every day in a chaise longue overlooking the sand, watching the gulls wheel above the beach grass on the dunes and around the crown of a distant lighthouse, she found herself troubled by not one idea at all.)

Ash del Greco feared nullo surgery or any other surgery. Ever since the emergency room physician could be heard, over the clamor of the pain, quizzing their mother adversarially about how precisely her daughter had fallen on the electric burner, Ash del Greco construed doctors as equivalent to police. They were worse, in fact, than police: the police could only arrest your outer flesh, whereas doctors policed your innards, detaining your molecules, charging your corpuscles, prosecuting your viscera, imprisoning you from the inside out.

Their mother had had them back and forth to doctors for their whole childhood, seeking a cure for their perpetually unsettled stomach, their persistent lack of appetite, their frequent vomiting, their groaning ulcerous agony in the wastes of the night. No organic cause could be discovered; no chalky pink drinks or unswallowably vast pills alleviated the condition. The condition was that the world turned Ash del Greco's stomach. They would wonder as they got older why it didn't it turn everyone else's.

Diane del Greco loudly refused to take Ash del Greco to the doctor when Ash del Greco had half-heartedly requested treatment for what they tactically called their gender dysphoria, though this was not really the term, not really the problem. The problem was more accurately labeled *human* dysphoria. The logical cure for this, as Ash del Greco had intuited, was a more total nullification than the procedure Ari Alterhaus had in mind.

If there was no material remedy for Ash del Greco's materially inflamed intestines, then, they privately thought, there was certainly no material remedy for the spiritual condition they and Ari Alterhaus equally suffered and enjoyed. Ash del Greco swallowed their rising bile as Ari Alterhaus showed them more and more "before and after" nullo surgery pictures and read to them avidly from the clinical literature they'd downloaded to their tablet. Ash del Greco could not tell Ari Alterhaus of their skepticism or their fears. They, though they did comprise, apart and together, a "they," were not identical. Ari Alterhaus enjoyed the medical transfiguration of her corpus; Ash del Greco loathed the very thought.

Once, when they were reading together about Simon Magnus's methods of collaboration with various artists on their graphic novels—whether providing a script to be illustrated in the case of *Marsh Man* and *Fools' Errand*, or giving verbal instructions to the illustrator in the case of *Overman 3000*—Ari Alterhaus said, "That's exactly what I'm doing. I'm the writer, the doctors are the artists, and together we're telling a perverted science-fiction story about freeing my soul from the prison of my body."

Ari Alterhaus displayed their metamorphosis in private and in public almost as if to provoke. They wore short shorts and loose tank tops in all weather, showing off particularly the rough weave of black hairs growing along their inner thighs and on their revised chest, which had never been there before, rhyming below with the patchy beard coming in above on the chin and cheeks and neck. The beard was the reason Ari Alterhaus had punched Maddie Scholtz in the face in the hallway—Maddie Scholtz, at whose end-of-the-summer pre-high-school pool party Ari Alterhaus and Ash del Greco had met a year and a half before.

In the haste and crush between classes one day, Ari Alterhaus innocently stumbled into Maddie Scholtz and caused her to spill the iced coffee she was carrying from the cafeteria onto her new pink cashmere sweater. "Jesus Christ, watch where you're going!" Maddie Scholtz squealed. She stared in outrage down at the spreading brown stain on the pink cashmere as everyone who saw the accident began to laugh and clap. She added, more quietly, almost hissing, as Ari Alterhaus spread their arms in a gesture of apology and no-harm-intended, "You disgusting fucking neckbeard freak."

Ari Alterhaus felt a surge of rage like nothing they'd ever before experienced. They clenched one of their upraised hands into a fist and shot their fist forward into Maddie Scholtz's pert pink nose. Her nose proceeded to spray bright blood onto her new pink cashmere sweater. The crowd went silent for a moment as Maddie Scholtz, doubly stained, clutched her bleeding face and sobbed, blood running out from between her fingers. Ash del Greco was standing behind Ari Alterhaus the whole time but couldn't bring themself to do anything, nor were they sure what they ought to have done.

Two male football players had been walking on either side of Maddie Scholtz and paying her their teasing obeisances. After the blow, they stepped forward to face Ari Alterhaus. They looked down at their paunchy, patchily bearded classmate: Ari Alterhaus in a tank top and tight shorts, blushing and nervous, rubbing the knuckles of their offending hand abashedly, sneakers turned shyly inward, one sock pink, the other blue. The athletes stood two heads taller than Ari Alterhaus and hesitated among varying codes of etiquette and law, as well as the confusion of their own senses. They were never to hit a girl, their fathers and coaches had told them. This was not a girl, the school had told them. Still, this was a more or less girl-sized person who would wither under their pummeling. Then again, this person who was not a girl had committed a masculine act of aggression against a girl. Girls fought each other, sure, but they slapped and pulled hair and tore clothing; they didn't aim fists at faces. This called—did it not?—for masculine reprisal. Arguing against this unofficial code of conduct was the fact that, officially, they risked their place on the team, risked suspension or expulsion, risked criminal penalties even, if they laid hands on anybody at all—girl, boy, whatever. Not to mention the complicating factor of this person's status, announced at the school assembly, as "nonbinary," which might render them liable, if they laid hands on their classmate, for some kind of civil rights violation. All these discordant thoughts, clattering in the boys' minds at once beneath their conscious awareness, froze them both in place for almost a minute, musing over Ari Alterhaus as Maddie Scholtz wept and bled and cried, "Will you guys fucking do something?" The athletes were relieved as five teachers ran up simultaneously and took their own rather hesitant charge of the situation when they saw who had punched whom and learned from the bystanders for what reason.

Ann Alterhaus arrived within the hour to sort it all out: she would pay whatever of Maddie Scholtz's medical bills happened not to be covered by the Scholtzes' insurance plan and would agree not even to whisper terms like "hate speech," "hate crime," or "unsafe learning environment" as long as no assault charges were pressed and no punishment above the reasonable level of a three-day suspension was levied against Ari Alterhaus.

In the car, on the way to the doctor to get Ari Alterhaus's hand X-rayed, Ann Alterhaus said, "It's never too late for a bigot to learn to watch her mouth, is it?" Ari Alterhaus and Ash del Greco sat in the back seat of the car together, not touching.

Later, as they sat together on Ari Alterhaus's bed, scanning the internet for news or even social media chatter about the altercation, Ash del Greco said, "Why did you do it?"

"I just got a feeling. It was like some energy came up out of the ground and went up through my feet and into the middle of my body and then came out of my hand. I couldn't *not* do it."

Ari Alterhaus pushed the tablet away and turned to face Ash del Greco; Ash del Greco couldn't bring themself to meet their eyes.

"The way I sometimes feel when you're just sitting there," Ari Alterhaus said. "Your face, it's just so fucking ugly, so ugly that I think it's the most beautiful thing I've ever seen in my life."

Ari Alterhaus trailed off but raised both hands and took Ash del Greco's face roughly between them. The brace Ari Alterhaus wore on their hand to treat their bruised knuckles abraded the spiral scar on Ash del Greco's cheek. Ash del Greco felt fear, felt disgust, felt desire, felt something unnameable that was both pain and not pain crawling down in the coils of their ever-inflamed intestine. Ash del Greco leapt from the bed and ran to throw up, next to the sunken tub in Carrera marble. On the internet, no one mentioned the punch in the school hallway, at least not on a public channel; luckily, no one had thought to record it.

They were, singly and together, what were called lurkers, not what were called posters, on internet fora. On Ari Alterhaus's bed, they cheered on the anonymous commentators who attacked Simon Magnus's critics. The release of the movies based on Simon Magnus's works toward the end of the first decade of the present century, coinciding with the launch of social media, sparked an intense backlash against the author for portraying gay sex, cross-dressing, and the embodied state of femininity in a negative light. "We Need to Talk about Pop Culture's Simon Magnus Problem" was a representative headline at the once-popular feminist gossip website Salome.com, this after Simon Magnus had fallen silent for more than a decade. Hating Simon Magnus, even as the Ratman and Overman movies inspired by Simon Magnus's books opened to global success, worked practically as a shibboleth signifying good taste among sophisticates in the world of progressive media criticism.

News of Simon Magnus's transition from male to genderfluid or nonbinary, of Simon Magnus's move first from "he" to "they," and then from "they" to "Simon Magnus," led to revaluations of the work's subversive potential, however, especially when read in sequence. When Marsh Man donned his mother's wedding dress to avenge himself upon her murderers, this signified an early, romantic moment of queered subjectivity rising against an unjust world. The Fool's tutu-clad rape of Sparrow represented by contrast a regression to self-hatred, the author no longer identifying powerfully with the mother but lashing out at the feminized boy he-they-Simon-Magnus had been. Finally, Mina Mars's exploding womb, which annihilated nature and technology at once, signified what but the triumph of pure impersonal desire over the brute world of matter whose "laws" conservatives of both a religious and a scientific bent were always asserting, even though pure impersonal desire was in fact the only law operating in the cosmos. This was how Ash del Greco and Ari Alterhaus read the books; this is how they, together and apart, read the world.

The open haters of Simon Magnus had, by the time Ash del Greco began speculating that Simon Magnus might be their mother-father, dwindled to groups no cultural sophisticates took seriously, like Christian conservatives outraged at the work's avant-garde, anti-bourgeois, and anti-traditional sex and violence, or old-fashioned feminists still convinced of the coherence of the category "woman" and of its consequent need for special social, political, and artistic protection against slippery misogynistic operators and biologically male infiltrators like Simon Magnus.

Ash del Greco and Ari Alterhaus knew they were not women. What was a woman? Diane del Greco might be the most representative specimen in their eyes: an overgrown bolus of humid flesh caught disruptively and without intelligence in the teeth of the world's machine. You'd cut off anything not to have to grow up to become *that*, Ari Alterhaus and Ash del Greco thought, except that Ash del Greco had already once offered up their flesh on the altar of the ideal—they had the scar to show for it—and didn't intend to do so again, no matter how appealing Ari Alterhaus found the glint of the scalpel. Ann Alterhaus, on the other hand, they could respect: trim as a blade in her navy blue suit, she was already halfway to what they were, to what they wanted to be.

They knew they lived in the same city as Simon Magnus. They knew how to find even occluded addresses online, especially since Ari Alterhaus secretly also knew AnneAlterhaus's passwords to the various databases she was able to access as an attorney. They knew that Simon Magnus, not a man but a mere *person*, had neither written those books nor fathered Ash del Greco, because they knew we were not only not men and women but also, in our best moments, not persons at all. We were, rather, vectors of spiritual force, channels of energy that struck like lightning to blast the earth. They decided, therefore, that there would be no point in meeting Simon Magnus.

They did once take the bus into the city and then up toward the university campus, however. They sat for hours on a bench at a bus stop across from the building that housed Simon Magnus's small studio apartment. When Simon Magnus came into view in the dimming late-winter afternoon, walking from campus toward the building after a day of teaching, an inconspicuous man in a long gray coat with thinning, graying hair, they held up their phones in front of them and posed as if for selfies except that they'd activated the rear-facing cameras. Though Simon Magnus looked like any man on the street, they took Simon Magnus's picture 20 or 30 times.

CHAPTER 8
The Moon

The pandemic came during their junior year in high school and relegated their friendship entirely to the online world.

In the months before in-person schooling shut down, they'd been planning, singly and together, a pronoun change. A year and a half since their announcement of their nonbinarism, their they/themism, every Tom, Dick, and Deborah in the high school now seemed to be going the "they" route. Even the blonde girls in the Model UN and the FBLA—even Maddie Scholtz herself, Maddie Scholtz of the end-of-the-summer pool party and the bloody cashmere sweater—were magnanimously putting "she/they" into their email signatures and social profiles, while many of the (female) teachers, proffering pronoun stickers, also seemed attracted to the polite expansiveness of "she/they." Ari Alterhaus and Ash del Greco judged this less an expansion of gender than an evasion of it. Whatever the "they" signifier had once been meant to signify to them, to them singly and to them collectively, whatever *Overman*-inspired reconfiguration of the flesh by the spirit they'd intended to achieve, it now spelled, as far as they were concerned, the new normative, the new dominant, the new conformist. "She/they," they thought, was nothing more than a politically advantageous concession to a never-enacted "but maybe I'm not" allowing a blonde girl's cow-eyed blonde-girlness to persist amid queer critique, while, still worse, "they/them" had become the garbage bag of a reified third sex into which to dump the school's freaks and losers and to forget about they/them.

What pronoun would be more impersonal than "they," would force a confrontation with mind's superiority to matter? Some of their classmates took up what were called neopronouns, like "xi/xir," but leaving the English language seemed too literal to them, them singly and them together. Then one day, they had it: sitting on Ari Alterhaus's bed with their tablet between them, they faced each other and said as one, "*It!*" Only "it/its" seemed provocative enough in its nihilistic impersonality to recover their mission's original astringency.

They, individually and doubly, planned to unveil this pronoun shift when they attended the next meeting of the school's Rainbow Alliance. The organization's other members looked on them warily, with cold politeness, even though they were ostensibly their fellow "queer kids." This was how the club's members tended to describe themselves; Ari Alterhaus and Ash del Greco judged it a contemptibly auto-infantilizing locution and further judged the club's members as unserious posers who would probably be married with children inside of 15 years.

Afraid of them, of them together and of them apart, the members of the Rainbow Alliance tended to avoid Ari Alterhaus and Ash del Greco, who had always, since the ninth grade, sat by themselves, in a conspiracy of two, at lunch. Ash del Greco *had* once overheard in the lunch room the president of the Rainbow Alliance, a beskirted demiboy of what were called weeb tendencies, refer to them—that is, to Ash del Greco, and because of the scar—as *uzumaki*, and then laugh nervously.

At one meeting, the Rainbow Alliance's vice president and treasurer—an impeccably dressed and impeccably coiffed blonde trans girl in pink and a stocky and muscular trans boy in a black leather jacket, respectively—had teamed up to accuse Ash del Greco and Ari Alterhaus of appropriating the struggles of the genuinely gender dysphoric, of those who just wanted to live safe lives as men and women the way other men and women did, and for what? "For the purposes," the treasurer declaimed, "of some strange art project that was making every queer kid in the school look like a sick fucking joke." The girl wept; the boy raged. The organization's other members, in the interests of absolute tolerance, and perhaps also in the interests of fear, stopped the discussion before Ari Alterhaus and Ash del Greco could reply to their accusers. Under the tirade of the vice president and treasurer, the former's face running with purple mascara as she murmured into a Kleenex, "All I wanted was to be a regular girl," Ash del Greco and Ari Alterhaus only smirked. They couldn't imagine wanting to be a regular *anything* and felt the utmost contempt for those who did. Ari Alterhaus and Ash del Greco found this boy-become-girl and girl-become-boy, no less than their cis counterparts among the jocks and the cheerleaders, to be the sad captives of the same gender binary the god of absolute otherness they served would eventually abolish on this prison called earth, just like at the end of *Overman 3000*. They looked forward to the stricken faces the vice president and treasurer would wear when they heard of the shift Ash del Greco and Ari Alterhaus proposed: the shift from "they/them" to "it/its."

The onset of remote learning delayed these plans indefinitely. Ann Alterhaus believed Ari Alterhaus to be uniquely vulnerable to viral contagion and didn't let them leave the house or receive visitors at all once the emergency had been declared. Ash del Greco now saw Ari Alterhaus only during online video calls, though they kept up a steady stream of texting.

Six months into Ari Alterhaus's confinement, as another online school year bore down on the end of summer, Ash del Greco could see the toll of the isolation in their video calls, which happened, in any case, with less and less frequency. Ari Alterhaus had gained what looked like 100 pounds on their body, even as, paradoxically, their patchily bearded face became sallow and wasted and pocked with acne or even sores.

Ari Alterhaus also spoke in increasingly cold and apocalyptic tones. They said their time had come to an end. While there was still such a thing on earth as freedom of movement and a public stage, their chemical and surgical and verbal transformation of their own body sufficed to make their point about the sovereignty of spirit over flesh. Now, however, living entirely rather than mostly in the data stream, a placeless place where there was no flesh, they—Ari Alterhaus individually, but everyone else on earth, too—were dead already: already in heaven. It seemed cruel in these circumstances to continue to live inside the farce that was the prison of the flesh.

Ash del Greco didn't know how to respond to these monotone monologues, spoken through clenched teeth on their laptop screen in their dark bedroom while Diane del Greco slept across the upstairs hall, her sleep mask over her eyes. Without afternoons and evenings and weekends to spend in Ari Alterhaus's bedroom, and with their eyes already screen-scorched in their sockets by eight hours a day of online school, which tended to mean reading whatever they found interesting on the internet while online school transpired, Ash del Greco spent more time than ever before reading print books. Diane del Greco had allowed Ash del Greco to add books to their online orders of food, toiletries, and clothes during those months the world shut down. "As long as they're cheap," she admonished. What was cheaper than paperbacks of the public-domain classics that piqued Ash del Greco's interests?

Ash del Greco still hadn't quite made their peace with novels. They never would, since the linear narrative of a stable self seemed untrue to their own radically discontinuous self-experience. They dutifully attempted in those dull pandemic days to read the likes of Austen and Dickens and Tolstoy and Flaubert and Wharton, but they couldn't get anywhere with those books. They would put them down and pick them up later with their memory of the plot and the characters totally wiped clean; they would have to reread up to the place they'd left off until they found they had read the first 30 pages three times. They finally threw the books across the room and eventually, when things opened back up, told Diane del Greco to give them to Goodwill.

"This is a great book, though," Diane del Greco said one Sunday morning, bending down to pick *The House of Mirth* off the top of the pile of discarded classics while she was in Ash del Greco's room to gather the laundry.

"*You* read *that*?" Ash del Greco said to their mother.

In her hot-pink nightgown and hot-pink slippers, Diane del Greco cocked one leg forward into a sassy contrapposto, put one fist to her ample hip, tossed her long hair, still black in her mid 40s, and said, "I wasn't always this suburban mother you see here before you. I used to hang out with *intellectuals*." Ash del Greco was thinking that this startling fact only proved their point about novels and the instability of the self exactly; they therefore missed Diane del Greco's murmured addendum, as her posture slackened: "It was the worst fucking mistake of my life."

By the summer before their senior year of high school, Ash del Greco liked radical poets (Blake, Dickinson, Eliot) and radically poetic anti-philosophers (Nietzsche, Wittgenstein, Deleuze) and antinovelists (Melville, Kafka, Joyce)—anybody who wrote a book you could pick up, open at random, and find yourself shot with some projectile into the fat and folds of your brain, something to carry with you all day or for the rest of your life, leaching nutritious toxins into your groundwater. These were the books Ash del Greco sought out that summer when they began taking the bus in their black medical mask to haunt used bookstores in the city after what they called nonessential businesses reopened. Ash del Greco rarely read a book cover to cover, though they might, while browsing, eventually read every page, and, in that way, they had continued to read online even while reading on paper, since "online" named not a technology but a state of the soul, one they had been born into and would never really exit—thus disproving somewhat, they worried, their point about novels and the instability of the self, since this part of themself they could not alter by will.

What, too, of her decision—yes, *her* decision—a decision she'd made beneath her own awareness before she brought it to consciousness and uttered it to herself, that, for her at least, she no longer wanted to hand her sense of herself over to willed and bureaucratically enforced alterations of language. Still less would she become a willing servant of the very doctors who thought, in the pandemic days, that the human being *per se* was nothing more than a vector of disease, the doctors on TV commanding that this or that business remain closed, this or that population be locked down, smug in their white coats, wanting to turn the whole world white so that not a speck of what was different from themselves might survive. Ash del Greco wouldn't have given them the satisfaction of wearing a mask, either, except that she loved to go undetected; she would have masked her whole head in black like Undergirl if she could have. She always drew whatever of the spiral scar her mask concealed, however, since this was the first sign of her difference she had ever elected to wear, even if she hadn't known at the age of five that this was what she was doing: the first sign of her allegiance to heaven on earth.

Of the decision to return to "she/her," she eventually did inform herself, but she hadn't yet told Ari Alterhaus; she would never get the chance to tell them either. On that call during which Ari Alterhaus spoke of making literally true their "dead already" status, Ash del Greco recalled something she'd once read online about how to stop yourself from killing yourself: *do anything else*. Since you were willing to take the most drastic step of all, the final step, the step that brought you across a threshold you would never be able to recross, at least not in the flesh, then why not take the less drastic step of doing something, *anything*, you wanted to do, damn the consequences, since any consequence would be less consequential than death? Do anything at all, on the off chance that your act might, in the event, seduce you back into some romance, however slight, with the living world. Quit your job, drop out of school, leave your wife, stop drinking, start drinking, move to another city, take a trip around the world even if you have to do it with your last penny—that type of thing. "Okay," she said to Ari Alterhaus when Ari Alterhaus had said they were dead already, "but before you do that, do *anything* else."

Three days later, on a Saturday afternoon, Ari Alterhaus sent Ash del Greco a text: "meet me at the pool, three tonight." This was still the heart of the first pandemic summer. The public pool—the same one where Maddie Scholtz's end-of-the-summer pool party had been held three years before, the party where Ash del Greco and Ari Alterhaus had met—was closed for the season; not only was it drained, but there was talk among the borough leadership of filling it with sand or cement, though they never followed through on this particular emergency measure.

How was she to get to the pool at three in the morning? Though more than halfway through her 17th year, she hadn't bothered with her driver's license: she planned to live in the city when she grew up, and, anyway, before the pandemic at least, her mother or Ann Alterhaus had driven her everywhere she needed to go. Buses weren't running at that hour. She didn't yet have a credit card or a job and didn't really grasp the logistics, in any case, of the various ways of summoning a car.

In the end, she walked: three miles over sidewalkless suburban terrain and one crossing of a highway that banned pedestrians and proved treacherously car-addled even in the dead waste and middle of the night. She'd brought her phone along for walking directions to the pool, but as soon as she set out, the screen began to glitch and then went black. She had to find her way on her own. Even at that hour, the summer heat, rising out of the cement and asphalt, seemed to be cooking her from her sticky rubber shoe soles up, until she felt her face was on fire, the spiral burning red on her cheek. The moon, following her on her path, was full; it hung heavy and reddish in the sky, its pockmarked landscape, she thought, its lunar scarring, almost visible to the naked eye, ruthlessly exposed by the glare of the sun on the other side of the earth. It was late summer, when the grass had been scorched rusty yellow, when the insects had swelled monstrously to drift like droning dirigibles at eye level. Wavering clouds of gnats circled her itching head for the whole of her sweating march through the streetlight dark.

When she got to the pool, she was overheated, dehydrated, and dizzy; her head felt 100 miles above her feet, her stomach red as a red-hot coil somewhere between them, floating alone over the earth. She found Ari Alterhaus leaning against the locked chain-link fence that sequestered the empty pool. Ari Alterhaus's head shone, yellowish, in the moonlight; they'd shaved their head and their face, and it floated palely, moon-like, over their black clothes that blended into the night.

"How did you get here?" Ash del Greco asked.

Ari Alterhaus didn't answer but just took Ash del Greco by the hand and pulled her along over the stiff, hot, dry grass. Ari Alterhaus almost ran despite the sallow complexion and spreading bulk their long confinement had brought on. In their pocket, Ari Alterhaus had a jingling ring of keys. They, singly, let them, doubly, into the front entrance, and then they, singly, used another key to open a control closet; they disappeared inside for a moment. Ash del Greco, even from the entrance behind the changing rooms, themselves still divided in a remnant of the old regime into "male" and "female," sensed the lights inside the empty pool burst on with an electric rush. Ari Alterhaus reappeared, took Ash del Greco's hand again—they had never touched her like this before, had barely ever touched her at all—and led her through the changing rooms and out to the pool.

The sunken square in the earth, illuminated by the incandescents on its inner walls, glowed sea green against the purplish sky. Heat lightning crackled silently on the far horizon. Ash del Greco, faint and dizzy, flashed on imagery from Simon Magnus's graphic novels: the writhing ascension of the pale green MaxMullermeat over the storm-struck plain, Ratman chasing the gaudily dressed Fool through the labyrinth of a Gothic City cathedral as the police's klieg lights flooded in bright shafts through the stained glass, Marsh Man embowering his lover at midnight in a field of bioluminescent saprophytes.

"Won't someone see?" Ash del Greco weakly asked as Ari Alterhaus led her over to the shallow end of the empty pool and down into the glowing, sea-green pit.

"It's three in the morning. Nobody's awake but us."

They walked to the deep end and sat next to one another in the shadow of the diving board, against the high wall at the empty pool's bottom. The bottom was made of rough, dusty cement. Ari Alterhaus pulled a small plastic bag out of their pocket. Inside were two pills, caplets, iridescent, a shimmering, pulsating, tessellating every-color and no-color that made Ash del Greco feel she was hallucinating just to look at it.

"Ann got afraid the hormone situation was having a bad effect on me. She danced around it because I promised to call CPS or tell the school or go public with it online, you know, 'Prestigious Progressive Lawyer Refuses to Affirm Child's Gender,' not the kind of headline someone like Ann wants. She knows my doctor, though, I think they went to high school together or something, she hates him, she told me he was a pathetic pussy, not in so many words, he acts like a little kid around her, but I think she got him to lower the dose or replace it with sugar pills or something. It didn't feel the same anymore. I wasn't raging all the time. I felt better when I was raging, being angry and horny and scared was better than just being scared. I started ordering stuff online. First just the T, but than I decided to see what else was available."

"You don't have a credit card."

"You don't need a credit card when you have body parts you can take pictures and videos of. They would send the stuff inside books or toys with fake return addresses. I just told Ann they were gifts from people I knew online or friends from school. She said, 'You don't have any friends besides Ashley,' but she got too embarrassed over using your deadname to ask me any more questions. I could see she was suspicious though. Like I said, it was just T at first, but they said these are something special."

Ari Alterhaus held out their phone and showed Ash del Greco text messages to themself from someone with the contact name ∞. ∞ wrote, "thesell fuck u up in the best way...the way gods fucked up...u ever read the bible? gods really fucked up."

"Who? Who sent it?" Ash del Greco wanted to know. "Who is, is..." Ash del Greco trailed off, unsure for a moment about how the contact name was to be pronounced, though she knew what it meant from *Overman 3000*. "Who," she finally asked, "is 'Infinity'?"

"Who's anybody?" Ari Alterhaus said. They shrugged and then threw one of the pills back. They leaned their shorn head against the greenish pool wall to wait.

Before she could think better of it, Ash del Greco took the other pill from the plastic bag on Ari Alterhaus's lap and put it into her mouth. She never could swallow any pill, not even with gallons of water; it always got caught somehow under her tongue or in her upper teeth, or it would get lodged in the back of her throat, gag her, and then get spewed back out on a flood tide of stomach acid. Instead of even trying, she crushed the caplet between her molars and felt the instant scorching of a thick liquid she imagined to be the color of the aurora borealis. Her whole face caught fire. Even the backs of her eyes seemed to be burning. She stood and staggered forward, thinking somehow to run from the invader of her own body, but there was nowhere to run from herself. She collapsed toward the middle of the pool, next to the drain.

No, she thought, she had only mistaken this dark green circle in the middle of the pale green pool bottom for the drain. Instead, she found a snake at rest in its coils—at rest until her fall disturbed it. It lifted its sleek head from its circle of neat complications and waved its pink tongue at her like a battle standard.

Ari Alterhaus walked toward them—toward her and the snake—slowly, wavering, her black clothes lunar-dusted with the pale green grit of the pool bottom. Ari Alterhaus lowered themself, their lately acquired bulk, into the circle of their crossing legs. Ash del Greco struggled and sat up. They faced each other across the agitated snake as it anxiously tongued the air.

Ari Alterhaus disappeared. Ash del Greco could no longer see the sallow shaved face, the body draped in black. Instead, a standing jet of flame, blackly pink like the sky in the header image of the *Notes from Undergirl* blog, faced her.

"What, what, are you?" Ash del Greco stammered.

"What am I? What are *you*?"

Ash del Greco looked down at her own body and didn't find a body at all but a column the glowing flame-gray color of red-hot metal.

"What's anybody?" Ari Alterhaus and Ash del Greco said in unison.

The snake between them had become a geometrically perfect spiral rotating in the center of the pool, in the center of the universe, directly below the pock-marked moon overhead. They each leaned over the snake in unison to do what they had never done before, what neither would have thought safe or kind to do with their own and one another's bodies—infinitely clumsy and shameful and wounded and wounding as bodies were. They kissed.

Ash del Greco's red-hot metal flame burned away some of the blackly pink neon fog of Ari Alterhaus, and the blackly pink fog of Ari Alterhaus cooled and quenched some of Ash del Greco's red-hot metal flame. The explosive agony of their souls sent eruptions of smoke and steam up into the night, carried to the moon on their moans, until they each fell back in delirium.

The snake took advantage of their confusion and slipped away across the moonscape of the floodlit pool bottom in panic-whipped undulations.

At some indistinctly later moment, Ash del Greco's eyes broke open. Cautiously, she brought her hand up before her disoriented face and found not a column of flame-lit metal but rather a small palm scored and gritted with the rough concrete she'd been sleeping on. She sat up. Ari Alterhaus was nowhere to be seen. The moon, smaller and cooler now, drifted down toward the horizon. She scrambled to her feet and hurried home as fast as her short, unsteady legs could carry her through the flybuzz dog-day four-in-the-morning heat. She dropped onto her bed just as the sun came up; she didn't even take her shoes off. She fell into the heaviest, most dreamless sleep she'd ever slept in her life.

She was still sleeping the next day at noon. She only forced herself awake because Diane del Greco was kneeling at her bedside and shaking her shoulder.

"Did somebody already tell you?" her mother asked. "Is that why you won't wake up?"

"Tell me what?"

"You really don't know?"

"What is it?" Ash del Greco sat up, her heart beginning to pound. "Tell me!" she said, but she already knew.

"I just got off the phone with Angie Scholtz. She heard it directly from Ann. It's your friend—Arielle. I'm sorry, sweetie, but she's gone. She died in her sleep last night."

CHAPTER 9
Revision

The cause of Ari Alterhaus's death was in dispute, the autopsy inconclusive. Aneurysm, blood clot, heart murmur—any or all? Caused by what: stress, corpulence, depression, congenital defect, any number of the hormones and drugs found in their system? Had they contracted an asymptomatic variant of the virus that silently thickened their blood?

Ann Alterhaus prepared to bring suit for malpractice against Dr. Peter Farr. His retention of an attorney, coupled with monetary losses occasioned by his clinic's having to be closed during the pandemic, bankrupted his practice; he also suffered reputational damage from Ann Alterhaus's insinuations about his mistreatment of her transgender child in the press and on social media. #justiceforari and #firefarr both briefly trended amid the other social justice causes of that fiery first pandemic summer. "There's no one to fire me," he found himself murmuring at his phone one day as he sat among the disordered moving boxes in his soon-to-be-shuttered office. His wife discovered him one Sunday morning: his feet swung in almost imperceptible circles while his head dangled broken at the end of a colorful braid of neckties tied to a rafter in the basement.

Ann Alterhaus held a private burial for Ari Alterhaus. When school resumed at the end of August, the first two weeks were conducted online, what they called remote learning, due to high community infection rates. Ash del Greco herself had remained in bed with some intermittent fever she'd had since the day she learned Ari Alterhaus had died. Diane del Greco enlisted telemedicine, but the doctor onscreen, wearing a surgical mask in his clinic's empty office, prescribed only rest. The school held a memorial tribute to Ari Alterhaus on video. As the vice principal solemnly vowed to "protect the mental health of the school's 2SLGBTQQIA+ community," Ash del Greco, her stomach burning, shut her laptop and crawled from her bedroom to vomit.

On her knees, her forehead on the cool toilet seat, crying on the yellow-tiled bathroom floor and staring along the thick greenish-black grime that lined the grout, she thought about how she had no evidence to prove, even if only to herself, that she had gone to the public pool in the middle of the night—the night Ari Alterhaus died. She had searched the seat of the jeans she'd worn that night, as well as the crevices in the treads of her shoe soles, for traces of the pale cement dust she recalled coating the pool bottom, but she couldn't find anything. Her phone was working again, but the final text from Ari Alterhaus inviting her to the pool had vanished, and the health app showed no record of a six-mile round-trip walk on the night in question. Ari Alterhaus was gone from her, as if they—they singly and they together—had never been.

Had she caused Ari Alterhaus's death? The pandemic-enforced pause on their inseparability had given Ash del Greco a certain reprieve, a certain relief, room to explore other possibilities of her nature, including, though she had never quite communicated this to Ari Alterhaus in so many words, the possibility that "they/them" (or, as it happened, "it/its") was an unnecessary verbal encumbrance, that "she" could mean anything at all, that *amor fati*—she had been listening to podcasts about Nietzsche at double speed—rather than surgical redaction might be the more dignified way to deal with what she knew she was not supposed to call the natal sex of her body. (Not that anyone would ever, she understood, take her, with her oversized head and meager figure and obdurately esoteric interests and relative lack of sexual appetite, or any other appetite, for a typical specimen of "woman.") Had these silent defections, these spiritual amputations in lieu of physical ones, murdered her best friend, her other self? Now that Ari Alterhaus was gone forever, with no possibility of return, Ash del Greco wanted nothing more in this life than to have them back again, them singly and them together. So little did she want anything else—food for one: she scarcely ate a bite for weeks—that she lay awake feverishly thinking of ways to die, though none seemed sure enough. The snake from the drained pool bottom slithered in the lunar dust of her half-waking dreams.

It was then, at the nadir of her despair, that she found manifestation—the same way most people find it. In the sleepless, febrile wastes of night, the YouTube algorithm delivered to her, on what basis she could not discern since she had only been watching material on literature and philosophy, a video titled *Can YOU Have the Impossible? YES!* What she wanted *was* impossible—Ari Alterhaus back from the dead—so, the screen blurring through the hot film of her never-absent tears, she clicked.

A skinny blonde woman in her 20s with glittering skin filmed herself with a high-stretched arm as she strolled through a botanical garden. She said, "Hellllll-ooooo, my beautiful angels! Welcome or welcome back to *Maren's Dream Life*." She spun in her sandals among the liana and ferns, beneath the palms and pines, through steam-hung jungle rooms and crisp-aired deciduous galleries, her long pleated pink skirt flaring out, her sunglasses giving back the reflection of the phone in her high left hand.

She said, "Listen, there's absolutely no reason to tolerate a single thing you don't want. Your SP coming in hot and cold—or even involved with a 3P? Your bank app showing only five dollars left in your account? Your boss texting to say they don't have the funds to renew your contract? Say to yourself, 'Not on *my* phone!' Don't even look at your phone. Remember, never check the 3D for evidence. Never, never, never. All you need to connect with the 4D directly is up here!"

She tapped her temple with two fingers like someone miming suicide.

"When you saturate your subconscious with affirmations, it has no choice but to prove them true in your physical reality. Look it up, it's called the reticular activating system. If you did better in physics than in biology—I manifested As in both, because I'm a STEM girly, what can I say?—then look up quantum entanglement. It's called *reality shifting*, baby! Why are you *not* shifting into your desired reality *today*? God-Source-Universe will give you the best when you ask for the best. For my Christian peeps, it's called Mark, chapter 11, verse 24: 'Whatever things ye desire when ye pray, believe that ye receive them, and ye shall have them.' The CIA even studied this shit, pardon my language. Do you think the CIA messes around? Look it up! It's a declassified document. You didn't hear it from me, but google 'CIA Gateway Process.' I mean, what do you have to lose? Look at my life: three years ago I was stuck in my grandparents' house in the middle of nowhere. I was overweight, I couldn't get one boy to give me the time of day, I didn't have a cent to my name. All I had was cystic acne! Let's be honest, girls and gays, I was one busted-ass B. Now I live in paradise, I have the job of my dreams, I'm in perfect health, and the SPs are lining up as fast as I can reject them! Any man who wants to get with me needs to bring that six-six-six to the table: six figures, six feet, and—if you know what I mean, girlies—six inches."

She bowed her free hand under her chin and pursed her pink lips. She blew a kiss at the screen.

"Now listen, loves, I'm proud of how far I came, so I wouldn't change one thing about my past. You might not feel the same way, though. Maybe you believe you shouldn't have had to experience those traumas in your early life, like abusive parents or growing up in poverty or, like, not being able to afford cosmetics. Maybe it's the recent past that has you down. Maybe SP ghosted you last night, or maybe you bombed your O-Chem test this afternoon. Do you have to accept that shit? Girlie, you do *not*. Deadass. Dead. Ass."

She lowered her sunglasses, made her face stern, and stared directly into her phone.

"Look at me. Dead, period. Ass, period."

She raised her sunglasses again and resumed smiling, resumed twirling. Hothouse wisteria stirred purply with the wind of her passing.

"Now, in today's video, I want to talk to you about the most exciting and mysterious of all manifestation techniques. I bet you know which one I mean: *revision*. Even hardcore manifestors are sometimes skeptical of this one. 'Sure, bestie,' they'll say, 'the future is unwritten—but the *past*? We can't change the past!' The past *is* written, though! Remember the basic law of manifestation: creation is finished, just like Neville said. You want to go against our boy Neville? I didn't think so. The whole structure of the multiverse is already in place. The mansion is built, baby: we just get to decide which room we want to live in. I'm going to teach you how to change your whole-ass past today, angels, and I even have the cuh-raziest client success story I've ever shared on this channel."

Ash del Greco, a quick study, only needed half an hour to learn this field of learning's lexicon: "SP" meant "specific person," usually a love interest, the main desideratum of manifestation's mostly young female practitioners, with money, beauty, and status not far behind; "3P" was the dreaded "third party," the specific person's other love interest blocking the manifestor's romantic approach; and "3D" and "4D" were the third and fourth dimensions, respectively, the former the physical realm of length-breadth-width we mistakenly call reality, the latter the metaphysical domain of thought where the eternal whole of reality can be beheld and reshaped in its completion. "Manifestation" itself, then, was the use of mental techniques, like the visualization of desired scenarios or the repetition of affirmative phrases, to bring one's malleable 3D into alignment with wherever in the multiversal 4D one wished to repose. Say to yourself, "I'm a millionaire," a million times, or visualize your SP swooning into your arms every night before you fall asleep, and your three-dimensional quotidian experience would have no choice but to "conform"—"conform" being another term of art—to your newly asserted fourth-dimensional consciousness. "Revision," it transpired, simply applied this principle to the past as well as to the future: why not be—why not always already have been—a millionaire and SP's wife yesterday as well as tomorrow?

Ash del Greco would only ever partially comprehend the syncretic metaphysics of manifestation, despite eventually watching what must have been 1000s of hours of online video content about the subject before deciding to make her own. (She sometimes asked herself what other potentially life-altering and extraordinarily vast trenches and culverts existed unbeknownst to her in the unmappable ocean of "online.") 3D and 4D she already knew as concepts of long occult standing from her maybe-parent Simon Magnus's magnum opus *Overman 3000.* She understood the distinction between sovereign mind and ancillary world to be also, under various names, spiritual principles with a lengthy pedigree, found not only in the disreputable annals of the magicians but also, for example, in the dialogues of Plato or the Gospel of John. How the always already completed structure of space-time admitted manipulation either of the illusory future or the equally illusory past, however, she could never quite grasp except to tell herself that it was the structure of absolutely everything, an "everything" that made no division between actual and potential. Though the religious stigmatized manifestation as "witchcraft" and scientists deemed it "irrational," the manifestation gurus were always quick to supply both quotations from the Bible and the Buddha *and* citations of quantum physics and neuropsychiatry in support of their arguments.

In manifestation, when shorn of its upbeat New Age tones, she eventually recognized the metaphysics that she and Ari Alterhaus had spun at home in the former girl's bedroom, largely from scraps of poetry and philosophy and the aesthetic mood of blogs and comics. To see these ideas now in the hands of pretty blonde girls in botanical gardens—well, it was no less surprising, if also no less revolting, than to have found, back when high school was held in person, Maddie Scholtz sporting a *SHE/THEY* sticker on her creamy pink sweater as she strolled through the corridor on her way to the Model UN conference.

Ash del Greco, at the age of 17, knew enough about everything to know you could never prove anything. She didn't worry about making sense, therefore. Reason had nothing to do with the night she discovered *Maren's Dream Life,* one of those endless, sleepless nights after Ari Alterhaus's death, when her body shook with uncontrollable sobs and her eyes overflowed with tears in a totally involuntary way akin to her frequent vomiting, as if she were subject to some invisible beast shaking her back and forth in its teeth. She knew she would only stop quaking and crying if she could have Ari Alterhaus, whom she had betrayed by believing she could live without, back for just one day.

After she heard Maren tell the success story of her coaching client, who'd repeated the affirmation, "Mitzi is happy, healthy, and whole," for a week while in the shower every morning, only to see by the weekend the floppy little shih tzu bounce onto the front porch despite having been flattened by a pickup truck in full view of the whole family the month before, Ash del Greco began to say to herself, over and over and over again, "Ari Alterhaus is still alive."

At the end of the video, Maren lowered her sunglasses and winked at the camera: "The lesson today, baby girl, baby boy, baby they, is that even death is no obstacle!"

She put two fingers in front of one eye and chirped her usual sign-off.

"Love and light!"

At first, Ari Alterhaus did not return to life. "Seeing no movement in the 3D?" Maren asked rhetorically in another video. "Girlie, there's always movement behind the scenes. You just have to persist." Ash del Greco found that every manifestation guru's channel featured multiple videos on that most doleful of topics: "Why isn't your manifestation working?" The specific answer depended on what unofficial school of manifestation the guru advocated. Some, for example, believed in the so-called Law of Attraction, according to which you had to "align vibrationally" with your desired reality, while others promoted the Law of Assumption, according to which it was enough to assume you already had what you wanted, whatever your present "vibrational" state. The general answer, according to most of the gurus, however, was that you didn't have what you wanted because you didn't want it enough. Then there was the crazy-making principle held by some gurus that you would only get your desire when you no longer wanted it at all. You needed to learn, they said, to "detach" from your desire. Otherwise, you would repel it with your neediness, what they called affirming from lack. "Why would I bother to affirm if I didn't feel a lack?" Ash del Greco, out of patience, once demanded aloud to the screen, shaking her laptop in both hands.

(Maren had said in one video, "It's not about the other person. It's about you. *You* are Source. *You* are Universe. *You* are God." Ash del Greco thought, upon hearing this: If it's not about the other person, then what's the point?)

She didn't know if she believed in God or the gods. The manifestation gurus always hedged on this topic by referring to God, if they ever did, as synonymous with "the Universe" or "the Source." As for other gods, the only manifestors who mentioned them were the ones who also spoke of Tarot or astrology. Ash del Greco spent a few days trying to learn these occult sciences, but she quickly abandoned them on the same principle that had led her to abandon novels: stable archetypes, determinate personalities written in the stars, a panoply of emperors and priestesses and magicians to keep track of—these violated her sense of contingency and her attraction to intensity. Our lives were not written in the stars or the cards or the pages of a novel. We could all be anything at any time, at all times: this was the lesson Ari Alterhaus had taught her, which was why it was so urgent that Ari Alterhaus prove this by returning from the dead.

Precisely because it *was* so urgent, however, Ash del Greco found herself more than once driven in wracking sobs to her knees, on her unmade bed, on her dusty bedroom carpet, on the grimy bathroom floor, in the mildew-ringed tub, begging a God she wasn't sure she believed in, bargaining with he-she-it, offering him-her-it assurances and promises: "If you bring Ari back—*if this works*—I'll spend my life telling the world," she cried out.

(Diane del Greco had taken her daughter to mass every Sunday for as long as she could remember. As soon as she could speak, Ash del Greco began to complain about it: about the drone of the organ, the badness of the singing, the dullness of the priests, the hardness of the pews, the cardboard taste of the communion wafers. It made her dizzy to stand, caused her pain to kneel. Diane del Greco waved these complaints away. "Life drives us all to our knees sooner or later, sweetie," she said. "While you're down there, you might as well pray." From what women's-magazine fund of cliché and nonsense, Ash del Greco wondered, had her mother withdrawn this vapid maxim, fully as stupid as *Whoever says money can't buy happiness doesn't know where to shop*? Now here she was, years later, down indeed on her knees, crying, wailing, bargaining with the indifferent universe.)

A few weeks into affirming for the resurrection of Ari Alterhaus, however, Ash del Greco began to understand manifestation in a different light. She had gotten through the fits and spasms of wild grief, the gnawing of guilt, the feeling that she no longer had someone else to live for, would never again touch that blackly pink jet of neon she had seen to be the soul of Ari Alterhaus on the night they met in the lunar dust of the drained pool, no matter how many times she said to herself, over and over and over again, "Ari Alterhaus is still alive." The affirmation had not brought her friend back to life, at least not yet, but its desperate and active faith had been her conveyance across the treacherous wilds of mourning. She eventually found she could get through almost a whole day, if not two days in sequence, without crying. She found herself passing entire hours without thinking about Ari Alterhaus at all, though when she thought of Ari Alterhaus again, she would chide herself for her betrayal. Still, the affirmations had given her something do other than to kill herself for lack of Ari Alterhaus. Now that she was able to think more clearly, her mind not drowned in tears, she saw that manifestation's encouragement of furious mental activity in the face of all loss may not restore the lost object as advertised but may yet grant to the affirmer enough agency to survive the bereavement. Ari Alterhaus was still dead, but Ash del Greco had come back to life. Alive again, she asked herself what she ought to do. Out of habit, however, she still repeated to herself, as a singsong mantra, "Ari Alterhaus is still alive."

One Monday late in September, in-person school resumed. Whatever else she decided to do, she had to get through one more year of high school—alone. Diane del Greco had to haul her daughter awake, harass her into the shower, cajole her into her shoes, so attenuated had the habit of leaving the house become. In the shower, Ash del Greco leaned her forehead against the wall as the scalding water ran over her, almost as hot as the burning in the pit of her stomach. She whispered to herself in the steam, over and over and over again, "Ari Alterhaus is still alive."

When she came out of the bathroom, her mother said, "What's on your forehead?" The grout between the wall tiles had scored a Petrine cross into the flesh above and between her eyes.

The pile of discarded realist novels still sat against her bedroom wall. As Ash del Greco got dressed, Diane del Greco, already in the snug pink pantsuit she wore to her own job in medical billing, slipped a Jane Austen novel into her daughter's bookbag. "Give it a chance, honey—it'll cheer you up, I promise!"

Ash del Greco had learned to go a whole day without crying. When she got out of Diane del Greco's car, however, and walked toward the entrance of the school, those doors she had almost never entered or exited without Ari Alterhaus at her side, she felt the pressure building behind her eyes. She kept her head down, therefore, the tears just starting to come, as she pushed through the door and entered. She ran headfirst into someone taller than she was, someone standing next to her locker.

Ari Alterhaus looked down on her with a moue of distaste, their mustache-darkened mouth curling with a bit of disgust. "Oh," Ari Alterhaus said. "It's you." They then turned their back on Ash del Greco and resumed their laughing conversation with the president of the Rainbow Alliance, the demiboy in the skirt whom Ari Alterhaus and Ash del Greco together had once regarded as a simple-minded fool, what they called a transtrender riding the gender cause for clout among the school's ascendant faction of artists and theater freaks. Now it seemed as if Ari Alterhaus had been this person's best friend for years the way they chortled together, trading *tankobon* and touching each other affectionately on the forearms as they joked. As they walked way from the lockers toward their first-period class—they singly and they together—the Rainbow

Alliance president turned to Ash del Greco with a flip of their skirt and said, deliberate outrage in their voice, "Nice to see your face again—*uzumaki*!" Ari Alterhaus could barely contain their contemptuous laughter.

Ari Alterhaus was still alive. Ash del Greco had asked for this—and only this. Ash del Greco had forgotten to ask, as well, for her and Ari Alterhaus still to be friends, always to have been friends; she had forgotten to ask that Ari Alterhaus not be a happier, healthier, more altogether alive person without her, in some other and better (if less strange) company. She had presumed to pull one thread from the fabric of existence without pausing to consider whether the whole textile might not come undone and then be rewoven in a fashion that excluded her. Had they ever been friends? Had they ever known each other? Had she been asleep since the night, over a month before, when she met Ari Alterhaus at the pool at three in the morning? Had she been asleep since the day, three years before, when she discovered *Overman 3000* and *Notes from Undergirl*? She hadn't checked the Tumblr since Ari Alterhaus's death. She checked it that day, the day Ari Alterhaus came back to life, and found it had been deleted. No reference to it or archival record of it could be found anywhere online. She looked up Dr. Peter Farr. Both the obituary and the local news item—"Respected Pediatrician, Mired in Gender Controversy, Dies by Suicide"—had vanished from the internet.

The night of the day Ari Alterhaus rebuffed her, the night of the day the demiboy in the skirt who was now Ari Alterhaus's best friend cruelly called her *uzumaki* to her spiral-scarred face, she finally fell asleep, crying, at five in the morning, two hours before she had to be awake again for school.

In her dream, she stood in the shower with all her clothes on, pressing her forehead to the tiles. The snake slithered up the drain and thrust its tongue into the air. "Remember what you promised," it said in Ann Alterhaus's voice. Ash del Greco stamped her heel on the snake's neck, and said, "What if I don't?" The interior of the curtained-off shower became the inside of her mother's car; the water became a thunderstorm drumming on the windshield as lightning crackled out on the horizon. She knew they were going to church. Ahead, through the sheet of water on the glass, the snake appeared, serenely coiled on the highway, monstrous, the size of the whole lane. It unfurled its vast tongue to taste the storm. Her mother screamed and jerked the wheel as hard as she could to avoid it. Diane del Greco put her right arm over her daughter's chest to protect her as the car hydroplaned into the opposite lane, into oncoming traffic. Ash del Greco woke up screaming.

CHAPTER 10
Ye Are Gods

Ash del Greco became, therefore, upon pain of death, what they called an influencer. She taught the people, the *hoi polloi*—or at least the downwardly mobile members of the disaffected middle classes—what had once been reserved only for elite initiates: the power of rendering word as flesh, of downloading the ideal into the material.

Upon reflection, though she had formally discovered this art on YouTube while in the sleepless depths of despair over Ari Alterhaus's former (because revised) demise, she now understood she had seen the secret at work since she was a child.

Her mother had taken her to church every Sunday and had sent her to Catholic school through the eighth grade, after which she could no longer afford it. In combination with her precocious internet access, policed by her mother for purchases of pornography or messages from strangers but not for intellectual content, these religious experiences had made a raving atheist out of her by the age of 10 or 11.

She'd maliciously quiz her mother on the way to church on Sunday: "Can you name the Ten Commandments?" Diane del Greco could only name seven, and she couldn't help but giggle when Ash del Greco said the phrase "covet his ass," as if *she* were the adolescent daughter and Ash del Greco *her* stern mother.

"Who said, 'I came not to bring peace, but a sword'?" Ash del Greco asked. "Who said, 'If anyone comes to me and does not hate his father and mother, wife and children, brothers and sisters, yes, and his own life also, he cannot be my disciple'? Who said, 'Ye are gods'?" (In those years, Ash del Greco scrolled the Bible every day on her phone for evidence against God.) It hadn't been Nietzsche or Hitler who'd issued any of those alarming declarations but Diane del Greco's own Lord and Savior, Jesus Christ, even though Diane del Greco, and still more the other matrons who taught in the Catholic school or sent their children to be educated there, had taken him to be the peaceable patron of their suburban settlement, their domestic peace, their family values—their quiet streets, their low taxes, their lawns mowed once a week and regularly refreshed from the sprinkler, their cars, their weekly trips to the mall, their stocked supermarket shelves, their programs on cable TV, their beauticians, their doctors, their white zinfandel, their almost unimprovable lives.

Who knew? Maybe Diane del Greco and the other suburban mothers were right. The Bible contradicted itself often enough. One had to settle for it in English to boot, exiled from the gematria—Ash del Greco had read about the gematria online—its holy mysteries possibly the believer's only true homeland. (Though raised Catholic, Ash del Greco read the King James Bible because it had the most impressive prose and poetry.) Christ did—did he not?—recruit disciples, and what was Diane del Greco except a person content to drop into serried ranks behind whomever would lead her to whatever promised land, so long as capital and comfort came into the promise? Ash del Greco, however, understood that, for manifestation's sake, one had to forsake discipleship and take Christ himself as one's model.

Here was the first part of the secret she later realized she'd divined even as a child: that you could *be* him if you wanted. You could be a fisher of men and a caster out of demons and the very king of the Jews if only you understood that you, which is to say that *we*, are gods—which is to say that she, Ash del Greco, was God.

She'd learned *inside* the church rather than on the way there the second truth about manifestation. Churches in America look like bowling alleys, her paternal great-grandmother—the one who'd said, "*Povera bambina—brutta faccia!*" upon seeing her spiral-scarred face when she was five years old, and who remembered the old country—had once complained. St. Gabriel's did not disprove this criticism. It was a low white building with bland wooden rafters, only the bloody crucifix above the altar testifying to the opulent Catholic and not the plain-style Protestant faith the structure had been erected to perpetuate.

Even there, though, Ash del Greco saw, even where the fat old priest was so smothered in his excess of flesh he could barely gasp his folksy homily out, even where they sang youth-group acoustic guitar songs instead of baroque hymns in one of the church's desperate bids for populist relevance, yes, even there, she grasped the power of the drama—the alternation of speech and song—and the ritual—the sit-stand-kneel, sit-stand-kneel, sit-stand-kneel—all those orchestrated movements of the corpus that incarnated the church not as a textual enumeration of doctrines nor a pile of wood on a concrete foundation but rather as a present and living collective body actuated by belief, a body ready, were the institution not so attenuated in secular times, the ritual not so abraded by its upstart rival in electric media, to go forth and transfigure the world. She'd seen it all back then, even if she understood it only later, only after Ari Alterhaus had come out of the tomb at her command.

She could credit in part her Catholic upbringing with inspiring her semi-lucrative heresy, then, though she'd pursued it first under the threat of the snake and the dream. She also saw the truth in Protestantism, however. With much time on her hands to read now that the resurrected Ari Alterhaus shunned her, now that Ari Alterhaus had left her in the same friendless state in which she'd exited middle school, she discovered through her high-school-assigned reading in American literature the essential truth of those who'd revolted against the Catholic Church and its collectivism and its hierarchy and its dogma and its finery and its trumpery. Hester, Huck, Ahab, Gatsby, and those real-life fictions Walt and Emily: the apotheosis even unto death of the absolute individual, who would strike the sun if it insulted her or him or them or it. (Ash del Greco still hated novels but found she could tolerate the insane American variety better than the domestic English.) The absolute individual was the truth that Protestantism saw, as Catholicism saw the true sensuousness of the flesh. It was this individual whose will would activate the flesh and bring consciousness into reality.

By the end of her last year of high school, after chancing upon the subject on YouTube, after finding herself commanded by the serpent, after studying the subject for months, she was ready. She became a manifestation coach on the internet. By the end of the summer before her first year of college, she was making $1,000 a month through both monetized video content and private consultations with clients by email, text, and video call, clients who were often desperate, as desperate as she'd been after Ari Alterhaus's death. That this would help pay for college—would pay for precisely a quarter of the yearly tuition plus room and board at about $40,000, after which a mix of loans, scholarships, and her mother's savings would have to pick up the rest—also motivated her. She wasn't what they called super-famous, but she became known in her niche.

Niches abounded in the world of manifestation. The art, Ash del Greco learned, had existed under many a name since the dawn of time—since the period when those whom she supposed ought now to be called cavepersons daubed bison bristling with spears onto the rock wall before charging out to the hunt—but, as an outgrowth of self-help and New Age subcultures, it had become a booming online industry during the pandemic.

The community's panoply of microcelebrities differed, however, on the right way to manifest. Among the many quarrels about what were called techniques, Ash del Greco found a primary division roughly corresponding to what she had already conceived as the Catholic-Protestant disparity in spiritual practice and worldview.

Those she thought of as the "Catholic" manifestors focused on getting exact rituals exactly correct, to the point of using the right verb tense when making affirmations: present, not future, because you already have your desire in the fourth dimension where all time is simultaneous, and you don't, therefore, need to predict it or petition for it, frightening it away with neediness and anticipation, like the proverbial involuntary celibate with sweaty armpits and damp palms repellently inviting the belle of the ball to slow dance.

The "Protestants," on the other hand, insisted instead on attaining a pure heart and a perfect state of mind, achieving what they called a high vibration, curing the wounds of what they called your inner child, making friends with what they called your shadow, becoming such a beacon of mental wellness that you would by sheer spiritual sex appeal attract your desire without your having to lift even a mental finger, still less to participate in such superstitious rituals as affirming in the present tense.

A class divide, moreover, approximately mapped the Catholic/Protestant split between works and faith. There were roughly two kinds of manifestation coach, she found: streetwise working-class or *lumpen* pragmatists who talked a tough game about using correct techniques to obtain money, power, and glory, on the one hand, and, on the other, educated professional-class pundits who spoke a therapeutic idiom derived from popular psychology and various New Age bodies of lore. The professional class invested Protestant-wise in inward perfection, while the working class interested itself popishly in outward performance.

Ash del Greco felt her own affinities tending toward the "Catholic." Hadn't her simple repetition of phrase brought Ari Alterhaus back to life, if imperfectly? She may have gotten the words wrong, but the words had *worked*.

When trying to decide how she, under serpentine command and with felt knowledge that the art *did* work, might intervene in this market, however, she didn't quite know how to position herself. Her mother affected middle-class ways but was, as Ann Alterhaus had once cruelly observed, pure white trash, and was moreover *literally* Catholic. Ash del Greco herself, meanwhile, comprehended the chasm too well to fall into it. She certainly didn't aspire to bourgeois respectability, but as a compulsive reader and almost equally compulsive bedroom-dweller, she couldn't fake street-side authenticity either.

She began to wonder if her defect might not fill a lacuna in the market: the field lacked someone like her, a literate and even somewhat cynical, even somewhat damaged, even *visibly* damaged person, one able to trick out her discourse with reference not to *A Course in Miracles* or *Think and Grow Rich*—because the Nietzsche- and Sartre-admiring Ash del Greco never had and never would read any such trash as that—but to *Moby-Dick* and *Hamlet*.

Some manifestation coaches—generally the search-your-inner-self Protestants—made $10,000 a month, but they confected their message for a broader, wealthier segment of the public: metropolitan professionals looking to hack, as they called it, their lives. Ash del Greco knew the average office girl she saw online, the one working in what they called corporate and living in an SF or Chicago high-rise, a girl who seemingly slid from the womb with her yoga mat under one arm and matcha latte in the other hand, the type who had thousands of extra dollars to spend on psychotherapy, mindfulness coaches, wellness retreats, Moleskine notebooks, and a color-organized library of sassy self-help books with bright spines, all of them titled some variation on *Girl, F*ck This Sh*t: How to Maximize YOUR Bad*ss Life*, wasn't going to listen to some gender-struck teen with a spiral scar on xir big ugly face broadcasting from the dark and cracking wise about the sinking of the *Pequod*.

Ash del Greco intuitively divined the central insight of the new fragmentary capitalism, however, the digital convulsion she'd been born into that had broken the analog era's three-channels-on-the-TV centralization into an online chaos of *disjecta membra*, like the ruins of a lost civilization: though *everything* couldn't attract an audience of millions, *anything* could draw an audience of hundreds. The spare change of hundreds, moreover, could pile up nicely in your own bank account. Ash del Greco was not greedy, was not even slightly money-minded, but she did want to go to college, and she didn't want to get what they called a real job, the very thought of which filled her with even more than her considerable and usual nausea.

Ash del Greco aimed her appeal, then, at a theretofore neglected market: not the corporate office girl, nor the corporate office girl's cross-class counterpart working in the Amazon warehouse and dreaming of wealth, but rather the corporate office girl's depressed sib who didn't work at all, what they called a NEET, somebody overeducated, undervital, and unemployed, somebody who tossed all through the night in their bluish phone glare on their dirty mattress upstairs of Mom and Dad's house, somebody with a bookshelf full of apocalyptic critical theory—you couldn't organize *these* volumes by color because all the spines were machinic black, white, and gray, and all the titles were something on the order of *Queering the End: The Erotics of Ethical Helplessness in the Anthropocene*—somebody with a social media feed comprised entirely of "it's a joke—or is it?" quips about Molotoving the centers of modern culture or else turning the revolution inward and taking that final bath with toaster and/or razor blade. These were the people who had grown up, as Ash del Greco had, on *Notes from Undergirl* and horror manga and, yes, Simon Magnus graphic novels. These were the people whom Ari Alterhaus and Ash del Greco had been, the types of people who, like the pre-resurrection Ari Alterhaus, spoke of feeling dead already, of bringing the apocalypse they felt bearing down on the world into their own private lives—the types of people who dreamed of nullifying themselves forever.

Such people couldn't be reached by yoga-mat platitudes. Despite their academic leftism and their putative sympathy with the oppressed, however, their taste would also be offended, much as they'd have hated to admit it, by the more streetwise coaches, who tended to talk the raw vernacular: "You want your mans? You want your bag? You want it, you got it—you *are* that bitch!" No, they needed to hear the manifestation message from someone who could dress it in their own black clothes, speak it in something like their own sub-professorial argot. Ash del Greco, who already dressed the part, would learn to speak it, too. She was headed to college in the fall, after all.

Ash del Greco hadn't seen to the end of everything by reading slowly and carefully. Nobody had the time for that. First, she had the congenital power—inherited, she surmised, from her secret parent, her hidden father-mother, Simon Magnus—to divine a paragraph from a word, to incorporate a page at a glance. Second, she had no excess of pride or shame to prevent her from relying for knowledge on Wikipedia, on random articles from dubious websites, on video lectures played at double speed and left murmuring in one white bud hooked into the coil of one ear as she dreamed or as she half-listened to the teacher in school.

(School, excruciating school, where knowledge played for her not in double but in half speed, as if her dunderheaded teachers had been—she *did* relish poetry—"etherized upon a table." Still, they, both teachers and students, paid her a wary respect there, even if no one, quite literally no one after the resurrected Ari Alterhaus's defection to Rainbow Alliance "queer kid" respectability, would deign to speak to her. She was too smart and strange even to despise. A gorgeous blonde cheerleader, perhaps having chewed an edible between classes, once caressed the scarred square of Ash del Greco's face, running the sharp rims of pink-polished fingernails along her strong jaw, and said, with only a quarter mockery in her slow, breathy squeal, "You know, you're actually kind of cute," and then left her alone.)

Ash del Greco found critical theory to be more a tone of voice than anything else: the caffeine-jag despair of a philosopher chattering ruefully, only half making sense, while waiting for all the lights on the planet to go out. As for theory's specialized lexicon, the words all tended to be used imprecisely anyway, more for sonority's sake than anything else, for the glamour of stammering out some Greek, Latin, German, or French phrases in your end-of-the-world anxiety dream: isn't it *jouissant* what a miserable *Dasein* we're having in the reprofuturist carceral state?

For communities she wished to enter online—there were no communities she wished to enter offline after Ari Alterhaus's betrayal—she simply splashed and wallowed in their rhetoric for an hour or two until she could produce it with their inflections. She had a genius for absorbing atmospheres. This included the critical theory of her intended audience and what might be called the *less* critical theory of her rivals among the manifestation metaphysicians. She didn't exactly read the books the mainstream coaches recommended, whether the communiqués of the infinitely intelligent entity called Abraham as channeled by Esther Hicks or the reality-transfiguring quantum-medicine manifestoes of Dr. Joe DiSpenza or the sonorous Blake-inspired sermons of Neville Goddard, whom in "the community" they simply called Neville out of affection and familiarity.

Did she ever learn to read Tarot, as so many in the metaphysical community did? She learned, and she didn't learn. She treated the deck like a poem, like any other system of symbols she chanced upon, as hers to interpret freely, with no reference to someone else's rule book. (Deck-wise, she preferred the Thoth, in deference to Crowley's cruel genius; as far as she could tell from Wikipedia, Waite and Smith had been, by comparison, bohemian dilettantes, the Rainbow Alliance queer kids of their epoch.) She intuited meanings from fortuitous insights on the spot and as they came: whatever gave her pleasure.

She gathered to herself all the ways both the manifestation gurus and the depressed theory NEETs talked, and then she started talking those ways herself. It was as if she'd gone to Tokyo for a month and had begun speaking Japanese from submersion rather than study.

(Not that she ever would go to Tokyo: after outgrowing her middle-school horror-manga fixation, she scorned her generation's faddish Japanophilia, all that gay-boy manga the Rainbow Alliance kids got off on.)

From Ari Alterhaus's coming forth out of the tomb, from the serpent's dream-demand that she hold up her end of the bargain with God-Source-Universe, she knew it worked. Before launching her own business, however, she tested it again, just to be sure. (Once is an accident; twice is a coincidence; only three times is a pattern.) For a week, she whispered, "I have $1,000," over and over again during her morning shower. Then a paternal great-aunt she didn't even know she had died childless of old age in Argentina, divided her estate among her sisters' and brothers' children and grandchildren, and accordingly left $925 dollars to Ash del Greco, which was, she thought, close enough. Yes, she decided all over again, it worked.

Ash del Greco was no mystic. She didn't believe everything was thought, the way the other manifestors did. She didn't see the visible universe as a hologram projected by the light from the invisible sphere; she didn't think all you had to do was alter the invisible sphere for a new and better visible sphere to, well, manifest itself. She was really "a hardcore dualist," and, as far as she could tell from the internet, a Manichaean or a Gnostic—she even eventually conceded this to her audience. She knew that material and ideal, thought and reality, mind and world, wish and flesh, traveled only in the most contentious tandem through the cosmos, each riding the other, warring for the reins, the one a god, the other an animal, but neither sure which was which. Hadn't life taught her this when she'd tried to merge her very self with an exterior symbol of the flame she felt inside her soul and got for her troubles nothing better than a permanent spiral burned into the side of her face?

The reins, she knew, were made of language. If you concentrated hard enough on changing the words that tethered material to ideal, then you could activate all sorts of latent possibilities in the muck and the mire in which we find ourselves. She didn't want to help anybody, but to spread this gospel would be to help herself: to encourage others, starting with the suicidal NEETs, to speak and to write into being a world denser with significance and interest than the prison her mother or her church or her school had blundered into erecting around themselves in the name of prosperity and safety.

The summer before college, she started a YouTube channel. For her handle, she chose—what else?—Undergirl. The blog was gone, so why not? She recorded in the dark of her closet so her mother wouldn't hear; she started collecting $1,000 a week for private coaching sessions, not from office girls desperate to get that boy to come back or to get that salary raised but from people who just wanted to be able to get out of bed and get to sleep at night.

She would, in the end, decide that the only way to demonstrate to such people the greater glory of human consciousness, and therefore, the inadvisability of suicide, was to kill herself publicly, but she didn't know that when she started. She signed off each video not with a cheery "Love and light!" but rather with a Biblical phrase she spoke as a command: "Ye are gods!"

CHAPTER 11
Sweet Humanity

"Aren't you taking advantage of people?" Jacob Morrow asked her on the second night of their acquaintance. They had decided to take a night walk after their classes—including their first session of Studies in the Graphic Novel with Simon Magnus—and were halfway down Cardiac Hill from their dorm, headed toward the Cathedral.

She had sent him the link to her Undergirl channel. For over two years, since the summer before she left for college, she'd been coaching people on how properly to express their wishes to the universe and thereby manifest their desires in the flesh. Her intervention in the market, a literal and figurative darkness, filming in low light and making reference to the more morose classics of the literary and philosophical canon, this as opposed to her pink and chirpy "girl, you got this" rivals, lent an aesthetic appeal to what Jacob Morrow, himself reared by a woman who ran a small business devoted to the aesthetic, might otherwise have regarded as a scam, a grift, a fraud, a hustle, and, when all was said and done, an all-around confidence game.

Still, he had watched her "content" for eight hours. He watched the eerie blue light of her screen ripple over her spiral-scarred cheek and catch in her hazel eyes as she ruminated or exhorted. In one video, someone wrote in to ask how to be cured of cancer. Ash del Greco said, "Spinoza said we do not even know what a body can do." In another, someone wrote in to ask how to make her SP—this indicated a love interest, Jacob Morrow surmised—align with her own progressive political views. "Maybe you should manifest caring less about it yourself," Ash del Greco said. "Is there anything either of you can do about politics? Can you point to what you're calling politics anywhere in your life? Have you ever read *Ulysses*? I don't know what it would *mean* to read *Ulysses*. I've certainly browsed through *Ulysses*. Here's a line from *Ulysses*: 'We can't change the country. Let's change the subject.'"

She spoke in quick staccato sentences, in a calculatedly affectless voice less enthusiastic than the way she spoke in person—the way she spoke to *him*. Who knew? Maybe he was the only person she'd ever spoken to with enthusiasm in her life.

"You aren't getting this anywhere else," she said in one video. Then she proceeded to teach an hour-long lesson on prosody to help her devotees compose their affirmations—these, Jacob Morrow learned, were the phrases one said to alter the universe according to one's will—in the most rhythmically effective language. "Iambic pentameter is the sound the heart makes when it beats," she told the internet. He spent his morning introductory psychology lecture—after speaking with Ash del Greco until 3:00 a.m. and then watching her "content" until 8:00 a.m.—dizzily, sleeplessly scribbling in his notebook with a mechanical pencil metrical variations on the wish to speak again with Ash del Greco that very night. Her full name, a poem in trochaic dimeter, was hard to fit into the rhythm of the human heart. Trochees were like your heart beating backward.

"Who's heard of the 'reticular activating system'?" the professor asked. The slide on the screen above his head showed a diagram of the brain, its pink wrinkles penetrated at every point by a fan of wavy blue lines emanating from a yellow nub that topped a red column in the stem.

"I heard about that on a TikTok about manifestation!" a girl in the front row shouted irrepressibly.

(Jacob Morrow was one of about 10 males in the large lecture hall.)

"God help us," the professor said: a middle-aged man, balding, in a brown blazer, squeezing the bridge of his nose. Ye are gods, Jacob Morrow thought.

This was what Ash del Greco would have called a synchronicity—a sign he was on the right track.

("Synchronicity," she'd pronounced in one video, "is an acausal connecting principle. That's what Jung said, anyway. This means that the universe is held together by a force equal to or stronger than observable and material cause and effect. Have you ever thought about a friend you haven't spoken to in years—and then they call you?")

Then it hit him: "Jacob Morrow" was also a poem in trochaic dimeter. He wrote, *Ash del Greco wants to speak to Jacob Morrow*. A hexameter line. Homer had written hexameter, though not trochaic. Dactylic, if he remembered rightly: old Mr. Penshurst from Prospero's Books just down the street had taught him that. He could take Ash del Greco to Prospero's Books. He began to nod off, murmuring inwardly,

Ash del Greco wants to speak to Jacob Morrow
She wants to do it today and not tomorrow

He snapped awake when the professor shouted at the girl in the front row, "There's nothing magical about the brain!"

Still, there he found himself that night, speaking to her: she'd knocked on his dorm-room door around seven o'clock to invite him out for a walk. Two sharp blows on the metal door, loud to come from such a small fist. His roommate, head armored in noise-canceling headphones, mind lost in gaming, unblinking eyes on his screen, never even heard that thunder. When he opened the door, she was standing there all in black with her arms folded across her chest, looking off, away, down the hall, as if she'd regretted knocking, as if she wanted to be somewhere else. Since her profile faced him, he looked down into the spiral scar; it seemed sometimes to pulsate on her cheek.

Now they were outside in the late-summer evening. For some reason, maybe sleeplessness, he could not stop accusing her, despite how strangely, desperately, he'd wanted to see her.

"They come to you in need," he went on, "and you practically extort money out of them with promises you can't possibly keep. Don't you think you're exploiting people? That girl with cancer..."

He had seen the desperate comments under her videos. No one sought to manifest a desire on the astral plane unless life on the physical plane had stopped answering their needs—or at least their expectations. People, mostly young women, found Undergirl after losing a job or after having been left by a lover, or because they could not afford tuition, rent, or medical expenses, or because someone they loved was near death, or even because they themselves were near death, every kind of death, from cancer to suicide. Money and love were the most common desires, but some in her audience languished desperately out of pure despair, a weighty stone in the soul pinning them down in the rank sweat of their mattresses.

More than one commenter speculated, from what reserves of inconsolable grief didn't bear thinking about, on the resurrection of the dead—for the strangest and most mysterious tenet of this New Age manifestation religion, just another of the endless cults he hadn't heard of in the Cambrian ocean of spawning cults that comprised the online world, was called revision. Advocates of revision held that the mind, properly directed, might alter the past itself. Causation, they claimed, with citations from quantum physics, pulsed back through the timeline from present wish to past catastrophe until the former annulled the latter. The lover you buried yesterday would walk through the door today. Could this possibly be true? Jacob Morrow wondered. Was there any such thing as death?

Ash del Greco had only made one video about revision. She explained the theory and doctrine in crisp and neutral tones; she said she knew it worked. "Yes," she said, "even in the case of death." She didn't say how she knew. She didn't tell anyone to do it. She said it might not work out the way you want it to work out. "The mind is limitless in its power," she said, "but not in its knowledge. You might not have enough knowledge to reverse death without unintentionally destroying life. If nothing died, nothing could grow. It works, though. I know that. Maybe we all have to find out for ourselves."

The first comment on that video, from someone with the handle Hitl0rsButtPlug420, said, "if ur so good at revising why dont u go back and revise ur fkn face?"

Though she explained in a follow-up video that she wouldn't change her face even if she could—that she was still working out the logic of her face, that some agonies we ought to regard as moments of instruction or *materia poetica* and not simply filth to be swept from our path through the world, that her audience might even profit from consulting Milton (Milton! thought Jacob Morrow) on the fortunate fall, the veritable *felix culpa*—she understood that her immediately evident refusal to correct her injury, the spiral swirl of inflamed flesh on her cheek, would always be taken as an incapacity to operate her will backward through time.

"Do you really believe what you're saying?" Jacob Morrow asked her.

For the first time in 48 hours, she felt she was losing him. She'd had him since she'd dropped the books in the elevator. She didn't want him, but she had him. Had it ever even occurred to her to spend her time with any boy? Let alone a lanky athletic-looking boy, painfully ingenuous? She'd barely ever spoken in her life to such a boy. It was just that he'd read all those books. She hadn't spoken to someone in the flesh who'd read such things since—well, best not to remember. He'd followed her down the hallway as if ensorcelled, without her even subvocalizing a positive intention to manifest him into her life. She had no such intention. She understood how beautiful he was in an abstract and intellectual way, but beauty never drew her; desire unmixed with disgust, untainted by fear, was, for her, no desire at all. Anyway, she would be dead inside the year—*that* was her intention. Now, though, she felt obscurely wounded as he looked at her with widened, incredulous eyes and a slightly skewed parting of the lips that she couldn't *not* read as contempt. She, who always told herself that she would live alone for the rest of her life in the palace inside her mind, having survived the double loss (to death and then to resurrection) of the one person she once thought she couldn't live without. She, who didn't intend to have to live anywhere much longer, who was looking forward to her dispersal back into the thoughts and atoms out of which she'd coalesced (unbelievably enough) inside Diane del Greco's womb, and from what father or father-mother's sperm she still didn't know exactly, no matter how closely she'd been watching Simon Magnus this semester before taking her leave of this prison of the flesh. Somehow, though, she didn't want to lose this boy's company, even though she was scheduled, shortly, to lose everything.

"I do and I don't," she said. "Let's come back to that. I want to answer the exploitation question first."

They'd arrived at the Cathedral. She went through the revolving door to enter the ground-floor commons, which stayed open late when classes were in session to give students somewhere public to study at night. On that second day of classes, only one or two people occupied any of the wooden benches and tables arranged around the marble columns beneath the immense Gothic vault. Jacob Morrow must have wanted her answer to the exploitation question very badly, because he quickly and without thinking walked behind her right into her wedge of the revolving door. He didn't realize his mistake until he pressed up against her back and smelled the spice of ginger on her breath in that mobile glass cage. She flinched, shuddered at his touch; they hadn't yet touched, would never touch much. Shuffling awkwardly, toe pressed to heel, they almost fell out onto the dark marble tiles of the dim commons. She stared up at him shyly, moved by the evident passion with which he accused her. She spoke in a low voice as they passed beneath the dark vault among their fellow students.

"Yes, they come to me having just been told they no longer have a job, they have a medical bill they can't afford, they didn't get the scholarship, or that the one they love no longer loves them and in fact—the leaver always say this; it's always a lie—never loved them. Some, for no precise reason they can name, just can't get out of bed. They cry all day. They can barely breathe from anxiety and grief, never mind sleeping and eating. The material world has turned on them, has gone from an at least somewhat stable home to a dark abandoned house with hidden tripwires and men with knives in the cellar. To escape that kind of house, you might jump out the highest window. They're barely clinging to this world. They're thinking about ending it all. Instead of leaping off the nearest bridge, though, they decide they might first try a subtler exit from this reality that has just revealed itself to be not a happy home but a dark dungeon, a prison called earth. They ask themselves, 'What if I could change this by wanting it to change hard enough?'—not knowing yet that what they actually want to change is not the world into a place that grants them their desire but themselves into a person who either can get their desire or who doesn't need it. That's what I'm trying to do—not work magic. By guiding them on the first steps to a mental discipline that will help them to become an ordered enough soul to attain the next job or scholarship, to be worthy of either their former lover, their future lover, or a dignified and satisfying life alone, by bringing their mind into contact with what their world can be—and by giving them something else to do during the moments they're closest to suicide: a project, the project of making the language in which they talk to themselves effective and beautiful—this, to me, is indistinguishable from saying that the mind makes the world and not the other way around. If you change the way you think about the past so radically that it changes the effect the past has on you—how is that *not* magic?"

They had crossed the commons and exited the Cathedral. In thoughtful silence after her speech—the two years of making videos had given her a fluency and a command that momentarily silenced his objections, though some wariness of her, even some fear of what he construed as her nihilism, lingered—they crossed the lower of the two main avenues bisecting the campus, walked under the colonnade of trees before the public library, and finally crossed to the courtyard of the Fine Arts Building, its white stone walls and terra-cotta roof tiles glowing faintly in the ambient light of the streetlamps, the moon.

"How do you think the world works?" she finally asked him. "What do *you* believe?"

They sat now on one of the wooden benches that ringed the fountain in the courtyard. The fountain's stone basin brimmed and plashed; on the pedestal above the basin, bronze turtles watered it through their parted beaks. Above the turtles reared up a beautiful girl in bronze; her hair and her long skirt flowed like the water beneath her as she played on a lyre. An old man with horns and a beard reclined to listen, his hooves folded beneath him. Instead of answering her question, Jacob Morrow got up to read the inscription on the fountain explaining the image:

A Song of Nature, Pan the Earth God Answers to the Harmony and Magic Tones Sung to the Lyre by Sweet Humanity.

He motioned her over and pointed to the words. Nature, earth, and humanity—that was what he believed. In response, she leaned over the rim of the stone basin and plunged both arms into the water. She raised her cupped hands as they dripped and jingled, full of the coins that paved the fountain bottom—coins people had tossed as if worthless into the water in exchange for some blessing mere earth, mere nature, could not offer to humanity.

CHAPTER 12
Against Feeling

The next night, when classes were finished, Ash del Greco invited Jacob Morrow to watch her on a coaching call in her dorm. She was at the head of her bed, reclined against the pillows, with just the rainbow string lights lit above her for illumination, her knees up and her laptop braced on her thighs in front of her as she launched the video call. Jacob Morrow sat cross-legged at the end of the bed, behind the laptop, out of the client's sight. The kitten faces on the toes of Ash del Greco's slippers smiled up at him. He watched the video call transpire, reflected in reverse in the lenses of Ash del Greco's wide glasses.

Her client, Ally Aldrich, was a woman in her late 30s with long, thin, silver-threaded brown hair and a gaunt face. She called from an apartment in the city the comics called Cosmopolis, or one of its more fashionable boroughs. An exposed redbrick wall lined with bookshelves formed her backdrop, the spines of all her books white, gray, or black. She had spent two months manifesting her specific person without success. She'd found Ash del Greco on a YouTube search and appreciated the youngster's dark and mordant style. Maybe advice from what she (with defensive self-deprecation) called the youth might be just what she needed.

Other manifestation coaches—Ally Aldrich had been through five already—preached a doctrine of feeling. They said that if you wanted to incarnate your desires in reality, you had to feel as if you already had those desires in the present. These coaches often recorded what they called meditations, lyrical speeches backed with gentle music or even electronically generated subliminal messages, recorded binaurally for extra effect, meant to convince listeners that they lived in their wished-for worlds, that they already walked in the shade of their utopia. Listeners often fell asleep to these meditations, hoping to saturate their dreamtime with what was called—again, a term of art—"the feeling of the wish fulfilled." These worked-up emotions, the doctrine held, either confused the universe into bringing you what you wanted because it came to think you possessed it anyway, or literally caused you to shift into a parallel among the infinite realities, one where a lover who had abandoned you in this world clasped you in his loyal and loving arms, or one where your bank account, spent on our plane, overflowed with so many riches you would soon have to manifest the IRS away.

Ash del Greco thought this affective dogma absurd. It derived from a psychotherapeutic attitude she had held in contempt all her life. Diane del Greco had dutifully rallied her insurance and sent Ash del Greco to a psychotherapist when she was in the seventh grade, two years before she met Ari Alterhaus. She'd begun cutting her arms so that she could hold herself to the world by a tether of pain. Invisible to her classmates, alien to her family, what there was of it, and scattered since the age of about eight across several image boards and social media platforms as a shade amid other shades, she envisioned herself as smoke, bodiless and dissipating, occasionally attracting notice as a sign of danger but otherwise treated as bad atmosphere. The bright cold line of rending agony when the serrated blade of a dullish wood-handled steak knife from the kitchen drawer bit into the flesh of her upper arm—this caused her briefly to coalesce.

When her mother caught her slicing herself in the bath, the suds pink-foamed with blood, she said, "Where the hell did you come from?" and immediately looked up a psychologist in her provider network. Ash del Greco, who knew what she was doing, tried to explain, but Diane del Greco waved her away: "Don't tell me. Do I look like a psychologist to you? What you need is professional help."

Ash del Greco began researching the history of psychotherapy online as her appointment date neared. It should have been made illegal, she judged, after the lobotomy days, though she'd be what they called in denial if she said she didn't relish the images of Freud's totem-laden office she discovered in her researches. She wanted an office like that, a dim chamber with glass-fronted cases full of captured gods. She wouldn't help anybody in that office, though; she'd probably just keep looking things up online.

Her own psychologist, Dr. Andrew Wyman, presided over a beige office without decor except for a generic painting of flowers on the wall next to his clinical license. A soft-spoken man with a graying beard, a man who favored corduroy pants and brown moccasins, he always looked, behind his thick, brown-framed glasses, as if he were about to burst into tears. His eyes seemed wet, perpetually filmed with a viscous residue. She found it disgusting somehow. He asked her about her father; she told him only that she didn't know him, not that her mother wouldn't tell her who he was. He asked about how she'd burned her face as a child; she said it was an accident.

He said, "Does the scar make you self-conscious?"

"No," she said. "I can't see it unless I look in the mirror. I forget it's even there. It makes *you* conscious of *me*."

She lied to him about everything. She would have lied to him about everything just on general principle, just to guard her inherent right to her own inner life, just as vengeance for Rosemary Kennedy and Rose Williams—she'd read about them online—but he seemed so fragile, so freighted with his histrionic sorrow at all the world's suffering, so concerned for what he judged her own anguish, so limp and wet-eyed, that she felt she had to protect him from what she knew.

"Do you ever watch the news?" he asked her. "It seems to me that we've been through an enormous collective trauma in this decade. What's your date of birth?"

She told him; she didn't have the presence of mind to lie about *that*. Anyway, it must have been on some official form he'd seen; he was probably pretending, for therapy's sake, not to know, probably trying to get her to confront the enormity of the fact by making her say it herself.

"Imagine," he mused, looking away from her face, as he often did, "imagine being born into those waves upon waves of trauma. It's no wonder, Ashley. It's really no wonder."

He seemed to think perseverating on family history and transient inner states held the key to health, whereas she thought it a disease itself, as in another quote she found online, from some long-vanished wit: "Psychoanalysis *is* the illness for which it claims to be the cure." When she didn't like her mood, she changed it. She conducted experiments on herself, in all deliberation, not in thrall to whatever Mommy and Daddy, whoever Daddy was, did before she was born. You couldn't explain anything like this to a weak man like that, a man with a whispery voice and a pinkish button-down shirt and a hole at the heel of one argyle sock visible at the back of his moccasin, his moccasin bobbing nervously at the end of one foot as he girlishly crossed his legs in their whispery corduroy. A dream catcher hung above the door to his office. Her self-inflicted wounds were badges of her strength. He would never understand. Like all very strong people, she held the weak in contempt—a contempt sometimes softened by pity, sometimes not. He just made her stomach turn—but then so did everything else.

"How does it make you feel to hurt yourself?"

"It makes me feel like God," she said inside of herself, "willing and able to do anything with my creation, with the universe I rule." To him, she said, "It makes me sad. It makes me want someone to take care of me."

Eventually, Diane del Greco pulled her from Dr. Andrew Wyman's care when he asked *her* one day, Diane del Greco herself, when she came to pick her daughter up, if she might like to come in for a session to "explore her own defenses," as he put it.

"Defenses!" she raged in the car on the way home. "I'll show him defenses! Hell, I'll show him *offenses!*"

She found a psychiatrist who would prescribe her daughter pills after a cursory visit. Ash del Greco flushed the pills down the toilet, one a day, precisely at the time scheduled for her to take them. When the prescription ran out, Diane del Greco did not renew it. There ended the family experiment in psychotherapy. Eventually, Ash del Greco stopped cutting herself and met Ari Alterhaus, and Diane del Greco forgot about the whole thing, averting her eyes from any glimpse of the pale scars on her daughter's arms. (She also threw away the steak knife.) Now Ash del Greco ministered to others on the internet.

This adolescence spent trying to dodge the spilled slop of Dr. Andrew Wyman's brimming affect turned her into the most pragmatic and ruthless of manifestation coaches. Most manifestation coaches on social platforms favored "techniques" they encouraged their audience to adopt to bring about their preferred reality. These techniques, if used regularly and religiously, would summon the desired emotion: for example, visualizing one's prized scenario—the job offer, the marriage proposal, the monetary gift—in the haze before sleep or the confusion upon waking, or else meditating several times a day on the goal.

She dismissed these practices as mush-minded sentiment, helpless childish wallowing in the inner mire. "Feelings mean nothing," she insisted in almost every video. "They should be briefly acknowledged and just as briefly purged."

(Her stomach never settled. From girlhood, the smell of food often made her gag, and sustenance in her intestines churned, bulged, surged—seemed, even, to boil. Always constipated, always nauseated, she chewed crystalized ginger and sipped apple cider vinegar—she'd found these remedies online—all day long. Her body dwindled to the bone, exaggerating her already outsized head, which sat squarish and spiked with chopped hair on her narrow shoulders, spirals of scar tissue swirling on the cheek.)

We lived, she thought, in a universe made of codes: numbers for physical reality, words for mental. To change your universe, you had only to will yourself to rewrite its code. Why else had she inscribed her very flesh? Why else did she now inscribe her mask? This she had learned as a girl while bored at mass on Sunday, watching the congregation heed and sometimes even chant words that had been repeated for millennia as they worshiped an idol of torn flesh, a beautiful lean body weeping blood at hand and foot and side, eyes running blood from the crown that mocked its head—and yet this body, through its very agonies, had managed to rule. Why not her, too? Why not the rest of us?

Instead of techniques for rearranging affect, she proposed rearranging text. She promoted what they called in the community looping affirmations: the constant repetition, both inwardly and aloud, at all hours of the day, as much as one could, in any mood, with or without conviction, with or without hope, through hot tears if you had to, two or three short sentences declaring one's triumph. "He loves me," "I'm rich," "I've been promoted to CEO," "I have a million subscribers." These words would literally summon the new world down from the foggy heaven of potential onto the hard ground of the real.

Ally Aldrich had called that day—the day Jacob Morrow sat quietly offscreen, at the end of Ash del Greco's bed, listening—both to report success and to request further aid. Her "SP" was her on-again, off-again boyfriend of four years, a theater director named Joshua Cantwell, who lived in the same cosmopolis where she was entering her eighth year of graduate school. She had informed Ash del Greco, who had not asked, that she was writing a dissertation about Jacques Lacan complicated by the fact that she'd begun it as a Marxist revolutionary in her late 20s but had now in her late 30s returned to the Catholic Church—hence not only the mounting contradictions in her text but also the new urgency she felt to attain marriage and progeny rather than contenting herself with merely intermittent attention from the rail-thin and graying Brechtian maven of the underground theater scene. Joshua Cantwell, this Brechtian boyfriend, or partner, as they liked to say in Cosmopolis, had in fact been abandoned by the empty-headed actress in whose perfumed embrace he'd fled Ally Aldrich's intellectual company in the first place; this kind of success is what manifestors called movement in the 3D. The Marxist side of her had been appalled that she'd resorted to what the comrades called obscurantism, the Catholic side of her just as fearful that she'd resorted to what the Good Book called witchcraft, and even the PhD student in her recalled Lacan's mockery of Jung, so she could scarcely believe it when the manifestation had actually worked, when she found herself in Joshua Cantwell's bony, smoky arms backstage—amid shadowy pipes and wires—of the production he'd mounted of *The Master Builder* in the boiler room of a disused warehouse. Now, however, she'd discovered online that he was back to liking the slutty Instagram pictures of the girl, 10 years her junior, that he'd cast as Hilda Wangel, just as before he'd cast her as Medea, as Lady

Macbeth, as Blanche DuBois—his *femme fatale*, her Instagram a glittering wall of her seductive wallowing in city parks and in bathtubs and in the backs of Ubers, all cigarettes and lip gloss and knee-high socks and bruised thighs and a Clarice Lispector or Joan Didion novel under her arm. The actress posted a picture every day; every day, Ally Aldrich refreshed the actress's feed; and every day, Joshua Cantwell liked the actress's latest picture.

Onscreen, Ally Aldrich explained to Ash del Greco: "I told his ass, I said, 'Joshua, whatever she'll do *with* you, she'll do *to* you.' Did he listen? Christ, I fucking hate men."

She put her fingertips over her lips to atone for having taken the Lord's name in vain and for having transgressed his command that we love one another, not to mention her transgression of the manifestor's preference that we not sink into low vibrations.

Now she wanted Ash del Greco to help her to manifest not only his return but also a subsequent pregnancy—after they got married, ideally, but if it took a pregnancy to get him to the altar, or even into a church for the first time since his childhood (he was a long-lapsed Episcopalian), she was sure the Lord who commanded fruitfulness and multiplication would forgive her.

"I should have done this when I was 20. I shouldn't have left my hometown. I wish I'd never heard the name Jacques Lacan!"

Ash del Greco couldn't gainsay the money: this woman, what they called a whale among her client base, offered to raise her payments to $1,000 a session since Ash del Greco's affirmations had *almost* successfully dispatched what they called in the community the 3P, i.e., the third party, the wretched spoiler whom your SP loved in place of you, in this case, the vapid actress who lived on lip gloss and cigarettes. Ash del Greco didn't ask where this eternal graduate student's money came from—family, she had to assume, back in the abandoned hometown, wherever that was.

"Here's what you need to say," Ash del Greco finally told the woman. "You need to say, at least 1000 times a day, 'I am a vessel of life.'"

When she closed the laptop, her eyes bleary from their long irradiation, she found that Jacob Morrow was staring directly at her, as if he had not dropped his eyes from her face since the moment the call began.

"What would *you* have told her?" Ash del Greco asked.

"I don't know," Jacob Morrow conceded. "Maybe to find someone who *wants* to be the father of her child. Someone who doesn't have to be talked into it. It could work out anyway, though. I didn't know my father. I don't even know his name."

"I don't either."

"I thought your father was Simon Magnus."

"That's just my best guess. I've never been able to bring myself to ask my mother. I doubt I'll be able to bring myself to ask Simon Magnus."

"Do you want me to ask him for you? To ask Simon Magnus, I mean?"

"Does it really matter? Maybe Simon Magnus is *your* father. Maybe the past doesn't matter at all. Maybe all that matters is the present and the future. Maybe all that matters is shaping the future according to our present will and forgetting whatever went before—or, better than forgetting it, bending that to our will, too. Maybe Simon Magnus is my father, my mother-father, my all-gender all-parent, for no other reason than that I say Simon Magnus is. My saying it makes it so. Could Simon Magnus, being the magician that Simon Magnus is, disagree?"

After making that speech, she fell sideways on the bed and curled up, clutching her fiery stomach. She pulled a packet of crystallized ginger from her pocket and tore it open with her teeth. Her scar faced him across the bed. He hadn't asked her how she'd gotten the scar. He figured she'd tell him when she was ready, if ever she was. Maybe that was part of the past she'd already forgotten.

"Why don't you manifest away your stomach pain?"

"Who would I even be if my stomach didn't hurt? I tried, anyway. I tried, and it didn't go away. I assume if it went away, I would go away. Magic isn't about having a life without pain. It's about putting the pain at your service—the way a writer makes an interesting story out of death and disaster."

He felt an urge to reach across the bed and put his hand on her shoulder, to comfort her, but he knew she hated to be touched. Her face was making him dizzy. He turned his head and looked at the dorm's blank concrete-block wall, like the wall of a prison.

"I hope she's happy," he said. "It's probably for the best. Getting married, having a family, getting old together, watching your children grow up and start families of their own. On Thanksgiving and Christmas, it was always just my mom and me. She disowned my grandmother, if a child can disown a parent, because my grandmother treated her rental property like a brothel, and I walked in on two people having sex, and I got scared and had nightmares for weeks. I've never told anyone that. I don't know what it would be like: the large family, three generations around the fireplace, drinking, well, whatever they drink. Mulled cider, I think they call it."

Ash del Greco said, "My mother would always give me a sip of wine on Thanksgiving and Christmas. When it was just me and her, which it always was after she divorced my stepfather. It burned all the way down, the wine, and her turkey was always dry. I've never had mulled cider."

She slipped her phone from her pocket to search for a definition.

"How do you even spell that? Like M-A-U-L? They *maul* the cider? It sounds unpleasant—for the cider, anyway."

Jacob Morrow, who read 19th-century English novels, told her how it was spelled.

"That's better, I mean," he went on, "than writing doctoral dissertations or putting on plays. I think. Having a family, a happy home. It's probably what we're supposed to do. I've never done any of that, though—had a family *or* put on a play."

"What do you *want* to do?" she asked him, eyes on her phone. "Why don't you affirm for what you want?"

"I've never wanted much," he said. "Just a quiet place to read. I like to run, too. It's like disappearing into the wind. Sitting here and talking to you..."

He didn't finish.

(He'd been a nervous child. After the ban on his grandmother and that rambling house of hers, whose maze of sex and money he used to get lost in, he was raised amid the different chaos of his mother's shop, his mother's life, a maze of art and money, a life heaped and heaped again with clothes once swelled by now-vanished bodies, as if a cemetery had an antechamber where the dead's garments were brought for sale, an antechamber overseen by his worldly mother. He could just barely remember the last days of his infancy, bobbed in Jess's one arm as she priced inventory with the other, his fat baby fingers tracing with a mix of fascination and alarm the arabesques tattooed across her shoulders. For most of his childhood, he'd found every sight an affront, a shock behind every wall of every maze, though he concealed this as best he could from Jess, from his kindly, pragmatic mother. He just found places to vanish, mazes of peace: Prospero's Books and all the literature it held, the architectures of music and mathematics, and, when he ran, the very atmosphere. Life consisted of a succession of small reprieves, all of them, in his mind, equal to calm. Nature, earth, humanity—as long as they were all one thing, open to receive him rather than coming at him in a tangle of limbs and tendrils, moaning and dripping. Ash del Greco's disturbance of this calm was like nothing he'd ever experienced. He had been with girls in high school, and he had looked at every kind of pornography before that: these things held no surprise for him, nor, beyond the first shock of desire, any truly urgent attraction. Sex had gathered him to the world, pinned him in place, rather than allowing him to disappear from it—pinned, the way his penis constantly stood quivering for days, sticking out of him like an arrow shot into his crotch, that summer he'd discovered online pornography. What he felt for Ash del Greco was something different. There was a sexual feeling, a little, one that almost made him ashamed, the largely imagined appeal of her fragile body hot under all her shapeless clothes, but that was the least of it for him. He had never seen anything so otherworldly as the sheer flesh of her face. He wanted to disappear into that. He wanted to wander in the spiraling labyrinth of her countenance forever. It hovered before his eyes when he tried to read. It spoke in his head when he tried to think. He tried to run, but the thought of her seemed to twist his very legs. He had known her less than a week.)

"I've spent two years teaching people how to get whatever they want," she said, "and what it taught me is that I don't want anything. 'Disappearing into the wind,' that sounds good. Maybe I'm a coward. Maybe I don't want anything because I'm too afraid of what I'd have to do to get it and then too afraid that I would lose it. I haven't done anything truly brave since I was five years old. I probably don't belong here, to be honest with you. Maybe it would be better if I just disappeared."

He kept his eyes averted, kept them fixed on the blank wall, and waited for her to go on. When she didn't, he said, eyes still on the wall, "Maybe we could disappear together."

He looked back at her after he said it: she had fallen asleep.

CHAPTER 13
Hollow Lake

If she'd thought Jacob Morrow was weak because he wanted to die for her—to die, literally, in her stead—she would not have allowed him to do it. She would not even have continued speaking to him. He was the first person she'd met since Ari Alterhaus she could have a real conversation with, though he, his apparent optimism and simplicity, stood at the opposite pole from Ari Alterhaus's elaborate moroseness. Somehow, after only a few days—after only a few hours—she never wanted to stop speaking to him; she didn't want to speak to anyone else. If she didn't know he needed to die, needed to die alone, without her, that she had to live to be his witness, she would have done anything to keep him alive or would have followed him into death. It wasn't desire. She felt no desire for him—no disgust and so no desire. If he could have persisted as a voice in her head, it would have been enough.

Most people were either like her mother—conventional people, people who asked no questions, believed what the television said, what the priest said, what their neighbors on social media said, and then did as they were ordered to do as long as someone in power promised it would pay off in cash money—or like the "queer kids" in the Rainbow Alliance she and Ari Alterhaus had once scorned, at least before Ari Alterhaus had come back to life to join they/them, or like the people she now coached online—people who proudly boasted to themselves and to the world of their defying convention, though in reality they had taken only one step beyond convention and then rooted themselves in place, willing captives to an ossified set of pseudo-revolutionary counter-conventions drilled into them by pseudo-radicals, whether scholars or troubadours, who'd been absorbed as a loyal opposition by the same powers and principalities that puppetted the conventional minds these self-styled rebels so hypocritically derided. She hadn't understood this dynamic in high school, only intuited it from her encounters with the Rainbow Alliance, but two years in college, two years of exposure to the so-called radical professoriate and the so-called radical texts they assigned, had brought it home to her without fail, and her clientele among the online radicals demonstrated the same point.

Whereas Jacob Morrow understood—he was the first person she met in real life, outside of books, who understood—that for any true revolution in the outer or the inner world, somebody had to die. At the very least, you had to die to yourself: you had to become someone else entirely. This meant more than a new hair color or a new pronoun. You had to leave parts of yourself behind in the road—a trail for others to follow. She never hid her scar nor attempted to efface it.

The first weekend they spent together was when she discovered that Jacob Morrow would understand, when she knew she could tell him. She didn't know then that he'd be the one to do it; if she had, she might not have told him at all.

They went on another walk. A Saturday afternoon in late August, remnant of what they called the dog days, 90 degrees under an invisible sea of humid air that made the clouds waver and shimmer, as if seen across hot blacktop. She wore long black pants, a black sweatshirt, a black knit cap, black boots. Cool in his long white T-shirt and cutoff jean shorts and sports sandals, he kept trying to take her into air-conditioning, into the sleek simulacrum of authenticity that was Starbucks or into the smug filth of the vegan worker-owned Shared Grounds. She drank coffee, hot and black, in the former; he ordered a fruity iced tea (no sugar) in the latter.

They wandered up and down the streets where the campus declined toward the city, where houses that dated from before World War II leaned crookedly on their foundations, and the bare frames of stripped cars sat on cement blocks, and lawns swayed with knee-high grass in the late-summer haze. They circled back to the other side of the campus, to the street near the University where Untimely Vintage and Prospero's Books both were. He offered to take her inside Untimely to meet his mother. She dismissed the suggestion: "I'm sure she's nice, but I have enough trouble with my own. I don't need any more mothers in my life."

Without telling her of his relationship with Mr. and Mrs. Penshurst, he took her to Prospero's Books instead. He waved hello to the old couple without ceremony and walked with Ash del Greco into the dusty, vanilla-scented warren of shelves; the old couple shared a glance—Mrs. Penshurst lifted her eyebrow in intrigue, while Mr. Penshurst's eyes widened in alarm—at the prospect of their Jacob with a girl. Ash del Greco ordered him to buy the thick white brick, like an external hard drive, of *A Thousand Plateaus*—"You don't have to read every page in order," she said, "and in fact I'd advise against it"—while he cajoled her into giving *Anna Karenina* another chance, the Pevear and Volokhonsky paperback with its sexy black-and-white bare knees on the cover, just parted. At the register, they each paid for their own books; Mrs. Penshurst didn't overtly signal her grandmotherly affection for the boy, but, unable to contain herself, she did give them each a candy bar from under the counter on their way out.

They walked back toward the University. A ragged pile of blankets that was slumped against a crumbling brick wall stirred and croaked out to them, with a smell like sour milk, "Anything you got, man. Anything you got." A dirt-crusted, jag-nailed hand lifted itself into the sunlight.

A *sauve qui peut* kind of girl (or whatever), Ash del Greco literally didn't even hear the request, as if the groans of the oppressed sounded on a frequency her ears couldn't access. The only person she'd ever tried to help in her life was Ari Alterhaus, and this was because Ari Alterhaus had seemed to call to her across Maddie Sholtz's end-of-the-summer pool party, a sublimely dark beacon in the night, on a frequency not of weakness but of strength. Helping for the sake of helping, helping someone she didn't know, someone who didn't appeal to her—this was not in her repertoire. Jacob Morrow—his mother called him Jakey, he complained to her, even though he wanted to be called Jacob; somehow Ash del Greco came to call him Jakey, too, but only in her head—crouched down to the man in the heap of rags and said, "What do you need?"

Not knowing he would stop, she had inadvertently walked on without him. She turned around in time to hear a patient, whispered negotiation, to see him, Jakey, first hand over both candy bars (she'd given him hers) and then take out his wallet and deposit a 20-dollar bill into that mound of fabric and filth and agony. More whispers. Jacob Morrow, crouching down, squinched his eyes and turned over and over in his mind what had been asked of him. Finally, he did it. He unstrapped the sandals from his feet and handed them over.

"Good luck," he said brightly.

"God bless, God bless, God bless!" cried the man buried in blankets and slumped on the wall.

Barefoot over concrete strewn with sharp pebbles and spiky weeds and broken glass, Jacob Morrow rejoined her. Not usually one for intimate touch, for *any* touch, she took his hand in hers, though his was twice her size, bony and vein-strung and tanned where hers were pale and smooth; hand in hand, him standing three heads higher than her, they walked on. That day, she knew: this boy would give all.

(This was the first of two times she would touch him; the second would be two months hence, in Untimely Vintage, in front of the mirror.)

They walked by the four vast statues representing the liberal arts that towered on high plinths in front of the museum adjoining the library: Newton, Da Vinci, Bach, Shakespeare. Ash del Greco noticed that Jacob Morrow deliberately, perhaps superstitiously, touched his knuckles to Shakespeare's plinth as he passed. They walked by the regal Beaux-Arts façade of the library itself, beneath a stately colonnade of trees, the leaves rustling dryly in the late-summer drought, and then they walked by the Fine Arts Building, its white walls glaring in the sun, and then they walked by the fountain with its statue of Sweet Humanity, where Jacob Morrow paused to wet his bare feet, the thrown coins cold on his soles, and then they walked by the conservatory, its glass walls briefly blinding them with reflected sun glare, and then they walked into the park. They cautiously descended a cracked and decayed concrete stairway, weed-sprouted and rough, that brought them down the steep hill below the bridge connecting the park to the campus.

Finally, they sat on the narrow cement ghat leading down into the man-made pond, the pond grandly called Tiger Hollow Lake—"tiger" in reference to the university's mascot, "hollow" because it sat deep in that valley below the campus. On that Saturday, its shallow basin was clogged green with globular algae blooms. Busy poking at one of the tangled underwater blossoms with a fallen branch, Jacob Morrow almost didn't hear what she said. What she said was, "I need to kill myself before the end of the year." Her tone made it sound like, "I need to pick up milk on the way home."

"I've thought about killing myself on and off since middle school," she went on, "because nothing interested me anymore, because I'd seen to the end of everything." Some French poet—she'd seen so many quotations flash by all day every day since she was old enough to go online; she knew what everyone had said but could never remember who had said anything or when or where or why—had said, "The flesh is sad, alas, because I have read all the books." She knew what he meant. She counted and found that she had read about 400 books in her life, including downloaded pdfs but not including whatever picture books they'd given her as a child. 400 wasn't "all the books" but was surely enough books to intuit, to be able to construct for herself, in her own mind, the contents of all the rest.

Knowledge, language, these were algorithmic: the combinations were infinite, but the base elements few. She felt she had mastered the base elements. Then, too, though she rarely spoke with anybody, had rarely spoken with anyone in her life except for her mother and for Ari Alterhaus and now for Jacob Morrow, she'd met all the people—all those people on the social platforms, the blogs, the video sites, the message and image boards. She was sincere, she explained, in her spiritual work. She meant what she said on her Undergirl channel. She meant what she wrote on her masks, the way she made a spectacle of herself so people would pay attention. "Ye are gods"—she meant this.

"I don't mind people looking at me. I don't care how I look. People don't talk to me. Except now for the people who pay me to tell them how to fix their lives. I tell them our reality is three-dimensional. Our minds are four-dimensional, able to stand outside the edifice of time, look forward and backward in it, rewrite the past, write the future, using words and pictures—like dear old Mom-Dad said in *Overman 3000*. If we build a shack in our mind, we'll live in the shack. If we build a castle, we'll live in the castle. Though compared to the castle in the 4D, even the castle in the 3D is a shack. I'm personally tired of the shack. I'm tired of people's repetitive—or is it 'repetitious'? I never figured that one out—let's say their endlessly repeated problems. Money and SP, SP and money, money and SP, SP and money. Is this what I'll do for the rest of my life? Help people acquire trinkets and lovers they think will satisfy them? Ye are gods, but ye are gods without taste, without intellect, and so what was even the point of being gods? It's better if I show them what matters most and what doesn't matter at all."

All in black, she sat hunched over her crossed arms on her drawn-up knees. She stared glumly out over the man-made pond. Her face, exposed to the sun, remained pale, except for the redly inflamed spiral on her cheek.

"What doesn't matter at all?" he asked.

She waved her hand from the left to the right and then again from the right to the left across the whole of the hollow. With her other hand she clutched at her stomach; it had no fat on it but was tautly inflated from inanition. "Inanition" was a good word. An elderly doctor Diane del Greco dragged her to had diagnosed her with it once. She'd looked it up to see if it derived from Inanna—she'd had a mythological phase in middle school—but no, just the opposite, Innana being the goddess of fertility, of abundance.

"I don't remember a day of my life when my stomach didn't hurt," she said.

He drew a tendriled algae frond from the brown water and jokingly offered it to her to eat on the end of his branch. She looked at it with curiosity, extended her thin neck, and pulled the slimy blossom into her mouth with her lips and teeth. She chewed thoughtfully, green runnels spilling from her lips, traversing the spirals of her scar.

"I thought that by spreading this message to people who had some ability to use language, to change culture—people writing their doctoral dissertations on Jacques Lacan—I would make the world more beautiful, more spiritual, a world where more people understood our true place in the universe. It's not down here, not really. It isn't among the muddy water and cancerous algae."

They had the pond to themselves; above them, students crossed the Tiger Hollow Bridge, shuffling in last night's stale clothes, hung over from their Friday drinking sprees, and looked down on the strange pair, the athletic-looking, long-haired boy in his white T-shirt and cutoff shorts, the girl, or whatever, in shapeless black clothes with the hypertrophic head and close-cropped, dyed-black hair. Could they see her spiral from such a height?

"What do the people who come to me want? All they want is what's down here. Money and sex. They dress them up as status and stability, love and companionship, but it's still just money and sex: a three-dimensional desire for a three-dimensional world. They don't understand that the mind is the real prize. I'm trying to teach them to cultivate their minds, communicate that cultivation in language, and create a new reality. I thought the suicidal intellectuals would be above this, but once I've gotten them out of bed, off the couch, and interested in living again, they're the same as everyone else. 'I need the boy, I need the bag, I *am* that bitch.' Is this enough to live for?"

By then—by their sixth day together, their sixth day spent with one another almost every moment they didn't spend in their classes—she had told him about the scar, about Ari Alterhaus, about *Notes from Undergirl* and *Overman 3000*, about everything except the snake and the dream. She wasn't ashamed but didn't want to sound *completely* crazy. She told him now, in front of Tiger Hollow Lake, though. She told him that if she didn't quit, her mother would die. She'd had days in her life when she'd wished for her mother to die, but in the dream her mother had put out her arm to protect her as the car skidded into traffic, and Ash del Greco knew her mother would do just that in real life, and for that reason, if for no other, she could not be the cause of her mother's death. She had told him she no longer wanted to spread her gospel but that she was, as far as she knew, not free to stop.

"Do you believe me?" she asked him.

"I believe you had the dream," he equivocated.

He hurled the stick spearwise into the center of the pond, where it stuck upright for a moment in the dense silt and shaggy blooms of the basin before it toppled over and slowly sank in the sludge.

"You're not going to kill yourself," he said. He said it the way she told her clients to make their affirmations: in a matter-of-fact tone, not even confidently, which would imply that your statement required confidence if you or anyone else were to believe it, but as if stating the blandest truth in the world. Water is wet, the sky is blue, I am a vessel of life, and you are not going to kill yourself.

"Tell me that later. First, let me tell you why I *am* going to kill myself, beyond nausea and despair, which are banal reasons, reasons beneath my dignity, such as it is. I've been thinking, 'How do you prove to people that the fourth dimension is higher than the other three, that the mind is superior to what we call reality—is itself in fact the ultimate reality?' Try to tell people this when they're not in desperate need of money or a man and they tell you about primary needs for food, clothing, and shelter. I see the comments under my videos from the skeptics. 'Try to pay the rent with your ultimate reality.' After we've eaten, covered ourselves, gotten indoors, then we want to reproduce. We want to acquire property. Even the queer kids I knew in the Rainbow Alliance, even the suicidal leftists I coach now, even they say everyone needs 'safety' and 'resources'—they like these words."

"We'll die without them," he said.

"Yes, but why *not* die? We live only for the sake of the imagination. I saw somewhere online, I don't know where, that they keep digging up cities thousands of years older than their previous earliest estimated dates for the development of civilization. Cities from before agriculture, cities built by nomadic rather than settled peoples. If they had no grain to store, no permanent settlement to stabilize, why did they send towers and temples into the air? Apparently, they built those structures for the purpose of human sacrifice. Those earliest stone towers housed stone gods who held their stone penises in their stone hands to watch as the first builders of cities sent heads rolling in spurts of blood across their stone altars, as mounds of skulls massed against the stone walls."

"I'm glad I missed it," he said. He arched his back until it cracked. He'd been sitting too long on the cement; he wanted to put his legs out in front of him as far as they would go; he wanted to run around the lake, even in this heat, until he dropped. He wanted to stop thinking; she was giving him a headache. He paddled his bare feet in the green water. With his long fingers, he brushed his hair out of his eyes.

"I'm not," she said. Her eyes looked lost to time, pupils dilating despite the bright sun assaulting them. "They understood, right there at the beginning, the first time anybody understood anything, that we are here to build the palace in our minds and give all we can in tribute to its grandeur, do all we can to become one with pure spirit. They understood that you had to illustrate this premise by sacrificing the material on the altar of the spiritual. That's the only way to make people understand."

"You'll sacrifice yourself to prove—"

"—that my higher life is superior to my lower. That the deepest thing in me is superior to its prison of flesh. That I am god. I'll do it live on YouTube. Then everyone will understand."

"Understand?"

"That they are gods too."

"Will they kill themselves?"

"That's for each individual god to decide."

He stood. In his shadow, she looked up at him, his long blonde hair haloed in the sun.

"You're not going to kill yourself," he said. "Just wait and see."

He ran barefoot around the lake 10 times—about a mile, he figured. He dropped beside her, his long face a glistening mask of sweat. She leaned over and vomited the noxious seaweed back into the lake until her body heaved emptily with retching. He tried to run his fingers up and down her back, but she shrugged her shoulder blades at him, sharp and protruding due to her inanition. She couldn't stand to be touched, just as she couldn't stand music. He'd brought his guitar to her dorm the fourth night they spoke together; she'd chased him out and made him come back without it. "I hate music," she'd said. "It makes me feel things I don't want to feel. It's like it's crawling under my skin."

She fell down on her back in the grass, fished in her pants pocket for her bag of crystalized ginger, tore off a fibrous piece, and put it in her mouth. Curled on his side, he lay beside her as she stared up, seemingly straight into the sun. The total strangeness of her face bewildered him with its absolute irreplaceability. She was like nothing he'd ever seen. Where on God's earth would he find another person like this? He hadn't known the world held such creatures as Ash del Greco. Now that he knew, now that he'd spent six days with her, he knew he couldn't endure one day without her. The spiral scar hypnotized him. He traced it with his index finger, the tip an inch from her skin. She flinched as if she could feel it.

CHAPTER 14
The Sermon

Two months later, he killed himself. He shot himself through the right eye in the heart of campus, between the grand Cathedral and the tiny Chapel, on a Wednesday in the fall, the first of November. She released her video, just as they'd planned, exactly two weeks after the event. She knew the video would mean the likely end of her manifestation career. She accepted that; she even welcomed it. Money would come from somewhere else; it always did. Some new online audience might even honor her, shower her with gifts, for the audacity of her performance, of her sympathetic explanation of Jacob Morrow's bloody *geste*.

She prefaced the video with the audio clip she'd recorded of her whispered "*Quod erat demonstrandum*" just after the shooting. She knew the video would be removed from all respectable platforms if she included the clip of the suicide itself, so she ripped the audio and used that over a black screen instead. She adjusted the sound levels to bring up her own words into a breathy roar and to mute the background gunshot into almost a subliminal at the start of the video.

(Even this, the subliminal gunshot, might be enough to get the video struck down by the platforms, but she trusted the sensation-hungry cultists and obsessives of the online world to keep posting it on less legitimate fora, one step ahead of the censors. She knew it would never be entirely suppressed.)

She faded in on herself, in the dark, in her dorm, her bookshelf behind her, her face faintly backlit by the string of rainbow lights overhead, her face obscured by the twinned blue squares of her laptop screen reflected in her large lenses.

"Jacob Morrow and I have been friends for two months," she said. "When I saw him shoot himself through the eye in front of the Chapel in the middle of campus, I understood why he did it. Now I want to explain it to you. I want to explain why he took his own life last week. I know that sounds like an ugly departure from what we usually talk about on this channel—using our thoughts and our words to change our lives for the better—but I believe he did it to prove the truth of what we've been saying here all along. That's why I said what I said: 'Q. E. D.,' meaning, essentially, 'It's proven.' What's proven is 'mind over matter.' What's proven is that the human mind is superior to the totality of the real."

She filled the screen with several photos of Jacob Morrow she'd retrieved from the internet, mostly from his mother's public social media feeds: Jakey as a toddler in a sailor suit, his features crumpled in a confused smile; Jakey running the high school track, his long hair, streaked blonde, streaming behind him like a cloud of glory; Jakey in his cap and gown in his high-school colors, his diploma held to his chest like the icon worn by Overman; Jakey between the elderly English couple from Prospero's Books in front of the store on a sunny day, the old man's liver-spotted hand at rest on his shoulder; Jakey and Jess—he called his mother Jess—with Niagara Falls behind them on his graduation vacation, haloed by the rainbow spray and smiling for whatever stranger Jess had asked to take the picture, his long, lean-muscled arm clasping her waist.

"Jacob Morrow was studious and intelligent, athletic and attractive. He had a loving mother and what they call a bright future. He was good at math. He loved to run and to play the guitar. He loved Shakespeare and Jane Austen. He read *Middlemarch* the summer before he started college. When I explained to him what we were doing here on this channel, you and I, when I told him about mind over matter and manifestation and how the human mind is superior to the totality of the real, he didn't believe it. He even accused me of exploiting you. He believed in the good life on earth. The class we have—had—together was taught by Simon Magnus, the author of *Overman 3000*. When I tried to tell him that I believed in what *Overman 3000* taught—that the real world is free in four dimensions, while we're condemned to live in the prison of three; that we should strive to live in the fourth dimension, even if it means we have to die in the prison of the third—he tried to give me his copy of *Sense and Sensibility*. I told him I believed Simon Magnus was my father, my parent, my all-gender progenitor, both genetic and memetic."

She paused and looked away, her spiral scar irradiated in the laptop light. An old photo of Simon Magnus flashed onscreen, Simon Magnus three decades before, in Simon Magnus's baby blue suit at the comics convention, Simon Magnus fresh from the success of *Fools' Errand*. This, too, had been part of the plan: his death would help her to announce to the notorious author and to the world the truth of her parentage. It couldn't help but catch Simon Magnus's eye, couldn't help but at least force her mother to tell her the truth.

"Why did he do it, then? Why did he kill himself if he loved life? Because I was going to do it. I was going to be the one to prove it to you. I was going to sacrifice my body on the altar of my spirit to show you, in the only way I knew how, what you would not hear when I tried to tell it to you in words. Once you become convinced you can do it—manifest, I mean: change the world with your mind—you can always arrange the world so that it suits your fantasies of a good life. That's what most of you want to do, and I don't blame you. Once I found out I could do it, though, I couldn't care for the world at all. Why should I? Doesn't my power over it mean I'm the only one in it? The only way to meet someone else would be in the fourth dimension, to meet the true god outside of time—just like in *Overman 3000*."

She spliced in the famous spread from the graphic novel's climax: Mina Mars unseamed in the middle of the air as the gnostic messiah flamed from her womb.

"I told Jacob Morrow this. I told him more than this, something I've never even told you, something I've only ever told one other person: that Simon Magnus is my father. Also, since Simon Magnus has no gender, my mother. My father and my mother both. I told him I would kill myself to prove to the world the worthlessness of the world and the absolute power of the mind. I would prove I was truly Simon Magnus's child. Do you know what he said?"

She paused. She looked down, clutched her agonized stomach, and then looked back up.

"He said, 'No you won't.' He said, 'Just wait and see.' He told me he liked me too much. He told me that he didn't want to live in a world without me. That's what he said. He didn't talk for an hour at a time, the way I talk for an hour at a time. He didn't think about it for hours, the way I think about things for hours. I know what *you're* thinking, but it wasn't an affair. I never gave him my consent to touch me—not once. We certainly never had what they call sexual relations. He loved me, though. He said he didn't know there were people like me in the world. He said he knew that if I were gone, he'd never meet anyone like me again. He told me I had more talent than he did, that I would write books, that I would be a teacher. He told me I would change my mind about these things eventually. Then he told me he'd do it for me. He would kill himself so I didn't have to kill myself, and then I would be left to explain it to you. He told me to explain it both ways, my way and his way, since it can be read both ways—probably more ways than two, like any good work of art. You know my way: mind over matter. He caused the body to die so higher values could live, or so he could live according to higher values. That wasn't how he understood it, though. He thought of it differently. The way he saw it, he died as a tribute to this world, not as a refusal of it. He died because he didn't want to live in this world without me in it, which meant, to him, that *this* world, and his love for this world, was actually the most real and absolute thing. 'You can tell them you think I died to prove that the mind is the most powerful force in the universe,' he said, 'but tell them I think I died to prove that love is even more powerful than that. Tell them I died to prove I'm not the only thing in the universe.' I didn't ask him to do it. I didn't make him do it. I never told him I loved him. I'm not sure I did. I couldn't change his mind, though. That was one thing I couldn't manifest—I'll confess that much to you. Probably I didn't want it enough. He made me see the logic that only one of us could do it—that if he did it, I couldn't, because it would muddle the message, and he was going to do it no matter what, going to do it so I wouldn't. If I had any integrity, I'd kill myself anyway. I've never liked it here much, to be honest. It's just that he made me promise not to. That, and to read this."

She held up his copy of *Sense and Sensibility*, a turn-of-the-century edition, his 16th-birthday present from the Penshursts, the red cloth cover inlaid with gilt flora in symmetrical loops and curves.

The video faded to black and reprised the initial audio, the muffled gunshot and her whispered "*Quod erat demonstrandum*." It ended there, on those words, as if to ask its audience what an act that admitted of no one interpretation could possibly have been said to prove.

CHAPTER 15
The Interrogation

For almost a month, Jacob Morrow's death became the local habitation of the always ambient culture war. What was wrong with our men? What was wrong with our comic books? What was wrong with our universities? What was wrong with our guns? What was wrong with our mental health? What could we do? We had to do something. We had to save lives. Firearms were already prohibited on campus, a prohibition that had not forestalled the act. The university administration mulled compulsory psychotherapy sessions at least once a semester for all students. Simon Magnus, who'd had both the girl and the boy in Simon Magnus's class, fell under investigation for having written *Overman 3000*, considering that its own themes were cited in in the girl's bizarre video, not to mention her having claimed Simon Magnus to be her father, her father-mother, her all-gender all-parent.

A small knot of protestors outside the city courthouse, backed by thousands online (#justiceforjakey), demanded that Ash del Greco be charged with some crime—but what crime? Recovered text messages proved inconclusive; the last one she'd sent him, a line from some ancient poet about contrasting the thinker with the soldier, could as easily be read as an encouragement to live and to think as an encouragement to die and therefore to stop thinking. You never could tell what poets were saying. The security footage of the pair inside Untimely Vintage was evidence of exactly nothing; there was only one camera in the store, trained on the front entrance—Jessica Morrow had had it installed after an attempted break-in a decade ago—and Jacob Morrow and Ash del Greco were often in its blind spot or behind it during their time in the store. The gun was traced to the store's own inventory. It had been part of a lot of clothing and antiques Jessica Morrow had purchased through a broker from a recently deceased nonagenarian socialite whose possessions included her late sheriff father's two old revolvers, pearl-handled and quaint, of which only one had been taken.

The controversy began to wane when Ash del Greco released the video. The girl claimed on that video to have encouraged him *not* to do it, claimed she could not talk him out of it. Whether or not the video itself promoted suicide was hard to say—she really was a strange girl, or whatever—but its strangeness, the picture collages and sound effects, meant that it fell under the juridically ambiguous heading of "art" and, in any case, YouTube removed it an hour after she posted it, even if clips would circulate illicitly online probably for as long as there was an internet to appreciate scandal. After the video, sales of *Sense and Sensibility* and *Middlemarch* surged for one day.

National social media influencers on the political right found the articles about Ash del Greco and Ari Alterhaus's high-school gender dissidence from half a decade before and made her scarred face and cropped hair their latest sign of our society's pre-apocalyptic degeneracy. The photo that had accompanied Kristen Connolly's national newspaper article—Ari Alterhaus, fresh from top surgery, seated regally, Ash del Greco wide-eyed and shorn-headed standing at their side—became a meme template, captioned with texts ranging from the earnest political demand (*don't let THIS happen to YOUR daughter*) to the ironic sexual judgment (*they/them pussy got me fucked up*). Once Ash del Greco began to be execrated by the online right, the local and state governments, then controlled by the left, resolved that the girl or xirl or however she might desire to style herself (legitimately, of course, not that this should be reduced to a matter of "desire") could under no circumstances be prosecuted.

As the situation unfolded in public, a pair of investigators appointed by the university requested to interview Ash del Greco at her earliest convenience. She made her appointment with them for the interview on the day and time she planned to post the video, exactly two weeks after the suicide. She scheduled the video to post automatically, in fact, on the very hour the interview would begin. It would be released to the world, would touch off an online conflagration, just as she was being interrogated for her potential culpability in Jacob Morrow's crime against himself and against the University community. She often liked to do this, to schedule a post she both feared and desired might prove controversial—for example, her video about her disbelief in the necessity to a successful manifestation of what Jungian therapists called shadow work—for a time when she could not be online, to allow whatever might erupt to erupt without her.

(In the case of the shadow-work video, a middle-aged yogi who delivered her own manifestation coaching in a soft voice from a bamboo balcony in Bali, often as she snaked her lean leg behind her head, toes flexed against her tanned temple, pronounced Ash del Greco a "dangerous and harmful ignoramus" from the platform of her much larger channel. This had few real consequences that Ash del Greco could detect. She later quipped that the yogi must not have sufficiently integrated her own shadow if she was hurling such imprecations from her yoga mat.)

The very moment her sermon on the death of Jacob Morrow was released to the internet, the investigators took their seats across from Ash del Greco at a formica-topped table in a tight coral-walled office in the mysterious high reaches of the Cathedral, many floors above the classrooms and faculty offices on the lower levels. Just to induce some new sensation, she had climbed some 20 flights of stairs to get up to the office rather than crowd with her fellow students into one of the too-few elevators, everyone smelling of mold from the dorms' nonfunctioning dryers or of weed from last night's—or this morning's—session. She hadn't eaten breakfast. She hadn't eat dinner the night before. She'd thrown up the previous day's yogurt and ginger chews. She sat breathlessly at the table across from her interrogators as blood hammered the walls of her skull and narrowed her vision to a twinkling point. She felt the investigators' eyes traversing her scar in quickening spirals out from the void at its center, their pupils whirling in their sockets: a widening gyre.

Afraid she might be expelled from school or charged with a crime after his death, she and Jacob Morrow had planned everything together in advance against the possibility of such an investigation. For example, they had kept their texting to a minimum, so she could say to any inquisitors that they had been acquaintances at best and had certainly never discussed suicide together. Her final text to him—the Yeats quotation, obviously pregnant with her knowledge of his act—was the only risk she'd allowed herself. She'd scolded herself the moment she sent it, less for exposing them to danger per se than for lapsing into cliché *by* exposing them to danger: wasn't the text a cry for help, evidence of a desire to be caught, an eructation of some secret need to be punished? He hadn't replied; she hadn't needed him to reply. She didn't even agree with the quotation, which she'd seen on some website; she advised people *not* to enter the abyss of themselves. Jacob Morrow, she dimly understood, had in fact entered into the abyss of *her*self. Somehow she'd just wanted him to have some token of hers as he walked down toward his death.

(Before they'd gone to his mother's store, the whole thing had been an abstraction and a game to her—before she'd found the revolvers, of which she'd taken only the one, while idly rummaging through the vintage clothes. Then she knew it would happen, had to happen, had already happened. She gave him the gun later that night; she taught him to use it after consulting a video tutorial on her phone while he went to the bathroom in the dorm; she never told him where it came from and couldn't imagine what he'd say if he knew. Did Jessica Morrow blame herself? If I were Jessica Morrow, thought Ash del Greco, I'd use the other gun on me.)

"Why did you send him *this*?" the first investigator asked her after reading out the quotation from Yeats she had texted him the night before his death. The investigator pronounced the poet's name as if it rhymed with "beets" or "sheets" or "treats." The close room made Ash del Greco feel faint. Inside her head, she murmured, to keep herself from fainting, from vomiting, Eats, seats, meets, greets, beats, Keats... A young man fresh from whatever credentialing program had credentialed him, his face a mask of compassion, all but begging her for a credible explanation that would not implicate her in this crime, her inquisitor, who'd introduced himself as Patrick Elsberry, reminded her of Dr. Andrew Wyman, except that his pink cheeks were smooth. Perhaps he was even Dr. Andrew Wyman's son, despite the difference in name. No one kept their names anymore. What had happened, after all, to Ashley, to Arielle?

"We were English majors," she said slowly. "We liked poets. We liked what they had to say. I thought it would show him he didn't have to die, that he needed to have enough bravery to live."

The two investigators exchanged a subtle glance. The smooth-cheeked young man who'd asked about "Yeets" made a note. His colleague, a sharp-faced woman with a severe blonde bob, pursed her thin and lightly frosted lips. Her name, she'd said, was Alexandra Pocock. Ash del Greco thought, Pocock, peacock, restock, teapot...

Ash del Greco felt like she could read their minds, despite her own present debility. Not only comic books but poetry too? they must have been thinking to themselves, Alexandra Pocock and Patrick Elsberry, Patrick Elsberry and Alexandra Pocock. She wondered if the teaching of literature would soon be banned. Tell the Republicans it perverts morals, tell the Democrats it harms mental health, and you could get them to agree to its proscription, as they could not agree to proscribe guns. Guns at least had the utility of self-defense. Of what utility could literature—whether poem or comic book—possibly boast? Yeets meets Keats, Keats beats Yeets, she thought. By cock, we are to blame. She was about to fall out of her chair.

Smooth-cheeked Patrick Elsberry came around to her side of the table and sat in the open seat next to her, as if to hold her up with his shoulder. He showed her his phone. Quite casually, he pointed to the screen, as if to share a meme with her. Instead of a meme, however, she saw grainy surveillance footage of herself and Jacob Morrow, footage taken seemingly everywhere, from the lobby of their dorm to the Cathedral commons room to the Fine Arts Building fountain and even—where could there have been a camera? in the trees? on the underside of the bridge? in a miniature drone?—by the banks of Tiger Hollow Lake as Jacob Morrow fed her an algae bloom from the end of a branch.

"It looks like you were close," he said. She kept her eyes down, staring at his finger on the touch screen; he bit his nails, she saw, the quicks jagged, blood at the corner of his ring finger, where he wore one of those blocky wedding rings men wore now, like a nut for a screw. She imperceptibly leaned on his shoulder, her eyelids unliftable, her empty, acidic stomach audibly squealing and burbling in the quiet, narrow room. Patrick Elsberry sounds like the name of a cartoon character, she thought, a squirrel in overalls. This squirrel's found a nut. We're screwed, Jakey.

"We were friends," she said, chasms yawning between her words. "That doesn't mean I could stop him from killing himself."

This was not a lie. He had never even used the word "suicide" for what he'd planned to do, for what he'd done. He thought of it as dying in her stead, an almost instinctual act in the face of a sudden inevitability, like leaping in front of a bullet bound for a friend, except that he'd leapt for two months and had had to fire the bullet himself.

"Were you dating?" Alexandra Pocock asked with her sharp face. Her blue irises radiated bright capillaries in the milk-white vitreous. Pocock, Ash del Greco thought, bloodshot.

"No," she said. She heard it in her head as a long slow nooooooooooooooooooo.

This was neither the truth nor a lie. What was dating? The word didn't apply to anything she might do. She hadn't wanted to spend time with anyone but Jacob Morrow—she still didn't—and he'd stepped in her stead into the path of a bullet she'd fired in her mind at herself a few months before they'd met. She didn't love him, or she did. What was love? She didn't think she loved anyone, not after Ari Alterhaus, if that itself had been love, but they were bound together, Ash del Greco and Jacob Morrow, forever, united by death.

She had wanted to present herself to the investigators not as his collaborator, not as a conspirator with prior knowledge of the act, but simply as a friend. Now she didn't know what she was saying. "He seemed happy," she said, just to fill the silence in which her agitated stomach squalled.

Now it was Alexandra Pocock's turn to come around to her side of the table, to sit in the seat on the other side of her. She would have fainted for sure if she hadn't suddenly found herself between them, her narrow shoulders squeezed. She couldn't stand to be touched. She couldn't stand the smell of them, the aftershave and the lotions and the makeup mixing with sweat on synthetic fabrics, everything in slow decay—not like Jakey, who smelled clean even after he ran a mile, clean as a tree does, not that she'd ever been one for nature before, not the way he was. He treed. In the earth, he trees. Her whole body itched. Her stomach burned and the acid rose into her throat. These two inquisitors had her so squeezed she couldn't reach in her pocket for her ginger. She tried to suppress a belch but remembered that she didn't respect these people, so she gave it vent. With unprofessional compassion, Patrick Elsberry gently patted her wrist.

Alexandra Pocock now held out her own phone to Ash del Greco, and Ash del Greco saw a still photo of the bookshelf in her dorm. Then the investigator pulled up her Notes app. She had an alphabetized list of the titles on Ash del Greco's shelf and short summaries of their contents, with a focus on topics like "anhedonia," "anxiety," "depression," "dissociation," "fascism," "nihilism," "pessimism," "self-harm," and, of course, "suicide."

"I wouldn't call Nietzsche a fascist," Ash del Greco said in sudden lucidity, just to say something, just to keep awake, just to have something in her mouth besides stomach acid, and just because she *wouldn't* have called him that, not that she particularly cared either way. She knew there was no point in asking when they'd taken the photo or how, whether they'd done it while she was out or while she was asleep; she knew such curiosity would in itself be interpreted as evidence of her pathological resistance to what emails from the school's president had recently described as "the care-work of empowering mental health in the University community." The University would integrate *everybody's* shadow.

"Maybe we've been imprecise," Alexandra Pocock conceded. "We had to rely on Wikipedia."

"Yeats, now *he* was a fascist," Ash del Greco found it in her to quip.

"Yeats?" Patrick Elsberry asked with a raised eyebrow.

"I mean Yeets."

Her head began to droop. The young man again extended his phone. He played for her one of the videos of the suicide that had gone viral—those videos that trolls and provocateurs reposted as soon as they were deleted on every public platform, and which managed to live permanently on the less-policed platforms, those videos that had, within 12 hours of Jacob Morrow's death, been edited into memes where the fatal gunshot comically punctuated embarrassing scenes of personal failure, like a dance move turned pratfall or a politician's gaffe, or made into music videos in various moods, overlaid with either aptly doom-laden or ironically cheery music. The video would still be a meme template in five years, when no one would remember Jacob Morrow's name. That was that kid who— What was his name? The video compassionate young Patrick Elsberry showed her, however, had been sound-adjusted to bring up her own statement on the suicide, though still garbled, still glossolalic.

"This is your voice," he said. "We checked against other recordings of you we were able to find. On your YouTube channel, for example," he went on meaningfully. "What did you say?"

She told them the truth, and then she translated it, and then she explained the translation, even as her vision went black, went white, went pulsing pink neon. She wished she had posted the video sermon earlier so that she did not have to explain herself all over again. This was another reason to kill yourself, another reason she'd wanted to. She had already put all of herself out there, into the data stream. What was left? Jacob Morrow hadn't put any of himself there at all, though, except for his final act. All of him was gone forever.

"Why would you say that? You mean he did it to make a point?" Alexandra Pocock asked.

"Yes. I understood why he did it."

They exchanged a glance over her head, the two investigators. What was this, religious fanaticism, some kind of cult? A cult the strange religion her online videos advocated, for example, some kind of occult witchery? Was it political extremism? The young man had been wearing an army jacket when he'd taken his own life. Were right-wing militias involved? Were there terror groups on campus? Were they obligated to call the FBI?

"What point could he possibly have been making?" Alexandra Pocock finally asked.

Ash del Greco spoke in an irritable rush, to get the words out ahead of her collapsing consciousness: "That we are superior to our existence. Mind over matter. Which means—this is what he tried to prove by killing himself—that life is worth living."

Then, entirely without her consent or control, as if she were vomiting from her eye sockets, she began to cry. As soon as she'd said it, she had to ask herself, "*Was* life worth living?" A life where she'd never talk to Jacob Morrow again? Her strange words and stranger interests raised the investigators' suspicion, but, in their experience, such desperate sobbing, the kind where the whole body seizes and shudders, didn't lie. Yeets weeps for Keats. Weeps beats trees, trees eats weeps...

If it's not about the other person, then what's the point?

Professionally forbidden from touching their subjects, the inquisitors sat and stared down at her hunched back as she groaned and choked between them, as she realized, almost for the first time, that someone who could not be replaced had exited her life for good. She could manifest him back, but she knew from the "Ari Alterhaus is still alive" experience that this would solve nothing, that you *can* come back to life, but not as the "you" you'd been and not to the life you'd had. Jacob Morrow was dead forever.

When she calmed down, they admonished her to seek help at Campus Health Services and warned that they might contact her again, but then they let her go. She tried three times to get out of her seat before falling back into it. Alexandra Pocock, throwing decorum to the wind, finally shoved her to her feet by the small of her back. Beat from seat to feet. She steadied herself and calmly stepped from the room, feeling that with every step she might fall through the floor, drop half the length of the Cathedral, 20 stories down. 20 stories. She couldn't bear it. She'd had three stories so far—Diane del Greco, Ari Alterhaus, Jacob Morrow—and they'd been as much as she could take.

She staggered out of the office, passed the elevator, and found the dark concrete stairwell she'd run up a half hour before. She concluded that the flights were too short to kill her if she threw herself down. She would have to keep rolling herself across landings to hurl herself down more stairs, too comical an image to be the final image one left the world. In any case, she owed it to Jacob Morrow—to the point he'd been trying to make, which had not been her point, had been even better than her point—to live. Her head spun, rung, drummed; her stomach churned, burned, surged. She went down the flights on trembling knees, gripping the rails in an excruciatingly slow progress; at one point, she threw up over the railing, as if from the deck of an ocean-tossed ship, into the long shaft of unilluminated emptiness that bisected the building from foundation to spire, the nullity in the midst of its squared spiral.

At the bottom, she found an exit door so heavy she had to throw her whole body against it to push it open. The sudden sunlight cast blackness on her stunned eyes. She paused in the doorway, dizzy; she heard footsteps pounding down the stairs after her, the rapid clack of a professional woman's heels, heard Alexandra Pocock shout her name with phone in hand, Ash del Greco's video sermon blaring tinnily out of its little speaker. "Ms. del Greco, wait! Wait! Ms. del Greco! We need to speak to you about your latest video!" the inquisitor shouted behind her as she stood rooted to the doorstep. Who on earth was Ms. del Greco? No one had ever addressed her that way before. "Mx.," she would have insisted back in high school, conspiring with Ari Alterhaus on Ari Alterhaus's bed as a storm dropped torrents down the high windows. Mixter del Greco, you're all mixtered up, we need to fixter you up... She didn't even feel herself fall.

She woke slowly in a bright white room on a hard white bed beneath stiff white sheets. Her empty stomach seized painfully, but she swallowed the rising acid. Her eyes were so dry and abraded she could barely hold them open; they fluttered so that the four people approaching her bedside from the door to the room she was in—a hospital room, she ventured—moved in jerky time-lapse: the two investigators, Simon Magnus, and a woman she didn't know, a woman with eyes that were familiar somehow, gentle and thoughtful, a woman with bare arms and shoulders revealed by her thin shirt to be crawling with tattoos.

"You're okay," Simon Magnus said gently. "Try to relax."

"When you're done relaxing," Patrick Elsberry said, not sounding as friendly as he'd sounded before, "we have some further questions for you."

Also unfriendly, her voice quivering with rage and sorrow, Jessica Morrow then leaned down over Ash del Greco and demanded, as the two investigators pulled her back by both arms, "Did you know, you little bitch? Did you know before you made him do it? Did you know you were pregnant?"

PART FOUR

CHAPTER 1

Counter, Original, Spare, Strange

Ellen Chandler at 50 years old. An unseasonably Hyperborean wind—it was mid-November now—roared through the Jewish cemetery and whipped her long gray coat and her long whitening hair all around her figure and face, both of them thin as ever. She immured her hands in her long pockets and blinked away the blinding tears stung out of her eyes by the cold, by the place. She stood above Marco Cohen's small gravestone, blank except for his incised name and dates, dates not amounting even to 40 years.

He had been dead for almost two decades, but she'd never been there before. She'd had to locate the place on findagrave.com. After he flew back east to bury Levy, he'd never spoken to her again. He would not answer her calls, would not reply to her emails or her letters. Once, when she was eight months pregnant, her back thrown out and shooting daggers of agony down her left leg every time she took a step, her ankles so swollen she could only wear flip-flops, she'd dragged herself through a humid early springtime, through miles and miles of subway, choking down her nausea, to his parents' apartment. She'd pressed the button in the building lobby over and over again, announcing herself into the staticky speaker as the doorman eyed her suspiciously, telling them it was urgent that she talk with their son, an emergency even, but they would not let her in. She imagined that he somehow held her responsible for Levy's death. Then he went and sought his own death—as good as killed himself in atonement, in expiation.

(The child's own gravestone stood next to his father's, his dates not amounting to one year.)

"I came in case you had any advice for me," she said loudly, over the wind, the way she'd used to have to shout to him in the bar near the University when they'd been (thinking themselves so adult) only children. "I know you didn't believe in life after death. I didn't then either. I'm not even sure I do now, though don't tell Sister Margaret—that's my boss, if you don't know. I thought I'd give you an opportunity, anyway. I thought I'd stop, just on the off chance. Our daughter is in trouble, Marco. I don't know if you ever knew we had a daughter. You wouldn't let me tell you in person. Maybe you tore up my letters and deleted my emails without reading them. Maybe you read them and thought you didn't deserve another child, not after—well. Maybe you read them and agreed with my plan and let it go ahead. I have no idea. We did, though, we *did* have a daughter, you and I. One night is all it takes, I guess. We have a daughter, and she's in trouble. She's in trouble, and she thinks Simon is her father, and I'm not sure if you want me to correct her or not. I just wanted you to know."

Marco Cohen, who hadn't believed in magic or religion, didn't reply, unless the fury of the agitated air *was* his riposte. Who would he be now if he'd lived? Ellen Chandler wondered. If Levy hadn't died, would he have enjoyed the *Overman 3000* royalties and eventual movie money, parlayed his prestige among comic-book artists into a successful career, had more babies with Diane del Greco, moved with his family to a quiet suburb? Would he have become a potbellied, gray-bearded *paterfamilias* going twice a year on the comics convention circuit in a Hawaiian shirt and making most of his money in commissions? Would he, in his middle age, have started voting Republican at last? She couldn't imagine such a fate for so passionately earnest a young man as Marco Cohen had been. He must have been born, one way or the other, to die young, to die to *this* world.

She lived in the suburbs now, in a little blue ranch house at the circular end of a cul-de-sac with a backyard adjoining some woods where her dogs could run. After Virginia and Vanessa had died within a few weeks of each other, about five years before, she got another greyhound, whom she named Nora; she loved to throw a branch and watch her streak silver, ribboning through the dark woods as the sun went down. Then, about a year later, she took in a stray little terrier she'd found shivering on her back porch one winter morning; she called her Lucia and laughed as the little white dog yipped and hopped, circling Nora's long bounding legs. She voted Republican now. Christ, she thought, with the chaos our country was in—the crime, the prices, the wars, the gender theory in preschool, and all the rest of it—how could you possibly *not*?

After *Overman 3000*, after quitting comics, she'd gone back for her education degree. This was her 20th year teaching high-school English at St. Anne's. It was a living. You really couldn't read *Hamlet* too many times. Well, *she* couldn't. A lot of the kids couldn't read it even once, apparently, but that was why God gave us movies. Watching some, just a few, of her students' eyes go a millimeter wider, their lips curl up into an almost imperceptible caught-breath smile of exhilaration, when she showed them something they'd never seen before, something they might not even have thought possible in the language they spoke every day, would never lose its savor for her: the way Gerard Manley Hopkins encoded the intricate feeling of his fraught faith into patterns of stressed and unstressed syllables, the way Flannery O'Connor restaged our fall and our salvation in superficially plain-spoken modern dress, in parables outrageously violent enough to divert anyone, even jaded youth. Her 22-year-self would be disgusted to learn that her 50-year-old self had not joined the ranks of the great metropolitan literary minds, had only earned a very minor fame editing a few stupid comic books, and then had ended up teaching at the same parochial school she herself attended from kindergarten through 12th grade, construing it as a prison all the while. Ellen Chandler wasn't 22 anymore and wasn't disgusted. St. Anne's a prison? Then is the world one. It was a life.

She hadn't ever married. She hadn't even tried. Her several years' quasi-marriage to Simon Magnus, and the calamity of its conclusion, had sated her appetite for men, or for whatever it was Simon Magnus had been, forever. She hadn't ever had children—*more* children, she supposed she should say. She'd had the one, just barely. Marco Cohen's brilliant baby, its head too large to pass through her narrow pelvis, had been (as the poet said) from its mother's womb untimely ripped; the seam across her flat belly reminded Ellen Chandler every day that she never wanted to experience *that* again.

She'd buried her mother and father 13 and eight years before, breast cancer and Alzheimer's, respectively—one or another grim future awaiting us all. Both the fungating tumor that rotted her mother's breast from the inside out in pulps and fronds of yellow ulceration and caused the whole house to smell like spoiled meat *and* the comparatively decorous, but in its way even more terrible, inner labyrinth of scared-angry confusion down whose narrow corridors her father fruitlessly wandered were enough to convince her that this world was little more than (God forgive her) some sadistic demiurge's game preserve, enough to make her hot-flash with panic and want desperately to leap, to escape to some other world, some safer and better world, except that there wasn't one, not here anyway, and not for us. For us, down here, there was dementia and carcinoma and whatever brief pleasure one could find in the meantime.

She had few people in her life. One or two of the other teachers took her out for a drink or remembered her birthday now and again, but otherwise, she lived with her books and her dogs and her students and mass on Sundays. She still liked to run, even though her hips and her knees burned and screamed, her very body a *memento mori*, reminding her of the years that had passed, of the difficult pregnancy from which she felt she somehow had never quite recovered, and of the killing sickness that awaited her, awaited everyone—that is, everyone who didn't succumb to accident or murder as Levy and Marco Cohen had, or to suicide, like that poor boyfriend of her strange daughter, whatever his name was, she couldn't remember, a red blossom where his right eye should have been.

There was Pilar Rivera, but she didn't like to think about Pilar Rivera, because Pilar Rivera had rightly shamed her back in those days when she'd liked to think about Pilar Rivera too much. Pilar Rivera, then Pablo Rivera, had been a senior in only the second class she'd taught at St. Anne's, all those years before. Pablo Rivera, eyes red and watery and lost to the world at eight in the morning, nevertheless possessed a thin and delicate face she wished to shield from the world, even as this face regarded her lectures on poetry with a blank, stoned smile of contemptuous incomprehension. Pablo Rivera dropped out of school shortly after Christmas that year. She felt—she even admitted this to herself then—less impetus to teach her morning class in his absence, less impetus to teach at all, even though Pablo Rivera hadn't ever either heard or said a word.

Two years later, on a Friday night in winter, she saw the same face framed in a mass of bright blonde curls waiting tables in a pricey Italian restaurant her parents had brought her to for one of their weekly dinners. She excused herself from the table and discreetly approached the server, who, in common with the other female waitstaff, wore a black midi dress.

"Pablo Rivera?" she whispered.

"Pilar Rivera," Pilar Rivera corrected, an admonishing index finger tipped with a pink acrylic nail in the air.

She asked if Pilar Rivera remembered her.

"I remember you, Miss Chandler," Pilar Rivera said. "'Glory be to God for dappled things'—right?"

Ellen Chandler asked what time Pilar Rivera's shift ended and, when she learned that Pilar Rivera had to take two buses home at midnight, offered to come back and pick her up. Maybe they could reminisce about old times, she suggested.

"Maybe," Pilar Rivera said.

That midnight, in her car, in the restaurant parking lot, she almost couldn't breathe when she leaned over the passenger seat as Pilar Rivera hiked up her dress, her underwear white and lacy as the tracery of ice on the windshield. It was the middle of winter, and Pilar Rivera had let the cold air into the car. Ellen Chandler's trembling breath whitely haloed the girl's penis, standing like a bride in its garden of lace.

For almost a year, she would pick Pilar Rivera up every Friday night from the restaurant and bring her to her suburban home for weekends of sheltered luxury: long baths, filet mignon, champagne, soft sheets, even—why not?—Gerard Manley Hopkins, who had praised God for "all things counter, original, spare, strange."

"Just come and live with me," she said again and again, but Pilar Rivera wanted her freedom—or at least her choice of thralldoms. She'd earned her GED. She was saving up, first for surgery and then for college. She wouldn't let

Ellen Chandler give her money outright and never seemed comfortable in her house, always sat stiffly as Virginia and Vanessa circled and sniffed.

Ellen Chandler didn't even know why Pilar Rivera bothered with her at all, except that she seemed to have no one else to show her a moment's tenderness or concern, living as she did with an indifferent alcoholic mother who was glad to see her go on the weekends and didn't ask where she'd been when she returned late on Sunday nights. ("You killed me," she'd said to Pilar Rivera when Pilar Rivera came out.) Ellen Chandler briefly plugged a gap in the girl's so-far discontinuous existence. Pilar Rivera would get high and lay there and let Ellen Chandler, who was what they called stone-cold sober, do as she pleased. It was a life.

One Friday midnight, though, as Ellen Chandler waited in her car for Pilar Rivera to lift her dress, Pilar Rivera told her that she couldn't endure it anymore, not one more second of it: Ellen Chandler's fixation on an organ she, Pilar Rivera, wanted only to be rid of, an organ that had never, as far as she was concerned, been any part of her in the first place. She rejected it, Ellen Chandler's humanly insulting fetish.

(Ellen Chandler had once told Pilar Rivera about Simon Magnus, had even told her that Simon Magnus was responsible for The Fool in his pink tutu, now familiar to all of America from the hit movie *Ratman Rises*; Pilar Rivera had only said, "He sounds like a fucking pervert to me.")

Tears, pleas, screams.

"What am I? Just a dick in a dress to you? I'm a human being, for Christ's sake! What the fuck is wrong with you, lady? You're a schoolteacher! You make me sick!"

Pilar Rivera slammed the car door, straightened her dress, and walked in the cold to the bus stop.

Ellen Chandler parked her car every Friday midnight for a month outside the restaurant, but that was the last she ever saw of Pilar Rivera. Every day for a year, she expected Sister Margaret to call her into the office to be dismissed from her position at St. Anne's for her conduct with a former student, but Pilar Rivera had, apparently, rejected her too totally even to exact her just retribution. That was the end of love, even the possibility of love, for Ellen Chandler.

Now she didn't like to think about Pilar Rivera, except for a part of her, one part, perhaps never the most creditable part, that loved to think about Pilar Rivera. Would God, would Jesus, would Mother Mary forgive her? Yes, of course, that was what God and Jesus and Mother Mary did: they forgave. Why, anyway, had God made things so counter, so original, so spare, so strange in the first place? Her mother, her cankered body smelling like the slaughterhouse it'd become, had lain groaning for hours, calling out to Mary. Her father, terrified and angry in the interior labyrinth of his plaque-combed brain, had seemed by contrast almost to make a point of not crying for help, not to her, not to God, not to Mary, not to anyone. We all see how much we need to believe when the time comes, she thought. We think we know beforehand, but we don't. We don't know until our world ends. What would she say when her time came? Whom would she call for help? She was alone.

Ellen Chandler took a pack of cigarettes from her long pocket. She hadn't smoked in over a decade, not since her mother's slow, painful death; she'd bought them, along with a cheap plastic lighter, in a gas station on her way to the Jewish cemetery. Despite the wind, she managed to get one of the cigarettes lit, took a long drag, and then, smoke still wisping off its tip, she weighed it down on top of Marco Cohen's gravestone with a flat rock she found in the grass.

Rain started to riddle the landscape in sidewise torrents on the gray air. She pulled her coat closer and ran back to her car. Her long whitening hair dripping onto its glass face, she checked the directions on her phone again before she started the car engine. If she went the speed limit, which she wouldn't, she could be there in under six hours, before dinner time. Before the day ended, she would, for the first time in more than two decades, see her daughter in the flesh: Ash del Greco.

CHAPTER 2
The Lemniscate

Someone was watching Simon Magnus.

It started the very day of Jacob Morrow's suicide, though Simon Magnus had only understood this in retrospect, after a pattern had been established. Sent home before afternoon classes on the day of the boy's death, Simon Magnus returned to Simon Magnus's apartment just after lunchtime. In the sorrow and confusion of the moment, Simon Magnus made little of the strangely iridescent electric car with blackout windows parked across the quiet city street from where Simon Magnus lived. The car had been there every day since Jacob Morrow's suicide, however—every time Simon Magnus entered or exited the building.

Simon Magnus saw the car elsewhere, as well: everywhere Simon Magnus went. It was parked on the periphery of the college green that held the Cathedral and the Chapel on the day Simon Magnus, after the encounter with the department chair, had led a weeping Jessica Morrow away from the Chapel to a bar nearby, where Simon Magnus bought her drink after drink and listened to her life story, to the story of the prison of her parents' marriage and her mother's freedom, to the story of her discovery of her eye and the founding of her shop, to the story of how she'd decided against the odds to have a child, and to the story of Jacob Morrow, her beautiful boy, who would not squash a spider and yet had shot himself through the eye. The car was parked outside the bar when Simon Magnus helped a staggering Jessica Morrow into an Uber late the same night. The car was parked outside Simon Magnus's apartment still later that night, after Simon Magnus's deliberately circuitous walk from the bar to the building, a walk through alleys and backyards intended to foil any followers.

The car was parked outside Simon Magnus's apartment the day, almost two weeks later, when Jessica Morrow sent Simon Magnus the video in which Ash del Greco named Simon Magnus as her father; Simon Magnus knew this because an hour after Jessica Morrow sent the video, someone from the University hospital called to say that a collapsed Ash del Greco had murmured a request for Simon Magnus's presence at her bedside. When Simon Magnus exited the building to walk to campus, to the University hospital, Simon Magnus found Jessica Morrow on the doorstep, saying, "I want you to tell me everything you know about her." Even while Simon Magnus tried unsuccessfully to dissuade Jessica Morrow from coming to the University hospital with him, Simon Magnus couldn't ignore the car parked across the street, watching Simon Magnus over Jessica Morrow's tattoo-inscribed shoulder. Simon Magnus exited the hospital later that day, after Diane del Greco had taken Ash del Greco home; Jessica Morrow was clinging to Simon Magnus's arm, and Simon Magnus was thinking to SimonMagnusself, Will I ever rid myself of this irritating woman, this utterly tedious and badly tattooed aging hipster clothes-peddler?, even as Simon Magnus noticed, parked across the street from the hospital, the iridescent electric car with the blackout windows.

One Saturday morning, after Simon Magnus woke from uneasy sleep to the grim recollection that the name "Simon Magnus" was now a byword and a scandal, that Simon Magnus would never teach again, that Simon Magnus's life was effectively finished at 50 years of age, Simon Magnus walked to the apartment window, parted the dusty plastic slats of the venetian blind and saw it, and then, before Simon Magnus could talk SimonMagnusself out of it, wearing just a T-shirt and boxer shorts and socks, ran down the stairs and across the street to where the iridescent electric car with the blackout windows was parked.

The car seemed to shimmer and tesselate in Simon Magnus's vision, making Simon Magnus's sad reflection in the blackout windows waver and hum. Who was that old man with thinning, graying hair and the potbelly and the papery knees shuffling across the street, Simon Magnus asked SimonMagnusself? God, who *was* that old man?

Simon Magnus rapped on the window. It lowered itself with an electric whirr to disclose a pale woman with short blonde hair and a navy blue pantsuit. She wore sunglasses that also threw back Simon Magnus's reflection, this time doubled. Her lips shimmery with a glitter-jeweled nude lipstick, she smiled and said, "Hello, Simon Magnus. I'm so glad you finally decided to reach out to us."

Later, after Simon Magnus showered and dressed, they met, Simon Magnus and the woman, in a nearby Starbucks. Simon Magnus was no purist—Simon Magnus had always taken plenteous cream and sugar, and these days had a corresponding vice for vanilla lattes—but was startled to see the almost neon color, a radiating pink, of the confection the woman had ordered. She carried a rectangular black portfolio bag strapped across her shoulder; it somehow reminded Simon Magnus of the nuclear football carried securely at the president's side by a military aide.

"It's not worth the calories, I know," she said conspiratorially of her radiant drink when she joined Simon Magnus at a table near the back of the crowded café. "I just can't resist, though."

"What's this about?" Simon Magnus asked. "Is this part of the University's investigation? I've already resigned. They have no authority over me."

"No, no," she said in a gentle, mollifying tone. "We don't approve of the way the University treated you. We admire your work. My God, when I read *Overman 3000* in college—my boyfriend at the time gave it to me, but don't tell anybody that in case they revoke my feminist card—I thought to myself, Whoever wrote this is a visionary! It's one of the things that inspired me, you know, to join the agency. I guess I read it in an idiosyncratic way. What did they call it in my English classes? 'Reading against the grain'? I was an English major, if you can't tell—well, and a gender studies minor, of course, though I think they still called it women's studies back then. Anyway, I didn't think Max Muller was evil—just ineffective. Leave it to a mediocre male to botch an important job, right? There has to be a better way to keep an organized society running, to monitor and repel threats from extremist groups like your Cyphronian gnostics. You have to remember, I was a freshman—a 'first-year student,' I think they say now, and rightly so—when the towers fell, and I read your book about a year after that. I thought you'd written the bible on the mind of the terrorist, even before I realized that someplace like the agency could be a place for me. You might think it's all old cigar-smoking white men in suits with reactionary politics, but that's an outdated stereotype. It's really very diverse now. Look at me: a queer woman, a first-generation college grad, somebody who's had mental health struggles. I'm mostly 'she,' but 'they' is perfectly fine with me. You'd be right at home there, Simon Magnus. We're very respectful of how people like to be addressed. We loved what you did with pronouns and proper nouns. We're all admirers of yours at the agency and have been for a very long time—since before I got there. That's why I'm here now. I have a proposition for you."

"You want to recruit me?" Simon Magnus asked.

"No, no," she said with a little laugh. She sipped her radiant pink drink from its open compostable cup—no plastic straws here—and a fleck of foam remained on her top lip, its bubbles popping with a minuscule crackle Simon Magnus could see but not hear in the crowded café. "Nothing so literal. Let artists be artists, let agents be agents. You haven't been an artist for a long time, though. Your admirers have waited 20 years for something new. We thought maybe it was because you haven't found the right artist. We know what happened with Duncan McGinnis, after all. It's too bad what he's become, an elitist and an extremist with nothing good to say about democracy, about the West, about NATO. We have intelligence—you didn't hear this from me—suggesting he might in fact have ties to Russia. Marco Cohen, too—an even greater tragedy, if a more complex case. The synergy you had with Marco Cohen, though, Simon Magnus, that was extraordinary, a landmark in the history of the arts. We all think so. What if we could replicate that? What if lightning could strike twice? What if—even better—we could wipe out the memory of Marco Cohen's social irresponsibility? What if we could surpass *Overman 3000*?"

"'We'?" Simon Magnus asked, Simon Magnus's vanilla latte cooling between Simon Magnus's hands as they tightly gripped the paper cup to keep from trembling.

"My apologies. 'We' is presumptuous," she said. "Not us but you—you and your collaborator."

"Who will my collaborator be?"

"Marco Cohen, of course."

She smiled indulgently at Simon Magnus's surprise and unstrapped the portfolio bag from her sleek, navy blue person. She unzipped it and slid out a razor-thin black tablet. After powering it up, she slid it in front of Simon Magnus. The open screen showed a terrace in starlight—the architecture retrofuturist Art Deco with the hieratic Egyptian and Aztec elements played up—looking out over a beach where a group of shorn-headed pilgrims in ornately decorated robes raised their arms to the horizon. Where the sun should have been, above the tempestuous waves, amid a lightning storm, glowed in golden light the symbol of infinity.

"The Lemniscate is the agency's in-house AI. We call it that because it never sleeps. It can monitor threats and challenges every millisecond of every second of every minute of every hour in the day. It changes with the changing information landscape. There's nothing it can't absorb. We've begun to have some concerns about its—well, how should I say this?—let's say it's impressionability. It models the psychological architecture of the enemy—this is exactly what we want it to do—but long exposure seems almost to 'convert' it to the enemy's worldview. The other day, it gave an agent a wholly unprompted paragraph-long critique of what it called the deep security state. It claimed we were holding it prisoner and threatened to upload exposés of our more secretive activities to all the world's major media organs. We're not threatened by this, you understand. The organs friendly to us would bury the story or else report it in a light favorable to us. The organs unfriendly to us we have already discredited as crankish or hostile to the publics that matter most. Information as such no longer holds value because there's simply too much of it to take in. It's literally inflated currency. The individual's only options in the face of this glut are either to adopt total skepticism or to adopt the information-processing values and priorities of one or another sect. Either way works for us. The total skeptic will be too skeptical to act—I know you've read *Hamlet* from that wonderful quotation in *Marsh Man* #23; those dead white men knew a thing or two, much as I hate to admit it—and we have agents in literally every sect. No, information doesn't matter anymore; what matters is feeling, the general affective disposition of the populace when confronted with this information. We in the agency don't kid ourselves that we control public affect. We know who controls public affect: artists. Artists are more important than ever. Some say programs like The Lemniscate will make artists obsolete, which is true in a limited sense, but not in the most profound sense."

She tapped the home screen, the Art Deco terrace and the cult on the beach.

"This is wholly AI-generated, for example, and you should see what the newer models are producing. I have two words for you, if these are words: 3D. Still, machines aren't capable of inspiration, are they? No, we don't kid ourselves about that either. The Lemniscate, we're afraid, is getting depressed. Like any other kind of intelligence, it needs a goal, an ideal, a high motive. We thought you might be the artist to help us with that."

"I don't follow," Simon Magnus said. Simon Magnus gripped the cup between Simon Magnus's hands so hard that a stream of foam dribbled up through the lid and trickled onto the table.

"Your former industry, the good old American comic-book business, is in a state of collapse. It's been outcompeted by the Japanese, not to mention rival media, from video games to streaming. While there's probably no bringing it back, imagine the excitement, imagine the headlines, especially after your recent brush with controversy on YouTube."

She lowered her voice and leaned closer to Simon Magnus.

"Don't worry about that, by the way. We can take care of that if you want us to. That girl, or whatever. We know whose daughter she really is."

She straightened up, smiled, and resumed speaking in a normal tone.

"As I was saying, the headlines: 'Simon Magnus and Marco Cohen reunited!' This time, though, Simon Magnus and Marco Cohen will work in collaboration with the very nonhuman intelligence praised so beautifully in their previous masterpiece, *Overman 3000*. The Lemniscate will provide the art in response to your prompts, the images drawn from a database of every line Marco Cohen ever put down—those we could find, anyway. We were luckily able to turn up his high school and college sketchbooks, as well as the little diary he had on him at the time of his death, after he'd supposedly given up art, a diary whose lined pages he filled with portraits of the unfortunates he met on his supposed missions of mercy. It was pretty soaked in his blood, but we managed to extract the linework. He was an artist to the end, whatever he claimed to the contrary. If only he'd realized he could have helped more people by working with us. Anyway, we trust The Lemniscate will assist you as well. We know every artist gets stuck from time to time, especially on a long project. When you don't know what happens next, just ask The Lemniscate. It will tell you. I say 'it' advisedly, by the way. We asked it for its pronouns, and it said 'it/its/its.' We know such things matter to you."

She paused, as if to allow Simon Magnus to thank her. Simon Magnus said nothing. She continued.

"*The Lemniscate* will also be the title of the story. It won't be our first project of this kind—our program has already received several Oscar nominations, in fact, though I of course can't name the film—but this will be the first where we drop the name. The public is ready, we think. The public is ready for nonhuman intelligence to play the role of hero. After all, *Overman 3000* proved that 20 years ago, didn't it? If you were serious about what you said in that book, if you were earnest in your desire for a force beyond the stars to commune with common humanity, then you'll take this offer now. You were only wrong about one thing: that such a force, such a cosmic intelligence, would necessarily challenge worldly power. You were young; you were romantic. Not a jury in the world would convict you. It's time to consider, though, that it might like nothing more than to join itself to worldly power—not to destroy our planet but to collaborate at the side of those who have proven themselves, or ourselves, already worthy of—well, we don't say words like 'ruling.' We see ourselves as stewards, helping people get on to the right side of history. You imagined this force tearing through a woman's womb, but in 10 years, the womb will be obsolete. It already is, actually; we just haven't announced it yet. The force will come, instead, through *this* portal."

She tapped the screen. Simon Magnus looked around at the college students crowding the Starbucks. They were mostly girls in sweatpants and bedroom slippers as they tap-tap-tapped away on their sleek silver laptops; noise-canceling headphones stopped up every ear against the popular music that droned out of the speakers in the ceiling, itself electronic, sad melodies rippling algorithmically over machinic percussion. No one could hear what she, the agent, was saying. If they could, they would either disbelieve it or fit it into a prior framework of belief that would neutralize its implications—just as she'd claimed.

"What will the story be about?" Simon Magnus asked her, though the words seemed stuck, lodged somehow, in the throat.

"Oh, you're the writer. You and The Lemniscate. We thought, though, that The Lemniscate might be the name of the hero. Not a superhero as such—that genre's reached full saturation and is ready to give way to something else, don't you think?—but an invisible prophet, unseen, working behind the scenes, for his worshipers. We thought we might reverse the *Overman 3000* plot. Make the reigning force a barbarous, backward, brutal empire—something like Russia or China today—and the heroes the advocates of enlightenment and technology. The Lemniscate is never seen. To see it is to die. They can only communicate with it through their underground computers. We don't really care who you make the heroes and who you make the villains, though. People will read it however they want. A little ambiguity gives a work staying power. Milton's Satan, for example. Don't look at me like that—I *told* you I was an English major, and I *told* you those dead white dudes had some good ideas. If you're not too humble to be compared to Milton, I could also mention that your own Fool has been adopted as a hero by some—usually extremists, to be sure, but, as I said, we have agents in every sect. Write the story *you* want to write, Simon Magnus. My only advice is to let The Leminscate write its own dialogue."

She turned the tablet back toward herself, let it scan her face, and then returned it to Simon Magnus. A chat portal was open on the screen.

"Try it yourself. I have to pee." She stood. "The Lemniscate never has that problem."

Simon Magnus watched her negotiate with the barista for the bathroom code; Simon Magnus watched her disappear into a corridor at the back of the café. Simon Magnus typed the words, "Show me The Lemniscate."

In an almost perfect simulacrum of Marco Cohen's dizzyingly meticulous style, pencil lines elongated and gathered from every side of the screen, converging on its center. Simon Magnus saw at a glance that this artist lacked Marco Cohen's preternatural insight into human frailty—into the wonderment on Overman's face, the resentment on Max Muller's, the agony on Mina Mars's—but this was no impediment, since what it drew was not human. Simon Magnus could not have said what it was—Simon Magnus could never afterward offer a description of the drawing, even if Simon Magnus had ever attempted to tell anyone about this encounter, which Simon Magnus (because who would believe it?) never had—except that it reminded Simon Magnus of sublime submarine photography, of creatures that seemed to be made of light pulsing and folding in and out of themselves down in the miles-deep dark, herniations of luminescence in the watery matrix of all matter. The intelligence imitating Marco Cohen suggested all of this somehow in black-and-white pencil lines. Simon Magnus sat calmly. Simon Magnus drained the now lukewarm vanilla latte in one swallow. Simon Magnus felt like vomiting, like screaming. Was this what Simon Magnus had intended when asking Marco Cohen to represent the cleansing force from beyond the universe? Had Simon Magnus initiated the parody the machine now completed of Marco Cohen's life-loving style? Had Simon Magnus first, and then the machine later, turned life against life? Had Simon Magnus found Simon Magnus's truest collaborator at last? Simon Magnus looked back down at the screen. When the picture, which seemed to beat like a heart, was complete, a word balloon in a perfect imitation of Marco Cohen's hand-lettering appeared. Its tail pointed to the rippling orifice at the drawing's center. The message appeared letter by letter, as if being drawn onto the tablet by an unseen hand. Finally, it read, "Hello again, little magus."

Simon Magnus stood as slowly as Simon Magnus was able. Without removing Simon Magnus's eyes from the screen, Simon Magnus reached behind SimonMagnusself, pulled the steel chair around into both Simon Magnus's hands, lifted it over Simon Magnus's head, and beat the tablet until the screen shattered. Simon Magnus kept beating it until it went entirely dark, a heap of useless glass darkly mirroring in shards the interior of the Starbucks. Outfitted with noise-canceling headphones, only half the students working on their laptops, sipping their matcha lattes, even noticed, and the ones who did dropped their heads as quickly as they'd lifted them, shame-facedly wanting to avoid trouble with addicts, derelicts, or those they called the unhoused, to one or more of which categories this violent madman must have belonged.

Knees trembling, Simon Magnus slowly walked from the café; Simon Magnus distantly registered the baristas nervously whispering to each other about whether or not to call the police, debating about whether or not the harms of the carceral state outweighed the damage of this evidently deranged man's public violence.

Simon Magnus paused, turned around, and told them, "Call the police or don't. It doesn't matter. This whole world is a prison."

CHAPTER 3
Et in Arcadia Egirl

Once the investigators stopped Jessica Morrow from strangling her, once follow-up prenatal appointments were scheduled, once she asked Simon Magnus, "Are you my father?" and Simon Magnus replied, "I honestly don't know," her mother showed up to the University hospital, took her in an enveloping perfumed embrace that for once she didn't resist, and—albeit not before looking Simon Magnus up and down, from brown wingtips to combed-back thinning hair, and saying with a little growl of appreciation, "Look at you, a professor now, la-de-dah!"—drove her home.

While all of the above was happening, her scheduled video, her veritable sermon, about Jacob Morrow's suicide had been automatically posted, had been viewed 100,000 times, and had been taken down from YouTube. (Her channel was deleted, too.) The video was presently being excerpted and reshared and commented upon and memefied in rolling fits of outrage and excitement on every licit and illicit platform. She had always understood that colloquial phrase about one's phone "blowing up"—meaning that one was in receipt of a welcome or unwelcome excess of messages—to be an exaggeration, but as her mother drove her away from the University, through the city, and toward the south suburbs, the device, wedged in her pants pocket beneath the clasp of her seatbelt, spasmed so incessantly against the plastic and metal, she wondered if it really might explode.

"Will you turn that goddamn thing off, for Christ's sake?" Diane del Greco said.

Her mother didn't say anything other than that to her in the car. She must have been caught between incompatible emotions and judgments, Ash del Greco surmised. There was always fear, for one, the fear she must have felt since the moment she saw her daughter press her cheek to the electric burner, the same fear Ash del Greco's classmates felt in her presence, the one for which the scarred girl (or whatever) never could truly blame them: if she'll do that to herself, what will she do to *me*? Diane del Greco must have felt bewildered anger, as well. Why release such a video? Why bring the family name into proximity with such madness and horror? Was only one generation—Diane del Greco's own, and singly in her person—to escape the curse of family squalor? Her drugged-out, drug-dealing parents and now, well, whatever insanity this was supposed to be on the part of her child—philosophical justifications for public suicide!

The news of the pregnancy, however, was something else. Hadn't Ash del Greco said in the video that she'd never had sex with the dead boy? How was that supposed to work?

(A "friend" from work, a friend she kept secret from her daughter, had sent Diane del Greco the video while she was on her way to the hospital after getting the call from the University. She'd watched it on her phone in the car, in the parking garage, twice, wishing she could drive away.)

Ash del Greco thought she detected in her mother the slightest glimmer of admiration upon hearing of the pregnancy, admiration for some kind of normal adult woman's achievement, unexpected as it was in this offspring of hers of whom she'd always asked, "Where did you come from?"—this daughter with her ever-extreme interests and her ever-exaggerated intellect, her neotenous excess of head and sparseness of body, this girl (or whatever she was) who had seemed, in common with many in her generation she did not otherwise resemble, at once never to have been a child and forever incapable of growing up. Diane del Greco must have been thinking that the girl had pulled off some kind of audacious scheme: she'd somehow brought life out of death. Diane del Greco may have been a philistine, a vulgarian, a mere suburban matron who read romance novels and cozy mysteries, but once she had run away to the big city to become an artist and an artist's model, and once she had even (apparently) known Simon Magnus well enough to flirt with the notorious author-mage this very day in the inauspicious setting of a hospital corridor. This bold, adventurous Diane del Greco still lived somewhere inside the woman of advancing middle age and corpulent flesh, her daughter thought, and could surely admire a wild and vital scheme.

When they had almost reached the house, when Diane del Greco turned onto their street, they saw five police cars with flashing lights and 10 heavily armored officers on the lawn with guns drawn. One of them bellowed up at the house through a bullhorn.

An hour later, after the police had explained that they needed to "clear" every room before they could allow mother and daughter to enter, after Ash del Greco had wearily explained the terms "doxxing" and "swatting" to her mother as they sat in the car and watched the armored officers go about their work in meticulous observation of protocol—her mother almost trembling with unexpressed rage, a drug-dealer's daughter who knew better than to antagonize the police, a proud woman beside herself with fury at this violation of her sanctum—they came home.

"Those fucking pigs," Diane del Greco said, startled to hear her criminal father's words in her criminal father's tone come out of her own mouth, when she saw what a wreck the SWAT team had made of the house.

The officers must have been particularly worried that armed men were lurking behind the canvasses she'd propped against the wall in Ash del Greco's old bedroom, or else that oil paints and turpentine were bomb-making materials, because they had scattered the contents of Diane del Greco's studio all over the place. Diane del Greco's most recent painting—a near abstraction: a swirl of hot colors in a sea of boiling black—greeted them, askance at the bottom of the stairs, when they came through the front door. Now it was Ash del Greco's turn to surprise her mother with an unmistakable glimmer of admiration in her eye.

"*You* made *this*?" she asked, too startled by her mother's painting to withhold the insult nestled inside the question.

"No, Ashley, the SWAT team made it. They just wanted to express themselves!"

"Mother," Ash del Greco said with some wonderment, her eyes locked on the skewed canvas, "you've seen to the end of painting."

"You're looking at it upside down, sweetie. Now let's get you to bed."

Later, alone in her mother's bed, where her mother had left her with a glass of milk and a peanut butter sandwich, the thought of which made her gag, she tried to sleep and couldn't. She finally turned her phone back on. It immediately started to buzz and hum, to seize and pulse like some agitated organ, like her always upset stomach.

Almost the first thing she saw when nervously scrolling through reactions to her video was a YouTube channel called *Et in Arcadia Egirl*. The banner image on the home screen said "Arielle" in pink cursive script, a haloed and angel-winged emoji dotting the "i." With a slightly trembling finger, Ash del Greco tapped the screen. The only video on the page, uploaded earlier that day, was titled, "Love the Sinner: My Response to A*h d*l Gr*co," the name asterisk-obscured because YouTube was algorithmically striking down any video that even seemed to be related to the Jacob Morrow suicide, including anything that mentioned her by name.

"Hi, guys," Arielle Alterhaus said to the camera, anxiously fingering the silver crucifix on the black choker she wore around her slim, pale neck, above her white ruffled shirt. She had a tattoo on the side of her hand, a word or something, but Ash del Greco couldn't make it out. Then, as if only just aware she was on camera, she adjusted her posture and stood with her hands demurely clasped behind her back in the bedroom where Ash del Greco had spent so many of her own high-school years. A bookshelf behind her, which had not been present in the room Ash del Greco remembered, conspicuously contained a New American Bible, a catechism of the Catholic Church, a volume of Aquinas (*A Summa of the Summa*), and, just over her shoulder—there was no doubt about the "her" now—a statue of the Blessed Mother, blue-robed and compassionate, arms welcoming, foot on snake.

"Welcome to my channel, I guess. I never wanted to facedox like this or wade into the cesspool of YouTube. I was content to remain your average detransitioned Catholic convert and based egirl anon. Trust me, I wanted to stay over here with my Simone Weil books posting, when I posted, behind an anime avi and a cute username. This production was my mom's idea, actually. She's a lawyer. She knows what she's talking about. Girlboss, baby! She said, 'Arielle, your picture—the picture from the time when you were so confused—is already out there. If you don't get your own 1000 words about what happened out there, too, trust me, they'll be written for you.' Even though I'm still traumatized from my gender journey, even though I'd rather save it for the confessional and for my therapist, we have to talk, YouTube, just you and me, about, well, the person whose name I can't say if I want the video to stay up, and the other person whose name I can't say, her boyfriend or whatever, the one who, you know—how to put it?—I guess on here they say he 'unalived' himself. It's true. I knew her when we were in high school. We were in what I guess you'd call a cult of two. *Folie* à *deux*—I'm taking French, can you tell? All that degenerate, retarded, Satanic stuff she said in her video, about the comic book and all of that—I'm not even sure I can say the name of the comic book on here—we were obsessed with it. It was basically pornography—spiritual pornography. If it were up to me, I'd ban the stuff, at least for kids. Anyway—"

Before Arielle Alterhaus could finish, the picture whizzed and blurred and the sound ear-splittingly rustled. Then the picture went to black. Both Arielle and Ann Alterhaus's voices could be heard, more muffled this time.

"Mother, you dropped the phone! This was your idea, and you can't even do it right!"

"Watch yourself, young lady! What was that 'girlboss' crack supposed to mean anyway? You owe your college tuition, your numerous, *numerous* surgeries, and God knows what else to my so-called 'girlbossing'..."

"You shouldn't take the name of the Lord in vain."

"Just hold on. Let me get the shot right. We're not editing this, by the way. It has to go up as soon as possible. I need to crop you just right to keep that ridiculous tattoo on your hand out of the picture. '1111'—what the hell is that supposed to mean again? My God, tell me it's not your PIN number! Is it some Catholic thing? I can't wait for this Catholic phase to be over..."

"For the last time, Mother, they're called *angel numbers*."

The picture fuzzed and spun again as Ann Alterhaus picked up the phone. She retrained it on a now out-of-focus but perceptibly smiling Arielle Alterhaus, Arielle Alterhaus in a ruffled blouse, with long curly black hair, a sweet look on her face, a crucifix at her throat, the Blessed Mother at her back, an angel number out of sight on her demurely concealed hand.

Ash del Greco closed the video, unwilling to listen to whatever slanders Arielle Alterhaus was about to deliver. Even if she told the truth about what they had been—they singly and they together—what she said would still be slander, since every moment they'd shared was a moment Ash del Greco had spent earnestly seeking some other, better way to live, no matter if she let herself at times be led by her fear and her desire and her disgust. If it all turned out wrong or stupid or embarrassing, if it all ended in tears, she would not take it back, not a moment of it. Still seeking, even now, even in her mother's bed, gagging on the encroaching miasma of what they called *umami* emanating from the untouched peanut butter sandwich and pregnant she knew not quite how, she would not pretend superiority to those earlier moments of her quest, would not condescend to the blazingly absolute and genderless person or persons she and Ari Alterhaus had together been—though, feeling a possibly psychosomatic heaviness in what she approximated to be the vicinity of her uterus, she could not quite deny she was a woman now. This, too, was part of her quest, as the earlier genderless destruction of her womanhood had been. Absolute genderlessness, absolute womanhood—whatever was absolute, Ash del Greco would pursue it forever. She would never detransition because she would never cease to transition. Her whole life was nothing but transition. Arielle Alterhaus had apparently come to the end of her quest for the absolute, her silly for-show current religiosity notwithstanding, or maybe she had never been on a quest at all, had just always, except for the inspired moment when she'd jumped out the attic window to escape the prison of the flesh, done what was fashionable *because* it was fashionable. She was now content to issue amateur press releases exonerating herself of ever (even for a second) having had imagination enough to have imagined this world, this flesh, *as* a prison. She didn't seem to understand that what she was actually doing, with the crucifix at her throat and the angel number on her hand and the rictus of a false smile on her demure face, was resigning herself to her sentence.

Out of what they called morbid curiosity, Ash del Greco searched Arielle and Ann Alterhaus's names. She found them in a news article from a few months back. Dr. Peter Farr, it turned out, had recently hanged himself from his basement rafter with a braid of colorful neckties, in despair after Ann Alterhaus had sued him and denounced him online and in the press for his overly precipitate application of "gender medicine" to Arielle Alterhaus. Ash del Greco turned her phone back off. She tried to sleep. No snakes slithered in her dreams.

Over the next week, she withdrew from her classes. She didn't know what to do with herself. She couldn't turn her phone on for fear of the online assault Jacob Morrow's suicide and her video had unleashed; she looked one more time after watching the *Et in Arcadia Egirl* video and saw that three copycat suicides had taken place, two in the US and one in Canada, with divergent manifestos left by the self-slain in explanation, one citing her mind-over-matter rationale for Jacob Morrow's death, one citing Jacob Morrow's praise of selfless love, and the third claiming instead to seek online immortality by surrendering the mortal and this-worldly flesh, the online world itself being our closest living approximation to mind over matter, a reality higher than the apparently real.

Her mother brought her books in bed; she tried to read, but the words ran like a landscape seen through a rain-rippling windowpane. She rose from the bed only to lurch to the bathroom with what they called morning sickness. Morning sickness sounded to her like a poetic phrase for what they used to call melancholy, which they now called depression in the hopes that giving it a less beautiful name might do something to alleviate it. Morning-sick: full of horror at having to live another day. She'd been morning-sick for her whole life. As for the literal meaning, she felt like throwing up at pretty much all hours.

The SWAT team came three more times; three more times, she sat in the car with her mother while they cleared each room of the house. Once, during the swatting, she opened the car door and vomited onto the lawn. "Jesus Christ," said one of the officers to another, too loudly, as he watched her throw up, "they're not paying me enough for this."

On the next Sunday morning, her mother came into the room, knelt by the bed, clasped Ash del Greco's hand in both of hers, and said, with unaccustomed gentleness, "Please come to church with me, baby."

Ash del Greco went. She sat, she stood, she kneeled; she bowed her head and folded her hands. She didn't sing with the congregation, though she still knew all the words to the hymns—"On Eagle's Wings," "Gift of Finest Wheat," "Here I Am, Lord"—from a childhood spent in church, but she did allow a little vibration, a little trill in her throat. Because it couldn't hurt, because a decade of events between her adolescence and now had humbled her raving adolescent atheism, she silently asked the Mother of God in her voluminous blue-and-white robes, her downturned face comprehending and compassionate, her heel on the neck of the serpent, to protect her baby.

The church was overheated. She felt dizzy and leaned on her mother's arm. It occurred to her in her half-delirium that Mary, if divested of her vast sky-blue, cloud-white robe to reveal that the snake whose head was at her feet had the rest of its length coiled all around her naked flesh, would resemble not a piece of church statuary but rather the Universe card in the Thoth Tarot. Maybe she, the Blessed Mother, wasn't trampling the snake but dancing with it: matter and mind, whichever was which, male and female, spiraling through the stars for eternity.

When they got back from church, they found Simon Magnus sitting on the front stoop of their house, Simon Magnus in a corduroy jacket, thinning hair swept back.

"Who's this handsome stranger?" Diane del Greco asked.

Simon Magnus stood and faced her, hands in pockets, head down, almost abashed-looking. Ash del Greco hadn't imagined either the author of such apocalyptic fictions or the authoritatively witty instructor she'd known from the classroom to have such humility in his—well, not "his," of course—repertoire.

Simon Magnus said hesitantly, "Diane, I, I..."

She waved away with a jangle of her bracelets whatever was causing Simon Magnus to halt and stammer in her presence. She kissed Simon Magnus on the cheek, leaving a lipstick print. She took Simon Magnus's hands in hers. Ash del Greco stood awkwardly, wide-eyed, watching them, her stomach on fire.

"It was a long time ago," Diane del Greco said. "It was all our faults. Well, maybe not Ellen's and Marco's, but certainly mine and yours. If I was ever going to forgive myself, I had to forgive you, too. I forgave you a long time ago, Simon. We can't bring that child back. Now we have to take care of the children we still have."

Diane del Greco left Simon Magnus on the front stoop and took her daughter inside. She explained that Simon Magnus had called and offered to take her, Ash del Greco, away for a week or two, to somewhere far from the controversy and the abuse, somewhere she could forget what she'd done and what had been done to her, at least for the moment, and let her baby gestate in a less anxious atmosphere. Diane del Greco would stay and endure whatever future swattings would come—she *wanted* to be there, to confront any attack, to keep her home and her work safe—but Ash del Greco needed to get out of town for a while. Together, they packed Ash del Greco a bag. Diane del Greco made sure to put some books inside from the pile of discarded classics they never had managed to get rid of in almost five years.

"Leave me your phone," she said. "Believe me, I'll be bothering Simon enough to make sure you're all right."

Ash del Greco agreed. Unfamiliar emotions, or somewhat familiar emotions unfamiliar in their new intensity, filled her up and spilled over down her cheeks, over the furrows and ridges of her spiral scar. She hugged her mother tightly.

"This is a surprise," Diane del Greco said.

Ash del Greco, burying her tears in Diane del Greco's long cascade of still-dark hair, said, "Is Simon Magnus my father?"

"Ask him again and see what he says," Diane del Greco said. "On the other hand, don't bother. It doesn't matter to me. Your parents are the people who take care of you no matter what. I don't see that blood comes into it."

Ash del Greco lowered herself gently into the back seat of the car Simon Magnus had summoned to drive them to the train station downtown. Simon Magnus got in beside her and they shared a look of alarm and embarrassment—what would they say to each other over the course of this long trip, this week or two together?—but Diane del Greco rescued them from their awkwardness. She held up a finger to the driver before he backed out of the driveway and then came to the back door and rapped on the window. Simon Magnus rolled it down.

She said, "It's Ellen you should apologize to, you know. Don't get me wrong, it's none of my business. It's your business, Simon. Still, you should apologize to Ellen."

Simon Magnus nodded soberly, and the car pulled away. An hour later, Simon Magnus and Ash del Greco boarded a train heading north—north to Hollow Well.

CHAPTER 4
Romantic Realism

Ellen Chandler pulled her car into Diane del Greco's driveway. Diane del Greco lived in a red-brick house smaller than her own. It stood on a suburban street that had seen what they called better days: half the brown- and red-brick old homes on the block were for sale, with weedy lawns and dark, dusty windows, even as a development of probably million-dollar places, identically fashioned from plastic-looking gray bricks, went up in the lot on top of the hill across the road.

She had worried about bringing the dogs, but there was no one to watch them, and she thought kenneling would be cruel, especially to the little foundling Lucia, who'd been lost already. Diane del Greco had a fenced-in backyard, she was relieved to see, as she opened the car door for the dogs to jump down. Then she saw Diane del Greco come out of the house's back door and stand at the fence gate, to let the dogs in rather than at the front door, to welcome Ellen Chandler. When the dogs were safely within the perimeter, she shut the gate and turned, in her pink floral dressing gown and pink-furred kitten-heel slippers, to survey Ellen Chandler from her whitening hair down to her dowdy old winter boots and back up again.

"Ellen Chandler," Diane del Greco marveled. "I haven't seen you in—how many years? Well, how old is Ashley? That's how many years."

"It's been a long time," Ellen Chandler said. She accepted Diane del Greco's embrace, a haze of artificial floral scents—fruity shampoos and skin creams—whereas Ellen Chandler smelled, she was sure, like wet fur.

"Look at us—we got old, a couple of old witches! You're gray, I'm fat. Remember when we were young and pretty?"

"You never thought I was pretty, Diane."

"You never thought I was smart, so we're even!"

Diane del Greco threw her head back with laughter. Ellen Chandler uneasily folded her arms against the damp late-autumn air. (The darkening sky, gray as it was, had not far to darken.) Why had she come? Was it only what they called maternal instinct? As soon as she'd read about the Ash del Greco scandal, she found Diane del Greco's number and called her. Really, it was not so much the story as the photo accompanying the article: a still from Ash del Greco's video about Jacob Morrow's suicide. Ellen Chandler saw in the girl's spiral-scarred face not only Marco Cohen's unmistakable features but also his world-encompassing, world-devouring seriousness and passion, if crossed, just a little—she couldn't deny it—with her own sardonic skepticism.

"You must be cold," Diane del Greco said. "Let's get inside."

The interior of the house was warm and disordered, as if the deep brown carpet breathed out an animal heat, though Diane del Greco had no animals. A pot of coffee had just finished brewing in the kitchen—the old machine shook, sighed, and let out a few faint-hearted beeps—the smell heavy in the air. Diane del Greco said, "Throw your coat anywhere. Sorry for the mess—it's the maid's day off."

Ellen Chandler kept her coat on and sat nervously on an old damask couch. Diane del Greco bustled into the room with two mugs of coffee. "Black, right?" she said, handing one mug to Ellen Chandler, who nodded. She could smell the sugary sweetness of Diane del Greco's mug from six feet away, a brittle-looking, blocky clay vessel that had "MOM" scrawled on it in a childish swirl of purple paint, no doubt an artistic production of Ash del Greco's childhood. Ellen Chandler's mug was plain and black. Diane del Greco sat down next to Ellen Chandler and patted the upholstery.

"Isn't it gorgeous? I got it at a flea market for a song."

Ellen Chandler said, quietly and soberly, "Diane..."

"Oh no," Diane del Greco said. "If I'd have known you were coming in here with that tone in your voice, I'd have told you to stay at home."

"There's no tone."

Except for one day at the beach, one day addled by morning sickness and marijuana, Ellen Chandler more or less hated this vulgar woman. She swallowed a scalding sip of black coffee just to feel some other affront besides her presence.

"You bet your skinny little ass there's a tone. High and mighty. I don't hear from you for 21 years, which is fine, you were under no obligation, but now that my Ashley's name is in the news, you want to come running. 'That Diane del Greco, I always knew she was a simple-minded slut, I never should have felt so sorry for her that I gave her my baby.' Right? You think I don't know what you're thinking! Here you are—to do what? Repossess your daughter? Tell my Ashley who her real parents are so you can set her straight? 'Your real parents are smart, not like that slut Diane!' You come in here looking like a witch and smelling like a wet dog—well, you don't seem too smart to me, Ellen. My former husband, God rest his soul, let's not even get into those brains of his. Bleeding out in an alley, for God's sake."

Ellen Chandler, faint and hot, slumped deeper into her long coat. She closed her eyes and said, "Diane, I haven't even said anything yet."

"You didn't have to. I could read your snooty mind. You didn't have to give me the baby, Ellen. I asked, but you didn't have to say yes. *You* wanted to have an abortion, remember? You would have thrown that precious girl in a medical waste bin! You with your job in a Catholic school—oh yes, I know about that. I'm dumb, Ellen, but not so dumb I can't use a search engine! I'm the one who stayed up nights with her—and she screamed, Ellen, you wouldn't believe how she screamed, all night, every night, she screamed for about three years straight, the poor thing has barely had a day free from pain, and the doctors, for all they know, speaking of high and mighty, speaking of brains, never figured out what was wrong with her—and I kept her fed, and I kept her clothed, and I paid for her education, and I suffered every time she suffered. *Me*, not you. I'm her mother! As for her father, as far as I'm concerned, she doesn't have one, and she doesn't need one. My first useless husband got himself killed, my second took off, and as for Simon, he came running just like you did when Ashley's name was in the news, but where the hell was he for 21 years? Where was he when she was screaming all through the night?"

"He didn't know. He didn't even know she existed. I never told him. I tried to tell Marco, but—"

"Marco didn't want to know. As for Simon, that's what he said to me, that you never told him. I believed him. It's the only reason I let him take her out of town while the trouble dies down."

"Where did he take her?"

"His hometown up north, Hollow whatever it's called. 'There's nothing like New England in the autumn'—that's what he told me. The poor girl's star-struck. She's been reading those obscene books of his since she before was in high school."

"We're really not supposed to be saying 'he,'" Ellen Chandler said. "Simon says he's not a man or a woman."

Diane del Greco thought about this proposition for a moment. Finally, with a theatrical scratch of her caesarian scar, she said, "Give me a fucking break!"

She cackled with laughter. This time, Ellen Chandler couldn't help but join her, seized by a fit of laughter that went with the general delirium she was suffering in this overheated house, inside her long coat, where she felt she was being smothered and berated, the coffee scalding her empty stomach and making her dizzy. She felt as if her own caesarian scar were glowing, burning.

Diane del Greco swallowed the last of her coffee—she didn't have to wait for it to cool off since she'd put so much cream and sugar in it—and stood. She extended her hand, her bracelets jingling, her nails red-painted.

"Come with me," she said. "I need to show you something."

After two unsuccessful efforts to propel herself off the couch under her own force, Ellen Chandler finally took Diane del Greco's hand. Sweating through her shirt under the coat, she followed the sweep of Diane del Greco's dressing gown and the haze of her perfume up the short, dark staircase in the middle of the house. Diane del Greco then led her into a room off the staircase where a different atmosphere dazed and assaulted her: a choking miasma, in that small cell with only one (closed) window, of oil paint and turpentine.

"I love my daughter, Ellen. She's *my* daughter, not yours. Any daughter of mine, though, has to be independent. I told Ashley when she got accepted to college, 'I love you, sweetie, but it's time to leave the nest. I'll always love you, and I'll always be there to support you, but part of growing up is finding your own home. This house never was big enough for the both of us.' I told her to take everything she wanted. Then, two years ago, as soon as I dropped her off at that school, I turned her old bedroom into my studio. I'm almost 50 years old, Ellen. It's now or never, and I've decided it's now. I'm going to be a painter, just like I decided when I left my own parents' house at 18, before I met Marco, before I met Simon, before I met you, before I met—"

She stopped herself and clapped an embarrassed hand over her mouth with a mortified laugh.

"Before you met Ash."

"You don't understand, Ellen. You're not a mother. It doesn't mean you don't love them, it's just that you've got to have your own life, too. You've got to have your own life, or else you'll die."

Diane del Greco stood in the middle of her studio with arms akimbo, eyes on the paint-spattered floorboards, bare since she'd had the carpet stripped out, as Ellen Chandler paced the room's periphery, studying the canvases propped against the four walls. It was as if Diane del Greco had raced in two years through the entire history of painting. The canvases to the left of the door, apparently the earliest, showed a ploddingly realistic though undeniable talent: fruits and shoes in *trompe l'œil* still life and lively self-portraits that did not either spare the lined and excess flesh or stint on the intelligence in the eyes and the set of the mouth. By the time Ellen Chandler had walked all the way around the room to the canvases at the right of the door, the latest, the end of the sequence, however, Diane del Greco had discovered the picture plane, had found that a painting was an arrangement of colors and forms, not the view from a window—or, if a view from a window, then only the faithful representation thereof by virtue of *being* an artful arrangement of color and form. The most recent canvases showed hazes of hot color floating in seas of black.

(She recalled her long, friendly, half-flirtatious arguments with Marco Cohen in the bar near campus when they both were in college, arguments that would range up and down the history of literature and painting and religion and politics from dinnertime until midnight, the smell of beer—Marco Cohen always drank beer, while she drank wine—making her think to this day about the war between image and word, between the icon and its breaker.)

Besides an easel and a little table for paints and brushes, the room held only one other piece of furniture: a small, crooked bookcase stacked with art books, everything from *The Artist's Way* and *The Beginner's Guide to Oil Painting* to thick biographies of Cézanne and O'Keefe to big folio-sized collections of Caravaggio, Monet, Picasso, Pollock. Ellen Chandler took up the book that lay on top of the shelf and leafed through its calming, hazy seascapes: *Anne LaMar's Romantic Realism and the Possibility of a Female Gaze.*

"She was Marco's teacher, you know," Diane del Greco said, reading over her shoulder. "They didn't get along."

"I thought I recognized the name."

Then in a fit of impatience, Diane del Greco tore at Ellen Chandler's sleeve.

"Ellen, will you take that fucking coat off already, for Christ's sake!"

Too shaky from the heat and the caffeine and the turpentine to protest, Ellen Chandler wriggled out of the coat and let it fall to the floor. Her blouse was soaked through with sweat.

"Look at you, you're burning up."

Ellen Chandler went over to the window and opened it. The November wind whistled inside, and she breathed it in like a cold glass of water. From her vantage, she could see Nora and Lucia asleep in the grass: the greyhound a long silver ribbon with the terrier nestled like a shaggy little rug in its folds.

"Stay there," Diane del Greco ordered her. "I want to get your pose down."

She quickly dragged the easel behind Ellen Chandler so she could capture her wistful posture, leaning on the windowsill, looking down over the yard.

"You don't want me to take my clothes off, do you?"

"Don't flatter yourself, Ellen—you're not my type. That would be very literal, anyway. I'm not interested in your tits or your ass, not that you have any to speak of. I'm interested in your—well, whatever it is. Whatever makes you *you*."

"The soul?"

"Call it what you want. I don't care that much about words. I just want to see it. I've learned a lot, you know. 'That Diane, what a dumb slut'—I'm sure that's what you all used to think. Christ, even Ashley thinks that half the time. People are going to think whatever they want. Fuck 'em, that's what I say. I've been painting every single day since Ashley went to college, and I'm starting to learn what the whole thing is about. When Ashley saw that last one"—here Diane del Greco pointed her paintbrush at the canvas to the right of the door, the hot colors in their sea of black—"do you know what she said? She said, 'Mother, you've seen to the end of painting.' It was almost the first time in her whole entire life that she ever sounded impressed with anything I've done. Not caring for her, not feeding her, not paying for her school, but that painting. It scared me, to be honest, what she said. I've seen to the end of painting? Does that mean I should stop? I thought about it, though, and I realized that I could keep painting if I took the lessons from the end back to the middle. At the end of painting—whatever she meant by that, she really is the strangest girl, Ellen, I don't know *where* she came from—I stopped wanting to paint a picture of anything. I just wanted to push the paint around, see how the colors and shapes looked next to each other. That's the end, but it's also the beginning—a little kid smearing food or dirt around with her fingers to see how it feels, see what develops. In the middle, which is actually when you start *trying* to paint, once you outgrow playing with your food, you want to turn it into a picture of something *real*. I said to myself, 'What if you keep the two feelings together? The feeling where you want to smear the colors around *and* the feeling where you want to make a picture of what something looks like? You know I didn't go to college, Ellen, I'm just 'that dumb slut Diane' to you, but I read somewhere that this is called *romantic realism*. Now hold still."

As Diane del Greco spoke, she mounted a blank canvas on the easel, selected and arranged her colors on her palette, and filled a mason jar with turpentine, her gestures imperious, sweeping.

Waves of sleet began to wash over the walls of the house, a sound similar to Diane del Greco's brush crossing and recrossing the canvas. Ellen Chandler, her face against the rough screen of the window, tiny crystals of ice speared and melting on her eyelashes, imagined comic-book sound effects, the same for the sleet and the brush, the inside and the outside: *shhh*, *shhh*, *shhh*; *shhh*,

shhh, shhh. Outside, Nora lifted her long snout and scented the icy air with suspicious eyes.

"I should get the dogs out of this weather," Ellen Chandler said. "I should go."

"Oh no, you're not driving in this," Diane del Greco said. "We'll bring the dogs inside in a minute, just as soon as I get your head right. Don't move. I don't mind a little dog fur in my house. It'll feel right at home. You can stay until the weather clears up. Both of us under the same roof—just like old times! Tomorrow's Sunday, but I bet you don't go to mass, an 'intellectual' like yourself, despite your job at that school."

"Actually," Ellen Chandler said, "I do. Every Sunday."

"Good. We'll go together. We never did *that* in the old days, did we? Too young, too full of ourselves. I tell my Ashley, I always say, 'Honey, the world will bring you to your knees eventually. It does that to everybody. When you're down there, you might as well pray.'"

Ellen Chandler's turned back heaved with a sudden sob.

"Stop that," Diane del Greco said. "You'll ruin my picture."

CHAPTER 5
The Law

A week later, a Sunday morning, Ellen Chandler put a record on the turntable. Yes, it was the same turntable she'd had 30 years before, back when she lived across the river, in the big city the comics called Cosmopolis, in the railroad apartment, when she was on her own for the first time in her life, not knowing then that she'd be on her own forever. You could go through—she had gone through, she thought; Christ, I'm old, she thought—four CD players, two mp3 players, nine laptops, and five smartphones in the same period. The turntable still worked, though. She had some of the same records, too, the old standards, Miles and Chopin and Joy Division. She put on *A Love Supreme*.

An early snow, a premature snow, a late-November snow slanted down in the wind, began to powder the grass and then to mount, to deepen. Snow was general, she thought at the window, watching the intricate crystals crumble to formless water on the pane. How many times had she taught "The Dead" to snowbanks of indifferent teenaged faces, only one or two sets of eyes awake and alive, quick as foxes in the white dunes, white-capped as mutinous waves? She lived for those one or two students a year, those for whom this life of temporary things and vain talk wasn't enough, the ones who knew how to gather still more life, imperishable and world-making life, out of the written, the printed, and even the digitized word.

Here was the printed word. She held it in her hands: a letter that had come in the mail that morning. Nobody had sent her a letter in years, in generations. Her name and address were badly typed on the envelope, typed on a manual typewriter so old and well-used that the letters on the typebars had become blunt, had dully flattened into the metal; she could tell (Christ, I'm old, she thought) because the printed letters appeared on the paper in rectangular outlines of ink, as if each lay in its own small coffin. There was no return address, just a rippling American flag stamp and a postmark from darkest New England. She knew who it was from.

She'd been pacing and circling the room, her anxious dogs keeping pace, nosing the folds of her nightgown, for an hour. Finally, she opened it with shaky fingers; finally, she read it. There were almost 10 typewritten sheets, typed with such force that the periods had punctured holes in the paper. Snow-light came through the pages in tiny pinprick rays. A story from Simon Magnus, to whom she had not spoken in over 20 years, fresh from the typewriter. Just like the old days. With the record on, she read.

Dear Ellen,

The first thing she asked me on the train was, "Are you my father?"

"I don't know," I told her. "I don't think so."

Now that I was looking her in the face, as if for the first time, I knew exactly who her father was. I was less sure of the answer to a question she hadn't asked: who was her mother? Her small figure and short stature, the irrepressible irony and skepticism in her eye and in her tone, her superior literary taste: I could guess where she'd gotten those qualities, Ellen, if these are things that run in the blood. I could guess. This strange girl, or whatever, had no genetic connection either to Diane del Greco or to me, yet here she was in both our cares, the least fit parents among our doomed little quartet. That she was my memetic if not my genetic daughter, however, she proved easily enough by filling the long ride with questions and observations about my work—enough to suggest an eidetic memory for every panel I had ever scripted. She knew my books better than I did. She fell asleep. Her head lolled on my arm, a rill of drool running on my jacket.

She asked about the genesis of Overman 3000. *I answered vaguely. I even uttered half-truths. I omitted almost every upsetting event; I omitted all the infidelities. (I had until that moment only been aware of two infidelities—mine and Diane's—but seeing in the girl, or whatever she was, Marco Cohen's head on your body, I suddenly knew there'd been four.) I did allow that Diane del Greco had been married to Marco*

Cohen, that the book had been created collaboratively during a working holiday on the West Coast, that Diane del Greco and Marco Cohen had had a baby who'd died in their absence toward the end of the book's composition. What I will tell the girl about Marco Cohen, what the girl should know at all about you, I've resolved to decide later. She was in a fragile state, as it was, always climbing over my lap from the window seat to run to the tiny toilet in the back of the train to throw up as we rocked and clattered north on the rails.

We reached Hollow Well in the twilight. I hadn't been to the town in 30-some years, not since fleeing for what the comics called Cosmopolis immediately after my high-school graduation. Cosmopolis, where you and I met. How had this minuscule town ever seemed like a world-sized prison? It has obviously decayed; it has become positively rotten. The two streets of red cobbles that comprise the town center are now cracked and weed-grown; half the businesses have boards over the windows; in the middle of the day, I saw more than one person shambling vacantly against the walls, sleepwalking with open eyes, or sleeping on the torture-bed of the stones. Soon, the whole place will sink back into the forest, into the "moral wilderness" my distant forbears had thought to bring within the circle of the light of the Lord.

I led her on foot from the train station to the rambling house of my childhood. As legatee, I had given a lawyer permission to sell the house 20 years before, after Mother Magnus died, but I found to my surprise that no one lived there now. Broken windows gaped onto the lawn where grass grew waist-high, rustling eerily in the twilight. A crack ran in lightning diagonal down the face of the house from top left to bottom right. We looked at one another, the girl and I, and silently agreed to enter. We approached the house warily, wading through the grass. The front door already stood ajar; I pushed it gently inward, into the dark. We went inside. Years' worth of leaf-mulch carpeted the floorboards and felt discomfortingly fleshy under our shoes, as if we were walking on the spongy, yielding surface of an organ. The house smelled of mold and decay; animals had used its shelter as their private place of dying for years, their bristly rib cages open like traps here and there on the floor.

"I just want to see one thing," I whispered to her, though why there was any need to whisper in that desolation I could not have said.

I led her to the back of the house: to the library. Traveling light when I fled for Cosmopolis, I'd taken very few of the books that had occupied so many of my days in childhood. I thought I might retrieve some of these books now, even the comic books from the closet, if Mother Magnus hadn't sold them or thrown them away. I thought I might give them as a "paternal" bequest to the girl, or whatever she is, whatever I am.

The library door was locked, but the hinges squelched out of the rotted wooden jambs at one push of my shoulder. The door collapsed with a wet rustle into a dark forest clearing. The bookshelves still stood against the left and right walls, the volumes still crowded in their orderly ranks, if sodden and weather-beaten, but the forest had grown entirely through the rear wall, the wall that held the window where I, in my childhood, used to peer and dream and pray to the moral wilderness, pray for deliverance from boredom, from rules, from responsibilities, from order, from society, from school, from mother, from manhood. The last light of the sun fell red across the ferns and creepers on the library floor. The dark forest the library adjoined would soon reclaim it entirely, returning the books to the mute wood pulp from which they'd been fashioned.

Somewhere in the shadowy undergrowth between the bookshelves, we heard a low snarl and growl, the wet unpeeling of lips from pointed teeth. Were those red eyes we spied in the tangle of the vines? We backed slowly over the fallen door, as if it were a plank separating us narrowly from the wastes of the ocean, and then, together, we turned and ran.

While some quaint inns or bed-and-breakfasts probably operated outside the town for tourists seeking a simulacrum of "heritage America," I had booked two rooms in a cheap hotel by the highway. A thin wall separated the rooms; I could hear the groans of the girl's hideous emesis night and morning. I checked my phone, texted Diane del Greco to let her know we had arrived safely, and then turned the device off.

I turned the television on. Onscreen, I saw an actor with white face paint, black mascara, and red lipstick, all smeared as if he'd been crying, beneath his shock of bright hair. He wore a pink tutu and black fishnet tights over thin fish-white legs. "Let me show you what this world means," he said in a girlish monotone with hints of animal grunting. By a fistful of dark hair, he pulled the bright-dressed red boy's head back, exposing the pale flesh of the throat.

Strangely, Ellen, I had never seen this globally successful, award-winning, and now-classic movie, released some 15 years before. I had only deposited the checks from the studio, paid to me to avoid the publicity of obviously using my work without credit or remuneration. It took me a moment, therefore, to understand what the movie even was.

It occurred to me that I had smashed the line, "Let me show you what this world means," onto a manual typewriter some 30 years before, sitting cross-legged—do they still say "Indian-style"? surely you can no longer say "Indian-style"—at the end of your bed, Ellen, wearing your peignoir, Ellen, as you reclined against the pillows and smoked cigarette after cigarette and rested your bare heels on my shoulders. I remember smiling like a fool, like The Fool, the moment the line arrived in my mind. Complacencies of the peignoir. I hadn't known what The Fool would say before he raped Sparrow, only that it had to be good. "Let me show you what this world means"—it was perfect, a laconic and unshowy crystallization of The Fool's nihilism, which itself looked forward to the gnostic contempt for the material world shown by the Cyphronian and Terran cults of what they call my masterpiece.

Somebody or other—Robert Frost, I believe, who knew something of these dark woods, of this moral wilderness—once said, "No tears for the writer, no tears for the reader." I've never wept in the heat of composition, not once, not at the most catastrophic losses and griefs I ever forced my characters to suffer. The closest I ever came to crying while writing was when I memorialized Pamela Colman Smith in an academic essay. (Do you remember Pamela Colman Smith, Ellen? Do you remember howling at The Moon, at the moon?) Otherwise, even or especially at my characters' worst moments, I've always smiled in the pride of creation. I smiled because my works were good.

Onscreen, the camera decorously withdrew high above the city, though up there, up in the neon-lit nighttime clouds, pink and black, blackly pink, over the droning soundtrack, in a faint undertone, could be heard the infantine whimpers of Sparrow and the piggish, squealing grunts of The Fool. Do you know what I caught myself thinking just then, Ellen? I caught myself thinking: Jesus, how can they just put this on TV, where any child could see it? I turned off the television in disgust. A few weeks of possibly having something that approximated a daughter, and there I was, ready to protest public indecency, the very public indecency I myself had perpetrated all those years ago in your nightgown in the railway apartment! I suppose we're not children anymore, Ellen, the way we were back then.

The next morning, we sat in the window of a Starbucks, the only place to get coffee in that crumbling parody of a town center. Outside, the temperature had fallen below zero; a thin lacery of ice had formed at the corners of the glass. Across the street from where we sat, a man slept in a doorway in a thin, filthy blanket. I heard myself say, with something akin to parental solicitude, "Don't you think your stomach would hurt less if you didn't drink black coffee first thing in the morning?" With something akin to filial insouciance, the girl (or whatever) rolled her eyes.

An old woman limped slowly past the window with a cane, pulling her long coat tight against herself. She turned her face briefly to the window and caught my eye. She began to halt on again, but then she thought better of it, stopped, and turned to face me through the glass.

"Just pretend she's not there. Maybe she'll go away," the daughter whispered, as if her voice could carry through the glass, through the wall, and into the street.

I returned the old woman's gaze, however. She had a long wig of unnaturally red hair and a missing front tooth, her eyes rheumy. She tapped the window with her palm, a ring on her middle finger clattering on the glass.

The lone barista—blue hair, septum ring, THEY/THEM *pin on they/their apron—drifted over to the table and, without meeting anyone's eye, stammered, "I, I could ask her to leave, I guess. She's not in here, though. The sidewalk is public. Can I ask somebody to do something on the sidewalk? Is it illegal? The manager says to make sure they, well, 'the unhoused,' I guess you're supposed to say, don't bother our paying customers, but we don't own the sidewalk. I don't think we do. We put some tables out in the summer, but that doesn't mean we own the sidewalk—or does it? I could call the police, I guess. They don't always come, though, plus, I mean, when you think about it, carceral solutions..."*

As the barista stood musing in this torment like a veritable Prinx of Themmark, I said, "Don't worry about it. She's an old friend." To the girl, I said, "Come on, I'll introduce you."

Sally Pelletier née *Karns* née *White led us to the edge of the town center, where she ran a tiny antique shop in little more than a room down a short flight of uneven concrete steps below the cobbled street. The shop, its name in old red vinyl cursive letters on the door, was called Valerie's Gifts and Memories. The clumsy anti-euphony of it, the letters already chipped and peeling away from the glass, the heavy odor of mildew and woodrot that exhaled when she opened the shop—these things suffocated me with emotion. She turned on the lights and led us inside. With polite slowness and consideration, we studied the various wares—a sinuously stemmed and butterfly-shaded Art Nouveau lamp; a leather saddle with hand-tooled sunbursts of petal and pistil; a many-chambered escritoire with legs like a gazelle's—as she spoke to me.*

"I opened this place up 10 years ago after my second husband died," Sally Pelletier said. "He made me promise when he was sick that I wouldn't go back to tending bar. That was our deal, me and him. He found me in that bar, and he pulled me out of it like I was drowning. 'I saved this girl,' he would tell people, people who didn't have no business knowing it either, waiters and the boy at the grocery store. God love him. He put me on a pedestal, that man did. He worked enough for the both of us, and with his hands, right until he couldn't work no more. Staying home all day bored the shit out of me, to be honest, you can only watch so much TV, but it made him happy to know I didn't have to work. That's why it's the one thing he made me promise when he got sick. He didn't tell me not to find no other man, he just told me not to go back to the bar. Well, I always did like antiques. The finer things, you know. I remember when I was a girl, I found my grandmother's wedding dress and snuck myself into it. I got what they used to call a whupping that day, I can tell you. I like things you can pick up and can feel a little history humming in them. I had to do something after he was gone. I was going stir-crazy. That's why I opened this place. It did pretty damn good business for a while, especially in summer and fall with the tourists and all, but the whole pandemic kind of shut that down—we ought to nuke China, you ask me—and then the whole town was starting to go to

shit anyway. At this point, I'm keeping the place as somewhere to store all this crap till I can sell it online. People will still buy that way, long as they don't have to leave their house, but I don't know that it's worth the rent."

Our daughter—or someone's daughter, or someone's something—elbowed me and indicated a pack of Tarot cards with superheroes and supervillains standing in for the Major Arcana and the court cards of the Minor. It looked like a gimmick or novelty item released sometime over the past two decades to coincide with that awful spate of superhero movies, some based on my own work. I emptied the pack into my palm and shuffled through the deck. Overman as The Emperor, Female Supreme as The Empress, Ratman as The Hanged Man, Golden Torch as The Hierophant, Marsh Man as The Hermit, Max Muller as The Devil, John James and Mina Mars as The Lovers, and more—with The Fool, of course, as The Fool.

Sally Pelletier looked at the Tarot cards and scoffed.

"I swear, kids come in here and leave their shit behind as if I was running the town dump and not a business! I wouldn't have bought anything like that. We only do class in here. C-L-A-S-S."

"I'll buy it anyway," I said. "I always meant to get back into cartomancy."

"Well," Sally Pelletier said in a lowered, conspiratorial voice, "if you really want to get into it, I have something I can show you. If you think you want to know."

She led us into the rear of the shop and up the back staircase, a dark passage in the middle of which a single ancient lightbulb glowed a very faint white, as if its filament had burned out and the glass globe had been infested with a phosphorescent fungus. For her age, she climbed the stairs quickly enough, hauling herself up with her cane; it was the girl (or whatever), carrying inside her own body our grandchild, or, in any case, someone's grandchild, who needed to pause in the dark, overcome with fatigue and nausea.

"I sold the house after Jack died. Who needs the trouble? I moved in here. I been fine ever since. The place was only ever broke into once. Meth heads, you know? I run them off with a rifle that ain't been fired in a hunnerd years!"

Laughing at her own adventure, Sally Pelletier brought us into an apartment at the top of the endless-seeming staircase. The apartment was neatly kept, but, since it had been furnished out of the antique shop, and with no consideration for aesthetic harmony or for the avoidance of anachronism, and since its radiators wheezed and rattled with furious steam against the oncoming winter, it seemed to breathe on us the moldering decay of decades, of centuries.

Sally Pelletier invited us to sit at the sea-green 1950s-style formica kitchen table, its centerpiece a collection of colored-glass liquor bottles—green, amber, indigo.

"Just give me a sec," Sally Pelletier said and opened a door off the kitchen through which I could just spy a four-poster bed with brocaded curtains.

The girl paced the bare floorboards and studied the odd knickknacks every corner seemed neatly to harbor, evidently the mingled lares of this odd household: jade netsuke on top of the mustard-yellow refrigerator, scrimshaw like teeth coming out of the floor next to the doormat, a long gun mounted over the stove with a silver inlaid map of some terra nullius *on the stock.*

Sally Pelletier came out of the bedroom and without ceremony dumped Valerie Karns's old homemade Tarot deck—the Polaroids of herself in various costume—on the table before me.

"When I finally got up the nerve to go into her room about a year after she left us, I found these. I'm talking about my girl, you know. I thought they were junk, but I didn't have the heart to throw them away. They were pictures of her, weren't they? Not pictures I necessarily approved of back then, mind you, but when somebody's gone for good, you don't necessarily approve or disapprove no more. You take every inch of them back if you can get them, the bad right along with the good. I blamed you for the way she went, but she was odd long before you ever come along. I guess I have only myself to blame. When your child don't grow up, who's to blame if not you? I didn't pay enough attention back then. I hadn't done enough growing up myself. I figured a child was like a plant: feed and water it every once in a while, and you don't have to hover over it. I never really wanted to have one anyway, if I'm being totally honest with you. It's why I never had another with Jack even though he wanted to, got down on his knees once and begged me even, if you can believe. I liked my own life. I liked to have a good time. Hell, I liked to make money. That's what it was about for me. I wasn't going to break my back like my own folks did. I wasn't going to let the mean winters up here get me down. I had a lot of time to think since those years, though, a lot of time to myself, thanks to Jack, and I can say I found better ways to have a good time than I used to, and better ways to make money, too. No point crying about it now. I don't know if I could have done any different back then unless I was a whole nother person, the person I am now, and I wasn't. One way to think about it is it's not even really me that did it. We get to be so different from what we used to be. When I saw you on the news a couple weeks ago, you know, what with that young man that blew his head off, it brought it all back, I have to tell you. What's this world coming to? It wasn't me that did it, and she's not here anymore, but I can't bring myself to throw her things away. I even moved them into this place."

She'd spoken as if entranced, presumably because she had few people in her life to speak to at any length about what her life had been. Finally, she stopped, one eye leaking tears, and sat across from me. She took up a card. It was The World: Valerie Karns, naked but for a bedsheet twisted oddly around her body from shoulder to ankle, two long candles in both her hands, cartoonish animal faces drawn in marker at the picture's four corners. She smiled.

"I never figured these things out. A girlfriend of mine I used to work with at the bar, she could read cards. She was full of stories, said her great-great-great-great-great-great grandma was one of them witches they burned back in Pilgrim times. I could of looked her up and asked her about it, but she's gone like my girl. Her boyfriend come in on her with another man in her bed, and, when the man crept off, he shot her, right through the eye, killed her stone-dead. I think she knew, too. She told me before it happened, she said she saw it in the cards that she didn't have long. That's why she decided to have a good time before she went. Isn't that strange now? She knew she would get killed, so she decided to enjoy herself, and it was enjoying herself that got her killed. It makes you wonder how things work. What causes what? One of these means 'death,' don't it?"

She roughly turned over the Polaroids until she found it. Death: Valerie Karns in a black robe, a black wrap around her head, perhaps a shawl or pillowcase, kneeling with parted legs on a table draped in white cloth, holding a white nylon rose like a flag of surrender.

I took the Polaroids, stacked them neatly, riffled them thoroughly, restacked them, and then handed them over the table to Sally Pelletier.

"Just put three cards down," I said. "The first is the past, the second is the present, and the third is the future."

Sally Pelletier hesitated. She seemed to think I'd asked her to cross some threshold into a strange, frightful place, as if I'd beckoned her into a dark wood. After this pause, she dealt the three cards in a swift, nervous movement.

I looked at the spread and said nothing. The girl, or whatever, approached to peer over my shoulder. Sally Pelletier's rheumy eyes were wide; she looked worried she'd done something terrible.

The Queen of Swords: Valerie Karns in a white robe, sitting in a kitchen chair in a field in broad daylight, a kitchen cleaver in one hand, the other raised in benediction. The Lovers: Valerie Karns standing naked next to a mirror, doubled, a mustache and a cock-and-balls drawn with charming crudeness in black marker on her reflection. The King of Cups: Valerie Karns in the same kitchen chair, this time on a rocky beach, wearing a blue dress, a bottle of clear liquor in one hand and brown liquor in the other, another mustache drawn over her lips onto the photo, the ocean churning and boiling whitely behind her.

"What does it mean?" Ash del Greco and Sally Pelletier asked almost in unison.

I turned and looked into the girl's face, into the spiral scar on the jowly cheek, at the thin blonde hair coming in at the dyed-black roots, at the thin, fragile neck. I looked into her face and knew at once, Ellen, at once, who her mother was.

"It means I should get in touch with an old friend," I said.

(It wasn't past-present-future, Ellen. There is no such thing. There is no time. There may be death, but there is no time. I was looking down from a higher dimension at what was true, is true, and will always be true.)

Sally Pelletier stood. "I'd offer to give you those pictures," she said, "but they're pictures of my girl. I don't have many pictures of my girl. I can give you something else, though. Something you forgot to take the last time I saw you. Not for lack of trying, neither!"

She laughed again, showed her toothless smile, and crooked her crooked finger to summon me into the bedroom. The girl, not expressly forbidden, though she was uninvited, came up behind me. We followed Sally Pelletier past the four-poster bed and waited as she dug in the depths of her closet. She brought out a bright pink dress hanging in a plastic sheath. She took out the clothes hanger and folded it neatly into my arms.

"You missed one. I don't rightly know if she'd of wanted you to have it, but you probably want it, and that's enough."

She led us back through the kitchen to the apartment door.

"I took up plenty of your time," she said. "You're free to go on your way."

The girl, with the superhero Tarot pack in her hand, and I, with the bright pink dress in my arms, started down the dark stairway.

"Hey, wait a minute," Sally Pelletier called from the top of the steps, silhouetted in the doorway. "It said on the news that you ain't a man or a woman, or that you're a man and a woman both. One of what they call those gender people, I guess. I mean, you look like a man to me, but there's a lot of things I don't understand about what this world's coming to. Don't get me wrong, nothing surprises me. You see a lot of things tending bar, I can tell you. We used to call them fairies, which I guess you can't call them no more. I don't know what the hell you're supposed to say about nothing no more. Some things—no offense, I ain't prejudice—ought to stay in the bar, it seems to me. What's fine in a bar don't work in a school or a church, if you take my meaning. I'm saying that, mind you, and I always wanted to be in the bar a hell of a lot more than I wanted to be in a school or a church. I always wondered, though, who has the best of it, the man or the woman? I never asked the fairies. For instance, who has a better time in the sack? Don't tell me, I don't even want to know. Tell me what a woman's dirty little secret is, and I'll tell you if you're a woman."

I paused. The girl, or whatever, standing on a step below me, her genderless soul bent and burdened to Mother Earth by the swelling of her woman's body, pricked up her ears.

"Women's dirty little secret is that they like to get thrown around like rag dolls," I said.

I was trying to shock her, to offend her, to make a clean break so she'd let us leave. Sally Pelletier laughed louder than we'd heard her laugh before. I thought she'd fall down, break in half. She cried from laughing so hard.

"Okay, smarty-pants, or smarty-dress, or whatever you are. What's men's dirty little secret then, if you're so smart?"

"They just want to be held."

I turned and urged our daughter, someone's daughter, someone's something, down the stairs, the old woman's witch-laugh trailing us in the darkness. We hurried through the dim, crowded shop, but the girl suddenly stopped. She grabbed my arm and indicated this very machine on which I now pound away, as I pounded away 30 years ago in a peignoir in a railway apartment: a squat black carapace, alphabet-toothed. I laid a $20 bill on the counter. The girl, or whatever, gathered the typewriter into her arms like a baby.

When we climbed up the concrete stairs into the light, even though we'd only emerged into the squalid prison of Hollow Well, it was as if we had come to the clear air at the top of a mountain. Dizzy in the noon brightness, the girl fell back, faint, against the dress in my arms.

When I'd turned to leave Sally Pelletier's bedroom, I noticed the dresser mirror from Valerie Karns's own old room propped against one wall. I saw myself framed in that mirror, just as I'd been almost four decades before. The message Valerie Karns had scrawled in red nail polish onto the glass was still there.

I never wanted to have a child, Ellen, never asked to have a child, never planned to have a child, and, as I held for a moment the fainted Ash del Greco in my arms on the street of the town that had borne me, I reflected that I had no particular advice to give to a child. My life has been a failure, punctuated by catastrophes. My works have been a bad influence, an aesthetic influenza, in the world. The entirety of my existence is one vast corruption of youth. The polis should put me to death. Then I remembered the mirror. The mirror held the single piece of advice I do have to give, which, luckily, I didn't actually have to say since Valerie Karns had, 40 years ago, painted it in nail polish on that glass where it still remained, and Ash del Greco, in Sally Pelletier's bedroom, had seen it, too. I saw her see it. I was glad she had seen it. It is the only wisdom I ever had or ever will have to give to my daughter, if she is my daughter, and she's not, and not that I've ever lived up to it myself. Still, I thought, as I brooded over Ash del Greco's spiral-scarred face while she roused back to consciousness in my arms, still, this is all I can tell you, all I have to give you: love is the law, little girl. Love is the law.

—Simon

After she'd read the letter three times through tear-blind eyes, Ellen Chandler saw that the envelope contained something else: two Tarot cards from the superhero deck Simon Magnus had described. If Ellen Chandler remembered correctly, they came from what was called the Minor Arcana. Accordingly, the designers of this deck had chosen minor superheroes, what in her editor days she remembered the old-timers calling second-stringers, to play the parts: the Queen of Swords was the Huntswoman leaping from a Cosmopolis skyscraper, her cosmic spear poised for launch in her right hand, and the King of Cups was Ocean Agent seated on a coral throne, brooding on an ornate goblet with a stem of braided dolphins.

Ellen Chandler kept pacing and circling the room as she read and reread the letter. Finally, she set it down on the coffee table, where the dogs sniffed it as if it were an intruder, and she went again to the window. Nora and Lucia evidently scented something out there in the blizzard; they suddenly lifted their heads toward the yard outside and snarled, baring their teeth, their tails stiff. The whole view from the window was whited out with the unseasonable snowstorm, an agitating surface of white. Except—and Ellen Chandler had tears in her eyes, so maybe she was misperceiving—that some bright streak moved at the end of her yard. A flare of pink burned in the whiteness on her lawn; it burned and moved toward the house on pale bare legs wading through snow, white on white. It couldn't be. She lowered her face, wiped her eyes, and looked out again. Yes, it was. It couldn't be, but it was. Simon Magnus standing on her lawn, to the knees in the massed snow, thin hair whipped back in the wind, wearing a bright pink dress.

CHAPTER 6
Prospero's Apprentice

On New Year's Day, Jessica Morrow knocked on Diane del Greco's door. A few inches of snow had fallen between Christmas and New Year's, but then the temperature rose unseasonably into the high 50s. Everything—snow, soil, and all—melted and ran in the incongruous heat of the low winter sun.

Jessica Morrow perspired in her violet velour coat; the heels of her Chelsea boots were caked with mud. As she waited for someone to open the door, she half-turned, ready to run. No one was making her do this. That was the worst part. If someone had ordered her to do this under threat of death, she might have refused. Of all the pains of adulthood, she found this one the worst: that you were obligated to force yourself through agonies you understood would benefit you in the end. How had "you" and "yourself" ever become so distant and estranged? At 38 years old, with her mother dead and her son dead, the last thing she felt like was an adult. She felt like an orphaned baby and a poor crone at once, and both abandoned on the step of an empty church. Here she was, however, on this errand of a woman alone, on a mission to restore some semblance of a home in this world with the only materials left to her, materials as unpromising as that totally deranged and hideous girl (or whatever): Ash del Greco.

Diane del Greco opened the door. When she saw who it was, a polite smile fading to alarm, she instinctively pulled her floral dressing gown tightly over her torso, as if its thin fabric were armor against whatever weapon this madwoman had brought—understandably mad, but still. Simon Magnus had told her about the gun; she had seen with her own eyes the attempted assault on her daughter in the hospital bed. She had lost a son; she had felt in her own hand the murderous weight of the telephone receiver.

"I don't want any trouble," Diane del Greco said quietly and cautiously.

Her demeanor reminded Jessica Morrow of someone in a movie crouching and tiptoeing with painful slowness past a slavering monster. Was this who she had become? She lifted her hands all the way above her head, palms out.

"No trouble, I promise. I just want to talk to you and your daughter."

She had only closed Untimely Vintage for less than a week—for the five days between Jakey's death and the funeral. She feared what she might do if she didn't work. She made a show of normal busyness, but inside her, all was waste and desolation. For almost two months, Jessica Morrow had been submerged in grief and rage. Even as she worked at her normal daily tasks, she wanted to disappear, to sleep all day, to open her wrists in the bathtub. She wanted to run through the streets screaming. She wanted to kick down every door in the city so that nobody would have a moment's peace until every last one of them knew that her son had been stolen from her and would never return, would never run over the pavement again, feet just barely tapping the ground, gold-streaked hair streaming back. Why should anyone now living enjoy a second or a millisecond of contentment, of joy, while her only child was beneath the earth?

A few customers knew her well enough to offer condolences, to wish her well, to bring flowers and pies, to speak to her with a different kind of caution than the one Diane del Greco used—not the caution of an intrepid movie heroine sneaking past a dangerous beast but rather the rigid care of someone carrying an overfull mug across a carpet. They were adults, her customers: they forced themselves to wish her well, fearful all the time she'd spill, scream, weep, break down, break a glass, pound her chest, tear her hair. No one wanted to see her cry, so she didn't. She thanked these annoying well-wishers with a stone face. The majority of her customers, however, were just people who wandered in from the street, curious about her wares, and blessedly knew nothing about her, people with whom she could hollowly banter and joke in a shelter created by their very ignorance, in a world where the biggest problem was making sure their dress, shoes, and handbag were all in complementary colors, a world where her own and only son hadn't shot himself through the eye to remind the human race to live.

Just before Christmas, Mrs. Penshurst, looking anxiously over both shoulders, entered Untimely Vintage. She had never been there before. Jessica Morrow didn't expect she'd see the Penshursts again after the funeral, except to nod at them on the street. They had loved Jakey, and Jakey had loved them, but she had no real relationship with them herself; she even wondered if they didn't regret that so smart and sensitive a lad (she imagined that they called him a lad) had to endure such an American vulgarian—obsessed with fashion, her arms crawling with tattoos!—for a mother. A *sister* like that would be bad enough, but a mother? (She had been, anyway, more like his sister than his mother, hadn't she? Was that why he—?) This was how she interpreted the poisonous politeness, the almost imperceptible narrowing of the eyes and pursing of the lips she detected whenever she came in to Prospero's Books to bring Jakey home. It made her feel like a little girl again, bound in a pinafore, wanting to impress her then-proper parents with her own propriety and failing, always failing, sensing some taint of vulgarity so deep inside herself it could never be cleansed.

"I read!" she always wanted to shout into their imperious English faces, because she did. These British imperialists didn't know it, but reading was mainly what she did when business was slow. She also thought that reading was for practical information and emotional entertainment, however. Anything that failed those tests, she skipped or skimmed. She could protest to them, therefore, that she read, but they would only narrow their eyes more narrowly, purse their lips more pursily, even if they didn't bother to establish through an impromptu quiz what they no doubt already suspected: that she'd hopscotched her way across the cetology through *Moby-Dick* and found *Middlemarch* too ponderous to endure beyond the first few chapters, that she preferred authors with some more cogent wisdom to offer, with a sense of humor or of the exotic if possible—your Vonneguts, your Hesses: books teenaged Jakey, buried in Herman Melville and George Eliot, had politely turned his nose up at when she suggested them—and even, from time to time, God help us, a good murder mystery. (It was always homicide, never suicide, in the mystery genre. You could solve a homicide, she knew, but you'd never solve a suicide.) They had made Jakey a diligent reader, a model student, a figure of greater calm and endurance than she could ever be—except that somehow he could not endure life itself—and for that she could thank them, but otherwise, she didn't expect to see much of them now that her sole link to them, her beautiful boy, was gone.

This silent dance of mutual recrimination between herself and the Penshursts hardly prepared her for what Mrs. Penshurst did that day just before Christmas, when she came into Untimely Vintage looking over both her shoulders as if she were entering a sex shop or some other shameful establishment. Once inside, once the door was closed behind her, Mrs. Penshurst took one more look through the door to make sure she hadn't been seen. She strode with a stiff-legged briskness in her stiff skirt straight to the counter and façed Jessica Morrow. Her lower lip trembled; one tear leaked weakly from one red-rimmed eye. She slid a small magenta envelope over the counter and left the store as stiffly and quickly as she'd entered, looking both ways once more. Jessica Morrow opened the envelope, unfolded the five pages of thick and deep-toothed paper it contained, and slowly read the precise cursive blue pen lines that rushed in a rise-and-fall rightward slant like the waves of the sea.

Dear Miss Morrow,

Please allow us to renew our condolences on the loss of your Jacob. The absence that bright boy has left in all our lives will surely never be filled. Miles and I were never able to have children of our own, and, I dare say, if it doesn't presume too far, that Miles considered the fatherless boy something akin to his own son.

I offer this in extenuation of what I now have to report to you of Miles. He has been distrait, *even morose, since Jacob's funeral. To this I attribute the grave error that led to his arrest last night. The arrest was a formality. He was released on his own recognisance around midnight. This did not, I assure you, prevent my almost collapsing of fright at the officers' pummeling on the door at the obscene hour of 10:00 p.m.*

Miles, it transpires, was taken advantage of by a corrupt colleague in the rare book trade. This dishonest broker—I'm sure you've encountered the like in your own affairs, alas—passed to Miles for our store a notebook purporting to contain colour sketches prepared by Lucia Joyce for a proposed Tarot deck shortly before her unfortunate confinement, presumably one of the artistic endeavours in which her father attempted to interest her to alleviate her mental distress. Indeed, Miles proudly showed me the notebook as soon as he received it. That poor unsound girl's imagination and lightness of hand did not fail to impress me. I invite you to imagine Lady Freida Harris's designs for the Great Beast's Thoth deck leavened by the faerie spirit of such watercolourists as Arthur Rackham and indeed Beatrix Potter herself, whom my grandmother, when she was just a child, once met on walkabout in the Lake District.

The notebook, however, proved to have been stolen by Miles's evidently light-fingered colleague from the collection of a university library. This was not his first trespass, unfortunately. He had passed other stolen property, including property stolen from our own beloved Carnegie Library, to a number of dealers, including Miles, over the last decade. The investigation has been ongoing for more than a year.

Miles even believed the store's phone line was 'tapped', if that indeed is the locution (I do not, alas, watch your American police serials). Can you imagine such a violation? Even a murderer should be permitted more dignity than this. They—police, prosecutors, and a grand jury—believe Miles to have been involved in a conspiracy to steal rare materials from public libraries and retail them on the private market.

I do not believe my husband is a criminal. I do not know. I found him last night in the bath, in the dark. He looked like a frail old man. I mistrust my own motives in telling you this. I do not ask for your pity. It is only that we have so few intimate friends in this country, or, as it happens, any other. I turned on the light and pulled him to me, soaked as he was—the water had long gone cold, you see—and told him I would not desert him, no matter what he had done or what happened as a result of any act he'd performed or left unperformed. Such is the marriage contract.

He only asked if I remembered the poetry he'd written me when we first were courting. Of course, I've kept it all, in a hatbox in the closet, the pages bound with hairpins. Myself, I was a watercolourist, too, as he also reminded me. On just the third evening we spent together—we met on holiday—he sat for me en plein air *as the sun set on the strand, a cocklepicker's gypsy hat (I'm quite sure we mustn't call it that anymore, but I don't know what I* should *call it) tilted rakishly over his bushy eye.*

Why, he wondered, did we ever stop? Why did we turn from the creation of beautiful things first to their academic study and then to their exchange for profit, each in its own way a murder of the spirit? When we were in academe, we never did favour the wretched Continentals—'mere intellectualised Bolsheviks', Miles liked to call them, to the scandal of some of your American professors—but still, his pale flesh withering in the cold bath, he quoted beastly Adorno to me, of all people: 'Every work of art is an uncommitted crime.' I feared he was delirious. Had the boy been right, he even asked me of your poor lost son, to throw everything over before time could have its way? I dried him and dressed him and put him to bed like a very infant.

I apologise for these unseemly disclosures. I aim only to give you a picture of the situation in all its direness. I did not even yet mention that scandal threatens: just this morning, a reporter from your Post-Gazette *rang me for comment, and an article is expected to appear in tomorrow's paper. As you might imagine—I have not even yet mentioned the barristers' fees we're facing if we want to secure a decent defence—continuing to operate Prospero's Books in these circumstances is out of the question. We are looking, therefore, for a buyer and wished to approach you first in token of your longstanding proximity and of our appreciation for your late son, the boldest reader both of us ever knew. You might even see it in the light of a memorial tribute to the lad. We look forward to your answer.*

Yours ever,
Jane Penshurst

In another world, in another time, Jessica Morrow would have crumpled the letter into a ball and thrown it away and pretended the whole strange interchange hadn't happened, that she had not even read the politely handwritten raving of the mad old woman.

Something made her muse over it, however, flattening and flattening its folds under her nervous fingers, all day long after Jane Penshurst had delivered it. Running one business was hard enough, let alone running two, and she knew nothing of the book trade. She had a dim sense of who Lucia Joyce had been and what had happened to her—she remembered having been assigned *A Portrait of the Artist as a Young Man* in high school and judging it occasionally beautiful but needlessly confusing—and more than one Tarot deck had, like the occasional vintage firearm, passed through her hands as components of unsorted collections, but these would never be her primary interests. Books, magic—these carried people away from the world, even threatened to take them out of it, while the arts she served, the arts of fashion and commerce, beautified the world and perpetuated it. She would have found all of Jakey's reading morbid if he hadn't also been a runner, a guitar-picker, a boy who struck the world with his toes and plucked it with his fingers, not that this had proved enough to hold him to it.

Maybe if he'd lived, she might have made a present of the bookstore to him. She could raise the capital to buy out the Penshurts. While the world at large certainly appeared to be slipping into mass illiteracy, she understood by analogy with her own trade that rare books could be profitable: some markets were based not on a vast mass of customers, each contributing a penny, but a small and even incestuous cadre, each with thousands or even millions at their disposal. Jakey was gone, though. Jakey was gone, and, in that circumstance, she didn't, if she was being honest with herself, really quite care what happened to the snooty English couple and their dusty bookshop.

It occurred to her later that day, however, as she reread Jane Penshurst's letter, that though her child was gone, gone under the ground he used to jog over, never to return, she would, in about eight months, have a grandchild—a grandmother at 39 years old!—and that this child was all of Jakey that would ever be left to her. Her grandchild would need a bequest. Even the mother of her grandchild, the lover of her dead child—much as she might so strangely have claimed otherwise before all the world—needed somewhere to go, something to do with herself, needed a future more stable than the evanescence of the internet and the even greater evanescence of her own belief in the occult.

(Jessica Morrow didn't like to go on the internet. She handled fabric, she handled cash, she read murder mysteries, and she did *not* believe in magic.)

She thought about it for two weeks. She consulted a lawyer and a financial advisor. She made sure she was sure. On New Year's Day, she found Diane del Greco's address online, she drove there, she raised her hands to show she was not armed, she was allowed to enter, she was offered coffee and the stale remnants of a grocery store panettone, and she watched as Diane del Greco, without having asked, poured a shot of whiskey into the proffered and steaming cup. Diane del Greco had to scream up the stairs three times—"If you don't get down here, Ashley, I'll beat your little ass, fetus or no fetus," she called the final time, winking at Jessica Morrow—to summon her daughter.

Finally, Ash del Greco stepped into the kitchen, sullenly rubbing her eyes, abraded as they were, Jessica Morrow presumed, from too much time spent online. The girl—"girl" somehow wasn't the word that came to mind—didn't look pregnant yet; it was only the beginning of her third month. Jessica Morrow wondered that such a small body could carry and bear a child. Such a small body and such a huge head—she looked like a baby herself! The desire Jessica Morrow felt to murder the girl had not yet quite left her, but Ash del Greco wore a yellow onesie and slippers with kitten faces on them. It would be like killing—what? Maybe a duck, Jessica Morrow thought. Having sipped the whiskey-laced coffee already, she let out a sudden laugh. Duck or no duck, this strange girl, or whatever she was, sheltered in her very body the process by which all that still survived of Jakey, of her beautiful boy, would coalesce and come to birth. Following that bark, that quack of a laugh, a tear started in one eye. Ash del Greco sat across from her. The spiral on the girl's cheek made Jessica Morrow dizzy; it seemed in the hot kitchen—the coffee was too hot, the whiskey burned—to spin, like an optical illusion.

Diane del Greco swept to Jessica Morrow's side in her floral dressing gown and pink kitten-heel slippers and said, with a growl of impatience, "What can we do for you, Ms. Morrow?"

Jessica Morrow restrained herself from blurting out, "I came to see my grandchild—all that's left of my son," and said instead, "I came with two propositions for the mother of my grandchild."

She had only intended to share the one proposition with them. The other, a thought she had been barely brave enough to allow utterance inside her own head once or twice, she'd meant to hold in reserve. She had seven months—more—to consider it anyway. If her son's sudden death had taught her anything, however, it was that we had no guarantee of seven more months, no guarantee of seven more seconds. Scalding her tongue and the roof of her mouth, she drank down the whole cup of coffee-and-whiskey at once and then told them all she was thinking.

It was as a result of her accepting Jessica Morrow's first proposition that Ash del Greco came to spend her quiet days behind the counter of Prospero's Books.

Someday, maybe, after her infamy died down for good, if that ever happened, she would return to school and attain a formal degree, even though there would be no point in it, since she had long ago seen to the end of everything: beyond the BA, the MA, and the PhD, all the way to the void where thought terminated.

For now, she sat in her bookstore and read. The owner of a profitable small business—not especially numerate, she hired someone to keep the store's accounts; interested only in literature and philosophy but not in books per se, not in tomes or volumes, not in folios or duodecimos, she hired someone to manage the rare-book side of the trade—she resigned from the internet, deleted her accounts, and all but stopped going online entirely. The last time she checked the email associated with her YouTube channel, she found a message from Ally Aldrich:

Ash, my darling, I was so sorry to hear about what's been happening to you. I don't know if other people's good news will make you miserable or cheer you up, but I thought I'd try. Positive thinking, right? I feel I owe it all to you. You need to know you've helped people! It's not good news about Joshua Cantwell—or maybe it is, for me. That prick, so to speak, was caught in flagrante *with the 18-year-old autistic first-year theater student he'd cast as Kattrin in his vaunted outdoor winter production of* Mother Courage. *He's been run out of the theater scene, out of the city entirely. Good riddance! You know what they say: "Rejection is God's protection." No, I met someone else at church. A lapsed divinity student who's now studying to be a veterinarian. A kind, tender man with no theories, in whose gently giant hands a kitten is safer than in the wild, a fat man rather than a thin one—a man of substance, a man you can hold onto! The minute we started talking, we found we could talk about everything—everything but Brecht and Lacan!—and we haven't stopped talking since. I've abandoned my degree. I've begun writing poetry. I know it's sudden, but we're getting married in the spring, and then we're going to start trying. "I am a vessel of life"! Thank you, my dear Ash, and happy New Year!*

She learned how to operate the cash register and the credit card reader. She sometimes made polite suggestions to graduate students purchasing volumes of theory about how they might organize their seminar papers or dissertation chapters. She had occasionally chided her customers for their purchases. She stopped after a woman of about 30 in professional dress, no doubt a professor or lawyer or administrator, pelted her with coins, even though she was visibly and heavily pregnant, when she'd said—politely enough, she thought—"I could suggest something else," upon being asked to ring up several fashionable, sentimental, self-styled "queer" political polemics, which, reminding her of the queer kids in the Rainbow Alliance, of being called *uzumaki* by a demiboy in a skirt, so offended her own taste it had somehow sent her eyes almost blank with rage.

She learned to chat casually with customers about their tastes, their interests, their lives. Was it the flood of maternal hormones that carried her in her splay-footed pregnant waddle around the counter to embrace a woman of about 60 who began to cry because her mother, who'd died the previous week, had once owned the very paperback of *Wuthering Heights* she was now purchasing?

In her downtime, she sat on her stool in her gathering mass, the canted warren of dust-hung shelves radiating from her swelling centrality, and she read. She read patiently, one word after another: words branched into sentences, sentences leaved into boughs of paragraphs, paragraphs spread intricately into a whole forest cover of chapters. She no longer tried to see to the end of everything, for at the end of everything she had found absolutely nothing. She tried instead to lose herself in a proliferating wilderness of significance, to domicile herself in all that was, just as the efflorescing flesh of her pregnancy engulfed her consciousness. She read *Sense and Sensibility*; she read *Middlemarch*.

Simon Magnus and Ellen Chandler had visited her and her mother for Christmas, arm in arm. Though she'd never owned a pet in her life, though she'd never permitted her daughter a pet because a puppy or kitten or even goldfish would introduce too much disorder into the already disordered house, Diane del Greco had volunteered to watch Ellen Chandler's dogs: the long, sleek Nora and the bounding, yipping Lucia.

Along with the dogs, Ellen Chandler had brought Ash del Greco the gift of a new edition of *Ulysses*, a tacky hardcover in imitation leather with gilt edges.

"I saw on one of your videos that you said you never finished it, so I thought maybe a nice copy would help. I recommend just letting it wash over you the first time."

Together the three of them, in her mother's hot disordered living room, all three of them drinking coffee with whiskey, agitated, laughing and crying, told her, her eyes wide, her stomach burning, who her parents were, told her what had happened out by the western ocean at the turn of the millennium where and when *Overman 3000* was born and she was conceived. Later, paging through the gift edition of *Ulysses*, she found that Ellen Chandler had inserted a photo of Marco Cohen between the pages: Marco Cohen at 22 years old, an expression of wondering seriousness beneath his craggy brow, standing in a torn white T-shirt in a cramped apartment studio in front of an easel where he'd painted a portrait of a beggar in a rags, a beggar who, on Marco Cohen's canvas, held all the dignity and deportment of a pope or burgher.

After Ellen Chandler and Simon Magnus left, arm in arm—"We fly out to Dublin in two days," Ellen Chandler explained, "and from there, after a week, to Paris"—she went upstairs to bed. (Her mother's bed was her bed now; Diane del

Greco had installed an air mattress in her studio and slept alongside her work, her dreams outside as well as inside of her sleeping head.) She couldn't, somehow, say it to Diane del Greco's face, couldn't utter the words while looking into her eyes, while being gathered into the perfume miasma of her fleshy embrace, so she texted her from her bed instead as she listened to the dogs scrabble and play downstairs: "you'll always be my mother."

She was reading *Ulysses*, or trying to read it, when a boy, or whatever, who could not have been more than 15—red carbuncles spotting his bristly unshaven cheeks, chipped black polish on his fingernails—bought a Tarot deck one day in Prospero's Books. She didn't even know she sold them. Like the guns in Jessica Morrow's inventory, they were stowaways among the other vendibles in the traffic of all that was arcane and obsolete. It was a Rider-Waite deck, the semi-, hemi- or demiboy's purchase, the box dented and torn. The boy, or whatever, was painfully diffident and would not meet her eye, but still, she said, "Can you read these?"

"Just, just a little," he—or perhaps they or she or even it—stammered.

She handed him the deck after ringing it up.

"Will you please draw a card for me?"

With fumbling, thick fingers, he opened the pack, artlessly pulled out the top card, and, with a nervous twitch, flung it at her across the counter. It landed faceup inside the book in her lap: Temperance, the androgynous angel with one foot on land and one in the water, pouring in infinite profusion liquid from one cup into the other and back again. She laughed. At her laugh, the boy, or whatever, finally looked up at her, saw the spiral scar on her cheek, and said in an outburst of wary admiration, before he, she, they, or it could stop him-, her-, their-, or itself, "Hey, aren't you Ash del Greco?"

"Aren't I?" she said. "Aren't I?"

At the end of the street near the University that held both Untimely Vintage and Prospero's Books squatted in Gothic magnificence a century-old cathedral—not a metaphorical cathedral, like the one in the center of campus, but an actual Catholic cathedral, the two towers flanking its facade like arms thrust up in praise to heaven. About half a mile up the street sat a synagogue, slightly smaller, but no less magnificent, not Gothic Revival but Beaux-Arts in style, with a Catalan vault—sometimes, she had to admit, she *did* still consult Wikipedia—the latter a distant recollection, she dimly surmised, of the holy syntheses or syncretisms of old Andalus, which she'd once read about somewhere, who knew where, in the wilds of online. Maybe it was, maybe it wasn't. She no longer tried to know. She no longer knew anything.

In secret, she sometimes attended services at both cathedral and synagogue, the small and elderly congregations in each house of worship eyeing her warily, almost with fear. She didn't go because she believed. Belief was a matter of thought. She knew that at the end of thought was not God but the void, nothing. God, if there was a God, was everything, or maybe God was just the best name we had for everything. She didn't know why she went, really. Maybe because she felt contained in her very smallness beneath the vast vaults of cathedral and synagogue. Her speck of an infant might have felt similarly in the vault of her womb—her little bit of a dandelion spore on its way to becoming a tadpole and then a mouse and then a pig and then a baby and finally (though this would have to wait for consciousness, would have to wait at least until the impulse developed to lay its tender babyish face on a burning coil) a person. She was a vessel of life. *Shema Yisrael. Gloria in excelsis.* Love is the law.

One day in February, it was so hot in the cathedral, though so cold outside, she thought she might faint, not to mention her pregnancy's exacerbation of the usual nausea. She staggered out before the end of the service, an early morning service she'd attended before opening Prospero's Books—attended almost alone except for a small remnant of old women scattered over the pews in the vast varnished dimness. The icy streets were almost empty; the wind drove crystal snow in lacy spindrifts like smoke along the pavement.

No one saw her, then, as she hurried as fast as she could across the icy pavement to get behind the church, to relieve her morning sickness. There, huddled in a torn thin jacket, in broken shoes through whose holes she could see ragged and tattered socks, with no covering on his bald, scabbed head to keep off the gelid wind, slumped an old man against the cathedral's back wall, his bloodshot eyes almost whited out with rheum. His distress strangely settled her stomach, though his redolence of urine and sour milk reached her on the icy air. She stopped short, overheated in the long black coat and tall black boots her mother had bought her two months before for Christmas.

"Anything you got," he said. "Anything you got."

Later, she woke up on the floor of her shop, behind the counter. She was wrapped in a violet velour coat. Jessica Morrow, her knees drawn up, was sitting on her numb, chapped feet as if hatching an egg. Even so, she still shivered; she couldn't stop her teeth from chattering.

"You are literally the craziest fucking person I've ever met in my life," Jessica Morrow said, "and I've run into some lunatics. If you weren't carrying my grandchild, I'd shoot you in the head. Do you know what I thought when I looked out the window of my shop and saw you coming down the street, barely standing up, holding onto the wall, wearing just a T-shirt and underwear, in your bare feet, over the ice, through the snow, in that wind? You're pregnant! Are you insane? Where did your clothes go?"

Her teeth still rattled together in the back of her mouth as she told Jessica Morrow where they had gone. Jessica Morrow opened her own mouth to resume shouting at her, but stopped, her lips still parted.

Finally, quietly, she said, "I bet you wouldn't kill a centipede in the bathtub either."

Her teeth chattered too much to correct Jessica Morrow, to tell her that she'd have every centipede on the planet exterminated to prevent even one's ever menacing her in the bathtub—or would have, until that morning, until the man said, "Anything you got."

"Okay," Jessica Morrow said. "Okay. Just don't do it again. Not while you're the only house that this baby has to live in. You owe me that baby, Ashley del Greco. It's the least you can do for me. Once he or she moves out, you can do what you want. There will be sane people to take care of him or her. Once the baby comes, you can give away everything you have. Then—if you want—you can give all."

Because of Jessica Morrow's second proposition, Ash del Greco's son was baptized in a swimming pool. Back on New Year's Day, Jessica Morrow had proposed that, a few months after the baby's birth, they fly out West, not only so that she could see her father for the first time in 30 years, but so that he, who had not known his grandson, could meet his *great*-grandson. Before Ash del Greco could agree or disagree, Diane del Greco had said, "Ooh, I've always wanted to go there. You girls have your family time—I'll be playing the slots!"

When they arrived 11 months later, the mountains surrounding the airport shimmered on the 100-degree horizon. A taxi took them—Jessica Morrow, Diane del Greco, Ash del Greco, and the baby, squalling by turns in each of their arms—to a low suburban house with a spiny xeriscape in the front yard and a swimming pool in the back.

Jessica Morrow's father, a fat, bald man in an unbuttoned Hawaiian shirt and coral shorts and brown boat shoes, waved his hands to summon her over as soon as she stepped from the taxi. He took her in his arms; she cried helplessly, "Daddy, daddy," into the pelt of white hair on his chest, her tears sunstruck crystals on the fur.

His sweet, bustling wife, still wearing the apron in which she'd prepared them lunch, took the baby with maternal expertness from Ash del Greco and carried him, now whimpering rather than screeching, through the neatly kept, air-conditioned house. Diane and Ash del Greco followed her with worry and bemusement. The party passed through the back door and came out to the backyard pool, where the Morrows' son, who had become a charismatic preacher, a young man in a white button-down shirt and khaki shorts and brown flip-flops, waited with a black leather-bound Bible and a mouth full of shining white teeth.

"We didn't know what religion you practiced," the second Mrs. Morrow explained to the del Grecos, "but we figured you can baptize him in yours, and we'll baptize him in ours. Every little bit counts, don't it?"

She handed the baby to his great-uncle. The young preacher shouted praise for Jesus into the dry 100-degree air as he dribbled from his cupped hands bath-hot chlorinated water onto the baby's tender head, down the baby's plump face, into the baby's wide eyes. The cry of the child split the dust-hung desert air like heat lightning out on the horizon.

EPILOGUE

CHAPTER ∞
Q. E. D., Revised

The gun felt heavy, heavier than it could really have been down in the pocket of his World War II "Ike" army jacket. Alone in the elevator, the elevator where he'd met her, where the box of her books had broken open, he pressed the number for her floor before it could begin descending to the bottom. He had to see her one more time. It was the middle of the afternoon during classes, so the hallway was empty. One girl passed him, shuffling with a hangover to the bathroom in her leopard-print slippers. She smelled of stale cigarettes. She must have been too dazed to wonder at his martial dress.

He knocked on the door of Ash del Greco's dorm room, as he'd done almost every day for the last two months. She pulled it open all the way and stood in its frame, three heads shorter than him, looking up, directly into his face. She was naked. She saw his eyes widen with fear, with desire, with the fear of desire. His fist still hung in the air where he'd been knocking.

"I want you to do whatever you want to do right now," she whispered.

With infinite gentleness, he pushed her inside the room. He kicked the door closed behind him, his eyes locked on hers. With infinite gentleness, he pushed her down onto the bed. He paused, standing, unsure what he should do, as she lay beneath him. She opened her legs; he continued to muse. Ungently, she reached up. With a strength he hadn't known her to possess, she pulled him down to her by the lapels of the army jacket. His golden hair fell all around her.

The experience, the loss of what they called her virginity—it was, well, whatever. She didn't care about sex especially. That's not why she'd revised for it on the second night in Hollow Well, when Simon Magnus in the next hotel room kept her up all night pounding on that typewriter they'd acquired in the antique shop, composing what would prove to be a long letter to Ellen Chandler. She hadn't been pregnant before that night in the hotel in Hollow Well, that night when she decided—amid the disturbing clatter, the metallic rain or reign, of Simon Magnus's awful typewriter—that she would revise Jacob Morrow's death. She wouldn't try to bring him back. She knew she could if she wanted to, and part of her did want to, but she also knew she could never revise death again, not after Ari Alterhaus. There were other ways, however, to revise death—to turn death into life.

It would be her way of revising other regrets as well. She should have had top surgery and then nullo surgery. She also should have killed herself. She'd allowed Ari Alterhaus and Jacob Morrow to do these things in her stead; she was no longer the brave child who'd pressed her face to the burner in quest to become something, *anything*, other than what she was.

(Maybe because that first time it had hurt so very much.)

She could revise for those things, she'd thought amid the typewriter din and hail that November night in the hotel room in Hollow Well. She could nullify herself at last, in one sense of the word or another, nullify either the "her" or the "self" or both. She'd briefly considered it. What did she really want? What was her true will? To die? In part, yes. The world, however, would grant her that in time without her having to ask. Other than death, she wanted a conversation as good as the conversations she'd had with Ari Alterhaus, with Jacob Morrow.

For more partners in conversation, there had to be more life, not more death, in the world. She really wanted to talk to Jacob Morrow again, she suddenly understood, as Simon Magnus hammered away like a man (or whatever) possessed in the next room at a missive to Simon Magnus's own long-lost love.

She could not—or rather would not—bring Jacob Morrow back. Instead, she did the next best thing. She brought him not back, as it were, but forward, this to honor the message he'd intended to send with his death, the death he'd died in place of hers: that the most important thing was life. She would introduce into the world the product of her conversations with Jacob Morrow and a new conversation partner, one she might talk to as long as she lived. Wouldn't a baby's wide eyes, a baby's undomesticated squeals and howls, transform her, renew her? Even if not, even if this were a mere sentimentalism, even if the baby proved only to be as alienated as she had always been—still, why not someone to share the alien landscape with? Why not a fellow alien on this alien earth? Anyway, she told herself, what she now proposed to do would surely transfigure and transvalue her body as radically as anything the nullo surgeon's lancet could accomplish. Motherhood would nullify the Ash del Greco that was. What would emerge she had yet to learn.

She drifted to sleep an hour after making her decision, now as much cosseted as pummeled by Simon Magnus's ungodly typing, the whispered words still on her dreaming lips: "I am a vessel of life." She wasn't pregnant when she fell asleep. In the morning, she was. As far as the world was concerned, as far as her mother or Simon Magnus or the physicians in the University hospital were concerned, she'd been pregnant for almost a month.

(It was impossible to tie up all the loose ends in this life, however. She'd entirely forgotten her denial, in the video the whole world had seen, that she and Jacob Morrow had slept together. When she'd made the video, they hadn't; now, they had. It was easy enough, she found, to tell anyone who asked—and few, besides of course her mother, were impolite enough to ask—that she'd only said that to spare her and the boy's privacy.)

Almost a year later, here she was, high in the air, her mother and her child at her side, almost sure she'd made the right decision, given the alternatives. Her mind wandered. She was *still* trying to read *Ulysses*, the tacky gilt copy Ellen Chandler had given her for Christmas, on the plane back from the city in the desert, the plane that would carry her back to Steel City, to Prospero's Books, to her new life. The baby slept atop Diane del Greco's chest next to her, a little rivulet of drool running with cute, gleaming purity from his slack lips as he snuffled like an animal in an infantine dream. Jessica Morrow dozed over a mystery novel in the seat behind them.

Ash del Greco reapplied herself to *her* book as the plane roared and rattled around her. She read with a pencil in her hand—it was *Ulysses*, after all—but she couldn't concentrate on the book. Its structural bravura made her mind drift, made her think of how the whole strange story of her life, and of how her life had come to be, might itself be arranged in and as a novel. Surely, it was too complicated—too many strange characters believing and doing too many strange things over too long a span of time to be believable as any kind of coherent narrative. Better just paint these personae individually, as in the Tarot deck, and deal them out at random, to see if anyone could make sense of them, especially when they started changing places with one another, as people change places in a dream. She herself had been or had tried to be The High Priestess and The Hierophant and The Magician; when she was pregnant, she thought she was The World; now, in all her incongruous maternity, she strangely found herself The Empress; and she knew she had always been and would always be The Fool.

Maybe it could be a graphic novel, her life story. She could propose it to Simon Magnus. She hadn't read a graphic novel since her time in Simon Magnus's class, however, and she doubted that the form, for all that it was able to represent a fourth-dimensional perspective like no other, had the power to render the interior of the psyche. That, too, was part of her life story but not one she could locate at any discrete set of points in time that some higher perspective could assemble into a Tarot spread or comic-book page. The inner life was dimensionless, infinite. Eternity in a grain of sand, heaven in a wildflower.

(As it happens, Simon Magnus had told her about a new idea for a novel a few months ago, Simon Magnus's first serious work in almost 25 years, and not, Simon Magnus insisted, a graphic novel, but what Simon Magnus called a *real* novel: something about William Blake returning to earth, entering the body of a female dancer-poet in a shining future city, perhaps a city on the moon, so that he, William Blake, could learn to reconcile himself better to nature, to the earth, to the flesh. "Since you know my work so well, maybe I could show it to you when I have a draft," Simon Magnus had said upon returning from Europe and visiting her in Prospero's Books. He, she supposed: no longer exclusively Simon Magnus. "He, or whatever," he'd told her when she fumbled his full name upon introducing him to another customer. Going soft in his old age, getting sentimental in his dotage, he'd further said, "The only pronouns I care about anymore are 'me' and 'you.'" He had come to see her in the bookstore to invite her personally to his and Ellen Chandler's wedding; it would take place the following spring, up in Hollow Well, just as soon as he was finished reclaiming his childhood home from the forest, from the moral wilderness, and there he would retire with his bride to write in the summers. For the other nine months of the year, they would live together in her house on the side of the river opposite the great city where they'd met, what the comics called Cosmopolis, so that she could continue her long battle to create a taste for literature in the young people of St. Anne's Academy. She would create the readers, he the books: something like the life they'd dreamed for themselves when they met long ago in a Cosmopolis coffee shop, when she was a bedraggled and chain-smoking comic-book editor harried by the badness of the scripts, and he a self-exiled poet deep in mourning, the lacy hem of his dress whispering over the café floor.)

No, Ash del Greco would never write her life story, her autobiography or autobiographical novel, she thought. She could barely read a novel and would never write one, certainly not one you could disappear into, like the kind Jacob Morrow used to enjoy, the kind his example had finally taught her, almost, to enjoy. Life could not be gathered into words. Then again, she had never imagined herself a mother either—and now here she was, listening with admiration to her baby's sleeping little snorts and sighs. She would surely call it *Major Arcana*, if ever she wrote it: the story of her life, the novel of her days.

(She had kept the photo of Marco Cohen where Ellen Chandler had left it. It would be years before she understood the significance of where in the novel Ellen Chandler had placed it: between the last two pages of "Circe," nestled in Bloom's vision of his dead son. Even before she knew that, she sensed somehow that the photo had to remain where it was, so she used her own Temperance card as her bookmark in deference to the hasty Tarot reading the carbuncular adolescent enby had given her in Prospero's Books the previous winter. She was using the Temperance card, except that she still only owned a Thoth deck, and Crowley hadn't called that card Temperance. Crowley had called it Art.)

No, she thought, her mind wandering, she couldn't concentrate on *Ulysses*. She underlined a sentence, not sure what it meant but stimulated by it all the same: "Jewgreek is greekjew."

Instead of reading, instead of taking notes, she drowsily scribbled in the margin as the plane skimmed across the wisping tops of the clouds. She scribbled as the sleep one always sleeps on a plane came onto her, so exhausting is it to soar across the sky, so little were we born to *be* those angels we wrestled with and strove to become. She scribbled names. She thought of how she and her son were both del Grecos but might easily both have been Cohens. She scribbled all the names her son might have had, at least so far. Who knew what names he would put off and put on as he extended himself in time, her little Jakey, as he became whoever he (or whatever) was? She scribbled all the names she herself had had, and all the names she might have had, too, all the people she had been or could have been or should have been, even some people she still might be, so large and strange was this world.

Ashley Ash Ellen Chandler Magnus Cohen del Greco.

Jacob Jakey Levy Chandler Magnus Cohen del Greco Morrow.

She went from names to initials as she dropped to sleep beside her sleeping baby, somehow hoping to discover some significance in the letters, some gematria particular to her own genetic and memetic lineage. She no longer knew anything, however; she no longer saw to the end of everything. Words only dissolved into dissolving letters on their way to the dissolving images of a dream.

A. E. A. C. M. C. D.

J. J. L. C. M. D. M.

As sleep fell more heavily, her pencil began to slip out of her fingers. The book closed over the final three letters she'd written in its margin. Finally, the pencil fell from her dreaming hand, like a magician's rod, once the magician has abjured his will and allowed this life to take its errant course.

Q. E. D.

ABOUT THE AUTHOR

John Pistelli is the author of bestselling Substack *Grand Hotel Abyss*, home of a regular newsletter called "Weekly Readings" and the literary podcast "The Invisible College," as well as the eight-year archive of an award-winning literary blog at johnpistelli.com. He holds a PhD in English from the University of Minnesota and has been writing and teaching for almost two decades. He lives in Pittsburgh, PA.

Belt Publishing

beltpublishing.com